Early morning, November the ninth. John Kline, tall, strong, pale of face, ducking out of the small gate in the big gate of Winson Green Prison. Shivering, turning up the now unfashionably cut lapels of a blue suit crumpled and creased from being bound with government issue string for the past two years, eight months, two weeks and one day of a four year gaol sentence for manslaughter.

Hearing the gate lock behind him and feeling like a matador who has forgotten to bring along sword and cape, Kline peered into the grey morning light. Seeing neither friend nor enemy pounding towards him, he put one foot in front of the other and quickly walked away from the prison, determined to give it nothing more, not even a backward glance. He reached the pavement, stopped, ran a wary blue eye over the cars parked within striking distance of him. Nothing. No threat. No sweat. Not much, thought Kline, feeling a few strands uncoil from the ball of tension inside his belly. Crossing the tarmacadam of Winson Green Road he experienced the relief of a small reprieve from the retribution promised by the brothers of the young thug killed during a take-over battle for the nightclub then part-owned by Kline – the Maverick. Probably couldn't gauge the amount of remission I'd earn; probably thought I wouldn't want *any*, Kline decided, so… yeh, say it. So far so good, Kline told himself, then remembered the joke about a man who said the same thing while falling from a twenty storey building. Worried again, he turned into Villiers Street and disappeared from the sight of an Asian who had been watching the gate of the prison for the release of John Kline.

By the time Khan had turned into Villiers Street Kline had disappeared. Hurrying along down into Wellington Road, Khan was somewhat disconcerted to still see no sign of the man he had set out to follow. Only when passing along a grimy row of shops did Khan relax once again, for there through the holes of a net curtain behind a cracked plate glass window sat John Kline. Khan glanced up at the letters painted across the window; they denoted both the proprietor and the shop's function: Ted's Teas.

Khan pushed the door that had affixed to it a bell that tinkled on being opened and jangled as the door stuck halfway through opening. Sidling in, Khan saw that the shop was empty of customers apart from the man in the blue suit and pink shirt sprawled out beneath a Vimto sign drinking tea. Approaching the counter behind which, huddled against the tall tea dispenser, was a middle-aged English lady wearing a turban. Perhaps it was the sleep in her eyes or the smoke from her Players No. 6 that obscured her view of Khan, for she showed no reaction to his presence. Maybe it was the wax in her ears that prevented her hearing his polite request for a cup of Ted's tea. Whatever it was, after seeing her heavy rump disappear through the door that must have led to the kitchen at the rear of the counter area, Khan decided he was not to receive refreshment. He turned his attention accordingly towards the figure of Kline, who seemed intent on examining a group of coins held in the palm of his large, square hand. Khan, taking this to be a good point of reference with which to begin a conversation, said pleasantly, 'Decimal currency. You'll get used to it.'

The tall man looked up, put the coins in his pocket, put his hands on the table, looked the Asian up and down and said, 'Woh?'

'You're John Kline?'

'Well?'

Khan sat down opposite to Kline. Looked at him, leaned forward, said earnestly, 'I'm looking for a relative of mine, last address a boarding house in Rotterdam, left for England...' Khan spread his hands in a slight gesture of bewilderment, '...not heard of since.'

'What d'y want me t'do?'

'Help me to find him. You will be paid well. In English money.'

Money, thought Kline, I don't need your money. Just need time to claim my own. 'Sorry,' Kline said, standing, picking up his cup and draining the lukewarm tea, 'got t'go. Got a travel warrant courtesy've HM Nick.'

Receiving no reply, Kline shrugged, turned away, was about to go

PHILIP MARTIN'S
GANGSTERS

The right of Philip Martin to be identified as the Author of the Work
has been asserted by him in accordance with the Copyright,
Designs and Patents Act 1988

Copyright © Philip Martin 1977, 2016

Published by Candy Jar Books 2016

Candy Jar Books
136 Newport Road
Cardiff Road
CF24 1DJ

www.candyjarbooks.co.uk

Cover Illustration
Copyright © Will Brooks

Printed and bound by 4edge,
7 Eldon Way Hockley, Essex, SS5 4AD

ISBN: 978-0-9954821-2-8

First published by Sphere Books 1977

Philip Martin has been writing professionally for over forty years. Television credits include *Z Cars*, *Doctor Who* and *Star Cops*, but his most famous work is the postmodern series *Gangsters*.

Philip has had productions of his stage plays performed at the National Theatre; the Royal Court Theatre; the Traverse Theatre; the Liverpool Playhouse; and his local theatre, The Duke's Playhouse, Lancaster.

He has also written numerous plays and adaptations for Radios 3 and 4, including *Dead Soldiers*, voted radio play of the year.

A Life for a Life

when Khan casually brought out the enquiry as to whether Rawlinson would allow him to use it. Kline spun on his heel, turned, reached in one sudden and savage movement for the throat of Khan. Caught it. Gripped it, dragged the by no means slight Asian across the blue-plastic top of the rickety table. Khan, choking, found himself brought closer and closer to the hard angry stare of the man above him. Kline, quivering with effort and bitterness, looked down into the brown-black eyes.

'From him, are y'?'

'No... uh... no...'

Kline tightened his grip. 'Why mention the twat then?'

'The other... other released men told me... about you... you and him.'

It might have been the truth but Kline doubted it. Lifting the Asian by the lapels, Kline imparted the message he'd spent near to three years formulating. 'If y'are from Rawlinson tell him this... all I want is out from this bastard second city of his. I've done time f' his brother; either we call it quits or I'll kill him an' any more've his bleedin' clan he cares t' send against me.'

Kline pulling Khan in, then thrusting him away, letting him go, watching him crash into and down amongst the overturned tables and chairs.

'OK? Clear enough for you, shine? Good!'

Kline turned, walked towards the door as the turbaned lady came running from out of the kitchen. Kline glanced at her as he opened the door. 'Can't even have a cuppa tea in peace these days,' he said as he left.

A man wearing trousers that had just been pulled on over pyjamas joined his wife to look down on the fallen Khan, now trying to struggle to his feet from amongst the scattered and splintered remains of chairs and tables. Ted turned accusingly to his wife. 'Worr'ave I told yow about servin' wogs.'

The turbaned lady glared at her spouse indignantly. 'I didn't serve 'im. I didn't bloody well serve 'im at all!'

*　　　*　　　*

The Maverick Club looked better than Kline remembered it. Even the metal escape ladder that climbed up the side of the tall building to the top floor gymnasium had been painted. Kline nodded to himself; nice to have one's investments cared for during an absence. The club, converted by Kline and his former partner Dermot Macavoy, had been a cinema and retained the push bar doors, which were now thrown open to allow a change of air pollution to take place.

Entering the nearest of these doors Kline walked along a short green-painted corridor, went up a couple of steps and approached the side entrance to the main section of the Maverick Club. Reaching the door and peering through one of its twin circular windows, he could see that the club was empty but the faint beat of music and the spill of light from the unseen stage area made him enter. The slight thud of the door closing behind him was well lost in the wails, grunts and cries that embellished what Kline remembered as the theme from *The Good the Bad and the Ugly*. Remaining in the shadows, to the side of the door, Kline focused his attention on the stage. An older, white performer was taking a young, slim, West Indian girl through the art of removing her cowboy outfit in time to the music. Kline's gaze shifted from the girls, now prancing and whinnying about, to the table nearest the stage. There, his bulk overflowing on either side of a slimsy gold painted chair, sat Dermot Macavoy.

As the strip routine ground along its bumpy way, Kline leant back against the wall and looked about the club. It had hardly changed. New fittings of oil lamps with electric light bulbs dotted around on the tables but that was all. The large square oblong with its central circular bar still had the theme of the old west predominating, with its crossed confederate flags, wanted dead or alive posters and large blow-up photographs of long dead Indians looking impassively at a pioneer camera.

Above and on either stage were the same two heavy bison heads staring ahead with their glassy eyes. A snort of Irish impatience jerked Kline back to the stage. Evidently the novice stripper had failed to make a dirty enough draw. Macavoy was on his feet. 'Cut it. Cut th' music!' At the sound of its master's voice the music ceased. Glowering, Dermot approached the stage. Sandra, the white stripper scratched her thigh, Dinah spun the chamber of her Smith and Wesson. Dermot looked from one to the other, from the brown skin to the white, shook his head in disgust at both of them. 'I've seen sexier sisters 've mercy. You, Sandra, y' supposed t' be teachin' her how t' stir th' punters' trousers... it looks more like she's just seen her father confessor in th' front row...!'

'Stranger things 've happened,' said Kline's voice from right behind.

Turning suddenly, taking in Kline then stepping back a pace until stopped by the edge of the stage, all Macavoy could jerk out was, 'T'ought you was doin' four years?'

'Don't time pass quick when y' havin' fun?' said Kline with irony and a glance at the women above him.

Dermot started to piece himself together. The green eyes stopped darting towards the various points of exit and assumed an expression of what he hoped was honest pleasure; he straightened the waistcoat of his black pinstripe, shot some cuffs, held out at large right hand, pointed it at Kline, spread his lips in a smile and made a welcome. 'Great t' see y' John... bloody great, *great*! Yeh...'

Kline touched the proffered hand and said dryly, 'I'm sure.'

'Ey, Dermot,' said the golden voice of Sandra from above, 'we gonna re'earse or woh?'

Kline looked up and stared at Sandra. Even under the lights and stage makeup he could see the ravages of time, sex, booze, pills, drugs. And only her memory could catalogue what else. Without a woman for almost three years, Kline decided that if Sandra was all there was he'd remain celibate a while longer.

'Derm...' started Sandra again.

'Yiss... yiss!' said Dermot, searching for time to think, needing an idea and then finding it. 'Erm... full strip dis time... and with what is known as your full frontals... music!'

The music started. The same sounds came through the speakers as before with the only difference being that Kline was now in the prime position of the front row punter. He wanted to turn away but Dermot stopped him with a friendly hand and the comment that the spade girl was worth watching. Unwillingly at first Kline found himself a spectator to the gyrations that he'd witnessed before. Despite himself he found his attention concentrating on the figure of the coloured girl. Looking at the expression of her face he was surprised by the absence of the contempt most strippers affect at the men and the whole ritual. In three months or three weeks she would be as one with the rest but for the moment it was as if the enticement was more than counterfeit. Sandra, having started out on the buckskin routine alongside her pupil, quickly realised that she was performing for no one but the glass eyes of the brooding bison and withdrew. Kline heard Dermot mutter the word 'drink' and realised he had gone away.

On stage Dinah looked down at the tall man intently. She knew this part of the routine well enough to work inside the music, moving a hip... there! And throwing the other half in... there... and moving in... and legs apart and... uum! Like that... she'd had a fantasy, for a time, of being naked in a dream of walking between rows of men, of turning them on one by one... not strangers... men she knew, who would look at her like this white man. Kline saw the girl reach behind, saw the brown breasts bob only to be caught by her hands on the cups of the brassiere, which made the released straps dangle down on either side of the restraining hands.

'Good dangler, very promisin'...' said Dermot, returning with two glasses full to brimming with whisky. 'Not bad, Dinah, not bad at all!' he shouted in encouragement. Dinah smiled, let her breasts go free. Kline took a swallow of whisky, forgetting it was stronger than prison cocoa, and choked on the difference. 'Long time between drinks,' said Dermot understandingly.

'Not only drinks,' said Kline watching the brown body of Dinah Carmichael move towards him, stop, shake and start to ease itself out of the low slung, heavy gunbelt.

Dinah let the gunbelt go, stepped out of its circle of leather, hid herself with her last piece of apparel – her cream coloured Stetson. Kline watched her. She watched him. Dermot watched them both as the music swelled to its climax.

'Want y' money, do y'?' he said casually.

Kline nodded. 'Soon as y' like.'

Dinah removed her stetson. Kline had time to take in the open thighs with the tight dark curl between before Dermot's reply reached him. As it did Dinah swirled the stetson towards him. He caught it by reflex, turned to the white face of Dermot Macavoy and asked him to repeat himself.

'Y' money. I 'aven' got it.'

Kline felt his desire for the girl drown in a cold hostility for the man. Dermot, sensing this and covering his fear, hastily said 'Not...

not here, that is, not *here*.'

'Where?' said Kline.

Good question, thought Dermot, looking for another diversion, however temporary, and seeing Dinah still on stage. 'OK, Dinah, same way t'night and there won't be a dry leg in th' house!'

Dinah nodded, picked up her items of scattered gear and walked off across the stage. Dermot watched her. 'She use' t' hustle 'til I converted her.'

Kline placed the stetson he was holding onto the Irishman's head. 'You'll get your reward in heaven, an' bleedin' quick if I don't get my loot.'

Dermot looked less than well. 'Thirty grand, John. Take me least a coupla days.'

'Two grand – t'night.'

'Das tough, John.'

So pretty under his hat, thought Kline, who smiled and pulled the brim down over Macavoy's ears so that the style of the stetson became that of a cloche, held onto the hat and looked into the green eyes with the reddened rims. 'Just you get it, Dermot,' he said pleasantly, 'or I'll take my half out in bricks an' mortar.'

Having said this Kline released his grip on the hat and Dermot. Turned, walked across the tacky carpet past the bar in the centre, out through an exit and out onto the streets of Birmingham.

Watching Kline disappear, Dermot eased the pressure from one ear and then the other, removed the stetson and tossed it from him. He was glad he was no longer the owner of the Maverick Club; Kline was a problem that could be passed on. He thought as to which telephone extension would be the nearer, decided on the one by the bar. On reaching it he poured himself a drink, took the phone off its hook and dialled a number.

In the main office that spread across most of the top floor of the tallest building in the city of Birmingham, Rawlinson was closing a deal after a long haggle with a booking agent about contracts for artists to entertain on the circuit of Rawlinson's night clubs. Rawlinson, a stocky man of forty, moved a paper knife along the top of the desk as he listened to the voice pouring adjectives of praise down his ear about a comedian that Rawlinson found particularly unfunny. Time to stop this bullshit, he decided, and cutting across the other's spiel he said curtly, 'Yeh, I remember your client...' Pause for effect, get the bastard's hopes up, add a twist of insult. 'Your artiste...' Rawlinson began to enjoy himself. 'Still calls hisself a comedian, does he? Last time he done my clubs he was as funny as terminal cancer.' Rawlinson grinned at the protestations at the other end of the line then got bored with it and cut in again. 'No... no... no dice...' Remembered a catch phrase that was a little more up to date '...Y' know what they say... no bleedin' way!' And put the phone down on its cradle. It buzzed once back at him. Like a bee farting, Rawlinson thought sourly, and picked it up again. His secretary, as usual, did not bother to announce the caller so Rawlinson said, 'Rawlinson...' rolling the first letters of his name, which he liked to do for effect. Hearing only the voice of the manager of one of his smaller clubs, his interest fell away, only to revive until he was all attention, both on the words of his caller and the photograph of himself with his full family of brothers that stood on the desk before him. 'Yeh,' Rawlinson said. 'Yeh... and?'

In the darkened bar of the Maverick Club, Dermot swallowed half of his drink and continued with the news of Kline's release. 'Jus' now... right now, he left jus' now... no... no... I didn't say you owned the place now... he wants his share of the money... I put him off... had to, didn' I... but Kline he said he'd be back t'night for it... and sure as fate he will ... that's right, t'night... yeh.'

Rawlinson felt an emotion not too familiar to him for the last couple of years – anticipation. He spoke calmly into the mouthpiece, 'You leave it to me, Dermot.' He replaced the telephone receiver, continued to stare at the framed photograph before him. He saw himself three years before: Short hair, streaked grey, grinning at a bar with his brothers. All three – Tommy, Billy and the youngest, Brian. He remembered the days and weeks that followed the taking of that photograph. What was there to laugh about then, at that moment when the camera went click? He'd forgotten. Nothing to laugh at later when he had reached the accident hospital to find his youngest brother in a coma that deepened until the only word for it was death. The police had already arrested Kline and had him, click, locked up safe inside a police cell. Lucky, the bastard, to click for that… and click… again click… what ? Rawlinson turned on the swivel of his black-leather executive chair, impatient to locate the clicking source of irritation. Saw the slim build of his secretary beside him clicking the mechanism of his gold cigar lighter. 'Worrisit?' he said fiercely.

'Someone to see you.'

'Let 'm wait.'

Anne Darracott shrugged, put the lighter down, started to stroll away back to the outer office. Rawlinson watched her, wanting to share with someone. 'Annie…' he said softly. She stopped, turned, looked at him. Rawlinson glanced again at the photograph then over and across to the cool of his assistant. He made himself speak calmly. 'He's out. The bloke who killed our Brian 's out an' walkin' th' streets… huh, stupid bastard must've earned hisself remission.'

'Yeh?' was all she said. She turned and went on her way.

Rawlinson frowned, annoyed at her lack of emotion. 'Ey!'

'What?'

'Who's outside?'

'An Asian guy.'

A sniff from Rawlinson. 'Tryin' t' curry favour, is 'e?'

Not a glimmer of anything from Anne, who simply replied, 'Says he's carrying information.'

'Better than typhoid,' rejoined Rawlinson, trying again, then, giving up attempts to amuse, 'Onc've ours?'

A nod from Anne; impatience at this from her boss.

'Why not send him onto Rafiq?'

'Won't have it. Insists on seeing you.'

'Insists? *Insists*, does he? Well, if he insists we must have him in, mustn't we… seein' as how he bleedin' well *insists*!'

Anne, at the door, beckoned with a slight movement of her head. An Asian with a carefully trimmed moustache appeared in the doorway. Rawlinson looked at him with distaste. Knowing it would annoy, Anne announced, 'Mister Khan.'

Rawlinson sat back against his chair, swinging back and forth, staring ahead, his mind running more on the release of Kline than the visit of Mr Khan. The movement Anne made to return to the outer office brought back Rawlinson's attention. 'Come in. You an' all, Anne. Now. You. Matey. I hear that yow've bin insistin' on it.'

Khan said, bewildered, 'On... on what, please, sir?'

'On seeing me, please, sir.'

'Yes, yes...' Khan nodded earnestly and moved forward.

'Stop there.'

Khan stopped.

'Now, fire away.'

'Please?'

'Yow info, worrisit?'

Khan paused, looked sideways at Anne Darracott, who had taken a seat over by the office window.

Rawlinson caught the glance, smiled. 'Don't yow worry, my secretary is privy to all confidential information – so let's 'ave it.'

Khan shuffled his feet. Looked square at Rawlinson and enunciated clearly, 'John Kline has been released from prison.' Having said this he looked from one to the other.

Rawlinson was playing with a paper knife. His secretary was examining the back of her hands.

Khan thought he'd try again.

'The release... took place this mornin'...'

'Yes, we know...'

'How...?'

Rawlinson chuckled to himself, stood up with a burst of energy that sent him across to the window to look across the spread of Birmingham.

'Know everything in this city, me. Everything in Brum that moves, breathes or speaks I know all about...'

He turned from the window, looked across at Anne Darracott. She could sense the excitement running through him. Rawlinson looked her over from the fawn silk blouse to the brown skirt and the darker brown of the underslip just visible beneath.

He smiled, allowed himself to boast a little. 'I've an all embracin' eye, n'all, one that sees all, knows all, right down t' th' colour've undies she's wearin'.'

'Oh,' said Khan, showing a little embarrassment.

'One thing I don't know, just yet, is what your score is, matey.'

'Sir?'

'What's Kline to you?'

Khan took a breath. 'Enterprise and initiative.'

This brought a grunt from Rawlinson. 'Ey?'

Khan continued in his most Asian manner. 'I am trying to show them to you, sir, by keeping an eye on the prison...'

'Just in case Kline was released early?'

'So I could inform you, yes, sir.'

Rawlinson returned to his desk. Sat down. Stared at Khan, frowned in an attempt at recall. 'I've seen yow... at one've my clubs... the Maverick with...' Rawlinson never could remember names and looked as usual towards his companion. '...Young wog... the nutcase... carries a blade... lipstick?' He brought out in a burst of inspiration.

'Kuldip,' Anne said, rearranging her skirt.

'With 'im, ar.'

'Kuldip allows me to assist him on occasion,' Khan explained.

Rawlinson, rapidly losing interest and wishing to concentrate on more personal issues, stood up, pointed at Khan and looked at his secretary.

'What's his name?'

'Khan.'

'OK, Khan,' said Rawlinson, 'yow've initiated y' enterprise very nicely, so how about urinatin' off out've it?'

With a succession of small bows Khan began his retreat from the office. Rawlinson, in time to these movements, said, 'Ta-ra... ta-ra... ta-ra...!' Then just before the Asian closed the door, ended the interview with a contemptuous, 'Obsequious bastard!'

Anne smiled, stretched her arms above her. Rawlinson looked down at her. He loved the veneer of arrogance about the bones of her thin body. He reached to help her to her feet, took her deliberately by the hollow of her inner arm. She winced and pulled away just as he knew she would. 'Drink?' he said softly, moving towards the wall cabinet. Pushing a picture of the unsaddling enclosure at Ascot racecourse so that it swung open to reveal a mirrored cabinet containing on its glass shelves a varied array of drinks. 'Drink?' Rawlinson repeated. Still rubbing her arm, Anne Darracott shook her head, once, vigorously. The blonde hair swirled. Rawlinson watched it settle back into place. His fingers unconsciously followed the curves and hollows of the Dimple whisky bottle he had selected. Taking a glass from the bottom shelf, he poured scotch into it and stared at his secretary. It was a look of pure calculation and one she knew covered the play of odds and chances, profits and loss, risk and safety, life or death.

'What?' she said warily.

Rawlinson gave no sign of hearing her question, He was playing the angle of taking the enemy's place. If I'd been banged up in prison for nigh on three years, he thought, what I'd most want after a strong cuppa tea is a woman who looked just like that. Tired of the silence, Anne tried again to interrupt the process of Rawlinson's thoughts.

'What is it?'

Yeh! Rawlinson thought. If I was Kline and I was given the opportunity of a bunk up with a smooth piece of arse like you, baby, I might just drop my guard along with my trousers. With the first move in his strategy of capture decided, Rawlinson realised his white queen was about to depart the board.

'Annie!' he called after her.

At the doorway Anne paused, not turning. 'What?'

Rawlinson smiled his smile. Anne Darracott turned, saw it. Knew what it meant.

'What do you want?' she said, resignedly.

Chapter Two

Dermot Macavoy, his bulk encased in the mohair of a black evening dress suit, was at his station at the corner of the central bar of the Maverick Club, scanning the incoming punters for the white face of his former partner, John Kline.

Nervous and in need of a drink he snapped his fingers the way he had once seen Edward G. do in a forties film. 'Mack... same... same!'

The barman poured the Guinness against the inside of the glass to make a head a face could have been inscribed on, then totted a Jamesons whiskey chaser to stand alongside its dark companion. Dermot grunted as the glasses were placed before him, nodded, fretted, wondered whether to knock the straight Irish whiskey back western style then sip the stout or to do it the other way round. Shrugged to himself, took a taste of each and looked about him; checked his bouncers were at their posts, saw they were then cocked an ear to the quartet of musicians playing background noise to merge into the foreground noise coming from a side table containing members of the firm. Dermot frowned, twiddled with his purple velvet bow-tie, smoothed the ruffles of his lilac dress shirt and adjusted the position of his claret cummerbund, and told himself that if you employed niggers and wogs you must expect a little over exuberance. It was how they were. Dermot sighed, looked again for Kline without success and wished it was his night off, when he could wear a decent ordinary suit with a collar and tie and take himself down to the Irish Community Centre, there to feel safe and able to bask in a reputation grown tall on whisper and rumour that he was in on the rackets and knew what was what about you know who... Another burst of laughter from the side table interrupted the Irishman's thoughts. That'd be Malleson, Dermot told himself – always jumpy before a job, always showing himself around trying to impress Rawlinson and all the more since losing his last three fights. Yeh, he needs to collar Kline PDQ for everybody's sake, including his own, Dermot thought, turning and looking across at the side table and its assorted members. There was Malleson holding court, just as Dermot had imagined, all brown and white – brown skin, white teeth, brown shirt under the white jacket that stretched across his muscular boxer's shoulders. His trousers, too, were brown – expensive, sharp of crease and cut. Only the shoes he wore failed to match the style of the dandy that Malleson affected; they were brown but low of heel with a serrated rubber sole for grip when running and a fortified steel toe-cap for support against the impact of kicking. Next to him sat a Pakistani, Kuldip, small but well set with big hands and forearms made powerful by steering the wheels of Rawlinson's transport and of the occasional need to hang onto the handle of a knife when its sharp end jarred against bone. Kuldip laughed a lot but his laughter was never unguarded. When he could he liked a wall at his back and a hand inside his jacket, just as it was now, with a finger to touch the knife strapped snug inside its sheath on the strap beneath his left arm pit. Next to Kuldip was his assistant, Khan, and beside him sat Dinah Carmichael, her features vivid with stage make up and the application of a gold star painted just below her right cheek bone by her tutor, Sandra.

Malleson, from across the table, watched the play of lights on Dinah's glittering lurex dress that just parried the thrust of her breasts. I'm not a tit man, any'ow, Malleson told himself. Only reason y' want that one with those two tits is on account 've, like, she found out about my *in*tentions before she got 'ooked on my *att*entions. Malleson smiled. He liked that. Dinah saw the smile. Looked away, disdainfully. Probably thought I'm at it, mused Malleson. Well, screw you an your smart arse, I've had you, seen you, hair out, legs up 'n'kickin', tits up like rocks... Malleson frowned. Was he getting mixed up with somebody else? It didn't matter; they were all the bleedin' same so no wonder he got confused. Malleson scratched the fuzz of his head, took a pull of his beer.

'When's the comedian coming on?' said Dinah to no one in particular.

'When's the *stripper* comin' on?' said Malleson, showing his teeth at her. Dinah, ignoring this, turned away and looked towards the empty stage beneath the brooding bison.

'I wish he'd come on, don't you?' she asked Khan.

'Sure,' Khan said.

'I could use a laugh,' said Dinah, wishing the night would go away, become a story to recount... when I did my first strip, she'd say, with a giggle... no... with a shrug... as if it didn't matter...

She became aware that Malleson was gazing intently at her. 'What you staring at?'

Malleson imitated a pop-eyed punter. Licked his lips, leered lasciviously at her body. 'Just imagining the delights t'come, hur-hur!'

Holding up her middle and forefingers, opening and giving them a swift jerk upwards into the air and across at Malleson, Dinah turned away in time to witness the entrance of Anne Darracott. Kuldip, too, saw the blonde secretary enter and nudged Khan. All of the table, including Malleson, watched her slow, calm walk towards the bar and Dermot's flurry of welcome. Dinah looked the white woman up and down, from the long fawn evening skirt and the expensive, deceptively simple, white blouse with the fawn tasseled shawl draped, oh so casually, across the thin shoulders. There's one cool lady, Dinah thought; any guy wanted to strip that one down would need an ice pick.

'Royal visit,' Kuldip spoke for the first time for over an hour, nodding as he did so towards Dermot and Anne at the bar.

Malleson, reminded of the task before him, drowned his tension with a swallow of Brew Eleven, smiled and indicated the seemingly sullen Dinah. 'Must've heard about the big dayboo...!'

Malleson cleared his throat as if prior to an important announcement.

'...Ladies an' gentlemen, tonight a new strip queen is about to reveal herself, naked an' unadorned... I give to you...' Malleson made pause to wet a finger with which write imaginary letters on the smoke-filled air. 'I give you Miss-Dinah-Carmichael, who will appear tonight for the very first time, complete with her own, her very own, pussy, tits an' arse!'

Dinah gave him a look made cold with as much indifference as she could muster.

'Piss off, why don't you?' she retorted.

To this Malleson made no immediate reply, his attention being focused on the tall man wearing a blue suit and a pink shirt who had just entered the club. The grin that had momentarily died came more or less back to life. 'Piss off? Why not… Always open t' suggestions, me, y'know …' he said, standing, picking up his glass of beer and drinking, holding John Kline in his sights, making sure that Dermot met Kline and introductions were fully made to Rawlinson's knocking piece, Anne Darracott. Once they were that was the signal for Malleson to go. He placed his empty pint glass in front of Dinah, looked down on her, said, 'What a pity I won't see y' come all spillin' out've y' dress… still, I've seen it all before. I know you inside an' out an' that's a fact.'

It was true enough, but Dinah preferred not to think about it. Seeing movement on stage, she reacted by clapping her hands together like a child at a circus. 'Here's the comedian!' she said to Khan.

'That's right,' Khan said, watching her profile. She was all attention on the stage, where Billy Brody, this week's compère and comedian, straight from the pub across the street, was trying to remember the first words of his act.

'Awright,' he said to someone he didn't recognise. 'Awright,' he said again and tried to remember where he was and what the club was called. He was about to say 'Awright' once more when he noticed a tall, muscular coloured lad in a white jacket about to go through the exit marked 'Gents' that was down below Brody to the left of the stage. Inspiration seeped into Brody's brain. He bent down to Malleson as he passed in front of the stage, 'Go first left, sir, that's where you'll find them all hanging out…'

Malleson, his mind fully occupied with the problems of deploying a strike force on a mission of capture that might entail amphibian manoeuvre, did not hear the shaft of wit directed at him but shouldered his way through the exit doors and disappeared from the view of the tittering audience.

On stage the comedian continued to follow the thread he had started, 'Roll on transplant surgery, ey, Missis… be some murders done then, ey, woh? Still, yow think yow've got problems… friend of mine was in this underground urinal…' Brody waited for the groans from the audience to come. When they eventually did he continued, 'this bog down th' Bull Ring…' This brought a few cheers, with which Brody joined in while trying to remember the end of the joke he'd launched himself on. 'Anyway… anyway… ah, yes, there he was, in this bog attendin' to his business, lookin' after the stall, so t'speak.' Here Brody did a fair imitation of a rather downtrodden man in the act of urinating and remembered while doing so that he should have passed some beer through himself before he came on... Enough of that,he thought quickly, get on... get through this bloody story, intro the next act, whatever that is, an' get off... 'This brummy bloke,' Brody continued, speeding the story up as he suddenly recalled the punch line, 'was just comin' t' th' end of a peaceful pee when 'oo should come pantin' up but a bloody big night... a rather large member of our coloured brethren. Well, this jungle bunny dives into the next stall an' gets on with it... oooh! Great expressions of joy and relief... ooh! Ooh! So the little white bloke peeks a look over the splash barrier. An' what he saw, ladies an' gentlemen, did 'is well bein' no good at all.' Brody hitched his trousers, mimed the shaking of a penis the size of an Anaconda and assumed an accent that was intended to be West Indian but got no nearer to those islands than the Victoria Palace and the Black and White Minstrel show. ' "Ah tells you what, white man, I only just made dat..." "Gor' blimey," said the little man, "I wish y'd made me one!" There was some laughter around the club, not particularly hearty from the white male members of the audience, and Brody, seeing the trio of black girl soul singers preparing for their entrance, remembered who they were, introduced them as the Shadettes and left them to cover his retreat with the opening bars of 'Respect'.

In the corner of the bar Kline was at the end of his patience with the Irishman in the mohair evening suit and had just said so. In the background Anne Darracott sank another brandy without blinking. Uneasily, Dermot ran his fingers along the serrated folds of his cummerbund and decided to make a small stand. 'Don't threaten me, Johnny...'

'I need it. I need that loot t' piss off out've it.'

'Later,' Dermot said soothingly, 'later, relax... meet sum female company why don't'cha... Anne...!' He beckoned her with a clumsy inward wave of his hand then whispered conspiratorially to Kline as Anne came across to join them. 'I'll see y'right, don't worry.'

'You'd bleedin' better,' said Kline fiercely.

'fighting talk?' said Anne looking up at Kline and hitching her shawl around her.

Kline continued to stare at Dermot, who answered Anne by patting Kline tentatively on the shoulder and saying, 'No. Not at all.

Everything's fine, just a slight delay in a transfer of funds.' Then, turning half away from Anne, he muttered to Kline, 'You'll be taken care of, Johnny. She's all right, this one, got a boat...' Macavoy winked an eye, turned back to Anne. 'Just tellin' John here about y' boat...'

Kline looked at the blonde opposite to him. She looked several classes above the Maverick. Kline had an urge to ask what a chick like her was doing in a joint like this but resisted it. Dermot watched some eye contact taking place and carried on. 'Aye, a boat... of 'er own... down the canal... yeh.' Kline's glance shifted to Dermot, who again came in close to Kline's ear. 'You'll be all right there. Come back later f'y' money...' Dermot made ready to walk away from what he hoped would be a very short courtship. The prospect of getting rid of Kline lifted his spirits and with a final encouragement for Anne to 'treat this boy right for wasn't he a partner of mine from the old days?' Dermot lumbered away to leave Anne and Kline alone. Warily Kline looked around the club. No one seemed to be observing him. All eyes seemed focused on the gyrations and soaring rhythm of the three girl singers on stage, who were bringing an old Supremes number to a close with the obligatory cries of simulated orgasm. Kline turned his attention back to Anne Darracott. He felt a little of the reaction he always had when seeing the fashion model figure – curiosity but no instant desire.

Anne, intuitively realising Kline's reaction, sensed that the only time to make a play was right now. She walked four steps to the corner of the bar, turned, leaned back against the side wall, put an elbow on the bar, shifted her slight body weight onto it and looked across at Kline, who, without moving to follow, watched Anne's fingers move to adjust her shawl and remain at her throat. He saw a long forefinger tipped with a sheen of pink polish extend in his direction then journey up towards the lips that parted to smile at him. The white teeth gave the forefinger a small bite of reproval and the smile widened. Kline realised it was all there for him if he wanted it and he did want it. He wanted nothing better than to feel the flesh of a woman under and all about him. But even with the onset of want and need, somewhere in his mind the question nagged of it being all too easy. This woman – why should she go for him? Still, there was an answer; she could be a lady who only achieves release from a bit of rough. So, that was feasible. But why here and why tonight? He did not come up with any answers and perhaps he did not want to, for the nearest he had been to a woman like this was the glossy pictures pinned up by his cell mates on a prison wall. He knew that he would have taken greater chances to achieve a lesser prize. When he reached the blonde at the bar he inhaled deeply as if to scent out danger but all he could realise was the perfume of her.

Anne said nothing.

Kline said, 'Where's your boat?'

Chapter Three

The Indian film ended with the hero and heroine reunited. They glanced meaningfully at each other, sang their final song, gazed at each other again as the music reached its crescendo and finally ended. Jashir Singh Mahal looked across to his wife, Mangit, seated two children away from him; she nodded, stood and led the sideways shuffle along the crowded row of seats that led to the central aisle. Once there Jashir and his family walked on the threadbare carpet towards the main exit and foyer. Behind them, on the screen, flashed a trailer for the next week's programme, which featured two Indian actors fighting throughout the length of an express train. While the frenetic sound track crashed and cymbaled, words traversed the screen and were repeated as a voice over, words like 'VIOLENCE!' And 'HUNTED!' And 'NO ESCAPE FROM THE GRIP OF CHILLING FEAR!' The words still ringing in his head, Jashir left the cinema, gathered his family about him and waited to cross the Moseley Road. Tomorrow, he thought, tomorrow you will live in another part of Birmingham. One that is safe and secure. A cream bus with a blue line along its side pulled into its stop, causing a slight delay in the traffic. Jashir took his five year old, Bela, by the hand; the fingers of his son took a firm grip. His daughter, the year-younger Ashi, held her mother's hand and the Sikh family hurried across the Moseley Road. Behind them, down in the distance, was the skyline of the city, dominated by the dark oblong shapes of the high rise tower blocks with their myriad of living room lights climbing the sky. Once, years before, Jashir had stood and looked at the same skyline and marvelled that he had attained the goal of reaching such a city. Now he did not even notice them as he turned his back on the lights of Birmingham and hurried down Highgate and towards the two rooms on Stoney Lane that for one night more he would call his home

*   *   *

Kline followed Anne Darracott along the banks of the canal that once had acted as the artery of the heart of Birmingham's trade and transport system. In the darkness, with light only from the street above, Kline admired the quick step of his companion. He was about to make comment to this effect when Anne reached a long, white shape alongside the overgrown towpath.

'This it?' said Kline.

'Right.'

'What's its name?'

'*Anne Carol.*'

'Like you?'

'No.'

'Oh.'

Kline followed her aboard, went down a hatch that led into a small compact kitchen with a gas stove. Kline wondered where the gas came from and presumed it was from a container. He was about to ask about this and where the power for the light came from when Anne pushed through a bead curtain into the next section of the interior. Kline followed and found himself in the main living space of the *Anne Carol*. Kline looked about him, at the pictures on the walls and the small, almost miniature furniture. Like their owner they looked small, slight, polished and expensive. 'Old,' said Kline, indicating a chiffonier, 'I mean, antique…'

'Yes,' was all Anne said. She went to the far end of the cabin to the sliding doors that allowed entry from the prow of the barge. She glanced down at the padlock outside; it was as she had arranged, seemingly secure. After pulling the heavy tapestry curtains across she turned back to the business in hand. Kline watched her sit down on the double bed that was as broad as it was long and reach for a rag doll propped up against a pair of dark red silk cushions. Anne stared into the black button eyes before placing the limp toy carefully onto a small circular rosewood table at her bedside. She came back onto the surface of the bedcover, shrugged off her fringed shawl, shook her hair so that it swirled, then lay back languorously against the silk of the cushions and looked invitingly across at John Kline, who felt suddenly alert in every tingling nerve as he anticipated the end of the short journey between himself and her bed. He walked carefully across the carpeted floor until there was only bed and Anne Darracott before him. He eased himself down alongside her. Supported himself on an elbow and eased himself down on her. Anne shifted so her thigh made contact with his; Kline felt the pressure and went down to touch her lips with his. He felt the contact, made the pressure, then closed his eyes and let his body experience what his mind had long imagined.

Malleson, from his vantage point on Bridge Street, saw the lights spill from the *Anne Carol* onto the waters of the canal below. He gripped the wood of his pickaxe handle and waved it once towards the car that contained his fellow workers. They came out of the car and joined Malleson at the wall. In the darkness away from the street lights the dark skin of their faces could have been masked, for no features were discernible. Malleson only recognised which was which by the white beret that Bryden habitually wore. He was about to administer a reprimand about wearing white on a night raid when he remembered his own jacket and its snow white elegance. 'I don't know which end they'll be rockin' th' boat from... so you, Bonny, come with me, n' you... Atty take the sharp end, up front... right?' The white beret nodded and Hunniford, the light heavyweight, said nothing but vaulted athletically over the wall and disappeared towards the towpath that lay below. Cautiously, Malleson and Bryden followed and lowered themselves from the wall into the undergrowth at the foot of the wall. I should never've worn this jacket, it'll be ruined, Malleson told himself... and cursed as he stumbled on what felt like an old bottomless iron bucket.

'Awright?' Bryden whispered.

'Yeh,' Malleson replied, then, gripping his pickaxe handle firmly, he began to walk stealthily towards the light that came from the windows and open hatch of the motorbarge *Anne Carol*.

On the bed in the front section of the barge Kline was exploring the body of the woman beside him. All his instincts were to delve and grab and squeeze and take. But knowing that the main bout would be of short duration he made himself extend the preliminaries to give the woman a chance to come with him. Anne Darracott murmured. Kline could not see her face, which was turned away from him. He kissed the length of her throat, ran a hand down her hip, thigh, went up inside the skirt. Anne writhed, moaned. Kline encountered the hot dry centre of her. The arid welcome gave Kline that split second pause in which he heard the footsteps in the kitchen. Feeling him shift, Anne Darracott put her hands to his head, brought it down. Kline felt the hands holding his head suddenly tense and that decided him to move; Kline pushed her from him and rolled away as Malleson brought the pickaxe handle down with maximum force into the middle of the square foot of bedcover that Kline's head had occupied not half a second before. Kline scrambled across the bed and headed for the prow of the boat and straight into the massive arms of Atty Hunniford, who charged in through the sliding door. Trapped between the two West Indians, Kline did the unexpected and went back at the one with the pick handle. Malleson, seeing him leap back across the bed, swung the hard wood handle. Kline ducked. The wooden club smashed into a hanging lamp, which disintegrated, leaving the main cabin in sudden darkness. Kline could hear Anne Darracott's screams. He felt a body cannon into his and hang on; bringing a knee up into the groin of his attacker, Kline felt the impact but nothing like as much did the recipient, who gave a shout of sudden anguish and released Kline to stumble away towards the kitchen.

On his way Kline tripped on what felt like a cushion, tried to keep his balance, grabbed for the wall, caught hold of a rail of pictures which followed him as he fell to the floor. As he was struggling to rise, something hit him in the back and went down over him. Kline, in a corner, found what felt like a large plant pot with a spiked cactus and smashed it down onto where the head of his latest assailant should have been. It hit something, cracked against a bone and brought an exclamation of pain and rage, and a delay that Kline used to regain his feet and to reach the still lighted kitchen, where Bryden, in his white beret, was posted to meet whoever emerged from the melee inside. Bryden made the mistake of waiting long enough to see whether the figure was friend or foe and in that time Kline hit him once and once again. Bryden rocked, went back onto a shelf that did not give as a rope would have done but collapsed and brought a set of pans crashing down. By the time the pans had clunked together on the floor of the kitchen Kline was through the hatch and running towards the wall and the safety of the street above. He heard running footsteps behind as he struggled through the weeds and junk towards the wall. Once there he jumped, got a grip on the brickwork, felt his nails stub and tear as he found a grip that allowed him to haul his body weight upwards. Kline turned his body at the top of the wall just as the West Indian with the white jacket came at his legs wielding a pickaxe handle with every intention of smashing the dangling legs against the wall with one savage crossbat stroke. Kline lifted his legs in an instinct of preservation. The handle zapped into the wall with a jar that shook Malleson from fingers to the blades of his shoulders. He stopped as the wave of shock went through him, which allowed Kline to give him a restricted kick that landed just below the black's ear. Malleson went down amongst the rust and rubbish at the bottom of the canal wall and rolled over far enough to complete the final ruin of the once white jacket.

When Malleson got to his feet and rubbed his head he found an ear somewhat enlarged and still ringing inside. He was joined by Hunniford, sore of skull and limping, and Bryden, unmarked except for a graze on his boxer's banana nose. When all three climbed back to the road there was no sign of John Kline. 'I want t' see that white man again,' said Hunniford, rubbing the area where he wished he had worn his protector.

'Yeh,' said Bonny Bryden, feeling the squash of his rubber nose.

Malleson said nothing but looked back at the *Anne Carol*. He had not expected much trouble and was apprehensive for the consequences of the wreckage they had left below. 'She all right?' Malleson enquired anxiously.

Bryden grinned. 'I have seen happier ladies…'

'We did leave her home in what you could call a state of disarray,' Hunniford continued.

Bryden nudged the scowling Malleson. 'Not to mention coitus interruptus…'

'Ah, bollocks on the pair of you… don't you understand she's Rawlinson's?' He saw by the change of expression on their black faces that they now did. Malleson thought he knew where John Kline would go next and wondered if it would be better to try and placate Anne Darracott over the visit just paid to her home. No, he thought, capture Kline, give him to Rawlinson on a plate with an apple up his arse and all that clobber on the boat won't matter. Yeh. 'OK,' Malleson said to the others, touching his ear tenderly, 'shall we go and catch up with this Kline?'

When they reached the borrowed Jaguar car, Malleson got in the back, Hunniford in the passenger seat and Bryden beside him at the wheel. 'Where to?' said the voice from under the white beret.

'The Maverick,' Malleson ordered as he lay back against the seat and closed his eyes. His arms ached, the fingers that held the pickaxe handle across his knees were still numb and inside his swollen ear was the throb of a tom-tom. He opened his eyes, looked at the broad shoulders of his companions in the front seats of the car and said venomously, 'I'm goin' t'mash that Kline bastard!'

Chapter Four

Dinah Carmichael looked at herself in the long glass of her dressing room mirror. She looked confident enough in her boots; short, tasselled tan skirt; neon yellow briefs; gun belt and gun; tan bolero jacket to match the skirt; yellow gloves and a kerchief of the same colour at her throat and on her head a cream coloured stetson hat. She checked her make-up, looked at the outline of the gold star painted below her left cheek bone and then muttered to herself in reproof, 'No one's going to be looking at your face!' and flounced out the dressing room ready to get on and get her debut over. Halfway along the corridor she remembered she had forgotten to lock her dressing room. Then wondered where she could possibly keep the key; then forgot all about it as she reached the rear of the stage.

Dermot, the manager, was waiting. He nodded, looked her up and down, the way another man would have appraised a racehorse. 'You right?' was all he said. Dinah heard the comedian in mid-spiel on stage; she heard the words of the joke about an immigrant who wanted to be a conductor so they nailed him to a chimney. Dinah did not understand anything of this and only registered that part of the introduction that followed because it ended with her name. Dermot saw her frozen at the side of him. 'Get on!' he urged '...On!' and put his hand behind her narrow waist and pushed her onto the stage. Dinah stumbled slightly; someone laughed in derision at a side table. Her music started, she picked up its rhythm and strode to the edge of the stage and stood right over the table where the snigger had emanated from. Once there she looked her contempt at the bevy of super salesmen seated there. She selected the one with the sickliest grin, turned her back, pulled her gun, spun the chamber, opened her legs, twitched her thighs, bent forward and shot the startled salesman with a blank bullet aimed through the archway of her beautiful brown legs. That done, she straightened, coolly blew down the barrel of her gun. Someone clapped and the rest followed suit. Dinah holstered the gun, moved her thighs again to the beat of the music and started to remove a leather glove.

Outside the Maverick John Kline prowled along the rear of the building seeking an ill fitting exit door. Finding a possibility he straightened a piece of rusty wire, picked up for the purpose of gaining entry, and bent one end to form a hook. This done he pressed against one of the doors and inserted the wire hook into the gap created by his pressure. Feeling for the push bar, Kline could hear from inside the theme from that morning: 'The Good, the Bad and the Ugly'. He remembered, in a flash of recall, those brown breasts with the black tips pointing at him and missed a chance to lift the bar. 'Good Christ!' Kline swore at himself. 'Half've Birmingham lookin' for you an all you're at is brown tits and black pussy!' He tried the wire probe again; this time its hook got under the bar and like a surgeon sewing a suture Kline drew it out and up as he pressed the door with a knee until it opened. Kline went inside, closed the door behind him. He followed the ever louder music towards the rear of the stage and there he was – Dermot Macayoy himself, watching the rear of Dinah Carmichael and indulging in a sly game of pocket billiards. Kline smiled tightly to himself, went up behind Dermot, put his mouth to the Irishman's ear and said, as a statement of fact, 'You double crossin' black enamel get!' Dermot blinked, turned. Kline remembered the woman on the bed in the cabin, the flailing pickhandle, the money he needed to escape, and the frustration of it all caused him to lash out at the bullet head of Dermot Macavoy, who half rode the blow but staggered back. Kline was about to follow up when on stage Dinah reached behind her and undid the hook of her brassiere. The movement caught Kline's eye and distracted his intention to hang another punch on his former partner's chin.

The music pounded on. Under the shrill cries and yells of the vocal accompaniment the audience held its breath as Dinah dangled her straps prior to boosting her breasts at them. A sigh came as she opened her arms. Dermot, realising he was not to be struck again, said to Kline, covering his injury with an air of innocence, 'I t'ought you'd gone off shaggin'.'

'Oh, sure. Me, the bird, and your three black gorillas!'

Dermot assumed a puzzled expression. 'What you on about?'

'You wouldn't know?'

'No.'

'Got my money?' Kline enquired pleasantly.

'Sure.'

'Where?'

'My office.'

If it was as bluff it was a good one, thought Kline, watching Dermot warily as he moved towards him. 'Relax, John,' Dermot said and went past Kline. Well, now, thought Kline, maybe the conniving bastard really has got the money. There, was, of course, only one way to find out so Kline followed the burly figure of the club manager along the passage behind the stage, catching him up as they passed the artists' dressing rooms. The only precaution Kline could think of was to stay one step behind Macavoy as they headed towards the far corridor that Kline remembered did lead towards the manager's office.

The bouncer standing sentinel outside the main entrance of the Maverick Club watched the blue Jaguar stop opposite to him. He saw the three West Indians climb out and confer together. He knew who they were – members of the firm. He tried to think of some pleasantry to offer but on seeing the expressions on their damaged faces he changed his mind and was content to stand aside to ensure that their entrance to the club was an uninterrupted one.

Malleson entered the club, looked about for Dermot. On stage, Dinah, naked above the waist, hooked a thumb inside each leg of the neon yellow briefs and glanced down to see if the wide leather of the gunbelt was slung low enough across her hips. It seemed to be, so she inched down her briefs far enough to give a start for the approaching problem of their speedy removal without losing control or balance. The audience whistled appreciatively, bringing a whiff of beer-soured breath up to her. She shivered; for the first time she experienced the psychic power that a group can direct at an object. She felt the crawl of a hundred hands upon her and shuddered. The mob took this for coy reticence and urged her to continue. Hesitantly, Dinah sought a chair, sat on it, felt the fingers of the many men tug at her yellow panties until they came clear from under her gunbelt and finished at her knees. She stood and felt the briefs fall around her ankles. Then, because it was what her masters wanted, she kicked them down towards a table below her. They landed on the lap of a white man who took them up as if they were a handkerchief and went to blow his nose. But then he stopped; an expression of horror followed by revulsion at an imagined stench caused him to hurl the piece of unclean cloth from him. Those at his table collapsed, each into a paroxysm of uncontrolled raucous laughter. Nearby tables cheered and those at the rear of the club who suspected something pretty droll had occurred whistled and stamped their feet. While doing this, a man whose wife was obsessive about hygiene found the yellow drawers beneath his feet and surreptitiously pocketed them as a prize to be sniffed at later. Dinah, brown skinned, naked except for stetson and gunbelt, stood still and watched her audience be true to itself. She understood then why Sandra and the other strippers kept their contempt to hand like a shield. It was some protection against the many-headed monster that bellowed and slavered below her.

Malleson checked the area of the bar as well as he could amongst the cheering, milling crowd of punters. Failing to see Dermot or Kline he returned to the doorway and his henchmen. Finding them grinning at the stage he punched the first one and then the other to gain their attention. They looked at him resentfully. Malleson indicated by a gesture of his arm that he required Bryden to patrol the reaches of the Maverick building and for Hunniford to follow him to Macavoy's office. The West Indian trio went their separate ways as on stage Dinah wondered just how much music she still had to work with.

In the passageway that led along to the offices and the entrance to the club Dermot Macavoy, with John Kline a cautious step behind, was approaching the door marked 'Manager'. He slowed, put a hand in his pocket; Kline tensed but all Dermot pulled was a bunch of keys. He stopped outside the office door, selected a key. Kline looked up and down the corridor. Looked one way – saw nothing. Looked the other and witnessed the entry of two of the black gladiators he'd last encountered on and around the *Anne Carol*. As he didn't wish to renew the acquaintanceship particularly, Kline used Dermot as a handy excuse and thrust that gentleman at the two others who were running with some enthusiasm towards him. Dermot collided with Malleson which allowed the limping Hunniford to take the lead in the pursuit of Kline, who had slipped his field and disappeared around the far bend of the corridor.

Malleson and Dermot looked accusingly at each other. Then at the empty corridor.

'What a balls up!' said Dermot.

'Relax. Bonny's on the other side. Kline won't slip him.'

'All Bryden seems t'stop these days is heavy punches, ' said Dermot, picking up his bunch of keys from the floor.

'He's been overmatched...' Malleson started but stopped under Dermot's withering look.

'I'd love t'discuss fight ratings with y', but if y'll excuse me, I'll have the chains round your number one contender...'

Malleson did not bother to reply but went off in the direction taken by Kline and Hunniford. Kline, hoping to escape through the exit door he had opened earlier had passed by the backstage before he saw the black man in the white beret barring the way. Unseen, Kline turned and went a few steps back the way he had come and caught a glimpse of Hunniford turning into the passage that would bring him to the side entrance that for the moment sheltered Kline. There was nothing to do but take a chance so Kline entered the club proper by the entrance at the side of the stage.

Kline was fortunate that his entry coincided with the climax to Dinah's debut and that the bouncer nearest to him was all eyes on the leather gunbelt as it was eased down the circumference of Dinah's hips and flanks. The belt finally fell. The stetson covered the area of the audience's attention. The music stopped. Dinah thought, oh, shit, here goes, and opened herself to allow five full seconds of appraisal by the sheiks of Balsall Heath. The lights went out to cover her exit and in the semi darkness Kline stepped back into the corridor, looked up and down and found it empty. Quickly and quietly he walked away, expecting to hear the running footsteps of pursuit coming from behind him. Instead, just before reaching the bend of the corridor, he heard the rattle of chains and the drone of Brummy accents and footsteps loud in the silence now that the music had stopped. Kline looked back the way he had just come. From this angle he could see the three West Indians talking and gesticulating at each other in the corridor beyond the rear entrance to the stage. They only had to glance his way and Kline would be in the grip of a simple pincer movement. Desperately Kline tried the door nearest to him, marked 'Artists - Men'. It was locked. Kline went to the next, again marked 'Artists' but this time after the hyphen was the word 'Women'. Kline tried the door, turned the handle, expected it to be locked and found it open! He hurriedly went inside and closed the door behind him, turned, saw the window was just large enough to allow an escape. Kline hurried toward it, pulled on the rusted lever. Pulled on it with all his strength until it moved, allowing the window to open a full three inches before it came up against against the steel bars fitted outside to prevent entry or, in this instance, escape. Kline looked about the empty dressing room; he could see his reflection in the lighted mirror. Hunted, pale, desperate. He moved a row of multi-coloured costumes along the chromed rail of a movable clothes rack and discovered a laundry basket. Scenes from innumerable comedy films reeled into Kline's mind only to stop with the realisation that this skip only had the capacity to hide a third of him. Kline listened for sounds from outside. Maybe the chain gang had rattled past. There was no sound of them so he opened the door an inch and saw two of the blacks, one on either side of the corridor, obviously intent on checking every room and testing every locked door along the corridor. They would, in the next sixty seconds, arrive at the door that sheltered Kline. He closed the door, leaned back against it. His heart seemed to want to escape from him; it pumped and jumped as Kline tried to think what he could do next.

Malleson arrived at a door marked 'Storeroom'. He turned the steel handle; it gave an inch until the mortice of the lock stopped it from turning further. It was the final door along his side of the corridor so he glanced across at Hunniford, who was about to try the handle on the door marked 'Artists - Women'. He did so, the handle turned a little then stopped.

Malleson joined him. 'Anything ?'

Hunniford tried again. There was no movement. 'No,' he said. Malleson looked at the last door on that corridor, which was a general dressing room used occasionally when the bill was heavy with male artists. If it opened that's where the missing Kline bastard would be. Cautiously he turned the handle. It did not open.

Malleson put his shoulder against the door in frustration. The lock held tight in its frame.

'Perhaps our boy got round the other side,' Hunniford said, wishing the ache that pounded in his head and hung between his legs would dull a little.

'You go 'n' see. Meet me Dermot's office if there's nothing...' They turned, about to leave, when Malleson saw a movement down the corridor. 'Wait,' he said... but it was only Dinah Carmichael humping her gunbelt and gear along, after giving her all in the cause of the Maverick. Malleson grunted in disappointment, jerked his head for Hunniford to leave and contented himself by calling down the corridor, 'Loada rubbish. I've seen more pussy in a dog's home!' Dinah, walking bare-arsed, did not bother to reply. As she approached the door of her dressing room Malleson threw a wink at her and went away, leaving Dinah alone between the painted walls and wooden doors of the deserted corridor.

Inside the dressing room, Kline still held himself wedged across the inner frame of the door jamb. The hands that had held the lock steady against the pressure from outside showed white as Kline listened for the footsteps to go from outside of the room next door. Hearing them finally move he left the door and took a breath then another. Felt his stiffened muscles ease as the relief from tension coursed through him. He heard a shout from outside. Waited. Listened. He watched the handle of the door and saw it turn, knew he could not reach it in time. All he could do was hide and hope so he dodged behind the clothes rack and tried to conceal his height behind the row of scanty costumes.

Dinah Carmichael entered her dressing room. Closed the door, leant against it. She felt drained, disappointed, humiliated. It's not the body... naked body. What's that...? Skin with a bunch of hair... it's... ah, screw it, screw *them*, she told herself. Think of the money you'll earn and what that will bring. Comforted by this, she pushed herself away from the door. Going to the rack, she moved some costumes along to make room to hang the gun-belt and found a tall man stooped behind. She stared at him

'We've got to stop meeting like this,' Kline said and followed it with a small wan smile.

Dinah remembered the preview she had given him that morning and the search going on around the building at that moment. 'You're the guy they're after?'

Kline could not deny it, so he said dryly, 'You could say that.'

*

Malleson, finding another locked door when he reached the manager's office, went on into the club, where he found Dermot questioning Kuldip's sidekick, Khan.

'Y've seen no sign...?'

Khan shook his head.

'What about Kuldip?' Malleson interjected.

'Not here. He's on a van job,' Dermot replied for the Asian.

The Irishman and the West Indian looked around the crowded club, scanning faces, willing one of them to be that of John Kline. Khan watched them. Bryden and Hunniford pushed their way across to join them. They didn't bother to speak but simply shook their heads. Dermot glared at them. 'You've checked everywhere? Everything?'

'Right.'

To Dermot nobody seemed worried enough. So he spelled it out.

'Check everything again.' He turned to Malleson. 'Get your lazy black sods outside. Cover the fire escape, the roof. If y' find a bleedin' chimney y'ave my permission t'look down it. Bloody move! Seal this place tighter than th' gates've hell. Let dat Kline get clear an' Rawlinson will have our balls f'breakfast!'

On the top of the fire escape Kline turned to his helper.

'Ta,' he said.

'No friends of mine, those bastards,' Dinah said in explanation.

Kline looked at her with the thin cotton wrap around her. He had her address but knew he would never use it. It was time to cut all losses by pulling out of Britain's second city. There was no point saying any of it. So Kline lifted a hand to her and said 'See y'. ' The woman made no reply but went back inside away from the cold. The wooden door thudded behind her. Kline looked across the shadowy rooftops in silhouette around him. He was trying to remember the geography of the buildings. He decided that a route across the roof and onto the nearby multi-storey car park would be safer than to descend down into the yard of the Maverick. Which was a wise decision, for not a minute later Malleson and Bryden came to check the fire escape as a last resort. They found the door open and yelled at each other and at Dermot. But by that time Kline was across the roof and had entered with a leap into the multi-storey car park. He had no means of knowing then that he had been seen against the skyline and that the yellow Datsun that nosed up into the first level of the car park was seeking to run in to him.

Chapter Five

As he walked from one level of dingy, grey concrete car park to the next Kline was enjoying the absence of danger and the sound of running footsteps.

He heard the approach of a car but paid it no attention until it entered the same level as Kline, swerved between two support pillars and came directly at him. Kline did not wait to see who was behind the wheel of the yellow Datsun sports car but sprinted for the box of concrete that ran through the centre of the car park. On reaching this lift shaft Kline jabbed the button again and again but no light showed on the indicator above his head and the only machinery to be heard was underneath the bonnet of the car as it picked up speed. To his left Kline saw another exit and made towards it. Five paces away from safety Kline heard the screech of brakes and found his means of escape sealed off by a shining yellow wing. There was nothing to do but to run again and Kline went back to the lift shaft, tried the button without success before he then spied in the far corner another pair of doors under a sign in red letters that spelled 'Emergency Exit'. He checked the position of the yellow car and saw that it had remained at the exit waiting for his move. Kline realised his chance of travelling across this diagonal route to the doors in the far corner depended on the speed of his legs and the reflexes of the unknown driver. It was odds against him but Kline had no other option to take so he edged out of sight around the lift shaft, kept its bulk between him and the car and then started across the park like a rabbit at a bolt hole. Behind him, the sports car came forward from the entrance to allow its driver to see the running man and to assess his intention. Kline, mouth open, arms flailing, legs trying to hold their pace across the oil-stained concrete, could hear the Datsun turning, revving, picking up speed and racing nearer and nearer.

Suddenly the adrenaline that had sustained him seemed to ebb; he felt suddenly sick, tired, leaden. The distance that lay between him and the doors seemed immeasurable.

He mustered his remaining energy and hurled himself clear from the path of the pursuing vehicle. He felt the swoosh of air as it rushed past, and he stumbled, went down on one knee, felt the temptation to go all the way down and out, resisted, forced himself to stand and to run. Where? Kline realised he was at a parapet; he looked over into the night air, felt rain on his face, saw, three levels below, the lighted facade of the Maverick Club. Kline swore, ran his hands along the smooth concrete of the parapet. It gave no hope of a hand or foothold. The yellow car was now opposite and moving over the ground towards him. There was nothing to do but turn and face up to the compact mass of metal that was rushing towards him. He felt the muscles in his thighs knot as if they could protect each femur from the grey concrete wall behind. With the car coming head on at him it took Kline several moments to realise that the speed was an illusion and that the driver was applying the brakes. Whether to lessen the impact or not Kline remained unsure right until the chrome of its front bumper stopped two inches from the dusty knees of his old blue suit. Kline went to move; his leg muscles twitched but wouldn't obey him. He swallowed, thought of cold beer, peered in the dim light at the driver behind the wheel and windscreen of the car but the features were indistinguishable. The figure moved in silhouette to lean across to the passenger side. The door swung open.

Shakily, Kline eased himself out from between the car radiator grille and the wall. He went to the open door, looked down at the brown, handsome face with its black moustache. 'Get in, Mr Kline,' said Khan, smiling with his white teeth.

*　　　*　　　*

Eight miles from the multi-storey car park, in the county borough of Solihull, Rawlinson, driving his Rolls-Royce Corniche, was entering the driveway of a large timber-framed Tudor house owned by one of his associates, Mr Rafiq.

Leaving the car, which was the colour of old gold, Rawlinson went up the stone steps and, knowing that his arrival would have been monitored, did not bother to slow or pause at the final step but continued towards the door, which opened as it always did. Rawlinson did not bother to acknowledge the bow of the young male Asian servant who had attended to the door's opening but continued along a panelled hallway with its scatter of Persian rugs on the black and white chequer of marble flooring until he reached the main reception room, where he was met by Rafiq.

'My dear Mr Rawlinson,' said Rafiq, taking his soft, bejewelled right hand from the pocket of the blue silk dressing gown that swathed his small rotund figure.

'How are you, my dear?' Rafiq continued as Rawlinson touched his hand of greeting.

'OK,' said Rawlinson looking into the room, which seemed more befitting of the residence of a Rajah than that of a Solihull businessman.

'Come in… come in… a drink… a drink…'

'Brandy,' said Rawlinson, going towards the gold-brocade four seater settee and tripping, as he always did, over a head of a tiger skin spread before it.

'Piss off!' said Rawlinson to the snarl of the open jaws but the snarl remained, as it always did. Rawlinson settled himself along the length of the settee, took a glass bowl of Remy Martin from the warming hands of Rafiq and put his nose through the bouquet and imbibed a little.

'It is alright, the brandy?' the Indian enquired most anxiously.

'Just hooch, inn'it?' grunted Rawlinson and looked at the screen of the large colour television set that, with its cabinet surround, could have occupied much of the area of a council house front room. The screen showed a linkman mouthing silently.

'Whassup with th' sound?' Rawlinson demanded, pointing.

'I did not wish that it should intrude, not until the programme itself had started,' said Rafiq in over-explanation.

'Well, it's on now,' said Rawlinson looking for the cigar humidor. Rafiq passed it to him. Went to the TV, adjusted the sound. The expression of professional concern on the features of the anchorman of the late news programme seemed to gain in credibility with the addition of his commentary. Rawlinson selected a cigar, rolled it between his thick fingers while he listened, all attention on the television.

'…The Commonwealth Immigration Act of 1968. In nineteen sixty-eight immigration to this country was again restricted by

Parliament but this Act had a flaw which enabled those who had entered the country illegally to remain if they managed to evade capture for the first six months of their stay. The nineteen seventy-one Act closed this loophole and in nineteen seventy-three the Law Lords confirmed that this legislation was retrospective, thus opening the way for the blackmail and exploitation of anyone who had entered the United Kingdom illegally since 1968. In later years Home Secretaries have tried to counteract this by making offers of amnesty, which few illegal immigrants have applied for. Our Midlands reporter…'

A well known face in Midlands broadcasting appeared on the large screen.

'Him,' said Rawlinson, biting the end of a cigar and spitting it at the tiger.

'Yes, him,' Rafiq replied, dipping into a silver bowl that contained a selection of nuts.

'Ey up, matey mine, y'on,' Rawlinson said, lighting his cigar with a table lighter. Rafiq smiled modestly as on the screen the reporter completed his introduction and in the background the portly figure of Rafiq eased itself down the steps of an old terraced house in the Asian immigrant area of Balsall Heath. Watching himself, Rafiq smiled fondly and spoke in his slow, mannered way.

'These television people, why is it that they always wish for my comments?'

'Perhaps it's your rapid fire delivery,' said Rawlinson as a joke.

'No. Oh, no…' Rafiq replied slowly, never taking his eyes off the screen and watching himself pat the heads of a few ragged children before being approached by the television reporter.

'Mr Rafiq…' He spoke rapidly for on the film Rafiq showed little willingness to stop and talk.

'What about extortion, racketeering, blackmail, misery and exploitation in the Asian community?'

Rafiq shrugged. 'What about it?'

'Does it exist?'

'No more than in the white community.'

'But the white community doesn't have blackmailers extorting money from illegal immigrants under the threat of deportation.'

'Such stories are, like your statistics on the influx of illegal immigrants, greatly exaggerated…' On the TV screen, Rafiq looked up at his interviewer and smiled his modest smile. '...Look, I tell you, I am one of my people's leaders here in the UK.'

He paused, took his pipe from his overcoat pocket, went on talking while lighting it. 'I do not want this honour, it is forced on me. Every hour of every day, it is forced on me.'

'Yes... yes... but we have reports that the so called Asian Mafia have told the illegal immigrants on their blackmail lists that the offers of amnesty are only a subterfuge used by successive Governments to trick them into revealing their presence and that deportation will follow at some future date...'

On the settee Rawlinson leaned forward, watching Rafiq come into close-up while shaking his head emphatically.

'No... no.'

'But there must be some good reason why so few have applied for amnesty?'

Rafiq smiled calmly at his questioner. 'There is. There are so few illegal immigrants!'

Rawlinson laughed. Rafiq smiled in modest triumph. Popped a nut. Watched himself wagging a finger politically at the camera. 'Let me tell you...' his image told him, 'that many of these assertions are made to stir up public opinion in the hope that the Government of the UK will restrict the immigrant quota even more savagely than...'

'Mr Rafiq,' the interviewer said hastily, 'thank you very much.'

Rafiq turned the set off, looked across at Rawlinson enquiringly.

'I like it,' said Rawlinson in good humour, not so much from the covering-over of what could have been an unwanted exposure but from the anticipatory feeling that this night should see Kline delivered to him here by Malleson. Rafiq had gone to the fireplace, filling a pipe and simpering a little. Rawlinson looked ahead. It might be as well, he thought, to inflate the wog with a little praise; the cellars to this house were deep and extensive. One of their number would make a perfect cell for John Kline to spend the last few days of his life in. Rawlinson stood, smiled, went across to the fireplace and patted Rafiq on the shoulder, said with admiration, 'That was bleedin' great. Yow worked that poncey interviewer's questions right back up him.'

Rafiq put his pipe into his mouth just as he had done in the film, then he spread his hands and looked down at their perfection. He sighed and spoke the truth, 'One has had a little experience with such matters, my dear.'

The two men stood in in front of the log fire burning in its dog grate. Rawlinson nudged his partner slyly. 'Down't come on all modest, Rafiq.'

'Was it really that good?' asked the Indian, taking a spill and bending to light it from the flames of the burning logs.

Rawlinson put a foot on the fender, a hand on the carved spandrel of the stone fireplace. Looked down at Rafiq lighting his spill. 'Good enough t'qualify you for an honours degree in advanced bullshit,' he said, and flicked his cigar ash over the glossy head of the Asian and into the fire.

The yellow Datsun proceeded at a leisurely pace down Bristol Street towards Holloway Circus. In the front passenger seat Kline twisted round to look for any signs of pursuit. Khan, who had already checked in his driving mirror, stated, 'Nothing'.

'Not yet,' muttered Kline, then added, 'Like me t'go in front of you with a red flag?'

Khan smiled almost primly. 'This is a built up area, Mr Kline. We mustn't exceed the speed limit.'

'Ah...' Kline started but then became distracted at seeing a sign that pointed the way to New Street Station.

Khan turned into Queensway and headed towards Paradise Circus. 'You're goin' the wrong bleedin' way,' Kline protested.

'We have to circle around the traffic system,' Khan explained soothingly.

'Uh,' was Kline's only reply and he slumped down into his seat as if to hide himself from the sight of passing motorists. As they went down through an underpass, Khan glanced at his passenger. He saw the haggard, drawn face, the blue eyes, bloodshot and weary, but still alive with the determination to escape. Khan waited until he had negotiated Lancaster Circus then expressed his opinion.

'I don't consider your running away like this to be a lasting solution, Mr Kline.'

Kline grunted again, said wearily, 'Up the 'Pool... down th'smoke – first train out, I'm on it...'

Khan shook his head like a chess master at the move of a novice.

'Rawlinson has contacts in both places and if not him then one of his many brothers; like Napoleon our Mr Rawlinson is a devout believer in nepotism.'

Kline hauled himself up in his seat. 'I don't care what his religion 'is,' he said dryly.

'He wants you dead, Mr Kline.' Khan made it a statement of fact.

'How would you know?' Kline asked suspiciously.

'I'm newly enrolled in the lower echelons of his organisation… quite an honour for a poor ignorant wog, wouldn't you say?' .

Kline rubbed his forehead. 'This missin' relative of yours is probably at the bottom of the North Sea…'

'Yes, he probably is,' said Khan cheerfully, then, sensing Kline's confusion, added, 'Sorry you earned remission ?"

'No,' Kline said defiantly and looked out of the window.

Khan saw his reaction to the realisation that they were travelling in the opposite direction to New Street Station.

'What was that sign back there?' Khan enquired innocently.

Kline gave him a sideways look. 'Aston.'

'Oh dear,' said Khan, 'we seem to be going the incorrect way.'

Rawlinson slammed down the ornate telephone onto its delicate cradle. 'Fuckin' hell!' he shouted and kicked the tiger, which was just within range.

Rafiq looked across anxiously. 'Trouble?' he enquired.

Rawlinson thought of Malleson and his blacks and the Irish joke called Dermot Macavoy and said, 'Not for you, matey, not for you…'

When the Datsun finally pulled into the cover of New Street Station, Kline found it hard to accept he could simply get out of the car, exchange his travel warrant and leave Birmingham behind. Together with his money, he thought, bitterly. And he'd never find out what this wog geezer was up to with his fancy chat and big words. He was still at it, rabbiting on and on. Kline looked around; there was no sign of the enemy. Just cars and taxis and blokes with girls who lived in Coventry or Wolverhampton, holding each other until train time. Khan said something for the second time.

'What?' Kline asked.

'I said that you have only two options: find enough money to escape or stand and smash Rawlinson here.'

Kline laughed. 'With whose army?'

'Double your numbers, come in with me.'

'As what, like?'

Khan turned to face Kline. 'As back up. I may as well tell you I intend to take over all of Rawlinson's rackets.'

The matter of fact tone made Kline pause before asking, 'How, by an act of god?'

'No,' Khan continued calmly, as if discussing something perfectly feasible. 'I'm inside. I need someone outside, someone who won't go wagging his tail to Rawlinson. Someone like *you*, Mr Kline, who, if you'll pardon the colloquialism, knows arse from elbow, would be ideal.'

Kline opened the car door and ducked out. Khan made no attempt to stop him but leaned across and looked up at Kline. 'Don't let them run you out of town.'

Kline looked down at the Asian. 'My name's John Kline, not Wayne...' he said, slamming the door and walking away.

After a moment Khan, too, climbed out and followed at a distance. He saw John Kline take out his travel warrant from his inside pocket and locate the position of the office. Khan watched him scan the few destinations listed for imminent trains and then look down and to the side of the long ticket barrier, which was the only way onto the platforms. There he saw what Khan had already observed – the figures of three West Indians watching every ticket holder who approached the barrier.

Malleson checked his watch, held it to his undamaged ear and went to check the station chronometer behind a stationary staircase. Bonny and Atty remained at the barrier watching the clutching and kissing and sly groping with some interest but not enough to allow an unattached ex-convict to pass through unmolested.

Kline looked about him for inspiration and noticed Khan grinning at him. He's a cool bastard, thought Kline, that... Then realised that he did not even know the Asian's name. He checked that he could not be seen from the barrier, then walked across to the man with the black moustache. They looked at each other for a few seconds before Kline said, 'What's your bleedin' name, any'ow?'

Khan held out his hand and introduced himself with polite formality. 'Khan. Zaheer Mohammed Khan.'

Kline took the proffered hand. 'John Wayne,' he said wryly.

Chapter Six

After Rawlinson's call, Dermot Macavoy sat in his office sweating. He wasn't worried, he reasoned to himself; couldn't he place all the blame onto that bungling black bastard Malleson? All the same it would be nice if that phone rang with the news that Kline was on his way gift wrapped out to Rawlinson. The Irishman swallowed; running round like that he was down on his nightly consumption. He'd put the phone through to the bar then; if the quare fella called again on Malleson, he'd be there an'... unless of course the boss came down to find him standing drinking 'stead've out looking. No, he had to have a drink, look round the Club. See what's what, see backstage, see if his artists were fulfilling their function. Right. Dermot clambered up off his chair. Pushed his telephone button to the bar extension, went out of the bare office, locked the door and walked heavily down the corridor that would take him towards the rear of the stage.

On stage Dinah took away her covering for the second time that evening. It had the same effect as before... four-five, Dinah counted, and the lights went out. In the darkness she felt her way to the exit door that lay just out of sight of the whistling and whooping audience. She felt a body brush past her before the lights came on again and smelt the sweet sickly smell of hard spirits from the breath and pores of Billy Brody. The lights came on, Dinah checked she was beyond the sightline of the audience, gathered her bridal apparel up to her and eased herself out through the door into the corridor. On the stage Brody blinked his glazed eyes at the audience trying to gauge its composition and also waiting for the spirit to move him. 'Awright...?' he said to a tableful of Asians. 'Awright...?' he said again, still waiting... then he thought of a gag. 'Oh, aye, I travel all over, me, y'know. Aye...' he tried to muster a few local names. 'Aye... Bordsley Green, Handsworth... Smethwick, you name it... even gotta visa to visit Bradford once... which reminds me...' Of what? Oh, yeh... 'Did y'hear about all the white men left in Bradford They had this mass meetin' y'see... but it started to rain so they went and sheltered in a telephone kiosk...' Brody waited. There was hardly a ripple. He helped it along. 'Think about it...' he said encouragingly. A little laughter came eventually and he decided to tell another, involving the problems of playing bingo in Bradford, where, he would maintain, every shout of house was followed by offers from immigrants wishing to buy it. The audience listened patiently as Brody tried to spin the story out to its conclusion.

In the corridor at the rear of the stage Dinah met the manager. 'How'd it go?' Dermot said, looking at the swell of her breasts, which she tried to cover.

Dinah looked up at him. 'Haven't you even bothered to to watch?' she said sharply, watching his eyes fish over her.

'Busy, love, busy... but I'll catch y'last slot from the front...' Dermot closed a leering eye. 'In fact, why don't you have a drink with me right now, ey?'

'No, thanks,' said Dinah and walked around him. Dermot turned to gaze at her bobbing bum but she'd covered it as if it was obvious that he'd have a sly squint after her. Ah, plenty of time f'that... it's a screw to have on a boring night, he told himself and lumbered along the corridor through the side entrance and into the club just as Billy Brody muffed the punchline of a complicated story involving a policeman, a Pakistani and the Race Relations Board.

'Rubbish!' a Pakistani shouted from nearby to Dermot, who frowned and looked up at the perspiring Brody. The comedian saw the presence of the manager and began to sweat a little more. Brown bastards... like Calcutta... Bangladesh... Pakistan... come on come up with a good one... 'Rubbish!' someone said again and a two pence piece clinked at his feet.

OK, thought Brody, OK. 'OK,' he said, 'I'll tell y' a story that will make y'all feel at home. Awright, sir?' he said to Dermot, who declined to return the sickly ingratiating smile from the stage. 'Awright... here we go,' said Brody and took in two lungfuls of the smoky air. 'It's a sad story is this. Can we have a bit of reverence for the starving millions of the third world if you please, thank you.' The audience quietened as he signalled to the lighting box to give him a spot. The sidelights around the club went out, leaving just the dull glow of the oil lamps on the tables and the red tips of the punters' cigarettes as they sat around expectantly. In the spotlight, Billy Brody wiped the globules of perspiration from a forehead made high by his receding hairline. This done he squeezed the damp handkerchief in his hands to dry his palms then began to speak seriously to the now hushed and attentive audience below him. 'This Asian,' he started, 'lived in this village on the subcontinent of India. Silly bugger, he'd had the lack of foresight to be born in an area that was difficult to cultivate. Even when things would grow on his patch of land they'd either die from drought, be washed away in the flood of the monsoon...' They're rapt, thought Brody, feeling for the first time the booze and boosters reach some sort of equilibrium with his metabolism. He felt a little of the confidence he used to have when he was thirty. Yeh. Go on my son, life begins at forty and you are painting pictures... 'Anyway...' he continued, his voice stronger and suddenly more confident, 'this geezer had it hard but things were lookin' up for him – his wife was pregnant, about to produce what he hoped would be a son to help him till the earth and tend the crops that at last were starting to grow on his land – but then, after giving birth to a crippled stillborn daughter, his wife died... Broken, weeping, the little Asian wandered out of his miserable hut and onto his patch of soil that contained the crop of rice that was his only hope of survival in this world. As he surveyed the few pitiable green shoots he realised that rain clouds were gathering and that a wind was rising. The rain came and brought a flood; the flood washed away his precious crops. The wind blew into a typhoon that smashed the hut and ripped the clothes from the Asian's back. Rolling over and over in the mud and filth and desolation, torn by the wind, drenched by the rain, the Asian clenched his skinny fists and shook them at the heavens and screamed, "Why... why... why...!" Suddenly the storm ceased and from above a voice said, "I don't know why but there's something about you, mate, that just *pisses me off!*" '

Brody waited; then it came – a shout of laughter. He glanced sideways and the manager too was cracking his face, so that was all right. 'Not bad, ey?' said Brody to where Dermot had been but the big man was heading towards the bar. The comedian took his round of applause.

'Awright?' he asked someone, 'pretty funny, ey?'

Rawlinson heard the scrunch of tyres on the gravel of the driveway, got to his feet, stepped across the skin of the tiger and headed for the door that led into the hallway. 'Wait...' Rafiq cautioned, 'if the sound is one of reversal into the garage that will be Kuldip.' Rawlinson paused and in that pause they heard the vehicle outside go into reverse and move away from the house.

'Ah,' said Rawlinson in disappointment.

The dark eyes of Rafiq stared at him. 'You were expecting someone else?'

'Maybe.'

'Would it be indelicate to...'

'We'll talk about it when the time comes, if it ever bleedin' comes,' said Rawlinson savagely.

'Very well.' Rafiq moved across to Rawlinson. 'You must excuse me, my dear. I must attend to my duties.'

'There a delivery?'

'I believe so.'

Rawlinson thought about his secretary. Macavoy would have passed on any news of harm done to her... unless he'd been afraid to...

'I'll take the stuff on,' Rawlinson said decisively.

Rafiq wondered why but said nothing.

'I'm dropping by the boat later on,' Rawlinson added, 'if anyone on the firm wants to contact me, that's...'

'...Where you will be, I understand.' Rafiq indicated the doorway with a discreet gesture. 'Shall we?'

Rawlinson did not reply but strode out of the reception room across the hallway towards the passageway that led past the dining room and kitchens and ended with the entrance to the garage area. Trying to keep pace with him waddled Rafiq, who before reaching the dining room door was a spent force and had eased back down to his customary careful gait.

Anne Darracott finally succeeded in bringing light to the darkness of her wrecked home. What she saw when she hung the lamp up on its hook made her feel the emotion of loss. She found herself unable to focus on any single smashed object. To shield herself from the realisation she concentrated on one thing. The nearest thing. Herself. She began to undress. Then shivered, naked, confused. Went to the peg that should have held her embroidered green silk kimono but it wasn't there... she began to cry, bent down, felt around the floor, the tears tasting salt as they dribbled down into her lips. Her searching hand touched the cool smoothness of silk and she hugged the kimono to her. She looked down. Examined it. It was undamaged. Or seemed to be. She put her thin mottled arms through one wide sleeve then the other and held the folds around her. The silk threads woven into a multi-coloured cord to tie the kimono in could not be found and she simply did not have the energy or will to look. She rubbed her eyes with the back of her hand and knuckles; her mascara smeared and gave her eyes the sunken look of an early screen siren. She began to experience the irritation of her skin. Her nose began to itch so she rubbed it and picked her way over the debris to the haven of her bed. At its side she went down on her knees like an orphan asking God to please return her parents. Then he did, for on reaching under the bed she located the gold-coloured tin and brought it out. On the lid daubed with black paint was the word 'Bait'. She opened the small oblong box and thanked God that her artillery remained undisturbed. She went again beneath the bed frame, searching, searching, then closed on her antidote to fear and depression.

When Rawlinson reached the garage area the grey transit box van with the red Rawco Transport sign painted along its sides was already parked inside and Kuldip, seeing Rawlinson, ran even faster to close the steel doors of the garage. The crash that they made reverberated from one wall to the other. Kuldip came back to the rear of the van jauntily, enjoying the clash and clatter. Rawlinson, knowing the noise was unlikely to bother anybody other than Rafiq, nodded a greeting to the smiling Asian. Rafiq entered from the side door, saw Kuldip and began immediately to shout at his employee. 'Where have you been, Kuldip? Where have you been?'

Kuldip also began to yell. 'Don't shout at me, don't blame me. Blame the Dutchman. He was very late in!'

Rafiq lowered his high voice a few decibels and spoke anxiously. 'But everything is all right? No roadblock, police checks, customs examinations?'

Kuldip bared his teeth in a caricature of scorn and strutted around to the doors at the rear of the van. 'Road blocks, police checks! You spend too much time at your telly, Mr Rafiq. Even if those policemen set them up... I see them, I take diversionary action, all right? Everything's all right...' He paused to strike himself a congratulatory blow on the chest '...With me in the driving seat it always is.'

Rawlinson watched Rafiq go to Kuldip at the doors of the van.

'The seal?' Rafiq said as a final cause for anxiety.

Kuldip showed him the metal foil and wires that twisted into the lead of the false customs seal. Touching it, he answered 'Foolproof. That Dutchman knows his stuff.' Breaking the seal, Kuldip unlocked the doors. As they opened he wrinkled his nose at the rush of stale fetid air before clambering up and approaching one of the two boxes that lay inside the steel container. Kuldip knelt and put his ear to the splintery wood, listened for a moment then knocked sharply once, twice before saying in deep, sepulchral tones to whoever or whatever was inside, 'This is the devil speaking,' and followed this pronouncement with his maniacal squeal of laughter, which ended as he kicked the top of first one box and then the other. 'Move... move... end of the line!' he shouted in Urdu. Slowly lids of the packing cases shifted and moved aside to reveal inside each double coffin the brown frightened faces of a pair of illegal immigrants. Painfully and with stiff and aching joints each Asian clambered out. Disorientated they looked in confusion around the van then down to Rafiq and Rawlinson. Kuldip, like an eager sheepdog, harried and pushed them along towards the edge of the van interior with exhortations to 'Move! Move!' As they clambered down onto the concrete floor of the spacious garage Kuldip caught Rawlinson's eye and indicated the heads of the hapless immigrants now below him. 'Stupid wogs,' he said. Rawlinson smiled slightly. You had to encourage them, he thought.

Rafiq went up to Kuldip, who vaulted down from the van. 'The package! One of them should have a package.'

'Package!' shouted Kuldip at the Asians shivering in their little group. One of the Asians, slightly taller and younger than the others, showed some reaction and Kuldip picked him to swagger up to. 'Package,' he said again in Urdu and attempted to pull the jacket of the Asian's coat open. Frightened, the Asian started to resist.

Rafiq hurried across as Kuldip went inside his own jacket for his blade. 'Please...' Rafiq put a restraining hand on Kuldip's arm. To the youth he said kindly in English, 'It's all right...' The young man looked even more confused and Rafiq realised that he only understood Urdu. 'It is all right...' he said. The frightened liquid brown eyes looked into his and Rafiq thought, how interesting. But said, 'Trust me...' in Urdu and the young man decided he would, for he brought from inside one of the two jackets he was wearing a small square package wrapped in oilskin. Rafiq took it from him gently, gave the rather grimy hand a slight squeeze of encouragement and turned to Rawlinson. 'Like children... They trust me.'

Rawlinson took the small square of oilskin from Rafiq's plump hands and pocketed it in the jacket of his brown suit. 'More fool them,' he said, turning back towards the entrance to the house.

'We must meet again soon, my dear,' Rafiq called after him.

'We will,' said Rawlinson.

Jashir Singh Mahal looked around at his possessions piled around one of the two rooms in which he, his wife and his two children lived. There was nothing more to do until tomorrow. Everything was ready for what he hoped would be a speedy and effective removal.

The four immigrants stumbled along the labyrinth of the cellars that lay beneath the large timber-framed house. Kuldip shepherded them along the dark passageways until they reached a barred door, where he called a halt. There the Asians huddled together terrified, not knowing what was to happen next. Kuldip advanced arrogantly towards them. 'Enjoy your five star accommodation,' he said, removing a heavy wooden bar from its supports and pushing the door open. 'Get in!' Kuldip ordered, switching on a 60 watt light bulb that just illumined, through its cobwebs, the outline of six rickety camp beds, an old wine rack with empty bottles and, against a mildewed wall, a cold water tap that dripped into a rusting bucket. The youngest of the four immigrants, who had attracted Rafiq's attention in the garage above, saw the drip of the tap and ran down the steps towards the bucket. The others, realising his intention, scrambled after him. The immigrants drank thirstily in turn from the bucket until it was empty. The last to drink looked askance at Kuldip bestriding the top step above, then put a tentative hand upon the crutch handle of the tap. Seeing no hint of displeasure from Kuldip he turned on the tap, put his head down to it and filled his shrunken belly from the rush of water. Kuldip, remembering his obligations as host, went outside to an alcove where stale sliced loaves from Rafiq's supermarket were dumped. Taking one from the heap he returned to his guests in their subterranean suite. 'Dinner is served!' he announced and tossed the sliced white bread with its green mould motif down amongst them. He used to enjoy the scrimmaging and the fighting over the goodies provided but now, with repetition, it had palled. So he left the four latest residents to dine unobserved as he barred and bolted the cellar door on the product of his night's work.

With the bar closed, its grilles down and the cashing up taking place at the tills, Billy Brody was signing off for the evening. At a discreet rear table a punter, who had been plying someone else's wife with too many drinks, was wondering how he was going to get her sleeping head up off the table without drawing too much attention. 'She drunk?' a bouncer asked delicately.

'Er, well, not exactly drunk.'

'Just pissed,' said the bouncer unemotionally and whistled for help to lug the unconscious female to a taxi.

The gentleman punter wondered if he should offer a tip for this removal service and if he didn't would they beat him up? He took out his Letts Businessman's Diary, tore out a page from the memo section and wrote down the lady's address. It was a pity but one had to cut one's losses. He wrapped the address in a five pound note and offered it to the bouncer. 'Would you mind... not too good myself...' The bouncer's hand licked out for the five pound note with the speed and adhesion of a chameleon's tongue; at the same time his manner became exceedingly civil, which pleased the punter for it allowed him to beat a civilised retreat, which saved him witnessing the heel-dragging exit of his lady love a few minutes later.

For Billy Brody spieling on stage it was his favourite time. In half an hour he would be inside his private drinking club and at peace with the world. To the drift of passing men without women he said cheerfully, 'Nearly through boys and girls...' To a couple of disgruntled visitors to the Midlands who had hoped to cop for a couple of soul sisters from the Shadettes and had lost out, he said, 'Have y'ever noticed how some joker always writes under a Johnny machine "Buy me an' stop one"? I leave you with this thought, why not buy two and keep one jump ahead?'

One visitor shook his head and his companion said, 'Let's get aht this poxy fackin' place.'

Seeing them go, Brody called, 'Goodnight, lads, an' remember, be nice to each other!' The drummer gave a final roll; the lead guitarist already had his guitar in its case as Billy Brody said, 'Good night and God bless,' and closed the entertainment at the Maverick Club for another night.

The mini-cab pulled up outside the dry cleaners above which Dinah Carmichael lived. The driver was under contract to the Maverick, did not need paying but she tipped him.

'Ta,' he said, unoriginally, made sure the black bint had closed the door after her then drove away to continue the conveyance of late night workers home to their beds.

Dinah, in the doorway of the shop, fumbled into her purse for the key that would unlock the door to the stairway that led up to her flat. She heard the footsteps on the pavement, turned and saw the figure looming towards her, large and anonymous with the street light behind it. Christ! she thought, got the key out, thrust it in the lock, turned, got inside, pushed the door almost closed before the man stopped it. She heaved in an effort to close the final two inches of the door.

'Ey...' said the voice outside.

'Fuck off, will you!' Dinah hissed at the force pushing from outside.

'That's nice, innit...?' said the voice in an accent not of the Midlands.

'Who are you...?'

'John Wayne.'

'John Kline?'

'Right.'

Dinah did not move from the door but stopped trying to close it. She didn't know how to play this one. It could be trouble. *He* could be trouble, you mean.

'Let's in,' said Kline's voice from outside.

'I said... only... only in an emergency...' Dinah faltered.

'It's an emergency... let's in.'

Do yourself a favour, Dinah told herself, close the bleedin' door.

She closed the door. Not nice but practical, she said to herself, then added, you bitch, just before Kline threw himself at the door; the screws of the lock in the old wood of the frame wrenched out under the assault and the door swung open. Dinah backed against the wall at the foot of the stairs. Kline closed the front door carefully then came across to join her.

Dinah looked at him, not knowing what a prudent girl should do next. 'What's the emergency?' she asked him.

Kline passed a hand through his tousled hair, 'Haven't had a woman for three years,' he said simply as he reached for her shoulders and pulled her to him.

The intensity and pressure of the embrace startled Dinah and when Kline kissed her she had to kiss him back to save being pressed against the wall. She could feel the swift movements of Kline's hands on the buttons of her coat, opening them quickly and coming inside to hold each breast briefly before encircling her waist, dropping on either side of her behind and exerting pressure to bring her belly up against his. Feeling the lift and pressure of his erection she swayed her upper body away to look at him. 'Three years you said?'

Kline looked down at her, could not get any words up out of his throat. Dinah saved him the trouble. 'I believe you,' she said and put an arm about him as they turned to go up the stairs.

In the street outside Khan sat behind the wheel of the yellow Datsun and watched the windows of the rooms above the Ace Dry Cleaning Co. He observed the lights come on in one room then another but in no time at all the light was extinguished and the windows were dark as they were before. Khan smiled, stroked his moustache, hoped his new partner would find a satisfactory climax to his first day of freedom. After having noted the address he started the car, looked carefully up and down the deserted rain-dampened street and then drove away.

Dinah heard the car pull away from beneath her bedroom window and idly wondered who it was at that time of night. She had this capacity to detach herself to consider what some of her lovers had termed trivia while being engaged in the most intimate of manoeuvres. Now she let her hand play down among the hair that surrounded the pillar that stood up and away from the muscular flat belly of the man in bed beside her.

Kline felt the cool touch of a woman's hand dip down and fingertip across his belly until his balls screwed tight in their scrotum and in anticipation of the oncoming touch; when it came he shuddered, held her hand to him as if it was the first time and he was fifteen all over again. He kissed her throat, could smell the musk of her as he ran his big hand down along the smooth, warm flesh of her waist and hip and realised as he moved to trace the curve of the plump rounded behind that this was the point where he had suffered with Anne Darracott. He stopped in mid-caress, leant up on an elbow, listened. There was a tick of a clock, Dinah's accelerated breathing but nothing more. 'Wha...' Dinah started to ask but quickly realised the interruption was only a momentary one. Kline placed Dinah on her back, opened her thighs and lay down between them. Having found the small closed door he knocked twice at the entrance then entered through the portals and up into the warm and welcoming clutch of her cunt.

Dinah lay still, understanding that the last thing he needed was help and only towards the end did she join in unison with him.

To Kline crying out in the final clench of his orgasm it was as if release had at last been granted to his spirit as well as his body. He remembered a last slow wave of ejaculation, before he eased his weight from his elbows, turned his head on the pillow. He just had time to speak the word thanks to Dinah before sleep came to him.

Chapter Seven

The rain, which had drizzled on and off throughout that night, had started again as Rawlinson left his Rolls to fend for itself on Bridge Street and descended down towards the towpath of the canal. Reaching the cinder path he walked towards the deeper darkness that lay beneath a bridge. In the distance he heard a faint sound of a motor cycle travelling at speed. The sound became louder and louder until he could see the beam from its headlight. It could be a cop. It could be a pick up. You never knew; you could never buy them all and therefore you were never safe. Rawlinson dug into his pocket for the oilskin package, tensed, ready to commit the small parcel to the waters of the canal. The heavy 750 cc engine roared towards him. The beam illuminated the wet glistening girders of the bridge; the beam wavered as the rider lost a little control on the change of surface and then was gone. The darkness returned with only slight reflection from the water of the street lights above. The grey-haired man in the brown suit on the path below the street relaxed, put the square of oilskin back into his pocket and walked softly beneath the bridge, around a slight bend in the canal bank towards where a motor barge, showing one dim light forrard, was moored.

On the square bed Anne Darracott came awake at the sound of the rear hatch being opened. She was sure she had locked it... unless... she sat up, turned to look across the sea of debris towards the bead curtain. Unconsciously, Anne hugged the rag doll she had held in sleep to her. The bead curtain was swept aside and she saw the black and grey head duck inside. It was him, she thought. God the Father. She watched him survey the destruction his orders had brought to her home. Following his gaze around, she realised the extent of the damage. To him it meant nothing – just old furniture that could be replaced by new. To her it had been the pleasure of secret trips alone to sales at country houses, of auctions attended, of dealers bidding, of restoration, of finds and catalogues. She lay back on the bed, holding the doll, Jenny, to her and glowering as Rawlinson righted a cactus, tried to push the drawers back into a small whatnot that had been partly wrenched from the wall. The tiny drawers popped out again so he gave it up. Amongst the heap of splintered wood he located a small thonged whip that had originated in East Africa; he put it back on its hook and looked sideways at his irate secretary.

'Stupid pricks,' Rawlinson said, looking around once more.

There were so many ways to attack him that Anne could not decide with which to start. 'You...' she choked.

'What?' said Rawlinson, coming towards her.

'You *bastard!*'

'We know that,' said Rawlinson, looking back at the room, not to assess the damage but realising that if the blacks could slip up like this once, they might miss Kline again. Looking down at his feet he saw a wooden drawer that had been pulled out from somewhere. Trying to weigh the odds of who to involve in the continuing hunt for Kline, he absentmindedly began to kick the feather banding along the front of the drawer. For some reason this drove the woman on the bed to distraction.

Anne swung from the bed, picked up the drawer and held it to her. 'You're paying for all this...' she said over-dramatically, waving her free arm.

'So will they,' said Rawlinson, unmoved. Then added, realising he had made the decision. 'I'm bringing my brothers in.'

Anne examined the damaged herringbone design on the drawer front and began to cry again. There had to be a way to get at him, she thought; shouting and throwing things only amused him. She threw the drawer across the cabin. Rawlinson didn't even notice the crash it made. She thought perhaps a few contemptuous remarks on his sense of strategy might reach into him. 'Spades,' she said scornfully, 'why use spades? What about this private army you're always boasting about?'

Rawlinson sighed, 'Politics, Annie, politics... I muster all the bouncers from all my clubs n'it calls attention.' Rawlinson pictured the scene. '...fifty Herberts in dinner jackets prowlin' the bleedin' streets after Kline... later, maybe, but we'll give our black brothers another chance first... '

Anne gave him one of her looks that she wished would kill.

Rawlinson said, 'Wash your face, you look like Theda Bara.'

'Who?'

'Never mind,' said Rawlinson, seating himself on the bed and noticing the bulge in his jacket pocket. He pulled the oilskin package out and tossed it onto the bedcover beside him. She saw it, of course she did, but wouldn't allow herself to show any special interest.

Rawlinson patted the bed beside him in invitation. Anne did not move.

'Kline,' said Rawlinson and cleared his throat '...how's he look?'

Anne remembered the pale face of John Kline. 'Needs some sun on his back.'

'And a woman under his front?'

Here was something, Anne thought, and held her loose folding kimono around her in what was almost a hug. 'I did get that impression...' she said and looked away as if indulging in pleasant recall.

Rawlinson watched her intently. 'Oh, yeh...' What's this? he said to himself. 'Good bunk up?' he asked, casually.

Anne tried to smile warmly at the recollection. 'Well... I mean... we'd hardly had a chance to leave the ground before...'

'Ar...' said Rawlinson, starting to remove his jacket, 'Pick 'andle Pete arrived t'prevent further intimacies from taking place...' He grinned at her, insolently. '...Well, seein' as 'ow y'still' a virgin, I may as well kip 'ere.' He held his jacket out to her.

She took it only so she could hurl it back at him. 'No way, I've been used enough f' one night. On y'way. Don't step in the canal on y'way out.' She turned, flounced away in the direction of the kitchen, her pale green kimono swirling out behind her. This was what Rawlinson wanted. Fight and fire and resistance to overcome. Not the lines of compliant girlies with their Yes, Mr Rawlinson, No, Mr Rawlinson, which way would you like to fuck me next, Mr Rawlinson?

He caught her up by the bead curtain, caught her by the inner arm so that she screamed with pain but still resisted; he saw the white, thin body with its tiny nest of flaxen hair waiting for him. He threw her down onto the broad circumference of a large leather cushion. As she lay across the cold leather she wondered whether to feign injury but realised the futility of such a ploy. Hatred for him and for herself made her struggle upwards in time to see Rawlinson remove the last of his clothing. She lay half across the round cushion waiting her opportunity. It came when Rawlinson stood astride her legs looking down not at her nakedness but at the strength of his own erection. She mustered all her strength for one savage kick up into the hanging testicles above her. Rawlinson simply blocked the upward thrust of her foot with his shin and caught the attacking leg behind the knee with his hand. Anne tried to force her knees back together but all her strength of purpose was insufficient to prevent the grinning Rawlinson forcing them apart. She stopped resisting, lay there as limp as her doll.

'You enjoy it,' Rawlinson said, looking down on her. Anne half closed her eyes, turned her head away feeling him touch her.

'Bastards,' she said softly,

'Who?' Rawlinson grunted, finding access far from easy.

'You and Kline,' Anne said, turning her head and arching her back in order to let her Lord and Master in.

Rafiq eased the band of his royal blue silk pyjama trousers up over his plump brown belly and crawled between the sheets of his four poster bed. He lay back against the dreamy silk of his pillows and closed his eyes on the cares of the day. How tired I am, he told himself tenderly. It is that Rawlinson chap; all his directness of energy tends to leave a fellow somewhat limp. Forcefulness was necessary, he knew that, but it was also tiring... tiring... So...

A discreet knock on the panelling of the bedroom door made him open his eyes. 'Yes... Come!' he called. The young servant who had opened the front door for Rawlinson earlier in the evening now entered through Rafiq's door and closed it behind him. Rafiq knew he had told the boy that he would require his services but now doubted if he could muster the energy to use them. While Rafiq was deciding whether or not to share his bed the boy had anticipated the command and had started to remove his white steward's jacket. For some reason this caused displeasure in the mind of the fat middle-aged Indian for he clapped his plump hands together once imperiously and uttered a decisive 'No!' The boy, about to remove his shirt, began rebuttoning it without pause or emotion. Rafiq watched him and wondered what he had ever found attractive in such a dull stupid fellow. He wasn't even beautiful. And another thing, Rafiq suddenly remembered reports he had received about this illegal immigrant asking the permanent kitchen staff the English words for objects and places. Yes, it was time for him to be transferred away from the Midlands. 'Go,' ordered Rafiq, with a dismissive wave of the hand. The young Asian fastened the final button of his white steward's jacket, bowed, turned and left Rafiq propped up alone on his pillows, eyes closed again, lost in pleasurable speculation about the youngest of the immigrants now safely sealed in their reception cell under the big old house.

*   *   *

In the bedroom above the Ace Drycleaning Co. Kline listened to the sound of the early morning workaday traffic on the street below. When there was enough light to distinguish the circular pattern of the curtains on the window he turned his head to see the time on the clock on the bedside table but the face was hidden. He saw instead his cigarettes and matches and felt how good it would be to light a fag and smoke it quietly while thinking of the night just passed and of the day ahead. Kline cautiously moved the arm on which Dinah was sleeping. She stirred, came awake. He could just see her hair in disarray from the night's doings. He chuckled at her, moved his arm, reached for a cigarette, extracted one and lit it. 'What about me?' said the sleepy voice from beneath the head of hair beside him.

'You said you didn't use them,' Kline said.

'No, I don't... that's right,' Dinah yawned and snuggled up against him with a sly hand slipping below to test for signs of tumescence.

'All gone,' she said, like a child holding an empty sweet bag.

Kline remembered the pleasures of the night with its occasional intervals of sleep. 'You surprised?'

'No,' she said and then removed her hand from his groin at the sudden surge of interest it showed to her touch. Kline smiled and smoked. Dinah lay with her head on his shoulder, slowly coming fully awake and starting to think sensible thoughts regarding her own future safety. Kline exhaled; he didn't know about the future but he had the past all sorted in his mind. He just wanted to tell someone about how it was. At least someone will know why if the worst happens and we don't make it to the end of this day. He tightened his white arm around her, catching a side of brown breast in the cup of his left hand.

'Asleep?' he asked. The head shook itself. 'Wondering what you're into?' Kline guessed. The head moved again, this time to express affirmation. 'Don't worry,' Kline gave her a small hug and wondered where to start. He knew the sequence of explanation. He'd been through it in one way or another time and again in the past three years. 'We'd converted this old cinema...' he started suddenly then stopped.

'The Maverick?' Dinah said, her voice still husky from sleep although she was quite awake.

'Yeh, the Maverick...' said Kline, grinding out his cigarette and leaning back again. 'Always Westerns... proper Westerns...' He realised he was digressing. 'Yeh, well, anyway, we opened the place to entertain the public and to make a few bob... no one noticed us an' no one bothered us, not until we caught on an' began to make a profit; like blood in the water, that brought the sharks... tenner protection, then twenty until it was a century a week off the top. I'd bin in the SAS...' He felt Dinah shift to look up at him in puzzlement. 'SAS,' Kline said, looking down at her. 'Special Air Service.' He frowned in memory. The girl felt his arm about her tighten as Kline continued, 'Saved that money, sunk it in the place. It was mine. My sweat, my blood. I decided no more bleedin' protection. This guy – Rawlinson's kid brother – tried t' prove how much we needed it. We fought...' Dinah felt Kline's hand leave her breast and clench in emphasis against her side. 'I hit him an' hit him 'til he went down... down f'good, 'f'ever, like, y'know. They called it manslaughter, stuck four years on me.'

Dinah remembered back to what seemed weeks ago but was only the previous morning. 'What about Dermot?' she asked.

'Must've sold out... probably to Rawlinson. A lump sum and a job as manager, that's how it figures.'

'And he won't pay your share?'

Kline looked down at her indignant expression, moved his hand across the muscles of her back. 'No. He's all for Rawlinson reaching me.'

Dinah made no reply but put her head on one side against Kline's chest and looked towards the curtained window. She felt his hand wander down her spine and trace circles in the dimples at the top of her buttocks. She shivered; Kline pulled the bedclothes up around her. She didn't know how to tell him what was running in her head so she remarked on the obvious fact that it was getting light.

Kline turned the clock face towards him. 'Bin out me kennel twenty-four hours.'

They went into their own thoughts. Dinah lay still, not looking at the man with her. Kline stretched in the warm luxury of the shared bed. Even if the coming day carried as much punishment as its predecessor, Kline decided that if it ended in the same way he could get through it. He was about to say this when Dinah reached a decision. 'You can't stay here... I... I... don't want to get myself involved.'

Kline said nothing to this abrupt statement but watched her move from him. He raised himself on an elbow and spoke to her gently. 'You are involved. You let me through their net, took me in... attended to my needs... all of them... you're involved right enough, kid.'

Dinah was bewildered by what she suddenly realised was the truth of the situation. She thought of Malleson and Macavoy and burst out petulantly, 'I have t'work there f'Chrissake!'

'Why?' Kline simply asked.

'Money. Bastard money!' She looked across at Kline and added defensively. 'What else, enjoyment?'

'Dermot said you used t'hustle?'

Dinah remembered a few encounters in hotel rooms, of cash before delivery, of simulated orgasms and every dirty trick used to bring about a premature conclusion and the maintaining of the difficult pretence that the body being sold wasn't really her own. She laughed in a way which she hoped was light and dismissive but obviously wasn't, for the man in her bed just looked steadily at her, waiting for words that would help him to understand. 'Hustling?' Dinah decided to reduce it all to economics. 'Tried it. Ask for twenty quid, settle for fifteen, go down for ten. Big-big deal. I earn more last night f 'takin' my clothes off in time t'the music.'

Kline understood. 'Yeh,' he said.

'Pays more for a night than a week in a shop.'

'Sure.'

The West Indian girl remembered the last time she had felt the need of self justification. Her eyes moved away from those of John Kline. She drew her knees up inside the bed clothes and rested her firm, determined chin on the hump of the multi-coloured patchwork of the quilted eiderdown.

'My parents were from Trinidad. Me, I'm from Brummagem. They call this home, not me. My father n'mother, I love them, y'know, but I can't live with them... I can't...' She paused, smoothed her unruly hair. Kline lit another cigarette. She took it from him, took a deep solitary drag and passed it back. 'You're lucky, you're a man; you can do things... all I can do is... I mean... what?' She uncovered her firm, outstanding breasts and displayed them to an imaginary audience, then covered herself and turned again to John Kline. 'My parents, they won't walk away, won't go home to Trinidad, won't admit they've lost out. Me, I don't care... me I just want out've this John Bull island...'

Kline reached across to touch first one of her breasts and then the other. 'Me n'you both,' Kline said.

Jashir Singh Mahal waved to his family at the door of the house where he had lived for the past three years. He wanted to call back that he would see them at lunchtime and to be ready but remembered that someone might overhear the information so he contented himself with a last wave of the hand before tucking his tin lunchbox underneath his arm and walking off down the street with its sections of derelict housing. Mangit watched until the turbaned figure of her husband had disappeared before withdrawing indoors with her children.

Rawlinson stood on the prow of the *Anne Carol* and pissed into the still waters of the canal. Watching the golden arc he remembered childhood competitions with his brothers about who could make the highest watermark up the back entry wall. Being the eldest he'd had a handicap mark of two feet from the bottom brick. He remembered his youngest brother trouser leg up and standing on tiptoe. What was the point of thinking about that? He watched the water settle back to its former stagnancy, adjusted his dress before returning to the cabin to find his secretary at her morning devotions.

Anne sat on the bed with her gold-painted bait box open before her. She had already cooked up a pill and had it in the dropper with this morning's selected needle. Rawlinson knew she had waited for his return and, knowing how he hated the ritual, was determined that he should witness it. He could have left easily enough but that would have been a transgression of the rules he and his helpmate played by. He watched Anne wind a thin leather belt around the small circumference of her left bicep and, after pulling it tight with her teeth, rub a vein in the hollow of her inner arm. Rawlinson suddenly found the centre button of his suit jacket undone and looked down to watch his fingers fasten it. When he looked up he saw Anne Darracott smiling, mocking his weakness. She took up the needle with its dropper and put the sharp point to the distended blue membrane. Rawlinson stoically watched the touching of the vein again and again before the final gentle insertion and injection took place. Anne released the pressure of the belt around her arm; the dropper hanging from her arm filled with her blood. She wanted it to do just that. Deftly she squeezed the dropper between finger and thumb, putting the blood and every last dreg of heroin back into her system.

On the other side of the bed Rawlinson pretended to look about him for any overlooked belongings then said casually, 'Don't forget t'distribute last night's stuff.'

Anne smiled provocatively at him, wiped a smear of blood from her arm, put the dropper, the belt and the needle back into the bait tin. She stretched across the bed, lay on her back, lifted one leg in the air and laughed.

'See you,' Rawlinson said and then turned and left her alone to enjoy her golden hour.

The morning was cold but Rawlinson took no account of subtle changes of weather. He left the *Anne Carol* behind and walked back towards his Rolls. There were things to attend to, inquests to be held and certain woolly heads to be knocked together.

Chapter Eight

The telephone extension beside Tommy Rawlinson's bed warbled. Tommy's wife, who Rawlinson referred to variously as 'her', 'that' or 'the shrew' lifted her roller-strewn head, stretched out a fat white arm and lifted the receiver. Hearing Rawlinson's voice she frowned. She didn't approve of him for leaving his wife all those years ago and she had a suspicion that he didn't like her for marrying Tommy. 'E's asleep...' she said in her crying voice.'

Well, bloodywell wake 'im up!' Rawlinson ordered forcefully.

'Charming,' was her standard reply, but she gave the inanimate lump buried beneath the bedclothes beside her a push. 'Tommy!' Nothing. She brought her knee into his back.

'Uh.' The object said and surfaced by standing on all fours so that the blankets on the bed lifted with him.

'Tommy!' his wife shrieked. The blanket structure collapsed and from underneath emerged a head so blonde and square that the skull could have been the archetypal model for the German helmet of World War Two. He rubbed the limited expanse of his low forehead against the outrage of being forced awake at 9.30 in the morning. He was glad that the gum sealing his top eyelids to the bottom was so strong for that ensured none of that daylight crap could filter in. Why was he thinking anything, why wasn't he asleep? Then the voice blared into his ear like a train horn in a tunnel.

'Tommeee! Tommeeee!'

'Woh!' he roared. And opened his eyes and closed them again like a mole forced up into the light of day.

'It's 'im... y'big 'ead brother.'

'Bloody 'ell...' groaned Tommy, taking the receiver and finally forcing eyes tinted red by yesterday night's bottle of vodka to stay open.

He listened until his brother had finished speaking, said, 'Right,' then put the telephone back to rest in its cradle.

'Worrisit? Well? Woh?' the shrew enquired in a voice shrill with suspicion.

'Our kid,' said Tommy, rubbing the knuckles of his right hand, 'he wants t'see me.'

' 'Ere in Coventry?'

'In Brummagem.'

'Y'not gooin?'

'I've got to… ' he said and put a thick hairy leg outside the bed.

Billy Rawlinson was between the ages of his two surviving brothers. In height he stood just under six feet, in intelligence he could add up a column of figures to his elder brother's satisfaction. In temperament he lacked stability, having neither Rawlinson's control or Tommy's bull-like assurance. After spending all night in the casino of his club on the outskirts of Wolverhampton he had, by dint of heavy betting, bludgeoned a miniscule profit from the night's poker and had returned to what the estate agents had advertised as a truly impressive and superb detached residence of supreme quality. As he parked his green Rolls Silver Shadow in the driveway between the lawns and landscaping he glanced up at the front bedroom window and through the double glazing caught a tiny glimpse of his lady wife before she withdrew. Billy yawned, looked at his watch: ten o'clock. The kids'd be at their school, their private school. He tried to remember what the state of play was between his wife and himself. Not that it mattered a monkey's tosser, anyhow; he'd forgotten to request permission for his all night absence so the welcome awaiting him would be cold enough to petrify a penguin's piss.

As he opened the front door he saw our lady of the severe silences come down the open wooden stairway and sweep into the spacious magnificence of the lounge. 'So what?' Billy said loudly. Then saw a note next to the phone on the hall table. He read in his wife's ten out of ten for neatness handwriting, 'Your brother Oswald called at 9.45 am. He wishes you to meet him at a place called the Maverick Club in Birmingham as soon as is convenient. I informed him that I neither knew where you were or who you were with.' Billy toyed with the piece of paper. It would be nice if his brother had decided to throw some action his way once again. Life was lucrative enough in Wolverhampton but it was also very boring.

'Our kid leave a number?' he called into the lounge and receiving no reply he thought why bother? But went inside anyway and tried again. The woman sitting with a magazine open on her knee looked up at him long enough to show the cold indifference in her eyes, then returned to scanning the property in her *Country Life*. Billy stared at the top of her carefully coiffeured head. 'Bollocks!' he shouted suddenly. 'I'm sicka all this silent sending t'Coventry type bollocks!'

Without looking up, she said in her matter of fact take it or leave it grammar school voice, 'To Birmingham, not Coventry. Your brother said to send you.'

Billy wondered if he should hit her, grab her by the throat, lift her up, take back his fist and smash it into her snooty, turned down, sour as a lemon gob. Ah, bollocks, he thought. Then shouted again in his black country accent that was never so thick as when rowing with his wife, 'Bollocks, bollocks... fuckin' bollocks!' which took him out through the front door, which closed behind him. Soddin' hell, he fumed at himself for failing to slam it properly. Still, there was the car. He bounced into it, started up, hauled the steering around and sped across her manicured lawn, turning at speed on the driveway so the hundred quid a throw tyres squealed past the front windows where the woman remained seated, calmly reading her magazine until she heard him race down the drive and into the road, leaving her alone in the silent architect-designed house with its idyllic setting and impressive corner position.

*   *   *

The gymnasium above the Maverick Club was alive with feet running, ropes skipping, punchballs springing and weights clattering. In the central ring two novice heavy-weights shifted around, blowing through their noses and threatening sooner or later to lay a glove on each other. Around the flaking walls were the experts, the trainers, the hangers on and one or two gentlemen who were on the wrong side of the law. The sections of wall that were unoccupied showed cuttings, photographs and old fight posters without which the guys who grunted and groaned would just have been working out in a large damp depressing room instead of *Bam!* a training gym for up and comers, contenders and future champeens! Malleson stood facing the heavy bag and pulling on his gloves for punching practice. He was in his gear: the boxing boots, the shiny red shorts with the ivory stripe. He felt cold and apprehensive. He'd considered doing some road work that morning but had decided that last night's pursuit of Kline would have been sufficient exertion. He pulled on the gloves, made a fist and threw it at the hanging weight in front of him. While going through the motions of assaulting the bag he kept an anxious eye on the entrance that led into the gymnasium from the interior of the Maverick Club. I'm not worried, he told himself, he can't blame me... anyway Atty an' Bonny are still deployed an' that mick Irishman has men out lookin'; probably they'd got Kline already and if the boss did look in it would only be to offer a word of congrats for masterminding the capture. Then he saw the door open and caught the hard expression of Rawlinson and the hangdog look of Macavoy and knew he was in it up to his eyebrows. He steadied the weight of the bag; he felt exhausted, like a fighter who had only trained for a quick knockout but now knew that the fight was going to go long distance. Hoping to impress he launched a vicious attack on the stuffed leather until it swung under the impact. He went in, hammered combinations and one-twos until his hands hurt and he could feel the presence of the men behind him. He mustered a final flurry culminating in a final thudding right hook that landed where an opponent's chin might have been.

'Terrific!' Rawlinson shouted in encouragement then added, so Malleson could hear, ' 'E's dead good at punchbags, in'e, Dermot?'

Macavoy, who had emerged unscathed from an uncomfortable interview only by blaming Malleson for every aspect of the previous night's fiasco, tried to adopt his employer's tone and after examining Malleson's muscular body with a critical eye pronounced that Malleson was 'a fast boy, coulda bin Olympic.'

Rawlinson noticed a fight bill for a promotion he'd had a piece of. The name of Malleson featured on the bottom line. 'That's what 'appens, innit?' he said regretfully, going to the programme. 'You show them the big time an' they can't take it, like.' Malleson mustered a few more punches, pretended he wasn't listening. Rawlinson leaned back against the poster and regarded the unhappy fighter, adding, 'They get slow an' fat, prefer to use pick 'andles!' Exhausted, Malleson stopped, panting and punched out. He watched out of the corner of his eye as

Rawlinson sauntered nearer to him. Rawlinson stopped within the range of a straight left and pointed an inviting finger at his own chin. 'Come on. Yow 'ave first swing…' The West Indian pretended not to hear.

'Come on!' exhorted Rawlinson again but still Malleson refused the invitation. Rawlinson made a derisory gesture and turned to the overweight Irishman. 'Dermot, Dermot, it's terrible. The jungle bunny's gerrin' deaf an'all!'

Malleson threw the punch, not a hard one, at Rawlinson, who had an arm ready to block the blow and another to pull the punchbag in so that it collided with the boxer. Malleson already off balance, staggered into the embrace of Dermot Macavoy, who turned him to face a series of short stinging slaps from the back of Rawlinson's right hand. 'Listen, "Cassius",' Rawlinson said, punctuating each word with another blow across the frightened brown face, 'You've twenty four hours t'find Kline, an 'e's gonna find 'im… inne, Dermot?'.

'Float like a butterfly,' snorted Dermot down Malleson's sore ear.

'Sting like rice puddin'!' said Rawlinson, burying his nails into the small brown nipples at the centre of the fighter's pectoral muscles.

Malleson's head went back in agony against Dermot's shoulder, who thrust him away head first into the heavy punchbag. 'Black puddin'!' he said contemptuously.

'Ar…' replied Rawlinson as he noticed his brothers, Billy and Tommy enter the gym.

Shaking his head, massaging his chest and wondering how he could have ruined a good white jacket in the service of this pair've bastards, Malleson muttered, half to himself, 'I don't even know if that Kline man is still in town.'

Rawlinson, about to move away with the intention of greeting his brothers, turned back to the boxer. 'Oh, he's in town all right; Dermot owes him money…' Rawlinson wagged an admonitory finger at his Club Manager, 'Now don't you pay 'im, Dermot.'

The Irishman gave Rawlinson the assurance that he would indeed do all and everything he could to resist such a temptation.

Rawlinson watched his two brothers bounce across the ring towards him. They arrived and leant over the ropes, grinning down at him. This was more like it. Rawlinson nodded a greeting at them. Billy said, 'Ellow, Oz,' and yawned pleasurably. Tommy showed his teeth in what was a friendly grin but which made him look like a wolf who had just spotted a lamb straying from the fold. What could Rawlinson do to amuse them? His eye roved around the gym and settled once again on Malleson. He'd do, Rawlinson thought. The unhappy boxer saw Rawlinson give a friendly smile and beckon him across. Cautiously, he went as invited. Evidently the heavy recriminatory stuff was over, for the boss was patting him on the shoulder, smoothing the red and roughened, smarting skin on the front of his chest considerately.

Rawlinson whispered something which the boxer's damaged ears didn't catch. 'Ey?' Malleson said, relaxed now that everything was forgiven, and moved closer in to catch the words of wisdom, but received instead Rawlinson's sucker punch deep into his solar plexus. The wind went quite out of his body, the brown eyes popped with surprise and pain. He doubled up, gut on his thigh, knowing that breath would never return to his body. In the ring, Billy and Tommy Rawlinson guffawed like kids on the first day of a long awaited holiday. For them it was good times come again with Ozzie dishing out coercion by the basin-full.

Rawlinson indicated the winded boxer to Dermot. 'Inform our deaf coloured friend here that unless he finds Kline I'm very much afraid that he will be unable to play with us ever again.' He turned to his flesh and blood. 'Right, Tommy, Billy?'

Tommy and Billy nodded in agreement with their big brother. Dermot Macavoy, who wanted very much to be one of the gang, said approvingly, 'I think y'makin' sense.'

The leader inclined his head with humble thanks, 'Thank you, that's what comes've dealing with intelligent people, Dermot.'

Malleson slowly straightened up to find Rawlinson still waiting. This time, Malleson told himself, you throw one this time and I'm ready, but neither a blow nor a word came. Malleson found himself staring into two eyes as hard and grey as quernstones.

Someone had to speak and the West Indian said weakly, 'When we find Kline, what happens then?'

A tight little smile of secret pleasure came fleetingly to Rawlinson's lips before he turned, caught a rope and joined his brothers up in the ring. All three looked down at Macavoy and Malleson before bursting into a round of harsh, malevolent laughter that died away to nothing as each thought of their dead brother. They exchanged glances as vengeful as any made across the open grave three years before. Then they turned and walked away across the canvas of the ring.

Malleson shivered.

'Cold?' said Dermot.

'Sumthin' like that.'

'You need a drink.'

Malleson knew he did. 'But I'm in training...' he said, unconvincingly.

After an hour spent re-arranging and sorting through the debris left from the night before, Anne Darracott was pleasantly surprised to discover that the cabin of her motor barge was at least habitable again. She moved back towards the bed, turned and surveyed her home; it wasn't too bad. She ran a hand through her blonde hair, smiled to herself; no, not so bad, not when you remembered Rawlinson's promise to stand the cost of replacing the damaged antique furniture. She'd certainly earned the concession. For, lying awake and itching for sleep, she had conceived of a plan to discountenance the snoring man at her side. She would wake him, pretend a sexual need, and he would be impotent, which would be a nice shot to keep in one's locker. Or, even if he did manage to hold it up, she could lie back in total boredom while he sweated and strained at her behest. But it hadn't worked out that way, for Rawlinson, flattered by what he had interpreted as desire, and inflated by that stupid male pride, by that overblown machismo, had coupled violently with her until the walls of the vent he was using so thoroughly became so hot and dry that each succeeding stroke, each poke and thrust became one of dragging torment. She had screamed and struggled but he took this for ecstasy and said, in the lassitude that followed, that it was one of the most satisfying fucks he had ever participated in. She tried to set him straight, to rob him of that smug satisfaction but he refused to believe in her pain and discomfort and drifted into a heavy sleep from which Anne could not recall him.

When eventually she slept she dreamt a scene of her childhood when her mother was still alive and free from cancer. She had watched the chop-chop of the steak being cut into strips for the dish of Chinese pepper steak. Saw her mother's deft fingers take the pepper and salt and sprinkle the raw red meat. 'I bet that burns,' she heard herself say to her mummy, who smiled and pretended to shake the salt and the pepper pots at her. 'Put those on your tail and you'd soon know it!' In the dream the seven-year-old Anna Darracott had looked wide-eyed. 'I bet it would itch and itch and itch!' She woke a second after in time but fifteen years later in body to find herself clawing the raw wound of her vagina with savage fingernails. She made herself stop and the burning pain returned, redoubled and remained until the early morning injection of heroin removed all aches and pains, all troubles and woes.

Anne, standing in the now re-arranged and partially restored cabin, tried to concentrate on what she was required to do that day. Her mind skittered here and there. She remembered the package from last night and also a sale of antique furniture at a country house near Stratford upon Avon. She could sail to the sale, she thought and giggled. Come on, come on, concentrate she told herself, then giggled again but then made her forehead frown so that any onlooker would perceive that she was taking very seriously the dangerous trade she was engaged in. I'd love a coffee, she thought, hot and sweet, saturated with sugar, enough to stand a spoon in. 'OK, baby, OK,' she said aloud and went towards the kitchen, where she discovered that her water container had not escaped disturbance from the previous night's visitors and was lying on its side dry and empty.

'Balls!' Anne said to the kitchen and noticed that she had left a gas jet flaring from before her fix. She turned it off, wondered if her kitchen cupboard had remained undisturbed, checked, found it was OK. She took out the coffee jar and a 2lb bag of sugar and placed them on the cupboard top ready for her return. This done, she picked up the plastic water container by its handle, searched around for its cover, found it then climbed up towards the stern. Coming up onto the small area of deck she rested a hand on the long arm of the tiller, her eyes blinking rapidly as she tried to adjust to the grey light of the morning. She looked about her at the black murk of the water, at the dirty greens and bracken browns of the overgrown canal banks, then along the dark-grey cinderpath that led away under the bridge and towards a cold water tap. Anne, dressed in tight blue denims, white polo neck sweater under a short velvet doublet dyed the colour of Madeira wine, jumped from the deck of the *Anne Carol* and went skipping down the tow path like a seven year old swinging a bucket towards the seaside. She did not look back, so missed seeing the long figure of John Kline straighten up from his hiding place among the damp undergrowth. Kline waited until the jaunty blonde lady had disappeared under the archway of the bridge.

He guessed, having seen the container, that she was after water. The trouble was he didn't know how far away the source of that water was. Deciding to gamble that it was far enough for his purpose, he moved stiffly across the path, jumped onto the boat and disappeared down the hatchway.

In the kitchen Kline looked about him wondering where to start and what to look for. The night before Khan had mentioned the *Anne Carol* and drugs, so Kline supposed he should be looking for evidence to confirm or contradict his partner's suspicions. He looked in a few cupboards but there was nothing apart from a few supplies of basic foods, cereals and such. He went into the main cabin; it looked more or less as it had at the start of his previous visit, except this time there was a definite lack of soft lighting and all the bed had on its cover was a rag doll with black button eyes. Kline went across to the bed, looked down at the toy, then knelt down to peer beneath the bed. In the restricted light he could see very little so he put his long arm under and found the shelf and a cold metallic object that, when out into the light of day, he saw was coloured gold. Kline opened the lid, which was marked 'Bait', and saw the syringe, the eye dropper, the assorted needles, the spoon and understood. Searching again under the bed he came across a leather pouch laced tight. The ruffled neck opened and revealed the white powder inside. Kline wondered what drug it was and guessed at pure heroin. An ex-addict in Winson Green Prison had once given him the SP for Class A drugs under the misuse of Drugs Act: for illegal supply fourteen years or a fine or both; for illegal possession seven years imprisonment or a fine or both. It was a fair bit of bird, a big bowl of porridge for something that looked innocent enough to stir into a cup of tea. Kline felt the bag and all its dangers and wondered what he should do with the stuff. Then he remembered the sugar packet in the kitchen and began to have the start of an idea. Kline pushed the bead curtain aside; he half expected to find King Kong in his white beret waiting to start round two but the kitchen was empty, both of black boxers and blonde junkies. Opening a waste bin by means of its foot pedal Kline emptied the pouch of its magic powder and stirred it out of sight beneath the exotic covering of tea leaves, potato peelings and onion skins. Kline then took the empty pouch to the cupboard top and replenished it from a 2lb bag of sugar imported legitimately by Tate and Lyle. He had laced the little pouch up tight and was on his way back to the cabin when he heard the sound of someone jumping back aboard. The bead curtain swished as he dived through into the cabin. He just hoped it would stop swinging by the time whoever it was entered down the ladder of the hatchway. Reaching the bed and replacing the pouch back on the shelf left only a second in which to get across to the other side of the bed before Anne came home with a full bucket to her kitchen. Through the still swaying bead curtain, Kline could see the blonde head, the red doublet and the blue jeans. If he could see her she could see him so he ducked down behind the bed. He could hear the sound of the kettle being filled and the gas jet being ignited as he squeezed himself between the floor and the frame of the bed. What the bloody hell am I doing here? Kline asked himself. What good was it going to do, all this undercover, undermattress stuff? Well, it was something, a small gesture. In the darkness, Kline smiled mockingly at himself – a gesture, all right, like trying to ward off dum-dum bullets with the palms of your bare hands. Still, it was better not to be seen or to be discovered; they might think he'd got clear of Brum if he kept what army jargon used to call a low profile. And the profile you're keeping now, kid, he thought, couldn't be any lower. Turning his head to the kitchen, he began to ease his position further towards the centre of the section of floor beneath the wires that held the mattress. Through the gap under the bed cover he saw a pair of slim legs in faded blue denim walking towards him. Kline stiffened, began to edge his way back to the far edge of the bedframe. It couldn't be, he thought, she couldn't have seen him, but it looked very much as though she had, for the feet in their brown moccasins had stopped and the face of Anne Darracott, framed by a fall of fair hair, came down into his view. Kline thought she was looking straight at him but with the bedspread hanging down between them perhaps she couldn't see anything much. A hand with long, slender fingers groped its way towards him along the shelf that ran under the head of the bed. Kline tilted his head away until the muscles of his neck began to cramp. The searching hand found something and withdrew. The cover fell into place and darkness returned to the world of John Kline. He wondered what the woman had been searching for – probably the pouch of heroin. So much for that ploy. But when Kline felt along the shelf, his fingers touched the pouch and beyond that came the cold touch of the gold baitbox. So what had she taken away? Kline wondered whether to stick around or find a more comfortable hiding place or maybe just piss off unseen at the first opportunity. What to do? Then the engines started under him and he felt the *Anne Carol* move away from her moorings and settle down to a steady chug-chug, throb-throb that added the irritation of noise and vibration to the dust and discomfort of the confined space beneath the square of the bed.

Hand on the tiller, breeze in her hair, heroin in her blood, Anne Darracott was thinking that she didn't give a shit about anyone. She had a packet of heroin stuffed down between her jeans and her belly and she would soon drop that, then point the boat towards Stratford and run up a bill at that sale, baby, that would turn Rawlinson's black hairs grey and his grey hairs white. 'Yeh! Oh, yeh!' she shouted exultantly and picked up her mug of coffee and drank from the warm brown sweetness. She put the drink down beside her and felt in her doublet pocket, took out a gold lighter by Dunhill and a packet of cigarettes by Lambert and Butler, selected one of the international size cigarettes, put it into her mouth, lit it, inhaled deeply, replaced the lighter and fags then pushed on the tiller to send the *Anne Carol* into a long arc that would carry a wide bend that led into the section of the canal below the heart of the city. Two white women, pushing prams filled with the consequences of celebrating the Lord's last birthday with too careless a rapture, paused on the street running alongside the canal and followed the long sweep of the green and white barge guided by the slim carefree figure at the helm.

'Like a bleedin' cigarette commercial...' said one sourly.

'Awright f'sum...' said the other enviously.

Seeing them, Anne waved gaily. For some reason this enraged the two mothers. One shouted, 'Bloody 'ippy...!'

The other, 'Soddin' student!'

Anne grinned up at them and for no good reason gave the clenched fist salute as she disappeared around the bend.

'What was that for?' said one, puzzled.

The other sniffed. 'Must 'ave a nigger down below,' then, catching sight of the companion's baby, she added hastily, 'Not that I've anythin' against them.'

'Fair enough then,' said her mate as they each recommenced the pushing of their separate prams.

When the barge emerged from the series of arches and tunnels and entered onto a stretch of open water, Kline carefully eased back the sliding door that led onto the front of the vessel, now moving steadily along, its chug-a-chug effectively covering any sound the door might have made. Kline went into the open air, closed the door behind him and relaxed a little when he realised that he was hidden from the view of the stern by the square edifice of the cabin. He knelt down and peered down the length of the *Anne Carol* and noted that there was a small ledge running along the side towards the rear. Kline supposed a determined man might cling to its support for a few minutes if he had to. The barge was moving more slowly and he realised they were now near Old Snow Hill. He could hear the traffic zipping by and could see the rear yards of small factories and workshops and on the black brick of the passing walls he read the notices that discouraged the use of the canal for bathing purposes. The barge slowed and stopped at the rear of what had been a small scrap yard that must have expired under the weight of its product for it was piled with a pyramid of car bodies long cannibalised. Kline felt the barge bump against the canal side and stop. He waited, tensed and ready for discovery, but nobody came to discover him so he ventured a peep across the cabin roof. The tiller at the stern was unattended; the motors still idled over but there was no sign of the lady pilot until Kline caught a glimpse of red and blue on the far side of the rusty mountain of car bodies. To obtain a better view he would have to move from his present position. Not wishing to lose the advantages of being an undiscovered stowaway he supposed the best course of action would be to jump into the water, swim the length of the barge and tread the canal while spying from the stern. Kline looked down at the black mixture of Birmingham effluents glugging against the side and decided to avoid immersion by edging halfway along the narrow ledge port side of the *Anne Carol* while keeping the width of the cabin between his perch and dry land. After five or six sideways steps he arrived at an uninterrupted view of Anne seemingly about to unfasten her denims. Kline smiled. Nothing like catching a lady with her pants down. But it wasn't to be, for what emerged from her waistband was something that could have been a package; it was difficult to be sure for it was quickly hidden inside an old square water cistern. This done, the red and blue figure turned on her heels and began to pick her way back towards the barge. Kline ducked down. This was going to create a problem. He could not get back to the prow without being seen. With luck he might be out of the line of vision from the stern but he couldn't possibly hold his footing on the narrow ledge for any length of time; already the muscles of his legs were transmitting faint signals of distress. The barge tilted slightly as its skipper returned aboard and quickly got the long vessel under way, heading for a right hand, curving bend ahead. Kline, clinging on to his side of the slightly pitching barge, looked down at the waves of disturbed water, then back towards the now receding scrapyard. He saw a small man approach the spot where the package had been planted. It was difficult to be sure from that ever increasing distance but if he had had binoculars to focus Kline was certain that they would have shown a gentleman whose features were Oriental in cast and whose skin was yellow in hue. He would also have been prepared to wager that the package, still warm from Anne Darracott's belly, would soon be on its way towards London's Chinatown, where it would be cut and cut again before being distributed on and around Gerrard Street to whoever felt the need and was able to pay the price.

The *Anne Carol* ploughed on and Kline's muscles ached more with each moment that passed. He looked up at his tired hands and fingers and told them to pretend they were limpets for a little longer while he considered the limited possibilities of his position. If he eased back along towards the front of the barge the movement would probably be noticed and if he launched himself into the waters by the time he had disappeared below the surface the stern of the barge would be alongside. What a bastard, Kline said to himself, and felt his weight beginning to pull through his hands, making his balance even more precarious. He felt the barge slow appreciably and then saw why, for looming ahead was a small humpbacked bridge and a narrow aperture of a tunnel just wide enough to take the dimensions of any fair-sized water craft that did not have a large man protruding from its side.

That's it, thought Kline, seeing the black brickwork of the bridge approach steadily. But then he realised that it he could hang until the last moment he just might escape unseen, for the woman at the helm would need all her attention to guide the barge into the black hole of the tunnel. Somehow Kline made himself hold on until the prow entered the tunnel then he let himself go. He felt the shock of the water, felt the immediate change from dry to wet, from warmth to numbing cold, and tried to stay down clear of the bottom the barge long enough for it to avoid smashing his skull. The wake of the *Anne Carol* bounced him against the wall and back down amongst the mud and the bricks and the tyres and the barbed wire that lay on the bottom of the canal. Finally he could take it no longer and brought his head up out of the stinking, churning water and into the air. Gasping, breathing in gulps and coughing out water, Kline realised that the *Anne Carol* had gone. Whether or not he had been seen there was no way of knowing. He started to wade slowly towards the bank, clothes sodden, hair flattened, face streaked with mud, clothes hung with slime and weeds, shoes squelching with each step taken through the gunge beneath. Almost at the bank, Kline had the distinct feeling that he was under observation. He turned, looked up and saw the feet dangling down from the small bridge that spanned the tunnel. The legs were covered in grey wool up to nut-brown knees. Kline continued his upward gaze until it met the dark, accusing eyes on a West Indian schoolboy of nine or ten years. They looked at each other for a long moment, the bedraggled man and the boy in his schoolcap and blue gabardine raincoat. Finally the lad remembered the big word he'd been cautioned with and said sternly to John Kline, 'You're not supposed to swim in the canal, mister, you'll get salmon... ell... lilla...!'

Chapter Nine

'What kind of shampoo do you use?'

'What?' said Kline, lying in the bath and watching the dirt of the canal float off him.

'I said...' said Dinah, looking from the bathroom shelf with its conglomeration of toiletries, unguents and perfumes, to the man who filled her bath to overflowing.

'Anything,' Kline said, sluicing the sludge from between his toes.

Dinah sighed. 'What sort've hair've you got, Kline?'

'Dunno.'

'I mean oily, dry...?'

'Dunno.'

'Well, what do you usually use?'

'Depends on who's bathroom I'm in...'

'Oh, here...!' She threw a bottle of medicated at him; he caught it before it smashed against the tiled white wall behind the bath.

'You're polluting that water, look at the colour of it...'

'Report it,' Kline said lightly, sitting up then easing back so the warm wave of water returned to wash over him.

This is better, he thought, better than catching, what was it? What the kid got tongue-tied on... oh, yeh... salmonellilla. Kline chuckled to himself.

Dinah watched him. 'Anything I can share?'

'If you want.'

'Oh.'

'Just some kid who couldn't pronounce salmonell... lill...' Kline laughed. Dinah gave it up.

'I don't want to know what you're at or where you're up to...'

'OK.'

'After you fell in that canal, how'd you get back here?'

'Found a phone box that'd been done over but still worked. I phoned for a taxi, stayed in the box until it arrived.'

'Didn't the driver say anything. I mean, when he saw you?'

'Yeh. He asked me if I wanted to go back to the Black Lagoon.'

Dinah laughed. Kline picked up the bottle of shampoo, unscrewed the lid and let a little of the blue liquid drool into the palm of his hand.

'Shouldn't you wet your hair first?'

'Oh, yeh…'

'Here…' Dinah brought out a pink stretch of rubber hose with a spray attachment and inserted the taps of the bath into its bulbous ends.

'Sexy,' said Kline, watching.

'You reckon?'

'Oh, yeh…' Kline confirmed as a surge from the hot tap reached his groin.

'Try this,' Dinah countered and turned the cold tap so that the stream through the spray turned to ice.

'Ah!'

'Shampoo,' she ordered, holding out her hand for the blob of blue that Kline still held. The transfer effected from the cup of one hand to the other, Dinah regulated the spray of water then directed it at Kline's head and began the washing of his hair.

The rhythm and the lather and the feel of other hands turned what had always been a necessary chore into something pleasurable and vaguely erotic. Dinah rinsed the big skull and Kline snorted water and lather and dirt and grease from his nose and mouth as the clean water ran over him. Halfway through the second application of liquid shampoo, Kline realised that the hands on his head had ceased their massage. He opened an eye and looked up at a tense and worried Dinah. 'What's up?'

'The door… I'm not expecting anybody.'

Kline stood up, the water cascading off him. He saw himself in the mirror of the cabinet, naked with hair plastered to his skull by streaks of lather. Ridiculous, he reached for a towel.

Dinah fought down her fear. 'It's probably someone from the shop downstairs.'

'Maybe. I'll see.'

'No.' Dinah turned and left the bathroom and went briskly to the front door but faltered for a moment on reaching it. The sound of the bell rang loud and long until Dinah opened the door to shout, 'Stop it!'

Kline held the bathroom door ajar and listened to the smooth voice of the caller.

'Good afternoon...' it said, 'I'm conducting a census of this area. Do you have a Mr John Kline residing with you?'

'Wha...?' Dinah said, startled, but by this time Kline had recognised the voice and wrapped the towel about him before emerging from the bathroom.

'It's all right, Dinah, he knew I'd be here...'

Khan sauntered in without being asked, looked coolly about him then at his partner of less than thirteen hours. 'Don't let me interrupt your ablutions, Mr Kline.'

Dinah stared at the Asian then looked towards Kline. 'He's OK,' Kline answered her unspoken question. 'He's a friend of mine,' he added, wishing he knew for certain whether or not that was a statement of the truth.

Khan sat down, noticed the pink shirt, white shorts, socks, sodden shoes all drying in the warmth from the gas fire. 'Where is your blue suit?'

'Downstairs, getting a two hour cleaning job.'

Khan raised an eyebrow, lowered it, then gave Dinah a charming smile. 'If you were to offer me coffee, I would be delighted to accept.'

Dinah opened her mouth. Kline said quietly, 'He wants to talk to me.'

Dinah sighed, said, 'All right, OK,' and disappeared into the small kitchen, there to create sufficient noise to express either resentment at having her home taken over or tact in order not to overhear any compromising information.

The Pakistani leaned back in his chair. Kline went into the bathroom, put his head under the tap to rinse his hair, then re-emerged rubbing his scalp vigorously with a smaller towel than that worn as a Dhoti around his waist. 'What have you been up to?' Khan said and stroked his moustache as Kline began to outline the events of his morning.

Arriving at the entrance to the Raj, Rafiq was greeted by the doorman and management with all due courtesy and effusive thanks for bestowing such an honour upon their restaurant.

'Yes... yes... I am expecting company,' said Rafiq, allowing servile hands to remove his camel hair coat.

'Guests, yes, yes, they are here already.' The manager, wearing evening dress at mid-day, bowed his way backwards and opened the way to the interior.

Rafiq paused before entering. 'Guests, you said. More than one?'

Rawlinson, when requesting this meeting, had not mentioned bringing anyone else, unless...? Ah, now he understood. 'A gentleman and a fair lady?'

'No, no... three gentlemen... you see... please.' The manager gestured and Rafiq entered, then stopped and waited for his eyes to become accustomed to the subtle lighting within the restaurant. Usually he enjoyed this pause like a lover who intensifies his ultimate pleasure by postponing consummation for just a few seconds more. But this time he felt uneasy. Not many people could afford to eat in such an establishment at lunchtime but there were a few businessmen and at a table near the glittering bar the wife of the proprietor, in a sari of coral pink with an edging of woven gold. She smiled to him; Rafiq bowed in return.

'I put the gentlemen at your usual table.'

'Yes... yes... that was correct, all right,' Rafiq snapped and followed the manager who led him through the tables, towards the long row of tiny silver bells that hung tendril-like from the gentian-blue ceiling forming a moving wall that effectively divided the restaurant into two sections. The Rawlinsons were at Rafiq's permanently booked table behind the wall of hanging bells. Rawlinson was leaning back in his gold and claret chair, drinking champagne, a bottle of which nestled in a bucket of ice at his elbow. Above him a figure of the god Shiva spread arms over him as if bestowing a benediction. Next to Rawlinson sat Billy, trying to yawn and drink from a pint of Brew Eleven bitter at the same time. Opposite to Billy, the other brother, Tommy, was absorbed in the problem of how to ring out the tune of 'For He's a Jolly Good Fellow' on the silver bells that hung down within reach of his chair. Seeing all three brothers at his table Rafiq was aghast. He waved the manager away and hurried towards the surviving members of the Rawlinson clan. He could not contain his indignation and his voice squeaked out in high pitch as he approached Rawlinson the elder. 'Why are they... your brothers, what are they doing in Birmingham!'

'Park y'bum an' I'll tell y',' Rawlinson said, indicating to the empty chair opposite to him. Rafiq sat down next to the would-be campanologist, who paid no attention but rang out tin-tina tin-tin... ting... ting!

Across the table, Billy Rawlinson burped as he opened a menu; after glancing disapprovingly down the listed items of Eastern cuisine he pulled a face and said to the Indian, 'Ey, Raffy, do they serve chips in 'ere?'

Rafiq ignored him and leant across the table to Rawlinson. 'I demand an explanation,' he said intensely.

'You'll get one,' Rawlinson replied, gripping the bottle of Lanson Black Label and filling Rafiq's glass to the brim with champagne.

Khan drained his coffee cup. 'This secretary of his...'

'Anne.'

'She must know a great deal about the drug market?'

'first hand,' Kline said and moved his bare skin nearer to the fire.

'You could use her to get to Rawlinson.'

'How?'

Khan smiled, placed the cup on its saucer carefully. 'By gaining information and turning it over to the law... solve your problem if Rawlinson got a ten year stretch for drug smuggling.'

'Fourteen,' Kline corrected him.

'You've thought about it then?'

'Yeh.'

'Good, good, all of this is... good, for it is all progress... progress...' Khan stretched luxuriously, like a lean brown cat, lithe and confident of gaining success in the game he was playing.

Kline watched him. 'Think so do y'?' he said, flatly.

'Irresistible progress.' Khan's voice became vibrant with enthusiasm. 'Yesterday we numbered one, myself; then two, yourself... Now...?'

Dinah Carmichael entered carrying a blanket for Kline. Khan looked up at her, letting his last word hang like a question directed at her. She answered with a shake of her head.

'Uh, uh, baby, you're still two.'

'As you wish,' the Asian said casually but surreptitiously indicated to Kline that he wished further persuasion to take place.

Handing the blanket to her near-naked lodger by the fire, Dinah missed the byplay and by the time she had hitched the woollen covering around Kline's shoulders Khan was bearing his coffee cup towards the sink in the kitchen. Dinah knelt down beside the figure in its blanket. 'That man...?' she whispered.

'Khan.'

'He crazy or what?'

'I dunno. I dunno who or what he is.'

Kline suddenly shivered.

'Cold?'

'Someone on my grave,' said Kline, brooding.

'Don't say...' the girl slipped an arm inside the blanket and held it around him for comfort. Kline lifted the blanket and she came inside as if to shelter from a sudden storm. Neither said anything and when Khan returned all he could see was the back of two heads showing above a bundle of blue blanket. He smiled fondly at them, paternal in his expression.

'Must go, my children. Kuldip, my immediate superior, says that today is the day that the golden eagle craps all over Birmingham.' Khan half held his hands out as if to catch a shower of golden rain, then looked down at the upturned faces of his audience. 'Children, Kuldip says that if he and I wish to collect an abundance of riches all we need to do today is hold out our hot little hands... so!' Khan held his hands out fully; then let them fall. He gazed down at the babes in the blanket. At one white face and one brown. One male, one female. 'Be good, children...' he said gently as he turned and left them, hoping, like a father in a fairytale, that all would be well in his absence.

When it was his turn to be paid Jashir Singh Mahal shuffled to the cashier's window. The wage packet that he signed for was thicker than usual but that was as it should be. Jashir thanked the clerk and moved away back towards his section of the production line. There was nothing else to do but continue the work that kept coming down the track until the final blare of the factory hooter would make it pause and signal the end of this his final shift.

The mind of Mr Rafiq was a whirlpool of bewilderment. Across the table from him sat his partner, Rawlinson, listening with half-hooded eyes while Billy, the vice king Billy, talked in a loud voice of tearing the city of Birmingham apart. Looking, no doubt, for this… this… what was his name? Kline. Rafiq shook his head from side to side as if to shake away the effects of a bludgeon blow. Why should they jeopardise all of their investments, their cover, their safety, their liberty, all for the petty joy of killing such a nonentity as this Kline person. And to involve such an important personage as himself! Rafiq's brown eyes rolled slowly from one side to the other on a wave of horror as he contemplated the consequences. The Rawlinsons on the rampage; it would lead to trouble, shootings, investigations, not only of the murder of Kline but also any accomplices who had the misfortune to be involved. The fat little Indian shuddered. He must do something. He looked down; in his agitation, he realised he had been crumpling his table napkin again and again until it was no longer crisp and clean but crushed and dampened with the pressure and perspiration from his chubby hands. He threw the cloth down onto the tablecloth before him. Rawlinson's eyes flickered across the table at the movement but he made no comment. Rafiq decided that during the forthcoming meal he would have to speak his mind.

'Ow's that secretary've yours?' Billy asked his brother.

'OK. How's that wife've yours?' was the reply.

'OK.'

'Where you movin' to next?'

'Dunno… I mean… we're not… are we? She say anythin'?'

'No,' Rawlinson paused, looked at the saturnine face of his brother; he'd forgotten this one had a yen for Anne Darracott – same basic type as Billy's wife, 'cept one was ramrod straight and the other… Rawlinson put the problem out of his mind. I'll needle him a little, he decided. 'I hear y'buyin' your own removal van, that right?'

Billy scowled. 'No, it's bloody not. 'Oo told y'that?'

'Ere's the grub,' Tommy Rawlinson said with relish, pointing a stubby finger at the quartet of white-jacketed Asian waiters bearing trays and pushing trolleys towards their table. The manager adroitly placed warm plates before all four.

The head waiter asked, 'Bhuna chicken?' Rawlinson raised a finger. 'Machchi curry?' Rafiq pointed at Tommy. 'Hara mircha?' Rafiq indicated himself. 'Tali machchi?'

'No, I ordered fish…' said Billy, just before the dish of fried fish was served to him.

'You must have some lemon pickle with tali machchi. It is the only true accompaniment to such a dish.'

'I 'ate bleedin' lemon 'n' I can't stand soddin' pickles...' pronounced Billy, glaring with suspicion at each new container that was placed on the table. The dishes that Rafiq had so carefully ordered included brinjal burtha, Bombay duck, naan, poppadoms, many mounds of rice, sliced peppers and an assortment of pickles including that of lemon. Rawlinson took in the apprehension on his brother's faces and decided to enjoy himself a little.

'Ey, Rafiq,' he said, with a chuckle of anticipation, 'tell them, y'know, what y'told me last time we were in here.'

'What was that?'

'About Indian food.'

'I don't recall...'

'Yes, y'do... about God's secret n'all that...'

Rafiq helped himself to a little rice, a little bread and a lot of aubergines.

'I said... that... mm... cookery was one of the secrets that the Gods have revealed to man...'

Rawlinson nudged his brother.

'Woh?'

'Listen.'

'Yes, cookery is an art divine or should be...'

Rafiq became expansive, unable to resist the temptation to expound before the manager and head waiter, who were still moving dishes, making adjustments, hovering around, doing everything to make the meal successful short of relaying the food from off the plate into their customers mouths.

'Cooking, cooking should be a sacred ritual...' Rafiq mused, 'part of the sacred life of any people... don't you agree?'

'Oo, ar...' said Tommy, shovelling rice onto his plate.

Billy Rawlinson had finished a careful perusal of the various dishes on the table and had realised that one was missing. He grabbed the head waiter by the arm and said, 'Ey, yow, where's me chips?'

The waiter failed to comprehend.

'Chips. *Chips*!' Billy repeated loudly.

His brother, Tommy, up from behind a hillock of yellow rice. 'Now chips?'

'Don't look like it.'

'Bloody 'ell,' Tommy said in wonderment. 'Now bleedin' chips.'

The manager looked at Rafiq who tried to explain what the missing order was. A puzzled look appeared on the face of the manager. 'Chips?' he said.

'Chips,' repeated Rafiq and choked on the word. Tommy took a helping of Bombay duck, commented that it niffed a bit, took a bite and expressed the opinion that it was the fishiest piece've bleedin' duck he'd ever tasted. Rafiq wanted to die, to have the shame over and done with. The manager, stiff with dignity, walked away to confer with the head waiter, who shook his head in derision and spat out the word 'Chips' the way Billy would have said 'Wog'.

Deciding that a little havoc was called for, Billy started to get to his feet but was restrained by his elder brother. ' 'Ave sum rice,' said Tommy from across the table. 'It's good as Vesta, nearly.'

'Ah, bollocks,' said Billy and toyed with his fish before picking up his pint of British bitter and draining it down. 'Want anything?' he asked the table as he stood up. Heads were shaken at him, so he left the table and walked aggressively towards the bar glaring from side to side in the hope that maybe an Asian would be foolish enough to contemplate the crossing of his path.

Rafiq watched him go, then turned back on Rawlinson. 'No!' he said vehemently.

'Y'what?'

Rafiq swallowed a piece of pepper with its stuffing of spiced meat, dabbed his lips with the crumpled napkin and made himself as calm and as reasonable as possible. 'We need silence and smooth waters. Send your brothers back to Coventry and Wolverhampton, there's a good fellow, *please.*'

Rawlinson ripped a piece of naan in half. 'I want Kline.'

'Use my boys then,' Rafiq said, offering the dish of brinkan burtha.

Rawlinson pushed it away with a gesture of contempt. '*Your* boys... if the spades couldn't get Kline to jump on the shovel, what chance've your dummies got?'

'*Your* brothers running round the Bullring turning it into a... a circus is *not* what is required,' Rafiq said heatedly, then paused while a waiter brought a chrome platter on which were scattered several underdone portions of chipped potatoes.

'Stick'm there! 'Bout bleedin' time,' said Tommy, helping himself to a couple and shouting across to the bar, 'Ey, our kid, chips're up over 'ere!'

Billy, a pint of beer in each hand, bellowed in reply, 'Right, down't yow eat any bloody more, yow bloody gannet guts!'

Rafiq winced at the upraised, unseemly voices and tried sweet gentle reason yet again. 'I do not think you realise quite how much money is involved, my dear...'

'Don't I now?'

The Indian looked serious. 'How many Asians in the Midlands?'

'Bleedin' millions,' sniggered Billy, returning and sitting down after placing a pint of bitter on either side of the rapidly cooling platter of chips.

'Please!' Rafiq held up his hand. 'Let us work on a figure that ten thousand are illegal immigrants prepared to contribute at least two five pound notes a week to my party funds...'

Rawlinson reached for his champagne glass. 'Hundred grand a week, I know.'

'five point two million a year...'

'Theory innit,' said Rawlinson casually before taking a mouthful of the bubbling amber liquid from his glass.

Rafiq tapped the table to give due emphasis. 'A possibility to work towards... Both of us are equal, both of us have much to lose – money, prestige, position, freedom, power... why jeopardise them all for the sake of killing this one Kline fellow?'

There followed a pause. Rawlinson's objectivity disapproved of the need for excitement, anarchy and savage revenge. The grizzled head bent over the glass and watched the bubbles rising like troubled thoughts. He pushed the glass away. 'He killed our kid,' he said simply, betraying no sign of the conflict within him.

Rafiq's attitude hardened at this apparent disdain for his logic. He pursed his soft, red lips. 'Any trouble, any publicity and we call a halt to our alliance.'

Rawlinson scowled. 'We stop Blackbirdin' when I bleedin' say,' he stated coldly.

The Asian smiled almost insolently. 'Drugs you can run, my dear Mr Rawlinson, but not the Blackbird. You may own a transport company but how would you operate in the Asian community? Do you speak Urdu, Punjabi?' He watched Rawlinson fidget at the thought. 'Do you have the contacts, the list of illegal immigrants? Do you know when and where they get paid and how much they will contribute to my party's funds?'

Rawlinson shrugged a shoulder. 'I can find out.'

The Indian shook his head. 'No. I know my value to you in money and I demand an equal say... I cannot afford trouble over this man Kline...' He stopped, simpered to himself, turned an elegant ruby ring around his index finger and paid no attention to his partner's growing irritation. 'I have to tell you... that independent approaches have been made to me about widening my political affiliations.'

Rawlinson threw his head back and laughed at the ceiling, then at Rafiq. Billy snorted. Tommy gave a peal on the silver bells.

'Vote f'Rafiq?' Rawlinson sneered.

'Only if you wish to...' Rafiq smiled at the prospect of becoming Britain's first Asian Prime Minister. He waved with a regal gesture towards the head waiter indicating that he, the Emperor, wished the table to be cleared. From the kitchen an army of waiters advanced to obey his command. The manager came to enquire if all had been to his complete satisfaction. Rafiq said the food had been superb. He apologised in Punjabi for the crass behaviour of his guests and insisted that the manager add a twenty-five percent surcharge to their bill to compensate for such unforgivable behaviour. The manager replied in his native Punjabi that he would be most happy to act on Mr Rafiq's kind suggestion.

Rawlinson watched the two Indians jabbering away in their monkey language. Political affiliations... that Herbert opposite was getting above his fat little self. He gave Rafiq his Basilisk stare and said, 'Yow might be 'ead serang 't'brown brothers...' He indicated the scurrying waiters, the smiling Manager. 'But t'me, you're just a *wog*.'

Rafiq did not like that particular word or the contempt and disdain with which the word had been heavily seasoned, but he made himself smile as if it were of no consequence. He picked up his shallow glass of champers. 'But a *significant* wog...' The oily smile remained as he made a concession. 'Kill this John Kline if you must but do it quietly and quickly, Mr Rawlinson, or do it not at all.'

*

Dinah Carmichael lay on her side and watched Kline asleep on the pillow beside her. She listened to the deep, slow measure of his drawing the oxygen in and sending the carbon dioxide out. Yesterday, she thought, her way was clear and bright as cut diamond. All she needed to do was hide her feelings and bare her body every night until she could afford the most satisfying take off of all, that of her jet flight away from this damp and dreary island to that other island on which her parents had been born. Simple. So how come she was dallying with this white guy Kline who wasn't even paying for her favours? She shifted onto her back, pulled the covers up around her bare shoulders. The movement brought a wave of the salt-sweet smell of him up to her. Semen. The scent, the presence of it inside her womb together with that morning's slow fall should have been warning enough. She suddenly realised that she hadn't given impregnation a second thought. Disliking spermicidal foam or the pill or diaphragm or anything like that, she usually insisted that the guy either sheath his sword or take his naked weapon elsewhere. Yet here with this stray from the street she had hardly considered it. And another thing, she thought grimly as she turned her back to Kline and looked towards the living room with its glow from the still burning fire running up bills drying his clothes... What other thing? Face it, she insisted to herself, fighting the attempts at her consciousness to repress the memory of what had occurred after Khan had left them to their own devices. They had decided to return the blanket to the bed. When this was done they undressed and climbed between the sheets without a word. During the foreplay and the act that had followed they had enjoyed an intensity of pleasure made desperate by the foreboding that there might not be another time. Kline, with his cutlass dulled slightly from the clash of their previous encounters, had climbed with her towards a peak of orgasm that had culminated with Dinah taking his hands from her breasts and placing them around the circumference of her throat in the hope that he would apply the same intensity of pressure to her windpipe. It had seemed the right end to it all, the final abdication of responsibility of her life. But later, after the fire had fallen and the pump of blood had slowed, she was frightened for herself and had said nothing, only hushed him and pretended a need for sleep so she could figure out whether to accept commitment or turn him back onto the street and return to the cold clarity of the day before.

*　　　*　　　*

The numbered balls clicked together and changed position on the small pool table that stood in a side room of the Maverick Club. Dermot Macavoy stepped back from the table smirking and waved his cue in invitation for the brown-skinned dandy dressed in tan-coloured gabardine to take his turn at the table. Malleson pored over the pool table, trying to assess the angles from ball to ball, from ball to pocket. Unconcernedly the Irishman watched the fuzzy black head bent over the table. There was no way that Pick Handle Pete was going to score, 'cos he, Dermot, had left him sweet FA.

'I can't win this game any'ow, can I?' Malleson said in frustration.

'Wanna quit?'

'May as well.'

'That's a fiver then.'

Malleson peeled a blue one from his depleted roll. It had been an expensive way to pass an afternoon. He'd been certain, was still certain that Kline would be captured here at the Maverick. All he had to do was to wait and keep himself ready. But then – Malleson tasted the bile in his belly – suppose he didn't show, what then? 'Where is he… that Kline bastard, where?' he suddenly burst out.

Dermot slipped the five pound note into his big black-leather wallet. 'He'll cum back,' he said soothingly. 'Count on it… count on it… I'm tellin' ya, he'll cum back here.'

Malleson banged the butt of his cue on the floor. 'How'd he wriggle out last night… How?'

Dermot shrugged. 'find that out 'n'y'might just be gettin' somewhere. 'Til you do, you're off the firm.'

'So?'

'So y'don't work no club, no string've girls, no outfit'll look at y'an' as f'future fights…' Dermot saw the eight ball on the table and remembered a scene in a forgotten film that would illustrate his thesis. He brought the cue ball onto its spot, made a bridge and stroked the ball down the table. It was supposed to strike the cushion and nestle behind the eight ball but he'd used too much elbow and it rolled back past the black and white ball. He decided to try again and to cover the execution he developed his theme. 'Y'might get a job 'umpin' bricks on th'lump… don't think th'quare fella's got that just yet.' He struck the cue ball again but this time not hard enough, for it only kissed the far green off the cushion. Oh bugger it, thought Dermot, the coon wasn't even watching, anyhow. He walked down the pool table, picked up the black ball, showed its figure to Malleson. 'That's what you're behind 'til y'find Kline.'

It was all lost on Malleson. ' 'Ow d'y'mean?' he said, squinting at the figure eight on the ball as if it was a clue to the whereabouts of John Kline.

In the doorway of a disused shop Kuldip pushed more paper money into his already laden pockets and impatiently watched while yet another stupid wog fumbled unwillingly for the two fivers that would guarantee freedom from the immigration authorities for another week. 'Here!' he said, snatching and making note of the payment next to the stupid wog's name. This only took a moment and his darting eyes missed no familiar face in the passing throng of factory workers. Someone joined him in the doorway. By reflex Kuldip held out his open hand, but then dropped it when he realised it was a fellow collector. 'All right?'

Khan nodded, fumbled in his pockets as if over anxious to pass on the payments he had collected outside the gates of another factory. 'Not now. I trust you. I trust everyone,' Kuldip said and gave a sudden squeal of laughter.

You need your brakes adjusted, my friend, thought Khan as he stuck a silly grin on his face as if the excitement was all too much for him.

Kuldip nudged his helper. 'There's one've ours...'

'Where ?'

'The Sikh... in the turban.'

Khan saw the man indicated trudging along with downcast eyes, a metal lunchbox tucked under his arm. He paid no attention to the men in the doorway but continued as if he had no obligations to anybody, as if he had a legal right to walk the streets of the UK.

Kuldip stepped outside, 'Hey, you... Jashir!' he shouted indignantly. The Sikh stopped but did not turn. Kuldip curled his lip in annoyance and put a hand on the handle of his knife and sauntered towards Jashir Singh Mahal. 'Think I wasn't coming?'

The Indian's eyes clouded with bitterness. 'It's pay day, isn't it?'

'So pay... pay!'

Looking down at the hand that Kuldip had thrust out impatiently Jashir slowly brought out his pay packet from his jacket pocket. Fishing inside for a ten pound note he realised that his blackmailer was staring at the unusual bulk of the brown packet.

'Lot of overtime?'

'Yes... yes.'

Kuldip, his eyes bright with avarice, said at the wages envelope, 'Maybe we should charge you more... everything's going up these days, even the price of silence.'

'No more!' Jashir shouted angrily.

'Shouting at me are you?'

'I cannot pay... I cannot pay any more!'

'Sooner get sent back to your Mother India?' The Pakistani came close in to the bearded man in the turban and spoke softly, 'It can be arranged... one telephone call and you are in Winson Green Prison, my friend.'

Agitated, Jashir walked away a few paces then returned to his tormentor. He pointed a trembling finger. '*You* get sent to prison! I tell the police how I was brought here. Nothing happen, not to me... they forgive me.'

Khan waited for the squeal of laughter to issue from the ugly, grinning mouth of Kuldip but instead there was only an expression of scorn. 'You are a child.' Kuldip looked at the Sikh with hatred and contempt. 'The amnesty trick is only played on immigrants brought in donkey's years back. No, for you it's fasten your seat belts and cheerio to England, wife and family.' He waved a hand towards an imaginary aeroplane and wiped a mock tear from his eye then grinned at Khan, who smiled and nodded to show that he appreciated his superior's sense of humour.

The ceremonial knife his religion required him to carry all times came into Jashir's thoughts. His hand went to its concealed presence. Kuldip saw the movement, reached inside his own jacket; Khan prepared himself for trouble. The Sikh, realising what was about to take place, withdrew from the conflict. This was no way for him to behave, to descend to the level of these thugs and gangsters. Without a word he turned and walked away down the busy street.

'See you next week,' Kuldip taunted, tucking Jashir's contribution into his bulging pocket. He didn't know what but something was wrong. That Sikh, he'd always been a protester but this time it was as if he didn't care too much about the threats of betrayal. 'Follow him!' he ordered and gave Khan a push in the same direction as that taken by Jashir.

*

It was still day, although the light was fading, when Kline came awake. He glanced at Dinah, who had turned on her side in sleep so that one brown shoulder was exposed. Kline pulled the cover over it and felt a touch of the warmth from her skin. He turned the alarm clock to him; it was six o'clock. He decided to set the alarm for later in case he should get tired of his thoughts and drowse off again. He reached for the clock but found its time switch already set so he settled back into the dry warmth of the shared bed and considered whether to lay for Anne Darracott, return to the Maverick Club or head for the hills. Or stay? Or go? If he was quiet and stealthy enough he could tiptoe into the next room, put on his drying clothes, collect his suit, which should have been placed dry and clean outside Dinah's door. That done there was nothing to do but walk away. Then there would be no comeback on the girl should the worst happen. Kline grimaced; so he wasn't heading for the hills. Well, come on, he urged himself, if he was going to take off and walk out now was the time. A minute ticked past on the luminous dial of the alarm clock. Kline placed an exploratory hand onto his genitals. Like the rest of him they felt warm and relaxed and for the present not inclined to stand up and fight. He thought for a while what he had to do. Tried to plan but realised there were so many wild factors that it was pointless speculating beyond any time but the present. So, that decided, he turned and gently pressed his thighs and belly against the back of the sleeping woman. Her murmur of acknowledgement comforted him and seemed to confirm the decision he had made.

From his vantage point in the garden of an empty house on Stoney Lane, Khan watched the 35cwt removal van lurch away from the house where Jashir and his young family had, until a minute ago, rented two rooms. As a member of Rafiq's boys his next objective was clear; he must telephone the number painted on the side of the removal van and pretend to be one of Jashir's friends, who had unfortunately mislaid his new address. Khan wrinkled his nose. He didn't like the turn the game was taking but what other course was there? He had to prove his usefulness and loyalty to Kuldip, Rafiq and Rawlinson. To do that he must first discover the new address that the Sikh now sought as a refuge from his blackmailers. Khan stepped out onto the pavement; he knew where there was a telephone kiosk; while following Jashir he had made mental note of its position. He hesitated for a moment, knowing that as soon as he discovered the location of Jashir's new address he would have to betray it. With a bleak expression on his face Khan began to move unwillingly in the direction of the telephone box.

Chapter Ten

The yellow Datsun 12oy went through the centre of Bordesley Green. Kuldip looked out at the empty shops with windows covered by sheets of corrugated iron. 'I know it round here... yes, Saltley... that's a reformatory, or used to be... maybe still is.' He scowled at the memory and picked up the piece of paper on which Khan had noted Jashir's new address. 'This'll be the next left. It is off Mansel Road.'

Khan prepared to turn left at the next opportunity. Kuldip watched him. 'Hey, you, Khan.'

'What?' said Khan.

'You did pretty good.'

'Thank you,' said Khan quietly as they turned into Mansel Road.

'There... over there.' Kuldip jabbed a finger at Floyer Road.

When they had stopped outside Jashir's latest home Khan turned to his superior. 'You wish I should come in with you?'

'Yes... he's bad news, this Sikh... I'm going to cut him up pretty bloody rough.'

'Kill him?'

'Not unless I have to,' Kuldip said as he climbed from the car and started his swagger towards the front door of the address given to Khan by the removal company. Khan waited until the Pakistani was on his way before unlocking the glove compartment and transferring the .38 Webley that lay inside to the holster that was concealed beneath his jacket. This done, he left the car and hurried to join Kuldip.

He arrived as Jashir opened the door then tried to slam it in the faces of these most unexpected and unwelcome visitors. When Kuldip blocked the closing door with his foot, Jashir gave a cry of anguish and ran down the hallway to where his wife and children were peeping from behind heaped furniture.

Kuldip flung the front door wide and commanded, 'Stay... you listen!'

Jashir covered his family with the spread of his arms. 'Touch them and I kill you.'

Kuldip strutted down the hall way towards the Sikh family. 'Kill, kill? I came to give you a message from the big boss.' The Pakistani waved a finger under the hooked nose of Jashir. 'He is very angry, my friend. He ask why that scoundrel Jashir run away. Does he think we cannot find him?'

The Indian looked from the sneering features of Kuldip to the impassive Khan. 'I've paid you!'

'A smirk came to Kuldip's lips. 'The payments are increased for you... for you, silence will cost another six pounds.'

'Six?'

'Sixteen a week.'

The Sikh waved his arms in frustration and anger. 'I cannot pay it... I go to the police now, tell about you!'

Kuldip stopped the movement that Jashir had been about to make by grabbing his shirt and throwing him against a stack of wooden chairs. Jashir staggered, fumbled for his knife and brought it out. Kuldip smiled and matched one blade with another.

'Go to the police, my friend... they put you on a plane for India pretty bloody quick. Not your wife, not your children – just you! They stamp your passport "Deported". You not get a job in India then, I tell you. You go back to your village, they laugh at you for your failure here in England!'

Jashir moved his head from side to side; he looked at the frightened face of his wife, Mangit, and at the wondering eyes of his children peeping from behind their mother's sari. Kuldip watched the play of expression on the bearded face. 'Your wife, she will have to work to send you money... your children, they...'

It was too much. Khan knew that the Sikh was going to react to Kuldip's goading in only one way. When the thrust came he threw himself forward in an effort to block the lunge of the knife at Kuldip.

'Wait!' Khan pleaded while holding the Sikh's knife arm with his two locked hands.

Behind them Kuldip became highly agitated and excited as he

hopped around looking for an opening past Khan. 'Him or me... him or me!' Khan kept hearing him shout. 'Not going to be *me*, I bloody tell you!'

As the flood of anger that had sustained Jashir began to ebb Khan felt the muscles that had been straining to burst free from his restraint slacken. Keeping himself between Kuldip and the Indian, Khan said to his colleague, 'What now?' Kuldip looked down at his knife then gazed sullenly around the family until it stopped at its breadwinner.

'You better pack your things, Jashir, I'm telling you... you are already on that plane!'

The clock on the bedside table was poised to strike. The big finger reached twelve and the little one said eight so it released the hammer and sent forth a clangour of bells.

The couple in the double bed stirred but made no move until the clamour had finally ceased. Then the woman yawned and said sleepily, 'I have to go and work.'

'You n'me both,' came the reply from the adjacent pillow. Dinah sat up. The movement made Kline haul himself onto the prop of an elbow. 'See you later?' he asked.

'Where... here?' Dinah's voice faltered as she turned her head away. Now was the time. Now was the time to duck out, thought Dinah. Now. But she said nothing. After a moment's silence Kline asked what was troubling her. She shook her head. 'Just trying to remember where I put the spare key.'

As he knew he would be coming back to this bed, Kline suddenly didn't mind leaving it. He swung out and hurried towards his clothes in the living room; Dinah watched as the white buttocks disappeared through the doorway.

'You seein' that Khan man t'night?'

'He's otherwise engaged, didn't you hear him say?'

Kline's head appeared around the door just as Dinah brought her brown skin into the cold air outside the bed.

'It's milkin' time...' Kline said, looking down at her breasts, watching one going one way and one bouncing the other. He steadied their sway and said gently, 'Ow now, brown cow?'

Dinah went past him. 'He's trouble that guy.'

Kline followed her into the other room, picked up his shirt and started to put it on. 'Who isn't... what isn't?'

Dinah said, presenting him with the spare Yale key, 'Me.'

'You.'

Dinah shivered. 'Stay here, Kliney, ey?'

Kline stood in his blue socks, his shorts and flapping pink shirt. 'I have to attack, get sumthin' on Rawlinson or go under...'

Dinah became angry at his lack of caution. 'Been under once today, haven't you?'

'You could say...' Kline had gone to the door, unlocked it and peeped outside; as promised by Dinah's friends in the shop downstairs, his suit hung on a wire hanger swathed in polythene. He came back inside, showed the suit. 'They did it.'

'Yeh,' said the girl on her way to the bathroom.

Kline came to watch her turn the taps on at the end of the bath. He raised his voice above the dual water splash. 'I'm going down that canal bank again t'night. I want to see what trash 'as floated since this mornin'.'

Dinah came out to the bathroom door, folded her arms and watched the white legs step into the blue trousers. Kline looked up.

'I'll be back later, don't worry.'

'Who's worried?'

Kline pushed his shirt down into his waistband. 'No one,' he said.

'Do me one favour. Try not to fall in the bleedin' canal this time, OK?' She turned, bent down to turn off the cold water tap.

Kline could not resist touching the suddenly revealed chink in her behind. 'Whoops!' he said as Dinah straightened with some alacrity.

'Keep y'bleedin' cold fingers t'y'self, Kline.' She reached up to the shelf and brought down a jar of blue bath crystals.

"And if y'do go swimming again take that Khan in with you. He could use a wash!'

'Don't worry about him.'

They watched the aquamarine crystals dissolve and cloud the clear water for a moment before Dinah turned to speak to him. He put his arms out to her but she stepped back a pace and looked up at him.

'Worry... worry. You use that word all the time. Think I don't know enough not t'bother about any man, black, white or brown? You go away,' she pushed him with no force at all, 'or stay... get killed or live on... I'm not worried about it. Clear? I just want out, away...'

'Away t'the sun?'

'Right.'

Kline kissed her, then said lightly, 'Maybe I'll come with you.'

'As what?'

The words 'white nigger' came into Kline's mind but he kept them to himself. He wanted to puzzle out what that description entailed. So, for the time being, he grinned, fastened his dry and clean blue suit jacket and said, 'See y' kid...' then went away and left the brown stripper alone to step into bath water now coloured blue as the Caribbean Sea.

The large table in the ante-room used to assemble the weekly take was covered by neat rows of green, blue and brown currency notes. Rafiq, seated at this table, transferred a mark of payment from the last of his collectors' paying-in books and closed his master ledger with a sigh. Beside him Kuldip gathered together a scatter of green pound notes and began to count their number to add to the total of contributions. Behind them, standing guard at the door was Zaheer Mohammed Khan, allowed to witness for the first time the Golden Eagle's Harvest Home.

Slumped in a corner of the same room, Rawlinson splashed whisky from a crystal decanter into a tumbler of the same stuff. He'd been drinking all day — champagne at the restaurant then brandy, and afterwards, with his brothers at the best of his clubs, the Aster... what had he supped there? Brandy, whisky, vodka? That was Tommy's tipple. Tommy. Billy. They'd spent the afternoon planning, early evening instructing Herberts in dinner jackets about the search for the missing Kline. He'd managed to obtain a photograph from one of his contacts on the *Evening Mail* and had had it photocopied. It was out of date but it would do. His belly burned inside. That bloody curry. He realised he was relieved to be away from his brothers for a while. Yeh, he was glad he'd made the excuse that he had to supervise the take here at Rafiq's, leaving to them the organisation and the labour involved in the search for John Bleedin' Kline. When they caught him he'd take over, then... he swallowed a mouthful of scotch. He neither felt drunk nor sober. Anyway, for tuppence, as his mother... The ringing of a small bell made him look up. Rafiq rang again. The young immigrant who had arrived the night before now entered diffidently.

Rafiq turned from the money table, examined the youth in his black trousers and snow-white steward's jacket. 'Turn around,' he ordered.

His new servant did so. How attractive he looks, thought Rafiq, feeling a delicious sensation of anticipation at the thought of falling upon that sweet brown bottom. 'My tea...' he said in Urdu. 'You may bring it.'

The servant understood and bowed before withdrawing. Khan folded his arms as the servant passed him and concentrated on Rafiq and Kuldip at the table. The ledger that contained names, addresses, record of contribution, time and method of illegal entry was being referred to by Rafiq, who located the section catalogued 'M' and ran the point of a silver pen down the list of names until he found the one.

'Jashir Singh Mahal?'

Kuldip nodded, snapped a rubber band around another hundred notes. 'That's him.'

Rafiq referred to the Sikh's record. It was not a good one. 'Mmm... tried to lose us once before... bad payer.'

'Yes, always excuses,' Kuldip smiled down at his master. 'Rent, clothes for his children. Make an example of him, why don'tcha ?'

Rafiq turned to his partner. 'That is what we will do.'

He turned back to his minions. 'We're putting up the payments. It would be as well to have this one fellow deported as a deterrent to all the others.'

Khan and Kuldip nodded their agreement then stood aside to allow the young Asian servant to re-enter with a metal tray laden with everything needed for the civilised taking of tea.

'That last cargo. All are placed in suitable employment... all are noted on the list. In the book?' Rafiq tapped the ledger laid out in front of him.

Kuldip jerked a thumb at the bent white back of the Asian pouring tea into Rafiq's china cup. 'All except him. And one other.' The cups and saucers, the pot and the tiny cakes were laid out neatly. 'Very good,' he said in Urdu, then added in English, 'We'll keep this one; his not speaking the English language is an advantage. About the other chap still lazing about in the cellar, you get him the job left by that scoundrel Jashir, all right?'

Kuldip nodded. Waited. Rafiq smiled, reached for two bundles of notes, one brown, one blue. 'Here,' he said and tossed them nonchalantly to his lieutenant. 'Thank you, Mr Rafiq,' Kuldip said humbly. His master wondered how much of the money gathered that day had remained in Kuldip's pockets but dismissed the speculation as pointless. Whoever he employed would take a profit; it was the way such people were.

Kuldip and Khan prepared to leave as the servant opened the doors into the hallway.

'By the way, Kuldip...'

'Yes.'

'See your helper receives a money bonus.'

Kuldip flexed fingers tired by the counting of much currency. 'I will.'

Rafiq looked at Khan. 'What is your name?'

'Khan.'

'Very well done, Khan,' Rafiq said before waving a dismissive hand.

Khan and Kuldip withdrew. The servant, too, bowed out and closed the doors.

'Good day?' Rawlinson said, coming to look over the table with its rows of neatly bound money.

'The usual.' Rafiq reached for the pot of tea. 'Tea, my dear?'

Rawlinson shook his head. 'Gotta go.'

'Where will you be?'

Rawlinson considered. If that blonde bitch of a secretary had a telephone he could have gone and waited on her bleedin' boat down the canal.

'Flat above my office.'

'Where are your brothers?'

'Aster and the Carlton.'

'Behaving themselves, I hope and trust.'

'Yeh, sure!'

'Good.' Rafiq picked up the telephone and dialled a number.

His partner turned to go. 'Might see you later...'

'Yes, yes,' Rafiq replied, then deliberately changed his voice to that of a tremulous, frightened stool pigeon at the declaration of the voice at the end of the wire.

'Bordesley Green Police Station.'

'Please, sir, I wish to report the presence of an... an illegal immigrant!' Rafiq gulped for effect.

Rawlinson laughed and started to leave the room. As he opened the doors he heard Rafiq continuing in his most-very-anxious Asian voice, saying, 'Yes, sir, I do have his latest address. My name does not matter, sir. His name is Jashir Singh Mahal!'

Billy Brody looked out on the Friday night audience at the Maverick and said, 'Awright?' He didn't feel too bad; he'd fallen asleep for an hour or so after the afternoon drinking session and felt fuzzy but conscious of his timing. That sense of panic would need a drink to assuage it soon but for the moment he could cope. What to tell this lot? 'Awright, awright...'

'Gerronwithit!' a voice shouted at him.

'Gerroff!' someone else added.

'I never do requests,' Brody rejoined, then said, with a glint of amusement, 'Which is why I'm doing nothing!' Nothing. 'Gerronwithit... gerroff... No?'

'No!' came the shouted reply.

'Awright, awright. I was just shufflin' some jokes that wouldn't offend the Race Relations Board. Y'know the sort've thing, don't you, sir...'

' 'Oo me?' said a driver from Liverpool truculently. 'No.'

'Course you do.'

'No, I don't.'

Brody gave it up. 'Aha, sort've gag I mean, ladies and gentlemen, is like the Pakistani who took a pig into a pub. He walked in with the pig wriggling and squeaking under his arm and the landlord said, "Where'd y'get that?" And the pig said, "I won it in a raffle!" ' Some laughter. Not bad.

'No need for that sort've thing... take Irish jokes and I wish somebody would... Irish jokes are the same. What's funny about an Irishman standing for hours on a broken down moving staircase?' They didn't get it. 'A broken down moving staircase...' A few titters. 'Or the other Irishman who got on a bus down Digbeth and shouted up to the conductor, "Sor, do y'moind if oi bring a crate've Guinness up?" "Course not," said the conductor, so the Mick went "Oooargh". ' Brody went on miming a man vomiting while the audience laughed in varying degrees of amusement.

Dermot Macavoy was not amused. He put down his pint of Guinness and said to Malleson, 'What's funny about that?'

Brody thought he'd milk the same gag one more time.

'Same joke, same bus, same conductor, only a Paki gets on and shouts upstairs, "Please may I be bringing my Alsatian up?" Same result… "Oooarghl"!'

That was better. Just like wogs, thought Dermot, and gave a grunt of mirth. He glanced at his companion; the brown face remained unsmiling. No sense of humour, decided the Irishman.

'Thought you was lookin' f'Kline?'

'I'm just waitin' f' little Miss Dynamite t'come on, then I'll smell around backstage.'

Brody finished his illustration of jokes the Race Relations Board might disapprove of with 'Like the West Indian on a zebra crossing… now y'see him… now y'don't. Now y'see him…' Needing a drink and trying as always to remember what came next, he glanced furtively over his shoulder to see Dinah Carmichael backstage, dressed for her virgin bride strip. Oh, yeh. 'So… carrying two cups of hot chocolate… whoops, sorry, love! Here she is ready t'reveal as much of her beauty as y'want or can take… put'm together an' I know she'll really open up for you. Ladies and Gentlemen, Miss Dinah Carmichael!'

On the tape the strains of the Bridal March started. Dinah slowly appeared; the scattered applause died as they looked her over in her white bridal dress and veil. Dinah moved to the front of the stage, lifted her veil to show her face to the mob, then opened the skirt, put a leg on the stool set for her and began to unfasten the suspenders that held up her white silk stockings.

Malleson detached himself from the bar and walked down the aisle that led not to matrimony but to the corridor at the rear of the stage. He paid little attention to the disrobing of the bride or the panting of her hundred grooms.

The canal remained dark and empty of the green and white barge named *Anne Carol*. Kline, leaning against the underside of the bridge felt cold and hungry. I'll get some jockeys whips, come back, give a once up and down the tow path then jack it in, he decided. He put his hand in his pocket, found enough coins to buy some fish and chips, then moved out from under the bridge.

Malleson prowled along the corridor backstage. He still couldn't fathom out how that Kline bastard had got clear the night before. How Kline had reached the fire escape from this side of the building, he just couldn't understand. Somebody must have seen him, for there was nowhere to hide, not on this corridor. All the doors had been locked; he'd tried most've them himself... most but not all. More or less for the sake of doing something the West Indian tried a few again; they were still locked, as they should be, right. You couldn't trust anybody. Then he tried another and it opened. Malleson blinked and saw the mirror, the lights and a wild west costume laid out for a later strip routine. He checked what the notice said on the door; it read 'Artistes - Women'. After thinking back to the happenings of the previous night he went inside, saw the window, pulled it open, noticed the steel bars outside, then turned back to the room and started to consider some possible solutions to the puzzle of Kline's disappearance from the Maverick club.

The bridal music now marched triumphantly towards its climax, with Dinah only a floral bouquet away from revealing the dark mystery that had sheltered within the pure white vestments. Wankers! Dinah thought contemptuously as she tossed the plastic nosegay aside, opened her legs and waited for the lights to blackout.

When the lights came back on Malleson returned jauntily to his drink at the bar.

'Anything?' the Irishman grunted.

'Maybe, but I'll need t'be sure...' Malleson said, finishing his beer. Maybe his future wasn't so bleak after all. 'Have another?' he asked his colleagues on the firm.

'Why not,' replied Dermot, wondering at the change in Malleson; from someone down and out and behind on points, he suddenly had the optimism of a man who had the odds on favourite in a sweepstakes draw.

The lower wooden panel of the door that lay between Jashir and arrest splintered under the impact of the kicks aimed from outside. A regulation police issue boot burst through and cleared enough space for an arm clothed in blue serge to appear and grope for the bolt on the door. As the bolt shot back, Jashir held his wife and children to him. He had always intended that should he be betrayed he would inform on his blackmailers. Now he knew that was an impossibility. As Kuldip had so thoughtfully pointed out, Mangit and his children would stay here, alone, unprotected and open to retaliation should he give information to the immigration authorities.

Two policemen stepped over the broken wood of the now open door.

'Jashir Singh Mahal?' one asked.

The Sikh nodded and detached himself from his wife and two young children. 'That is me.'

'Do you have a passport or an entry permit giving you a legal right to reside within the UK?'

Jashir shook his head.

The crushed newspaper that had held the fish and chips floated like a water lily on the black waters of the canal before it waterlogged and sank. Kline stuck his hands into his pockets and started to walk slowly back along the tow path towards the far bridge where he had hoped Anne Darracott would have moored her barge. Walking along the cinder path Kline was thinking of nothing in particular.

Had the *Anne Carol* appeared he wasn't exactly sure what he would have done. Perhaps attempted a little clumsy interrogation as if he were the Old Bill.

Kline snorted to himself. 'Where were you on the night of…' And 'We have reason to believe that you can assist us with our enquiries.' It wasn't funny, all that crap. Not when he had it to come. And it would now that he was down on their sheet with classic form. Yeh, fair game, someone to be pulled in on spec. Someone to be fitted up, disbelieved on principle, a prime suspect for any GBH.

His Regular Army service, all the work done after demob, all the money pooled with Dermot to set up the Maverick Club, all gone, all pissed up the wall. Bad enough news without this vendetta piled on top. Kline speculated about Rawlinson; he'd never met him, only exchanged stares briefly in court at the time of his trial, only received notice in prison that suitable revenge was to be exacted upon his release. In the darkness, a dozen paces from the arch of the bridge, he stopped and clenched his fists against the wave of anger that suddenly passed through him. He'd told his woman, Dinah, that he had to fight back or go under. Now, an hour later, he realised in full the truth of that statement. Maybe she was right about Khan being bent as a dog's hind leg but when the Asian said there was no alternative but to stand and smash Rawlinson he was right. It had to be attempted and the place to start was right here. He turned and looked back along the glinting watery ribbon of the canal.

Nothing disturbed its waters but he determined to wait until something did; silently he moved to his vantage point under the bridge and settled down to keep vigil.

Kline leant back against the brickwork, decided to smoke a cigarette and had one between his lips and ready to light when he heard the murmur of voices nearby.

'No.'

'Why not?'

'Cos.'

'But why?'

'I don't love you.'

'C'mon.'

'No.'

'Christ!'

'What?'

'You know what you are!'

'What am I?'

'You know.'

'I don't.'

'PT.'

'What's that?'

'Never mind.'

'What?'

'Prick teaser.'

'Who says that?'

'Everybody.'

'Well, I'm not...'

'Yes you are.'

'No, I'm not.'

'Come on then.'

'No.'

'Why?'

'I don't want a... you know.'

'No.'

'A baby.'

'Don't you... you know, use things?'

'No.'

'Why?'

' 'Cos I don't like... I like y'.'

'Yes. All right.'

'But not enough, y'know to...'

'I missed me last bus f'you.'

'That's not my...'

'Oh, f'get it!'

Kline watched the two shadows move onto the path at the other side of the bridge. He smiled to himself as he watched the dark figures merge into obscurity. Permissive society, was it? Same old scene he'd gone through when he was fifteen. Then he stopped the process of recall. Something was happening; yeh, he recognised the chug-a-chug before the lights of the long, low vessel appeared from around the far bend. He put the unlit cigarette back into its packet and waited for the motor barge *Anne Carol* to come and berth at her mooring.

The music of *The Good, the Bad and the Ugly* shrilled out as Malleson approached the door of Dinah Carmichael's dressing room. If it opened he could be in business; if it was locked, well, perhaps he'd still check her out, anyway. He turned the handle and opened the door. The boxer whistled a snatch of the theme that little Miss Dinahmite was peeling off to and strolled inside, pulled up a chair, picked up a hairbrush and began to push the bristles of nylon over his scalp and through his hair.

The trip away had been disappointing; the sale was of furniture as massive as it was ugly and of no use to Anne. On the long pull home, she'd felt the familiar symptoms of need but had allowed them to grow ever more insistent in the knowledge that on reaching home waters there would be splendid relief.

Anne Darracott shook the white powder from the pouch to the spoon and held it over the flare of the gas jet and began to cook it up. She felt itchy, irritable; a yawn started, she stifled it, made sure her hand didn't tilt the brown liquid. *Brown* liquid? She looked down in consternation; it looked... looked like... She put the spoon down and pulled the pouch again, saw the coarse grains she hadn't thought to notice before. She wet a finger, dabbed, and tasted the result. It was no longer 'H' for heroin but 'S' for sugar. She blinked. Rubbed her nose one way, then the other. Yawned, tried to think. Her supply... her supply... she had no supply! Who? She ran to the bed, felt underneath, thinking perhaps Rawlinson had put a dummy pouch under for a joke... yes, that's it, a gag... she felt right along the shelf as far as her searching fingertips could reach. Nothing. Other side...? That was where he'd put it... She scrambled across the bed and dropped down to grope along the remaining section of shelving. There was nothing to touch; perhaps it had fallen down. She was about to put her belly to the floor and crawl when a voice from the other side of the bed drawled, 'In a fix, sugar?'

Anne looked up, saw Kline smiling innocently at her distress. She knew it, knew it was him. She stood then threw herself in fury across the bed, scratching, kicking, clawing, gouging at his eyes... biting at his throat... The force and the unexpected speed of the assault took Kline aback. He caught the wrists of the thin arms and eventually contained the efforts to break his grip, dodging as best he could the kicking feet and pointed knees that tried to make mincemeat of his groin. When he felt there was nothing more to come, he threw her away onto the bed, where she lay panting, covered in perspiration, showing all the symptoms he had hoped for when substituting her drug supply.

'What you here for, Kline?' she said, bringing the words out jerkily.

'Your connections.'

Anne laughed. 'Go an' screw your little nut!'

Kline sat down on the circumference of a large leather cushion. When he spoke it was after a calm appraisal of the sweating, distraught woman lying opposite to him. 'You'll tell me... when you need to fix so bad you'll tell me... I've seen druggies like you in the nick... kicking, screaming, puking... they'd start like you, itching, snotty, sleepy, tired and yawny...'

Under the suggestion of his words Anne started to experience the beginnings of a huge involuntary yawn. Kline noticed her desperate effort at control.

'Yeh. Sometimes they'd get the yawns so bad they'd dislocate their stupid jaws...' Kline stretched his legs and continued to keep his voice at a conversational, matter of fact level. 'Course, I wouldn't want anything like that to happen... I don't want anythin' t'stop you having your heart to heart with me.'

Anne glared defiance at him. Sat up, folded her arms tight, looked down at him, secure and straight. Mr Straight Fucking Normality. She wouldn't give in. She would die first. She'd fake, lie, say anything to find out where he had hidden her stuff. Kline lit a cigarette. Inhaled blue smoke, blew grey smoke out. He glanced across at the thin blonde, white-faced and rigid with hate and determination.

'Take your time,' Kline said, dropping a spent match into a small bronze urn. 'Take all the time you can take...'

Anne looked away; the hate for him was burning her eyes. She wanted to yawn. She wanted to sneeze. She wanted to scratch herself all over. Her jaws ached with the effort of holding the yawn in... she fought it all the way but the bones forced themselves apart until she yawned and yawned to the limit of her jaw's extension. Kline made no comment but drew on his cigarette as Anne Darracott closed her mouth, rubbed her eyes, then began to yawn and yawn again.

Collecting up her gunbelt, stetson and the rest, Dinah heard the Shadettes hitting the opening bars of 'Satisfaction Guaranteed'. Heard the opening words of the lyric as she backed out into the corridor with an armful of attire.

'*Satisfaction guaranteed or take your love back,*' the voices sang behind her. '*So good... so good... so good... Let me put my arms around you, oh, baby, please...*' then the words trailed away into the beat of the music as she humped the gear towards her dressing room. '*So good... so good...*' she sang to herself as she opened the door. She went in to find Malleson smiling up at her with his best 'Who's a sexy boy' grin on his face.

'What's this?' said Dinah suspiciously. The white teeth showed a little more.

'You should lock your door. Anyone could walk in.'

Dinah smiled scornfully at his stupidity. 'Where would I carry a key?'

Malleson frowned. 'Hadn't thought've that.'

'You wouldn't.'

'So, with this door open, just anyone could walk in, right ?'

Dinah became wary. He seemed pretty dense, but you never knew. She stepped behind the clothes rack, slung her stuff over, reached for her cotton wrap. In the mirror Malleson saw one hanging breast in profile for a minute. He wished he could remember why this chick had split with him.

'Who's screwing you these days,' he asked casually.

'Not you.'

'You mean, not any more.'

'That was a screw we had?'

Malleson frowned. He was pretty good usually unless he'd been smashed or stoned or both. Yeh. That's why he couldn't remember the details. Anyhow, get back to the Sherlock stuff.

'I just wondered y'know...'

Dinah came out from behind the clothes rack. 'None've your business.'

Malleson got to his feet, went across and put on his deepest, most sincere act. 'I just hate t'see a good field lyin' fallow...' He touched her arm, gave it slight squeeze. 'Why don't we try for it one more time?'

'So you can end up runnin' me like your other chicks?'

'No, baby, no...' The hand on her arm became a soothing and, he hoped, a welcome caress. 'Let's back t'your place... right now... let's go back, mm?'

'I've another spot t'do.'

'Later then. Afterwards.'

Dinah looked through his charm and removed his hand from her breast. 'No. No way. None!'

Malleson stood away, surprised by her vehemence. Why should she react like that, come at him that way. Unless she was keeping someone at home. Keeping someone all to her greedy little self. He'd try again. just to be sure. 'Ah...' Malleson said, closing in and crowding her into a corner. 'Ah, y'don't mean that at all.'

Dinah looked up at him coldly. 'I'd sooner hustle a leper colony than go with you.'

Malleson's eyes flared with anger. His hands flexed but she stared him out. Malleson wanted to spill a little of what he suspected but that good time would come if he kept cool.

He clenched his fists, swallowed his anger and stalked out slamming the door as he went.

Left alone Dinah looked in the mirror. She must be getting old; two years previously she'd really rated that guy. Until she'd overheard him using her telephone and referring to her as 'meat for the street'. Forget it. Forget him. Dinah sat down, pulled a tissue from a box, rubbed make up remover onto the gold star painted across her cheek, then wiped it away. She wished she had a cigarette. That Kline, he'd have some. She sighed, wishing the long evening away, wishing it was time to climb the stairs that led to home.

*

The cigarette would not meet up with the flame of the lighter. It wavered around, was scorched a half inch length, lit with a small eruption of burning tobacco. Kline watched the woman suck in the smoke as if the only need her body had was for nicotine. She dragged on the cigarette again before wrapping her arms tight around her body as if laced into an invisible strait jacket. She began to rock to and fro, to and fro. Kline said nothing to break the silence that he thought must have already lasted an hour. He crossed and uncrossed his legs. Eased his position on the leather cushion. Waited.

Rawlinson sat at his desk with his chair pivoted around so he could brood over the city of Birmingham. He watched the lights, smoked his cigar, occasionally drank from the tumbler that stood beside the half full bottle of Dimple whisky. The city bored him. The office bored him. The silence and inaction bored him. He turned the chair and stared at the silent telephone and the photograph of his family that stood beside it on his desk. He drained the scotch, poured another, drew on his cigar and waited.

'You.'

Kline, startled by the word, looked across to the bed.

'What?'

'Nothing,' Anne said picking the skin on her face as if to remove insects. Her nose began to pour with hot, watery mucus; she wiped it away with the back of her hand in an attempt to stem the flow long enough to find another clean handkerchief from the cabinet at the side of the bed.

'Talk...' Kline said, quietly and firmly. 'I want you to talk.'

Anne stood, shivered and shuddered as a wave of inner convulsion passed through her. 'You... you... you sneaked in... in here...' She unwrapped an arm, waved it jerkily around. 'Substituted...'

'Right...'

'Dump it, did you... overboard... I expect... in the water so it'd be well ruined?'

Kline fought down the urge to pity the sweating, shivering, suffering woman before him. 'No, your stuff's still around. Should we play I Spy? Now let's see...' He moved his head and began to focus in turn on various hiding places.

Anne began to follow his shifting line of sight then realised what she was doing.

'Ah, fuck you... fella. Fuck you!' she said and slumped back upon her bed.

Rawlinson stood up from his desk, swaying a little. The bleedin' phone wasn't going to ring. So much for caution, so much for keeping out of it. Result was... nothing. No news... no Kline. Maybe it was best. Maybe Kline'd run out've town. If so, well, he had contacts in other towns. Sooner or later the bastard would surface and be sighted. So, for the meantime, life would go on its same old way. Perhaps he should expand, get into some new area. Trouble was his clubs were making a legitimate profit. The bleedin' transport firm was even breaking even. Huh. He picked his glass up and poured the whisky down his throat. It burned all the way down into the gut that insisted he get out there, find the enemy, maim and kill. Rawlinson reached for the Dimpled bottle, found it empty, threw it across the room; it bounced on the cushion of deep carpet pile and rolled silently under the leather couch. Rawlinson growled in frustration and told himself to get that bottle, take it to the window and hurl it twenty floors down towards the street. With a little luck it might splinter the skull of John Bleedin' Kline. Halfway across the office the hooch finally reached him. He staggered, swayed. Made an effort of will and managed to reach the couch. Lying face down, feeling the room recede, Rawlinson felt like a dead man. He mumbled about power, about sense and caution and what did they matter... about sex. No need great enough to interest him, he thought, 'cept one. The need to kill and, by that act, renew oneself... The thoughts muddled and reformed and repeated until he let them all go and succumbed to sleep.

Kline stood and looked down at Anne Darracott, her fair hair now dark and sodden with perspiration.

'I know how you drop the drugs but how d'you bring them in?'

The woman on the bed stopped the shaking of her head and looked up at him. She opened her mouth but it was only to sustain another jaw-wrenching yawn.

'Rawlinson finances the operation, you distribute. Who supplies the merchandise... and from where?'

The head shaking started again.

'Who?' asked Kline, doggedly. 'Who supplies the stuff?'

*   *   *

Anne lay on the bed. She felt her bowels start to open and she clenched her sphincter muscle hard and harder. Her belly felt full, with a coil of snakes writhing, twisting, bursting in their anxiety to be free from her. They seemed to be sliding inch by inch through the tube of her large intestine... writhing and inching slowly and inexorably. She heard someone screaming and screaming. Anne shivered, rubbed skin bumped up and cold as a frozen turkey. That someone screamed again as the snakes slid one by one towards her rectum. She summoned all her strength to resist and only made the leading serpent recoil an inch. Someone came to hold and comfort her. She opened the slits in her face that contained the stones of her eyes.

'Here,' said Kline and pushed a cigarette into her mouth to stop her screaming.

Anne coughed out smoke and spittle. 'Cold... cold!' she said.

Kline removed his jacket and placed it around her. 'Your boss, Rawlinson?'

The reddened eyes peered through water at him.

'Rawlinson...' Kline repeated, hugging her to him like a sick child.

'Him?' she said, yawning sleepily.

Kline shook her. 'Him and you and just who else. Who?'

Anne felt her bowels start to void. 'Ahh!' she said. 'Give me... give me my stuff, please.'

'Tell. Tell me and I'll go away,' Kline urged.

'Two trips...'

'Yes?'

'On the Blackbird run, that's what they call it.' The words came tumbling out in a stream she could no longer contain. 'This Dutchman...'

'Dutchman?'

'Rawlinson uses him... uses him... from Rotterdam.'

'What's his name?'

'I don't know... I don't know... please. I don't know!' She lied desperately, clutching the warmth of the man and shivering.

Kline said gently, 'Just one name. The Dutchman? What is the name of the Dutchman?'

The face cradled in his arms gazed up at him, its expression made bitter by the knowledge that the information it had to give to find immediate relief might jeopardise the supply from the primary source. The lips, white from compression, slacked and parted to form a name.

'What?' asked Kline, bending down to her.

'Van der Staay...' she breathed, then, seeing his frown of incomprehension, she began a chant towards a crescendo. 'Van der Staay... Van der Staay... *Van der bloody Staay*!'

It was something, thought Kline. Anne began to descend into the brief respite of the yen for sleep. Kline lowered her head down gently, and replaced his jacket by folding both sides of the bedcover overhang across her twitching body.

As he turned to leave a voice came plaintively after him.

'Where did you put my stuff... where?' it pleaded.

Kline made his way through the cabin towards the kitchen, picked up the white plastic bin into which he had poured the heroin and placed it inside the cabin where she could see it, then withdrew without a word.

Anne Darracott hauled her body upwards and struggled from the bed to the floor, then began the long crawl towards the rubbish container.

In the dark at the foot of the stairs, Kline listened to the silence and moved from one foot to the other. No suspicious sound carried to him. No light showed beneath the door of the flat above. Good. Kline went up the stairs, listened outside the door. Nothing. He inserted the key into the Yale lock; he could have opened it with a strip of celluloid but a key was more fitting. Ha-hah, Kline acknowledged to himself as he groped around in the darkness inside. He found a switch, pressed it down and the bathroom light came on. There was the bog, black plastic on a white pedestal. He lifted the seat, unzipped a banana and began to urinate. He thought back to the woman on the barge and the ordeal he had forced her through. No fun. Why, he wondered, had she got on the junk. It didn't just happen; you had to work to build a habit. Anyway, by this time she'd have scraped enough heroin from the garbage to ease the pain of withdrawal. By this time she was probably on the blower to her boss and they'd know he was still in town and fighting back. Kline gave himself a shake and wondered when Dinah would be home. Van der Staay, he repeated to himself as he pulled the fly zip upwards, Van der Staay. Rotterdam... Rotterdam... the cistern gurgled after he had flushed its contents away. After rinsing and drying off his hands he left the bathroom and noticed in its light that he had left the front door ajar. He went and closed it, put the snip on and turned towards the living room without noticing the small reflection of the dim light from the white beret of the man standing in the far corner.

Kline entered the living room and was about to locate means of bringing light to darkness when he felt an object block and restrain the movement of his arm. Kline looked down and could just discern in the semi-darkness the blunt head of a pickaxe handle. At the other end, seated in the shadow of an armchair was a dark face whose only visible feature was the smile of its grinning teeth. Kline knew who it was. He swept the handle away and ran towards the front door only to cannon into Bonny Bryden. In the darkness, the men skirmished, Kline throwing a right that missed and Bryden jabbing with a left that connected and sent his adversary back towards the living room door and into the path of Atty Hunniford, who was charging towards him from the direction of the bedroom. Wishing to avoid head on collision the white evaded the black by a last side step that took him alongside the armchair that was now empty. But before Kline could ask himself where the former occupant had gone, the need for questions was ended by a clash of heads. One belonging to Kline and the other to the pickaxe handle wielded by the West Indian.

To Malleson the impact of the smash into Kline's skull was similar to that which had bounced from the wall by the canal. It jarred and tingled but the recipient this time did not remain unmoving. Malleson watched with enjoyment as Kline went into a drunken sideways shuffle. Malleson set himself for another hook shot. Then lowered the hickory shaft as the stricken man stumbled into the back of the chair, tried to hold onto its support, missed and started to fall.

'Nine!' said Bryden, watching their opponent's knees hit the canvas.

'Ten!' said Hunniford as the kneeling figure pitched forward to assume the horizontal.

'Out!' said Malleson and aimed a kick of triumph at the ribs of the unconscious John Kline.

Chapter Eleven

The light hurt his eyes; the effort to sit up on the camp bed caused the clapper in his head to increase its toll. Kind hands helped him to rise from the bed. He swayed, still unsteady from the effects of the blow that had caused the flow of blood from the wound on the side of his head. Rawlinson looked at him, all mock sympathy.

'There now, that's better, innit?' he said soothingly, stepping back to look at the man swaying before him. 'I'm the same when I first wake up... Feel better?'

'I'm all right,' Kline lied, becoming aware of a pain in his ribs to go with the one in his head. He went to sit down again. Rawlinson caught him by the narrow lapels of his suit jacket and held him upright. Kline blinked into the cold grey eyes then stared around at the cellar with its other camp beds, its dripping tap and bucket, wine rack and, standing on either side of the man he recognised as Rawlinson, two sharply suited gentlemen who were unknown to him. Kline tried to sit down again.

Rawlinson spoke in his soft, calm voice. 'No, stand up. Yow've got company... come a long t'see yow... know my brothers, do yow? Billy...'

Billy stepped forward to hold out a hand. Confused by the politeness of it all, Kline foolishly went to grip the hand, which turned into a fist that struck him hard between nose and lip. Shaking his head, he fell back against Rawlinson, who caught hold and turned him to face another introduction.

'Tommy...'

Tommy showed his wolf-like teeth. 'Pleased t'meetchow!' He feinted to hold out a hand but brought his knee up into Kline's groin instead. Kline yelled under the shock of the pain. He tried to double up but Rawlinson grabbed the matted hair and pulled the pale-blooded face up. He wanted to witness the anguish in the eyes of his prisoner.

Rawlinson's control suddenly snapped. The hatred became naked, the manner primal and savage. 'We usta have a fourth brother but you took care've that, didn'tcha...?' He threw Kline against the wine rack and launched himself into a two-fisted assault on his prisoner that only abated when his strength ebbed.

When the frenzy passed and the blows ceased, Kline crumpled to the dirt of the cellar floor. Rawlinson, exhausted by the orgasm of rage and hatred, watched an empty wine bottle roll from the top of the rack and smash beside the unmoving head of John Kline. Tommy went and examined the body. His square face expressing disappointment like a child with an overcompressed kitten.

'Ey, Oz... 'e's out cold.'

'Chuck some water over 'im.' Billy said.

'Let me,' said Tommy eagerly, 'I've always wanted t'do that.'

Rawlinson realised he had Kline's blood on the sleeve of his soft brown-leather jacket. Feeling in a pocket he found his silk handkerchief and wiped it away. While his brothers waited impatiently for the bucket to fill, Rawlinson knelt down unobserved over the unconscious Kline and dabbed his forefinger into the run of blood from the smashed mouth. He tasted the warm thick salt of it and sucked it down as if to make it his own.

The bell in Rawlinson's flat buzzed once.

Anne Darracott, dressed in a long white towelling robe came from the bathroom, checked the spy hole and saw in its distorted circle the brown face she had been wanting to see. When she opened the door, Malleson nodded to her. Anne looked beyond him at two more blacks. 'The wrecking crew,' she said, remembering a glimpse of their beaten up faces.

'Yeh,' one said and the other grinned sheepishly.

'Come in...' she said, standing back from the door and allowing Malleson to enter.

'Won't be long,' he called to his henchmen and entered cockily.

Anne closed the door. He had better deliver. Already she could feel the re-emergence of the panic from last night's trip into chaos. 'Well?'

Malleson grinned, sat down before a low glass and chrome coffee table and produced two small packets, which he examined carefully. Anne found herself down opposite to him, ready and eager to open presents. She took one with trembling fingers.

'Hey, not that one, that's virgin pure… this one… Santa sent this one for you.'

'Chinese?' she said suspiciously.

'No…'

She tore open the packet, checked over the heap of 10mg tablets. Relaxed, smiled at him. 'You did all right.'

'It'll cost you you… er… him. It's, you know, the best.'

'Yes,' said Anne.

'You got equipment?' He took from his black and white -check sports jacket a leather cigar case that opened to reveal a collection of hypes and needles. 'You want…?' he started, indicating the contents.

'No. I brought my artillery along.'

'fine.' Malleson stood. This was him now − equal terms with royalty. Boss's chick, boss's flat. He looked around at the cool white decor and at the expensive tubular chrome supports for the black leather chairs and the circular glass table. This was him. He was on the up.

What had Rawlinson said to him on delivering Kline to that cellar… 'Y'in like Flynn.'

He didn't know what that meant exactly but it could not be bad. He'd already been given other jobs. This dope for blondie. And the other. The other job that had to be done.

He had to push on.

'Gotta go.'

'fine. I'll tell Mr Rawlinson you did a good job. That you delivered on time.'

'Thanks.'

Anne watched him walk purposefully towards the door. When it closed behind the West Indian she hurried across and slid the bolt in and linked the chain. She felt safe. For the first time since the abyss of last night there was safety. She smiled to herself and moved back to the low table where she squatted down and played pretty patterns with the white tablets, which were so clean and free of dirty things like tea-leaves, coffee grounds and nasty potato peelings.

Kline regained consciousness when the first bucket of water washed over him, but for some reason there had to be a second.

'There,' said Tommy when he had soaked Kline with as much water as had his brother Billy.

' 'Ow we gonna kill 'im?' Billy asked his elder brother.

Rawlinson rubbed his bruised knuckles and looked down at the battered face of John Kline. 'When l say. I want him to talk first. I want to know why yow...' he kicked the body of the man at his feet, ' 'Ave been askin' questions've my secretary.'

Billy smiled. 'Puttin' th'fix on 'er, sow t'speak.'

Kline wiped the ooze of blood from between his swollen lips and shook his head as an answer.

Billy looked enquiringly at Rawlinson.

'My turn?' he asked politely.

'Ar.'

Billy lifted Kline to his feet, propped him against the wine rack, held him with one hand and drew back the other.

Malleson put the plug of the hair dryer into the light socket above the bed, pulled down a switch and felt a wave of hot air blow onto the palm of his hand. Satisfied, he jumped down from the bed onto the floor. Hunniford and Bryden had completed their task and Dinah Carmichael sat against the foot of her bed, arms spread along the rail and bound by knotted nylon. 'Take this off me, please. It hurts,' she said, wide eyed, frightened, beginning to cry...

Malleson ignored the tears. He knew women – they could turn the tap on and off. He played with the flex of the hairdryer hanging from the socket on the ceiling. Dinah watched its sway, terrified. Malleson looked down at her in her thin purple wrap. She's been screwing that Kline bastard, he thought, here. Here, right here on this bed. Dinah watched him scowl in sudden anger and yank the leads from her hairdryer then tease the naked copper wires into two loops around his fingers. He kept looking at her as if in anticipation... of what? Sex? What else could they possibly want? She craned her neck and looked across at the alarm opposite to her on the bedside table. The shop downstairs would be closed for lunch. The bastards had picked their time all right.

'Kline...' Malleson spoke quietly.

'I'm not involved,' Dinah repeated yet again.

'Kline stayed here?'

'Know that, don't you?'

Malleson put one leg on either side of her body and looked down at the helpless frightened girl below him.

'My boss wants t'know what he was at... why he'd want t'ask certain questions about certain things...'

'Y'talkin' double... uh!' She yelled in shock as the man dropped down onto her thighs, reached for the front of her gown and ripped it from her with one savage movement. Malleson motioned Bryden to the light switch then placed a wire loop of each lead from the flex around her blue-black nipples. Dinah strained in fright and fear but the knots in the nylon only became tighter and the weight of the man on her made movement impossible. She turned her head and watched Bryden's hand stray towards the switch that would send electricity charging through her body. She opened her mouth, began to pant as if she would never take in enough breath to carry the sound that would express the depth of her fear.

Malleson looked at the heaving heavy breasts with their nipples coiled around by the copper wire. 'One more time... why?'

Dinah stopped gasping for breath. 'Nothing. I know nothing! Only what I've already said... they came here.'

Malleson frowned. 'They?'

Dinah shook her head in answer then stared at Bryden's hand playing nonchalantly with the switch. Malleson grabbed her face, twisted it back to him. 'Who was with Kline... who came to see him here?' he demanded.

Dinah did not know what to do, if the name of the Asian mattered. Malleson suddenly lost patience. He moved his haunches away from her, and the brown hand by the door went to flick the current on. Dinah screamed and her legs kicked up and down like a shot rabbit in anticipation of the pain. 'Pakistani,' she said, 'a Paki!'

'Name?'

'Khan... Khan!'

'Tall? The mush who runs with Kuldip?'

Dinah nodded and began to sob with relief as Bryden touched his beret to her mockingly and moved away from the light switch by the door.

Malleson regarded her and considered his course of action. 'I'll see to her. Wait for me outside.'

Malleson thought it all through. She was involved. She knew him, she knew Kline and Khan. Who knows what they'd talked about. She'd know names and if Kline's body was ever found they would have this woman's finger pointing at them all. A constant danger. A danger that could be eliminated. Eliminated easily enough. He reached into the inside pocket of his new sports jacket and took out the cigar case and opened it.

Dinah watched him. He's going to burn me, she thought, before he showed her the selected needle and its charge of pure heroin. When he inserted the needle into her vein she began to scream so loudly that he had to pause and stuff a hand towel into her mouth; after that it was easier and soon the transfer of the virgin powder into her bloodstream was complete. This task completed, Malleson busied himself with the housework of brushing down any surfaces that could carry finger prints. When he returned to the bed the figure tied to its foot was inanimate, which made things a great deal easier. He stripped the trim brown body naked and placed it across the bed. Then carried on with the gathering together of all the items that could bear witness to their visit. Everything, that is, except the syringe and the packet of pure stuff, which he left on the bedside cabinet. He wiped the syringe and pressed it into her hand hard enough to leave prints. Then there was nothing else to do, so he picked up the towel, the knotted tights, the hairdryer, the shredded purple robe and bunched them all together into a bundle that disturbed his well cut coat as he closed the front door of the now peaceful flat and hurried away down the stairs, past the dry cleaning shop with its sign saying 'Closed', across the pavement and into the waiting car.

'OK ?' asked Hunniford from behind the wheel.

Malleson's mouth and throat were dry and full of dust. He didn't trust himself to reply, so he nodded and stared out of the window at the Saturday lunchtime passing scene.

*   *   *

The extension on the wall of Rafiq's kitchen went 'Ting!' as whoever was using the telephone in the main reception room took up the receiver. Kuldip looked up from pouring cream over his third piece of chocolate gateaux and nodded at the telephone above his head.

'Lot-of phone calls... lot going on, I tell you.'

Khan took a sip of tea. 'That man the spades brought in... ?' he asked casually.

'Kline.'

'What will happen to him?'

Kuldip laughed then swallowed a forkful of cake while he considered.

Might as well ask the leading hound what would happen to the fox, Khan thought. 'Those Rawlinsons.'

Kuldip said, sitting back, replete, 'I expect they will send Kline on a short sea voyage.' He laughed again.

'I do not understand...' Khan started but was interrupted by the young Asian servant retreating into the kitchen before three burly West Indians, one of whom carried a pickaxe handle.

'They...' the servant began in Urdu.

'It's all right,' Kuldip replied in the same language.

The servant bowed, took away cups and plates from the table and carried them to the sink.

'Where's the Rawlinsons?' Malleson asked Kuldip abruptly.

'Cellar... why?'

'Show me...'

Kuldip bristled. 'I am not your servant.'

'Show me!' Then Malleson looked at Khan, 'Bring your mate... what's your name again?'

'Khan.'

'Yeh.' Malleson tapped the end of the pickaxe handle against the palm of his left hand. Bonny Bryden sauntered to a position behind Khan's chair.

Kuldip put a hand inside to touch his knife for comfort but the blacks for some reason only seemed interested in his helper, Khan.

'You goin' t'take me to the Rawlinsons, Kuldip?'

'All right.'

The West Indian turned back to Zaheer Mohammed Khan. 'You come along as well. I'm sure your mate Kline will want t'see you one more time...'

'Move!' shouted Bryden and hauled Khan to his feet and pushed him towards the door that led into the garage area and towards the entrance down into the cellars.

The Rawlinson brothers were at the foot of the steps conferring as to the merits of execution by firing squad. On the bed nearest the dripping tap, Kline tried to hold his resolve together through a bombardment of pain. Rawlinson heard the tramp of marching feet coming along the passage towards them. The party came into view, led by his boy Malleson.

'What?' asked Rawlinson.

Khan was produced and shoved roughly down the steps towards the brothers Rawlinson.

In the background Kline sat up, saw Khan and realised his only hope of rescue had gone.

Malleson nudged Khan with the end of his club. 'He's the one who helped our boy.'

Rawlinson looked the wog over, tried to recall his name.

'You. Enterprise and initiative 'imself.'

Khan looked bewildered. 'Please, what is happening?' he asked.

Malleson took a step forward, addressing Rawlinson. 'The girl, Dinah, spilled. Him and Kline... like that.' He tucked his index finger beneath the one in the middle, held them up to Rawlinson, who nodded.

'Where's the girl?'

'fixed.'

'Dead?'

'Heroin's a tricky thing,' said Malleson with a tiny smirk that disappeared as Kline found the strength to catapult himself from the bed. The intensity of rage and shock took him into the group; he aimed one blow at the brown face, got a grip on Malleson's throat... but someone held him and the West Indian broke the grip by bringing the axe handle up with the force of two hands. Kline went on fighting, kicking, clawing until they pulled him down. Malleson, rubbing his throat, raised the hickory shaft to the ceiling and was only prevented from crashing it down on Kline by Rawlinson's intervention.

'Enough. Not yet. Yow mustn't damage our property...'

He watched as his brothers dragged Kline to the far end of the cellar.

'Now,' he continued, looking around the cellar full of faces. 'You...' he indicated Khan, 'what yow bin up to... why 'elp this Kline bloke?'

'Please, I just felt sorry for him, sir.'

Rawlinson laughed incredulously. 'Feel sorry f'y'bleedin' self!' His gaze shifted to Kuldip. 'You...' What was his name? 'Lipstick, what d'y know about 'im?' He indicated Khan with a jerk of his greying head.

Kuldip shrugged, 'Not much... I met him in a bar... he seemed willing... OK... y'know.'

'No,' replied Rawlinson, staring at Khan and beginning to feel a vague disquiet. 'I don't know. He been searched?'

'Not yet,' Malleson said.

'Do it.'

As the man carrying the pickhandle started to come towards him, Khan reached for the gun inside his holster. He pulled it out, straightened his arm, was about to squeeze the trigger to fire a warning shot when Malleson hit the outstretched arm with his club. The gun went from hand to ground and exploded on impact, sending a bullet into the cobwebs of the ceiling. When the smoke cleared only Rawlinson remained in his exact former position. 'Tommy...' He motioned at his crouching brother to join him in an examination of the gun. Khan, nursing his arm, watched.

'.38 Webley... type of gun the law issue,' Tommy announced.

'Y'what?' said Rawlinson sharply, looking at his brother, then at Kline; finally his hard eyes rested on Khan. 'I don't like the smell of this curry,' he said quietly.

Chapter Twelve

As soon as it became light on the Sunday morning the garage area of the house in Solihull became alive with activity. Kuldip backed the grey Rawco transit box van towards the Rolls Royce Corniche, put the handbrake on and jumped down and ran to open the rear doors to be ready for the passengers. Kline and Khan had been separated through the night and now looked at each other as they were brought out by Malleson and two of the Rawlinson brothers. Khan smiled encouragingly at Kline, who dulled by pain and grief could only nod in reply.

'C'mon, c'mon!' said Billy pointing at the van and pushing the prisoners towards its interior.

'Right, any more f'the Skylark!' exclaimed Rawlinson, arriving from the kitchen and surveying the scene as Kline and Khan were bundled inside the box of the van.

Rafiq trundled out after his energetic partner. 'Rawlinson!' he called, 'suppose the Dutchman will not agree to dump their bodies at sea?'

Rawlinson smiled. 'I'll use a very persuasive word – money.'

Rafiq drew on his pipe worriedly. His partner nudged him. 'Cheer up, Rafiq, worse things 'appen at sea...' then strode down to his brothers at the rear of the van.

'Right, 'op in!' he ordered. They looked at him in consternation.

'I'm not ridin' next to no wog!' Tommy said.

'No,' Billy backed him up.

Rawlinson put a hand on each of their shoulders, pressured them towards the inside of the van, where the prisoners sat opposite to each other. 'Shut it!' he said.

Tommy shook off Rawlinson's hand. 'Why can't we take some

soldiers?' he complained.

'Why don't we phone the police?' was the sarcastic reply.

Tommy remembered what they were going to do. 'Oh, yeh. Yeh.' He suddenly glared at Kuldip. ' 'Op it... goo on!'

Kuldip shrugged and went to join Rafiq at the kitchen door. Rawlinson noticed Malleson about to leave. 'Not yow!' he called, then said, as an aside to his brothers, 'C'n trust 'im now.' Malleson approached. 'Yow 'c'n drive th'Blackbird van...' He turned to Bill. 'Yow c'n chauffeur the Rolls... and yow, Tommy, yow c'n get in' th'bleedin' box!'

The group dispersed, leaving a disgruntled Tommy Rawlinson to draw his gun and point it warningly at Khan. 'Yow move up well away from me,' he said threateningly as he climbed up into the van. The rear doors closed behind him. The engine started up.

Kuldip opened the garage doors and watched as they drove out and away with the Rolls following silently behind. Kuldip pulled the garage doors down with his usual force and went to catch up with Rafiq, who had gone back into the kitchen.

As Kuldip entered, Rafiq turned and opened his mouth to speak but paused when the telephone on the wall went 'Ting!' Kuldip frowned as Rafiq pointed at the telephone and mouthed the question, 'Who?'

Kuldip spread his hands palm up and carefully led the way from the kitchen along the passageway towards the reception room door. He opened it carefully and quietly, not wishing to disturb the user of the telephone. He and Rafiq heard the words in English: '...That's all I have... I...'

Kuldip flung the door fully open and glowered across at the young servant, who was supposed to speak only Urdu.

'Picked up English all of a sudden, have you?' said Kuldip, drawing his knife.

Outside the container base the van pulled in and the Rolls came and parked alongside. Rawlinson, carrying a walkie-talkie set, left the Rolls and came to speak to Malleson. 'Change over. Yow stop out 'ere and if y'see owt suspicious toot th' 'orn.' Malleson nodded, climbed down to allow Billy Rawlinson to take the wheel. Rawlinson climbed in next to him and the van drove towards the container base. Left alone with the Rolls-Royce Corniche, Malleson opened the door, slid behind the wheel, looked at the gadgets, pressed a button, watched with delight the windows slide up and down as he settled back, a watchdog in a luxurious kennel.

The man on the gate yawned and acknowledged the arrival of the Rawco van and released the pole barrier to clear the entrance to the square mile of container base enclosed within barbed wire fencing. The grey box transit van left the checkpoint behind and travelled past line after line of containers, past the giant legs of the Carricon crane and through the deserted yard towards the large covered warehouse that Rawlinson had chosen as the site for the execution of Kline and Khan.

The long blue container lorry nosed away from the motorport and re-joined the early Sunday morning motorway traffic. The driver knew the route well and as he powered along he hardly bothered to notice the signs that directed him towards the city of Birmingham.

Kline and Khan sat dejectedly on the rear edge of the open van. The long warehouse with its stacks of crates and boxes was as silent as any grave. The daylight as grey as the paint of the transit van filtered in from an open loading bay that looked down onto a section of the yard below. Khan wondered how long it would be. Kline went on blaming himself for Dinah's death.

Rawlinson extended the aerial of the walkie-talkie. 'Sinbad... Sinbad... Sinbad!' he called into the mouthpiece, then held the set to his ear. Nothing, only crackle.

He tried again with the same result. Everyone looked towards him. Billy took the safety catch off his automatic, turned to the prisoners.

'Not yet...' Rawlinson said. 'We'll wait until Van der Staay comes through – just in case...'

Rafiq hurried into his kitchen, out of breath and panting from the exertion of tidying up the cellar. The tigerskin rug on which that servant fellow had expired would be ashes now, the ledgers were safe elsewhere and arrangements for the movement of currency through the black market to India would need to be carefully handled should it become necessary. He heard footsteps outside. It wasn't staff; he'd given them a day's holiday.

'Who... ?' he quavered.

Rafiq heard a squeal of laughter.

'Kuldip?'

'Who'd you think it was – the devil or that servant fellow come back to haunt you?'

Rafiq's heart slowed a little. 'Where have you put him?'

'In the boot of that Khan's car. I dump it, abandon it, don't worry.'

'But...' Rafiq started.

'They find it, sure, sooner or later, but who the car belong to?' Kuldip answered himself, 'To Khan... Police not going to find him to interview, are they?'

Rafiq supposed not.

'Sinbad... Sinbad... Sinbad!'

'P'raps it don't work, ey, Oz?' said Tommy.

'It's the Dutchman. He's just late in,' said Rawlinson, leaving the channel open and looking towards Kline and Khan. Behind the van a double packing case crashed onto its side. Rawlinson turned, gun in hand towards the noise.

'S' only me...' said Billy, pushing the whitewood double coffin towards the condemned men seated on the edge of the van.

Rawlinson checked the automatic. There was no need to really; he used a good armourer. But it passed the time.

'Blackbird... Blackbird... Blackbird!' a distorted voice said from the walkie-talkie set.

Rawlinson pounced on it, replied, ' 'Ello, Sinbad, 'ow'd yow like to dump some special cargo overboard on y'way back to Rotterdam? Over.'

'How special, please, Blackbird?' said the disembodied voice.

Rawlinson smiled. 'Nuff t'rate a special bonus, Sinbad... over.'

'That is good enough for me. I will come on in, yes? Over.'

'Soon as you like, Sinbad. While everyone's at Sunday School... out.'

He pushed the aerial down into its socket.

Khan watched it disappear like their chances of escape. A gun barrel prodded him from one side and beside him Kline stood to face the guns of the Rawlinsons. For a split-second Khan's spirits rose at a sudden noise but it was only the sound of a car horn in the distance. He made his legs straighten and he stood up beside Kline. The three Rawlinsons formed a line and began to level their guns. Kline stared at his death.

Khan saw the car a moment before its squeal of brakes caused the Rawlinsons to scatter. White, screaming to a stop in the section of yard visible through the loading bay, 'POLICE' written along its side. Khan pushed Kline to the side and dived for the yard below as Billy loosed a shot at him. Kline, sent staggering out of the line of fire, saw a chance at safety and took it, running through the lines of crates and boxes of the warehouse.

Rawlinson saw his direction and followed, leaving Tommy to run for the far door that led towards the exit gate, pursued by police and Special Branch officers who had entered from the opposite end.

Billy vaulted from the loading bay and ran for a gap between two containers. He was engulfed by officers who had left the way clear in the hope that he would accept the invitation. Billy tried to clear a pathway but there were too many hands that held and forced his arms back against the steel of a container standing on the wheels of its trailer. The gun fell to the concrete of the yard. As Billy was marched away a brown hand appeared from beneath the trailer and grasped the gun. Khan scrambled out from his hiding place and went to lend what help he could in the round-up taking place.

Under the shelter of the Carticon crane Tommy Rawlinson, gun in hand, watched the police muster in two groups on either side of him. Tommy fired one way, then the other but soon they started creeping nearer. He crouched behind one of the four large legs of the crane and wondered how he could get clear through the gate, into the Rolls and away. Then he heard a rumble and saw the blue container lorry, driven by the Dutchman, enter the gate and rumble at speed towards him. It was a chance – if he could get in front of the lorry the driver would jam the brakes on, block the law long enough to allow him across and over the wire fence. Just a question of timing, he encouraged himself as the huge wheels propelled the lorry towards him. Wait... wait... wait... and... *now!*

Van der Staay saw the white cars and the running police and knew that this was no place to be. He decided to accelerate, hoping to get clear in the confusion. He put his foot down and headed for the other exit gate just before a fair-haired man ran in front of his cab. The Dutchman felt a bump of impact and braked hard until he stopped. He ran back to the group now formed about the man. The English policemen stood aside. He thought at first the blonde-haired man on the ground was merely unconscious until he saw the blood from the crushed skull.

The corner of the yard that lay diagonally opposite to the gate seemed deserted as Rawlinson, gun in hand, hunted along the lines of containers. Dropping down to his knees he scanned beneath. There, on the far side, between wheels was a pair of legs in blue trousers. Just standing still and waiting for the police to solve his problems. Rawlinson smiled tightly and began to open up an angle of fire, moving across from one row of trailers to another. He knew he should be thinking of his own escape but he couldn't let this chance go.

He saw Kline but not before Kline saw him. Rawlinson fired. He heard the shot go *spang!* against the metal but his target had vanished before he could fire again. He dropped down. Nothing. He must be above. Christ! Rawlinson swore as he ran towards the group of containers that must be sheltering his quarry. Arriving he clipped the pistol into its shoulder holster, began to climb up the small ladder that led to the top of the containers on which Kline was at that moment leaping from one to the next, one to the… But there wasn't a next, only space. He flattened down to minimise the target, crawled to the edge and dropped over to hang by the strength of his arms as Rawlinson reached the top of the ladder and surveyed along the line of containers. No Kline. Which didn't mean he wasn't up there.

Rawlinson was about to haul his weight up when below a Rolls Royce Corniche swerved around the corner with a squeal of brakes then hurtled towards the container on which he was perched. The Rolls pulled up, bouncing on its springs. The front passenger door swung open; Rawlinson jumped to the ground and dived inside. Malleson hit the accelerator.

Approaching the corner at the end of the line of containers, a white police car suddenly swerved towards them. Slamming back into reverse, sending the Corniche back the way it had just travelled, Malleson cursed. A police Range Rover was speeding towards them from behind.

'Stop the car!' Rawlinson yelled. The West Indian jammed on the brakes; all sorts of green warning lights appeared on the dashboard but he did not pause to read them but joined Rawlinson, who had burst from the Corniche and was inviting the driver of the police car to hand over his vehicle under the threat of a gun. 'Get in!' his boss urged and

Malleson pulled the cop out, got behind the wheel and took off with Rawlinson by his side. Within yards of reaching the white Triumph 2000 Police car, John Kline could do nothing except watch it disappear around the far corner of the warehouse. He ran a little way then stopped. Pointless, he thought.

The white police Range Rover cruised up alongside. A brown, handsome face with a black moustache looked out at him from behind the wheel.

'Like a lift, Mr Kline?'

Kline ran round to the driver's side, pushed the Asian towards the passenger seat.

'Let me give you a lift, Mr Khan.'

When Kline cornered and accelerated past the warehouse he could see the Triumph passing between the glass offices of the main exit gate but when the Range Rover arrived the barrier pole was down. 'Come on!' Kline yelled at the guard, who saw the word 'POLICE' on the white car, lifted the pole, saluted then stared open-mouthed at the battered face of the driver and the brown face of his passenger.

For Malleson it was all a little confusing; this was the third steering wheel he'd been behind that morning. This dashboard had more bleedin' attachments than had the Corniche. He pressed a few. The horn sounded, the wind-screen wipers came on, making a squeal of noise as they scraped across the dry glass.

'Why th'wipers?' Rawlinson snapped.

'Just came on.'

'Just purr'm off then.'

Malleson pressed a few more switches up and down. Nothing happened as far as he could see. The wipers went screeching on.

' 'Ere,' said Rawlinson, depressing a switch. The radio came on and announced cryptically, 'Last seen East of container base...'

Rawlinson began taking his anger out on the dashboard; Malleson tried to help but only succeeded in turning the siren on. Pedestrians in their Sunday best turned apprehensively. Rawlinson jumped up and down in his seat. 'Turn it... turn it... turn it bleedin' well off!' Malleson got lucky – the switches he hit turned the siren off and the wipers stopped halfway.

Rawlinson relaxed a little; at least now he could think. 'Right...

that's it,' he said, looking behind and failing to see the Range Rover hidden behind a cream and blue bus. He turned back to the road. 'Yeh. Everything's OK.'

They drove on towards the junction called Spaghetti without realising that the sign on the roof of the Triumph was flashing its insistent message of 'Stop Stop Stop'.

The Range Rover moved up alongside the Triumph approaching Gravelly Hill; Kline jerked the wheel and bumped the Triumph so it careered off the road and bisected a corner of pavement, seeming all set to smash into a wall beneath the layers of flyover that comprised the complex series of motorway interchanges above them.

Inside the skidding 2000, Malleson tried to hold the wheel, miss the wall and smash through a wooden gate that led he knew not where. Rawlinson saw 'WBA' and 'Villa Wankers' painted in blue Aerosol before all around were flying splinters of wood and the car was flying through the air. It landed on an incline that led down to the red dust and cinders that lay beneath the supports of the motorway. Malleson lost control of the steering wheel and the stolen police car headed straight for the waters of the River Tame.

'Turn the wheel,' Rawlinson roared. The West Indian did so and the car turned broadside, throwing a cloud of dust that obscured the view of the driver of the Range Rover, which had followed into the dusty precincts beneath Spaghetti Junction. The two cars sought each other in the red swirl of dust in which the concrete pillars loomed at every turn.

Rawlinson suddenly saw a route back to the gate and pointed. Malleson put the Triumph towards the exit and tried to throw enough dust as he went to blind the driver of the Range Rover that was trying to overtake and head them off at the gate.

'They haven't a bleedin' hope,' Rawlinson encouraged his driver, waving the hand that held his gun.

'Shit!' shouted Malleson as he felt the wheels fail to grip on the incline that led up to the smashed timber gate.

'C'mon... c'mon!' yelled Rawlinson as the Range Rover came nearer and nearer, its clouds of red dust swirling out in a typhoon wind behind. g

'No... no... won't grip... she won't grip!'

The other police car was now alongside and Kline was trying to open the door. Rawlinson beat him to it. Stood between the two cars he levelled the gun as Kline thrust open his door. The world turned over for Rawlinson; as the door struck him, he went somersaulting back over the bonnet and windscreen of the Triumph, hit the slope beyond and rolled over and over until stopped by a concrete pillar.

Kline ploughed down towards Rawlinson, as Malleson tumbled out the other side of the Triumph and ran away towards a canal bank and bridge. Khan aimed his gun and fired a warning shot that only made the West Indian move all the faster. Khan ran in pursuit.

Rawlinson and Kline struggled; the gun dropped from Rawlinson's hand as his opponent banged his wrist against the pillar. The combat became hand to hand and they rolled in each other's embrace down the cinder slope towards the muddy banks of the River Tame.

Malleson had opened up a lead on his pursuer and was running across a bridge that for some peculiar reason had steel struts stretching across at head height so that he had to think and duck after every second stride. One-two... duck, one-two... duck, one-two... duck...

'Stop!' shouted Khan pointing his gun from the other end of the narrow bridge.

'One-two,' said Malleson, waiting for the sound of the bullet being fired, 'duck, one...' He stopped and looked back when no sound came. Khan was looking disgustedly at the empty pistol in his hand.

Malleson saluted his good fortune by giving the Asian a jubilant 'V' sign. Right, let's get outa here, he told himself, and turned, said, 'Duck...' but did so out of sequence so that when he half straightened and went to hit his stride, his forehead went crunch into the next steel bar. Khan watched the West Indian fall back and even at that distance could see the sudden downpour of blood from the damaged forehead.

Rawlinson lay on top of Kline with an iron bar across his throat. Kline blocked the downward press of the bar with either hand. Each looked into the other's face; both knew that the other would grant no quarter. It was a contest of will, of which man had a greater desire to survive than the other. The bar touched down on Kline's gullet; he felt the gasps for air become difficult and painful. Rawlinson felt the advantage and threw all of his strength down onto the bar of rusted iron. Kline took it, wavered, swallowed, resisted and began to turn the bar from the right hand side. He felt a slackening and with a last effort threw Rawlinson from him. Both men scrambled in the mud at the side of the river before Kline landed the punch that sent Rawlinson into the fast-running river. Choking and coughing out the filth of the water Rawlinson waded towards a small island of silt and stones and tried to recover some strength to resist the man surging through the water towards him. He saw, half buried in the grey sand and pebbles, a shovel with a broken handle, dumped, no doubt, during the construction of the motorways that soared in all directions high above. Rawlinson gripped the shovel as Kline grabbed his legs and pulled him back into the deepest part of the river. Rawlinson brandished the shovel with its jagged metal edge and swung; Kline ducked beneath the arc of the shovel and his adversary stumbled off balance, lost his footing and went under the water. Trying to surface, to reach the air from under the water, Rawlinson felt hands close on his throat and try as he might he could not seem to break their grip. Kline looked at the face under the water and made himself hold on against the strength of the panic that came to the drowning man... the bubbles rose and burst then stopped. The hair floated, the face, distorted by the water, surfaced then submerged again as the body turned in the current of the river and drifted away. Kline looked about him. Saw the small island at the side of the bridge and reached its sanctuary with the last of his strength.

Chapter Thirteen

The Airport workers wheeled the coffin out of the hangar and towards the jet that stood on the runway of Elmdon Airport.

Kline, in his new grey suit, turned and looked towards a middle-aged West Indian couple. He'd already asked their permission but wanted to confirm it. The father nodded and held the mother, who searched her bag for another handkerchief.

'You must go now…' Khan said. Kline walked out of the lounge and approached the coffin on its way to the waiting aircraft.

When Khan arrived the tall man was looking down on the grey face of Dinah Carmichael, dressed in bridal white for her journey home to Trinidad.

Kline said something to the dead woman. What it was Khan never knew for the wind whipped the words away. Then Kline replaced the lid and gave the trolley back to the porters to wheel away. Kline watched them go. 'Just wanted t'see her… that's all.'

'It's all right,' Khan said as they turned back towards the airport and the faces of Dinah's parents at the glass.

'They're sending her home, y'see.'

'Repatriation.'

'Something like that.'

From the Immigration Office Jashir Singh Mahal was taken outside with an official on either side to ensure that he boarded the right plane for the first stage of his deportation to India. Jashir looked around for his wife but could not see her. One of the officers jostled him along towards the Trident waiting to wing him away.

Outside the airport lounge Kline and Khan looked at each other.

'Going back home?' Kline asked.

Khan smiled. 'This is my home.'

'You're police, aren't y'?'

'In a way.'

'Special Branch?'

'More or less.'

'Suit yourself.' Kline wasn't that interested. Law was law and he'd be having enough problems with them in the near future. They'd already been smelling around his club.

Khan put a hand on his shoulder. 'I had to recruit you to help flush Rawlinson out. You understand?'

Kline looked through the glass; there was no sign of anything, just people climbing aboard a jet plane. 'Yeh,' he said. 'Well, everybody uses me... why not you?'

Khan held out a hand. Kline took it. Then Khan said, 'Excuse me,' and went away.

There suddenly seemed nothing to do. Kline put his hands in his pockets and went outside. A little rotund Indian carrying a suitcase hurried from a taxi and bumped Kline slightly in passing. Kline had never seen Rafiq so no recognition came as he wandered into the car park nearby to the observation platform, where an Indian woman with two young children was waving frantically as a plane taxied down the runway with the noise of its jets rising and rising. Kline hated goodbyes, so he walked away.

When the plane carrying Dinah took off and climbed away from Birmingham he only allowed himself to watch until it finally disappeared.

Vendetta

Chapter One

Inside the interview room of a Birmingham police station, John Kline prepared to face the consequences of killing the man who had ruled the Midlands underworld.

Newbold closed the door of the room behind him, indicated to his sergeant that the prisoner should be seated and stared at Kline in much the same way as he viewed the world and its people – without enthusiasm.

Kline looked from one to the other, from the middle-aged inspector to Sergeant Ede. It was time to make a stand; he opened his mouth, formed half a word. 'Wh…?'

Newbold raised a hand in weary protest. 'Let's cut all the fifty-seven varieties of "Who me?" crap,' he said in the bored, flat monotone he affected. 'We've had a body washed up from a weir. It's bin identified as Ozzie Rawlinson. You killed him an' y' goin' down for it.'

Ede came in on his cue. 'Shall I get the charge sheet?'

Newbold yawned. 'Save a lot've effin' about.'

Kline, not wishing to spoil the burly sergeant's purposeful exit, waited until the door had closed before again attempting to speak. Again he was told curtly to 'Shuttit'.

Kline took a deep slow breath, watching while Newbold took out a tipped cigarette and lit it.

'What was your other stretch for, Kline?'

'Manslaughter.'

'You've graduated to murder, congratulations.'

Kline said nothing.

'I knew Rawlinson,' Newbold stated.

Kline thought he heard an echo of some regret.

'Miss him?'

'Not particularly.'

Kline smiled; it was time to enter the game.

'Just his kickbacks?'

Kline saw the backhander coming, moved his head away but still suffered the impact of the blow, felt the pain and tasted the salt of blood in his mouth. Here we go again, he thought.

Anne Darracott, four hours away from shooting the last grain of her last supply, stood before the boarded windows of what had once been the Chanticleer Chinese Restaurant. She rattled the padlock on the door, rang a dead bell, stepped back and looked upwards at the dark windows above the empty arteries of begrimed neon that formed characters of Chinese that could have signified anything, even goodbye. Anne felt a surge of bile in her belly; she'd heard of inter-Triad rivalries and knew arrests had been made, but that hadn't stopped her hoping that this, her best source of supply, might have remained untouched by misfortune.

Kline dabbed his damaged lip and stared up at Sergeant Ede, who grinned and enquired whether or not Kline was down in the mouth. Kline smelt the beer on the CID sergeant's breath and noticed the tensing of the big right hand into a fist. Like that, is it – this must be the hard man sent in when there's a tough nut to be cracked against a station wall.

'How'd y'come t' do that?' Ede went on, indicating the injury to the mouth of John Kline.

'Fell down some station steps.'

'Smart arse.'

Kline tensed for a blow which did not arrive.

'Where's this charge sheet?'

Ede smiled with enjoyment. 'They're putting your name on it.'

'Your gaffer is?'

'Right.'

Kline dabbed his lip again, examined the smear of blood. 'He's one've th'old school.'

'Yeh, won't take lip from anyone.'

Ede grinned at his joke. Kline saw the door behind start to open. Seeing Newbold he couldn't resist the reply.

'But he will take dropsy, kickbacks – the little presents for big favours received?'

Ede threw a right hand, which Kline anticipated, moving left and rising from his chair. Ede, off balance, was open for retaliation but Kline resisted the temptation and allowed the sergeant to recover and raise his fist again.

'Don't do it,' Newbold said wearily, holding the door open to the corridor.

'Not here, he means,' Kline said sarcastically.

Newbold said nothing, but jerked his head at Kline then at the open door.

Kline moved away from Ede and towards the CID Inspector. 'Many steps to fall down?' he asked.

'Never counted,' Newbold replied, his face expressionless.

What is this? Kline asked himself, sensing that in some way, for some reason, the situation had changed. For better or for worse he would soon find out. He stepped forward, looked up and down the featureless corridor.

'Which way?' Kline asked.

'What?'

'To the flowery dell – cell.'

Newbold sighed and looked at his sergeant.

'What's he think this is – open day?'

Ede, not knowing his cues in this game, made no answer but scowled at Kline instead. Newbold for the first time showed his frustration by rapping out, 'Go on, piss off out've it.'

Kline could not believe it. Another trick, a trap. Killed while trying to escape? Ah, come on. Kline watched Newbold turn away and slap his file against the chest of the disappointed Ede. Kline decided to test his luck and began to back away and out into the corridor. Remembering the way he had been brought in, he turned and quickly made his way down the passage and towards the front entrance, waiting all the while for that bored Brummy voice to sound behind him with a 'No walkies today, put him back in his kennel', but nothing happened. He turned a corner and saw an open passageway to the street.

Outside the interview room Ede glanced enquiringly at his boss and indicated the file in Newbold's hands. 'Back to CRO?'

Newbold considered. 'Uh huh. He's only lent out. Don't file th' bastard under "K", put him under "P" f' "Pendin' ".'

*

Even though he had emerged into the daylight, Kline still expected to be apprehended. He just couldn't figure it. No reason, no caution about leaving town; one minute down for murder, the next walking along this empty pavement alongside a dual carriageway with a belt of green grass between. Kline suddenly felt like running, just for the hell of it. Like a horse turned out into a strange field he wanted test the limits of his unexpected freedom. OK, Kline told himself, turning towards the kerbside. The strip of grass that divided the carriageway only ran for a little way before it dipped down into an underpass but it was better than nothing. Kline glanced back at the oncoming traffic, sparse at this time of early afternoon. A cream-coloured bus with a royal blue line along its side pulled past, followed by a slow-moving yellow car. Come on, thought the tall man at the edge of the pavement, then realised with a sudden shock of recognition whose the car was and what it all meant. Kline's long legs did his thinking for him; they obviously did not wish to have any further truck with the driver of that ill-remembered yellow Datsun car. Kline felt the hard road surface as he crossed the carriageway, then the soft, yielding going of the grass strip beneath his feet as he galloped towards the underpass ahead. Behind him, the Datsun moved up to challenge the running man who, arms pumping, legs driving, entered the descent of the underpass with a diminishing lead, but with just enough time to vault over a metal dividing rail onto the adjacent traffic lane. The Datsun, imprisoned, could only accelerate away. 'Bye bye,' said Kline as the departing vehicle surfaced on the other side of the underpass, where the green middle strip recommenced. As he watched, the car driver slowed, turned, bumped across the turf and lurched down onto the tarmacadam then accelerated to come hurtling back towards Kline.

A retired engine driver in a sedate elderly Ford Anglia could not possibly believe that anyone would choose to drive at speed down the upside section of a dual carriageway, so he shut his eyes and when he opened them the way was clear – the yellow car had shot past him and swerved into a side road in pursuit of John Kline.

Two parts down the length of the side road was a small access entry linking each road with its neighbour. It was sufficient in width to take a man or a woman with a pram but not the yellow car from the island of Japan.

The Datsun, thwarted, stopped with a howl of sudden brake

pressure and its driver emerged in time to see, through the entry's end, the figure of John Kline crossing a main thoroughfare towards an island that contained not palm trees and thatched huts but bus stops and public conveniences. The Asian stroked his moustache, slammed the door of the yellow car and followed the direction of his quarry.

On reaching the refuge in the centre of the traffic, Kline turned and scanned the different routes and roads that converged upon his island. He saw a bus approaching but it was heading out of town and it was out of reach anyhow. Then he saw across the street the handsome features and black moustache of the ubiquitous Mr Khan. For a moment the two men stared at each other. Then between them came the intervention of the outward bound bus.

When the traffic cleared, Khan could no longer see Kline but knew the only place he could have gone.

After crossing to the island, Khan regarded the twin brick buildings, one marked 'Ladies', the other 'Gentlemen'. What would Kline expect him to do? Go into the gentlemen's lavatory, obviously. Go into the ladies? No. Kline would expect him to act without thinking and go into the gentlemen's, so therefore… Khan went into the section designated as 'Ladies'.

Inside the white-tiled washroom, Khan moved in for the kill by approaching the only cubicle with a locked door and announcing.

'Caught in the act, Mr Kline?'

From inside the cubicle came a sudden intake of breath then the sound of a swift evacuation followed by much hurried adjustment of under and outer garments.

The cistern flushed, Khan waited. The door opened, a long nose with a pig eye placed high on either side regarded him with belligerence.

'What?' the high pitched voice hissed. 'What did you say, boy?'

The door opened fully and a middle-aged, tweed-clad armadillo of a woman sallied forth. 'Bad enough seeing your kind on the streets, now must we suffer your intrusion even here?' she said, her long nose quivering in outrage.

'Sorry… sorry,' said Khan, backing away in confusion and failing to notice her rolled umbrella until he felt its impact across his left ear. Driven back into the street, Khan fended a two-handed backhand smash with his forearm then gave ground towards a bus about to pull away from its stopping place. The irate armadillo charged; Khan began to run and found himself parallel with the moving bus. Glancing at the window alongside, Khan saw the profile of John Kline looking calmly ahead. If Kline noticed the panting runner outside he gave no sign but settled even more comfortably into his seat as the corporation bus outstripped all pursuit, turned a corner of Alcester Road and started the descent that leads towards the centre of the city of Birmingham.

Anne Darracott, in a telephone kiosk near to her houseboat on the canal, tried the last number in her blue book. It rang out. A voice answered. She made her plea. 'No,' the voice said. Anne held the buzzing receiver to her ear for a long time, then replaced it. Thought what else she could do to score. Saw a card advertising TOA Taxis before her and decided to take a trip into town.

Chapter Two

When Kline returned to the Maverick Club, he found himself looking over the swing doors into the main area of the club with its confederate flags, wanted posters and Western decor.

Above the stage the bison heads brooded over a lithe brown stripper who, in Wild West costume and with her back to Kline, could have been a lady he used to know. The music of *The Good the Bad and the Ugly* came on to the sound system. Kline remembered that at this juncture of her act Dinah would start the wriggle that would end with the discarding of her neon yellow briefs. The West Indian girl gave neither shimmy nor shake but remained still as death.

The music pounded on. No stripping took place. Below the stage, in a ringside seat, Dermot Macavoy finally lost patience, hauled himself to his feet and enquired in ringing tones of exasperation, 'What in the name of Jesus God is holdin' dose yeller knickers up *now!*'

Up on stage the slim brown figure shrugged its shoulders and began to turn.

In the shadows by the doors, Kline felt his gut tighten as if, despite all logic, the face that was about to reveal itself would be that of Dinah Carmichael. He saw Dinah but it was only the flash of memory that recalled her face set in a coffin bound for burial in Trinidad. Dead. Dead because of you, Kline forced upon himself in the remaining moment it took the stripper to turn and reveal herself as someone unknown.

As if to end the limbo between past and present, the music stopped. Kline began to move towards the stage where Dermot was expounding his theory of revelation in relation to the mystery of the female form.

'Punters want pussy, love. Show th'fur n' hear them purr. Stripper before you near let'm stroke it. 'Course, she knew I wasn't runnin' no monastic monks' retreat...'

'That's *all* she knew,' said Kline bitterly.

The Irishman's head jerked round in surprise, his sea green eyes registering apprehension as he acknowledged Kline's sudden presence. He nodded then turned back to the business of the stage.

'Take five, why don't y'. Think it over, love. Decide t'put all y'goods in the window n' we got sumthin' t'talk money about.'

The girl nodded without enthusiasm, gathered up the discarded pieces of cowgirl costume and withdrew.

Dermot turned to Kline. 'Law've bin lookin' f'you. Seems Rawlinson's body washed up from a weir.'

Kline remained impassive. 'Yeh, they said.'

Macavoy's expression showed surprise. 'They seen you?'

Kline touched the thickness of his upper lip. 'We had a chat.'

'An' they let y'go... just like dat?'

'You sound surprised.'

'Aren't *you?*' Dermot shook his head in disbelief. 'Your killin' Rawlinson has made a lot've people the poorer. That fella had an army've dependants both sides've th'law.'

Kline smiled tightly. 'Such as you?'

Dermot spread his hands in a plea for understanding. 'John... John... you got four years for the manslaughter've his kid brother but me... me... I got him leeched on to my back here.'

'Signed the place over, did you, Dermot?'

Macavoy snorted in derision at Kline's innocence. 'Rawlinson'd never put his name t'anythin'. His funeral's tomorra – two t'one y'find a phoney name on the gravestone.'

'I haven't been invited,' said Kline without regret. He regarded the Irish eyes thoughtfully. 'So, legally, if you'll pardon the expression, Dermot, we're still partners, right?'

Dermot could not think of a way to deny it. 'Yes, right... erm... what is it you'd be wantin' exactly, John?'

'Cash t'scarper. You owe me thirty grand, babes, my share of this place. I want it.'

Dermot's mouth opened, closed, opened again in an effort to articulate the extent of his disbelief.

'Right now, I'd be pushed t'raise thirty quid, Johnny,' he stammered.

Kline gripped his partner by the waistcoat front and pulled him in close. Dermot offered no resistance but began to babble a little.

'Rawlinson ripped us off. Took every penny've profit. Paid me a wage, a pittance, nothin' more. I'm not lyin'...'

Kline tightened his grip. 'Just holdin' back with my money an' the truth.'

'No... times change, John. Y'need more than a few quid in y'arse pocket. There's tax n' depreciation, insurance, cost've artists... inflation... willingness of the bank t'grant a loan...'

'What's in that old joint account've ours?' Kline interrupted.

'About a fiver.'

'And *your* account?'

'Not much more,' said Dermot with bland sincerity.

Kline found it difficult to believe but he had been out of touch.

'I'm going' t'check every statement've yours against one from the bank, Dermot,' Kline said, relaxing his grip on the Irishman's waistcoat. 'If it's true what you say, th'Maverick will have t'go on the market. If you're lyin', you're up excrement creek without means of propulsion...'

Kline's partner spread his arms. 'As God's my witness...' he said dramatically.

Kline cut it short with a snap of his fingers. 'Safe keys.'

'Sure... sure...'

Watching Dermot return to his jacket draped over the side of a chair, Kline suddenly felt bone weary of it all. He wanted to ride out of town, start anew somewhere. Now Dermot was about to give him the keys to his bankrupt kingdom; there would be books to check, accounts to go through, bank managers to see. Up onstage, a movement caught his eye but it was only the overly modest stripper, now dressed in street clothes and carrying the costume that once had been Dinah's.

Dermot Macavoy handed the bunch of keys across and then watched Kline stare at the girl. As if reading Kline's thoughts he said quietly, 'I heard about Dinah Carmichael. She was one've the best... difficult to ever replace.'

Kline, surprised at this unexpected show of understanding, could only nod in agreement.

Dermot pulled on his jacket, indicated the girl standing on stage and added, 'I'm tryin' but good strippers are born not...'

This was more like it: heartless, hard, uncaring – this was the Dermot Kline knew. Taking one step away Kline sent a right cross into the Irishman's jaw. Dermot staggered back and fell, the momentum of the punch sending him careering along the dance floor to bump headfirst against the apron of the stage.

'What was that for?' he yelled in shrill, hurt outrage.

Kline tossed the keys up in the air and caught them. 'It's the only way to start an audit,' he said and turned away.

Macavoy scowled as he watched Kline stride away in the direction of the offices. From above, the West Indian girl looked down upon him. Dermot glared up at her. 'Well, are you goin' t'strip down t'y'assets?'

The young lady shook her head from side to side and gave added emphasis to her decision by dropping the Wild West costume, boots and all, down onto the sweating, unhappy face below her.

Pete Malleson, stocky, athletic, his boxer's shoulders straining against the seams of his black leather jacket, strode along the Brighton Road towards the pinball parlour below which lay his basement flat.

A sudden breeze on his brow made him explore the chain of stitches that marked his forehead's collision with an unyielding iron strut on a narrow bridge below Spaghetti Junction.

Malleson frowned. He still could not figure why he had been given the chance to escape the consequences of that mistake and why his pursuer, Khan, had failed to follow up. Still, he should worry. Maybe Khan was more interested in copping Kline for drowning Rawlinson. Malleson hoped so. He wondered how deeply Kline felt about the death of that stripper. Maybe not very. Maybe not enough to seek revenge against her killer. Him. Malleson shivered, stopped, looked up and down the street. No avenging angel pursued him. Kline would be inside anyway, Malleson told himself, waiting trial. Yeh. Up ahead the sign 'Del Rio' glowed in dull red neon. To the black it signified home and headquarters, security and safety. He hurried towards it.

Across the street, in a doorway, Anne Darracott watched the West Indian approach the pinball parlour and push on inside. She shivered, felt goosebumps rise; did not wish to cross the street but had to. Had to. Did not want to open the door of the Del Rio but had no choice at all. Her thin hand pushed. The door opened. Inside was a dark pit lit only by juke-box glow and the multi-coloured glass panels that flickered garishly as steel balls propelled by shadowy players collided with circuits and caused the numbered totals to climb towards the dizzy summit of a 'Free Play'.

Anne heard the thud of the door as it closed behind. Her heart went bump and her legs said run as she peered around the parlour at the black shadows and tried to decide which dark spider was Malleson.

Kline came down the steps of the bank. He disliked all officialdom and bank managers in particular. He should have known when he heard Dermot referred to constantly as *Mister* Macavoy that his request for scrutiny of the Maverick accounts was likely to be denied. Kline thought next of the money seen in the cashiers' tills, of green and blue and brown notes of exchange – exchange for freedom, peace and escape from this city at whose heart he now stood.

At the foot of the steps he turned and looked back and upwards at the curved Rotunda building above and wondered what to do next. No solution came so he decided to walk somewhere, anywhere, until it did.

From the shelter given by the curve of the bank building, Khan watched Kline mooch moodily away. Whatever had transpired inside had obviously done little to help. Good, thought Khan as he moved to follow the tall figure now threading its way through the multi-racial crowds along New Street.

Malleson sprawled on his bed beneath the grotesque picture of a nude twenty-stone woman and snapped his fingers one to five and waited. He liked where he lived: the giant-size bed, the ivory coloured telephone to hand, the wall to wall carpeting, the hanging wicker chair, the glass bar, the tubular steel furniture he had noticed at Rawlinson's flat and copied slavishly – so what? He didn't care; it had class and that's what he wanted.

The door to the bathroom opened and Anne Darracott emerged, now transformed from the nervous, itching, fearful creature who had walked into his parlour into this cool, attractive white lady, who had been the ex-bossman's secretary, among other things. Malleson watched intently as she pulled one of his neckties from around her thin, bruised arm; he admired her as she sent her blonde hair all a-swirl.

'Thanks,' Anne said, and grinned, all confidence, all fear gone of the man on the bed.

Malleson lifted a casual hand in acknowledgement but said nothing.

Anne, remembering the rules of the pusher-fixer situation, fumbled in her handbag for the readies. Peeling away two fivers from her roll, she offered payment.

'I don't want money,' the black said.

Hello, Anne thought, squash this right away. 'It's the only payment that's on offer,' she said, her voice laced with warning.

Malleson looked her over, then spoke the coarse truth. 'Ten minutes ago, you'd've put anything and everything on offer, baby.'

'Bollocks,' said Anne arrogantly, tossing her head. The man on the bed, knowing where that over-bearing confidence came from and who had obtained the means, remained unimpressed.

'Ten minutes ago, you were way down the handicap. Now you're back in the pattern races.'

Anne was not listening. 'Mmm?' she said. She was feeling so good. So good.

'Class,' Malleson explained patiently. 'You're back in your right class, above me, out've mine?'

Anne shrugged. ' 'Course.'

Malleson, animated by the sudden run of his thoughts, sat up on the bed. 'Not n'more. See, your boss, Mr Rawlinson, that was. He isn't any more, right. There's a gap... who's goin' t'fill it?'

To Anne it was the only joke of the day.

'*You*?'

Malleson frowned, his stitches tight.

'Why not?'

'Why not... why *not*... you've got... what...?' Anne searched into her memory. 'Yeh, a pick-axe handle and an IQ that doesn't hit three figures.'

The dark brown eyes regarded her. 'I should've talked to you before I got you the stuff. Before you fixed.'

Anne really could not be bothered talking further. 'Got to go,' she said gaily and drifted away in the direction of the door.

Seeing his chances slipping away Malleson restrained her by means of an upraised leg. Anne stopped; Malleson looked up at her.

'Listen, you know who's friend and who's foe in this town, both sides of the law.'

'Forget it,' Anne said impishly.

'Remember,' said Malleson, sliding his hand up her inner thigh and hard into the soft of her crotch. Startled, Anne pulled away.

'Stick to pinball,' she said coldly.

Malleson gave her his insolent grin. 'I keep gettin' "tilt".'

'I'm not surprised,' said Anne, picking up her bag and wishing to be away from this basement and the hard flash of its interior decoration.

Watching her turn to leave, Malleson dropped all pretence. He stopped his grin and let his expression show all the determination and aggression he felt. 'I won't be so bleedin' polite next time y'come t'call. Next time I'll want somethin' more in exchange for your medicine.'

Anne gave him her stone stare. Malleson took it. 'Eight hours is a long time in the life of a junkhead,' he said softly.

Anne shrugged. It seemed an eternity. 'Long enough.'

Malleson decided he really wanted to lay into this cool white bitch. 'To score again? To find a supply? No,' he said, shaking his head in reply to his own questions. 'Only line you could hook into that isn't black, baby, is methadone at the rehab unit, and you'd sooner not get involved with all those white coats.' Malleson left the bed and moved to her seductively. Anne stood her ground. 'You go out, try an' hustle the street for your supply. If it doesn't happen for you... well... come back here, Annie, an' we'll play a game for just we two. It's called we'd better be nice t'th'nigger.'

Malleson pulled the thin blonde towards him, looked into the dilated pupils of her tawny eyes. The eyes blinked lazily back at him, expressing nothing but euphoria. Malleson escorted her to the door, opened it and pushed her out into what he hoped would be a cold, cruel world. Anne did not even look back at him but began to climb the stairs to the parlour and the street, looking like a sleepy child going to its bed.

Behind Malleson, the telephone began to ring. He picked it up – a Dermot Macavoy in dire need of an ear to tell his troubles to.

Malleson quelled the excited Irish voice. 'OK... OK, Dermot, I'm in now... OK. Calm down. What's the matter, they declared peace in Ulster?'

'No,' said the voice, 'worse than that. Kline's out. The law didn't even give him th'once over twicely.'

Malleson's fingertips played along the irregular line of stitches on his forehead. 'He mention me much?' he asked casually.

Across the city, inside his office in the Maverick Club, Dermot leaned forward to give unconscious emphasis to his embellishment of the truth. 'Mate, *mention* you? He talked of nothing else. All th'time on an' on, like a man obsessed... How you killed his bird Dinah... Yes, I know he's only one guy but don't forget he's trained – ex-SAS... Listen, I think he's smellin' around my bank. He'll get no change out've them but my bet then is that he'll try the bent-money loan sharks... I've tipped them off Kline is bad news.'

Malleson could not disagree. He wondered what to do. Listen to Dermot, anyway.

'Now they'll let us know when Kline shows,' continued the Irishman.

'Then what?'

'I suggest you take the best form of defence and attack.' Down the line Dermot's voice became shrill with warning. 'I'm tellin' you, Malleson, Kline wants two things – my money and your life.'

'Yeh,' Malleson said.

'When and if Kline shows at the loan sharks, d'you want t'know?'

Malleson decided on a policy of attack.

'I want t'know,' he said abruptly and replaced the receiver.

Chapter Three

The dingy office oppressed Kline. It seemed hours had passed since he had made his case for a loan. Kline stood up from the wooden chair and said to the middle-aged secretary, 'Hey, where's this Smiley gone to, the IMF?'

The secretary showed her dentures. 'No. Though they might apply to him.'

'Tell your boss I'm still here, will you?' said Kline quietly.

'Yes.' She pressed a button.

After a minute, there emerged the miserable runt of a man nicknamed Smiley because he had never been known to crack his face – not even when calculating compound interest on an over-secured loan.

'Yes?' he enquired of Kline.

'The loan. What about it – yes or no?' Kline asked.

Smiley rubbed the dry flesh on the back of one hand with the grasping palm of the other. He had done what he could to hold on to this person as Mr Macavoy had required. He had done a favour that could be repaid. No point keeping this bad risk hanging around cluttering up the office like a bad debt.

'Collateral?' he suggested.

'I own a club.'

'I meant something more portable or convertible – jewellery or some such thing of realisable value.'

'If I had that, would I come to you, Smiley?'

'What can I say then but forget it?' said Smiley.

'No loan?' Kline said bitterly.

'No,' replied Smiley, not even adding the word 'Sorry' but standing and enjoying the sensation of seeing Kline march angrily from his office to meet up with whatever fate awaited him.

Kline walked down Albert Street towards Masshouse Circus, lost in his thoughts. There was of course Yeadons. That really was a last resort but he remembered stories of dubious finance deals. It was a chance. Where was he? Albert Street. Yeadons's office had been about here but now... Kline scanned a block of new building under construction. Time. He'd had a lot of it taken from him. So what to do now? He felt for his jacket pocket and a cigarette only to discover that he could no longer move his arms. Strong brown hands had taken a firm grip on each elbow.

'Hello, white bastard,' said Hunniford.

'Well well, hell hell,' said Bonny Bryden, black and ugly under his white beret.

Kline resisted every step of the way but only succeeded in slowing their progress, the two blacks leading him down a flight of steps to the dust of an underground car park.

Malleson stood at the bottom and waited patiently for Kline to be brought down one slow step at a time. He opened the doors of the car so that bundling in could take place and leaned back, cool and elegant in a canary yellow jacket with chocolate brown shirt and trousers. When the trio was within range Malleson raised an admonitory finger and waved it in displeasure at the face of the still struggling Kline.

Through the final few yards before reaching the car, Kline launched one final effort to free his arms but it was beyond his strength. Then he noticed the position of the open car door and Malleson's pose as he leaned casually against it. Kline stopped resisting the pressure exerted on him from either side. The sudden release sent all three men rushing forward and into kicking distance of the car door.

Using the grip that still hung onto his arms as a support, Kline lifted both feet from the ground and drop kicked at the car door with all his strength; he felt the impact of steel on the soles of his feet and saw the door slam shut on Malleson's dangling hand.

'*Eeyow!*' yelled Malleson, finding his hand crushed in a press of pain.

In the turmoil that followed his surprise action Kline broke free of Bryden, but Hunniford threw his arms round him like a brother bear.

Watching Kline and his hanger on swing this way and that, Bryden waited for his opportunity for one solid punch at the white, sweating face bobbing around before him. During this scrimmaging Malleson kept repeating in agonised tones that perhaps someone should find the time to open the door of the car and kindly release his hand. Finally, Hunniford held his prisoner more or less still. Bryden drew back his fist but was then sent staggering by the onslaught of an intruder – the handsome and immaculate Mr Khan.

With this unexpected help to hand, Kline felt the grip about him weaken, and with one final surge of strength he burst the lock of Hunniford's arms.

Each pair stood panting and facing the other, the scene orchestrated by Malleson's howls and entreaties for someone to get his bleeding hand out!

Khan, not absolutely certain whether or not the blacks had other help in the vicinity, suggested retreat to the tall man at his side.

Weary and crapped out, Kline agreed. But he could not resist enquiring of Malleson, 'Do you need a hand?'

Seeing his henchmen start forward, Malleson called them back. By the time they had opened the car door and he had made terms with the pain, Kline and Khan had disappeared.

On stage at the Maverick the Shadettes swung into 'When Will I See You Again', their brown flesh and brightly coloured dresses of yellow, pink, green shimmering in a spotlight hazed with cigarette smoke. At the bar Kline sat with his back towards the stage and drained the best Scotch that Archie the dwarf barman could find. Next to Kline sat Khan, perched upon a bar stool, a full glass of Britvic orange before him.

Kline beckoned to the seemingly empty space that lay within the four sides of the central bar.

'Archie.'

A head progressed along the level of the bar. 'Boss?' the head asked.

Least someone remembers my place in this can of beans, thought Kline. 'Scotch and, what, orange?' he asked Khan.

'No.'

Kline smiled, mocking Khan's abstinence. 'Not while on duty?'

Khan shrugged. 'The taste does not appeal.'

'You should try prison cocoa,' Kline said bitterly.

'No, thank you,' Khan said politely. 'I'd really rather not... given the choice,' he added with a sly glance at his companion.

Kline took the glass filled to the brim by the diminutive barman and gulped a double down to sluice his mouth clear of the sickly taste brought back by unpleasant memory. The drink went down but the thoughts bobbed back. Kline turned and with his voice tinged with aggression said flatly, 'So, you're a cop?'

'Not really.'

'Special Branch?'

'Not quite.' The Pakistani waved a fastidious hand to shoo some ash from the bar before him. 'Let us say that I have access to a section of the security services that has some influence with the forces that govern our society.'

'What does that mean?'

'It means that I can request that some stones remain unturned in return for assistance and aid from you, Mr Kline.'

'Oh, yeh?'

Khan finished his drink and shifted his stool a little closer, lowering his voice.

'Judge Brian Bush said, not so long ago, that Birmingham is in danger of becoming synonymous with corruption.'

'Even a judge can get it right sometimes,' said Kline dryly.

'He also said,' Khan continued, 'that only the tip of the iceberg of corruption has been revealed, and my investigations confirm this, for I believe that sums of money made from corrupt practice are now being used to finance criminal activity.' Khan sipped his soft drink then went on. 'I suspect that a consortium has been formed that invests in illegal immigration, prostitution, drugs.' Khan paused for effect, took a few more sips of orange then added without a change of tone or emphasis, 'I also believe that the man I saw you drown, Rawlinson, was managing this consortium's various illegal enterprises.'

'Naughty of him,' Kline said lightly.

Khan smiled slightly. 'Well, he has been adequately punished but the men behind him, their identities remain unknown, though I feel they must hold positions of influence in business, the civil service, local government and the law. So...' Khan spread his manicured brown hands. 'Thanks to you, these gentlemen must have a sudden vacancy for a chief executive.'

Kline played with his glass, sending the amber fluid into a slow swirl.

'You got me out've that nick?'

Khan considered, then spoke with calm assurance.

'In the past I needed you as bait to dislodge Rawlinson from an entrenched position. This time I will require you to take his place in order that I may discover the identities of the men who encourage and profit from the spread of crime across the Midlands.'

If Khan expected gratitude or instant acceptance he was to be disappointed, for John Kline seemed to be following a stream of thought that flowed from resentment into anger.

'I knew security agents when I was in the SAS,' he ground out. 'That was in Ulster. Some seven hundred killings ago. When the Littlejohns were about and the runner – oh, an' that guy who ended up dead in a ditch down Surrey, the Special Branch informer, Lennon.'

The Asian smiled blandly. 'Propaganda, Mr Kline. You mustn't believe such stories.'

'I'd sooner believe them than your mates in DI6,' Kline said savagely.

'You wish to return to police custody?' Khan asked.

'I will anyway,' Kline said. 'Agents like you protect their helpers as long as use or information lasts, but when the guy wants out or has nuthin' else t'give, it's turn the stone over and the law must take its course.'

The smile under the black moustache faded. 'You refuse to assist me?'

'Right.'

The smile disappeared entirely from Khan's face.

'We have shared sorrow together,' he said seriously. 'For you the concealed murder of a loved woman, for me the loss of a colleague; need I remind you that the men responsible remain unpunished?'

Kline did not want to think about it so he swallowed the last of his drink and shrugged.

'I dunno.'

The Asian sensed Kline's uncertainty. 'Dunno what, Mr Kline?'

'The name of the man who killed Dinah is Malleson. The same man tried to abduct you today. For what, do you think – a quiet talk of shared experience? No, Mr Kline, he requires your death as a guarantee of his future safety.'

'Why isn't *he* inside?'

'No witness to his misdeeds. The official cause of death for Miss Carmichael was drug overdose.'

'Yeh,' said Kline, slumping a little on his stool, feeling for his cigarettes, then remembering.

'Archie...' he called. 'Get us some fags.'

Khan gave the big man beside him a sidelong glance.

'Rawlinson smoked cigars.'

'He could afford to.'

'You will have money soon,' Khan said, as if assuming cooperation between them had already been agreed. 'Your criminal activities will attract the corrupt money that must be floating around the Midlands.'

'When these... what... Consortium guys reveal themselves, then what happens?'

Khan nodded happily. 'That is when you and I fade into the background and allow the more orthodox agencies of law enforcement to take the credit for revealing corruption in high places.'

'How far would I fade away?' Kline asked. 'Right through the doors back into Winson Green nick?'

Khan put a friendly hand on his companion's shoulder.

'The police need witnesses. Only one person saw your fight with Rawlinson.' The Asian indicated himself and smiled winningly. 'I suffer from bouts of amnesia. I find a successful outcome to an investigation brings forgetfulness of many things.'

Kline did not believe him but there was no other possibility left open. He knew it and so did Khan.

In the corridor that led from the offices to the club proper, Dermot Macavoy paused outside the swing doors and said, 'Fuckin *hell*!' to himself. Kline and his smoothy wog mate were seated at the bar. Very friendly, they seemed to the Irishman, more than matey-matey, for wasn't the brown fella buyin' the Kline bastard a fat cigar and wasn't Kline taking it and weren't they talkin' to each other like new-found friends?

The Irishman rubbed the slight stubble on his Desperate Dan chin and asked himself why, if his partner Kline could form an inter-racial alliance, why in God's name couldn't he?

Dermot turned away and returned down the dimly lit corridor to the main office and its telephone.

Chapter Four

Anne Darracott came slowly down the curved steel steps that descended from the pinball parlour above and approached Malleson's front door. Her élan had long since evaporated, leaving only fear, need and desperation in its place. She rang on the bell, knocked on the door, kicked it with her small-size shoes but no one answered, no black face appeared. Anne wiped her nose and settled down to wait, an urchin off the street, hunched against the wall, waiting for her new black daddy to come on home.

Around Rafiq's round table of walnut wood they sat – Dermot, Malleson, Kuldip. Irish, black English and ex-Sikh. Behind each man, seated in the penumbra of shadow thrown by the glass, art nouveau shade that hung low over the table, were two representatives of each community, guarding the back of each leader.

From the mantel shelf above the stone fireplace a photograph of fat, jolly Rafiq waved a pipe in farewell to a newspaper cameraman. In the photograph his smile beamed out, giving a radiance of self-satisfaction to the smooth plump face of the Asian community leader.

Kuldip, his aide and dogsbody, kept glancing at this photograph as if the smile might just change to a scowl of displeasure at the use of his opulent home for this clandestine underworld meeting.

Across the table Malleson, elegant in grey pinstripe (it was to be a business meeting, after all), noticed the Asian's furtive glances towards the image of his master.

'When's the Maharaja due for a comeback?' he asked, pointing a finger from the hand that was undamaged, unbandaged and without the constant throb of pain.

Kuldip cleared his throat, trying to choose his words carefully. 'Mr

Rafiq has business in Rotterdam, to do with the Blackbird run, I think. He is low-lying but unpredictable. You see?'

Malleson enjoyed listening to the Asian's English. With some facility for the turn of a phrase himself, it amused him to follow the tumble and jumble of Kuldip's crazy mind, the circumlocution of his sing-song speech.

'But when's he comin' back?' Malleson repeated.

Kuldip shrugged. 'Could be another week, month, day.' He paused, looked at the photograph then apprehensively at the heavy, carved wood doors that led from the hallway.

Tonight even... He does not share his uttermost... confidences, not always with me, you understand?'

Malleson saw the look of unease and understood that friend Kuldip had made no mention of the meeting to his master.

'I understand,' he said and watched Kuldip turn to jabber in Urdu or Pushtu or some such to his two bodyguards, one a fierce Pathan, massive in girth and height, the other a small, alert brown man who twitched his nose and darted his eyes to and fro like a weasel on the lookout for a passing dinner.

Next to Kuldip sat Dermot and behind him Sturt and Cary, two bouncers from the Maverick whom Dermot could trust to stay on his side as long as it remained a winning one.

Cary was a stocky little man, Brummy, with a penchant for kicking people when they were down. Sturt, a natural middleweight veering towards the heavy had across his throat, from ear to ear, a white run of a scar tissue, a memento from the slash of a cut-throat razor. Sturt played idly with a voice box, a tube-amplifier that gave him speech, for although prompt medical attention had saved his life nothing could make the severed vocal chords do more than emit a raven's croak at best. Sturt prodded his leader in the back, held the voice box to the base of his damaged throat and boomed out in Dalek-like metallics, 'WHERE'S-THE-BOG?'

'Just shuttit,' said Dermot, who was lost in the contemplation of his plans for the demise of John Kline.

'Through there,' said Cary, pointing to a small door set in the wall opposite.

'TA,' the voice box intoned as its owner pulled himself to his feet and lumbered past the pair of blacks who flanked Malleson.

'HELLO-HOW-ARE-YOU?' boomed Sturt.

'What the hell was that?' Bryden asked Hunniford, startled.

'Voice of the Obeah man, man,' replied Bryden, transferring another five fingers of Rafiq's best brandy from a cut glass decanter into a crystal goblet.

Waiting for the meeting to begin Malleson tried to lessen the pain in his left hand by thinking of just what he would do to that white man Kline. Dermot had said on the telephone he had a plan and had also suggested that maybe a triumvirate could be formed to fill the vacuum left by the late Mr Rawlinson. Malleson thought about it and liked where his thoughts took him. To the top of the heap? Why not? He'd said as much to that blonde bitch earlier but now, now he was really beginning to fancy some expansion. He had a house of pleasure that gave a good return but maybe, just maybe, he had become lazy, complacent. Yeh, could be, could be the time was just right to do an Alexander the Great and conquer all the known world from Smethwick to Handsworth, even out to the far-flung frontiers of Balsall Heath.

The silence around the table brought him awake from his dream of conquest. He realised that all around the table were eyes intent upon him.

'What?' he asked with an imperious upward jerk of his bearded chin.

'I said, we got a problem,' Dermot repeated.

'Y'mean Kline,' said Malleson, becoming alert and businesslike. 'What about him?'

'I don't think he trusts me.'

Malleson shook his head in mock wonderment.

'I wonder why?' he asked sarcastically.

'Don't get me wrong,' said Dermot, scowling. 'He can't pin nothin' but it's, y'know, a feeling.'

'So?' said Malleson.

'We want Kline laid out as the centre of a funeral arrangement... Everyone agree?'

The furtive green eyes glanced around the table. All members of the board nodded in agreement with the exception of Kuldip, who frowned at the Irishman.

'Please to explain one thing, Mr Macavoy,' Kuldip said. 'Why is it you wish this chap so dead?'

'I wish this chap so dead,' Dermot mimicked, 'in order that I might own a whole Maverick night club and be left to run it at a quiet profit for nobody's advantage but my own.'

'Simple greed,' said Malleson casually. 'You can understand that, Kuldip?'

Kuldip nodded firmly.

Malleson smiled. 'He understands that.'

Dermot clasped his hands together and leant forward purposefully. 'We have to set Kline up again. In a way he's got to believe in.'

Malleson grinned. 'I'll send him a couple of my chicks – maybe he'll screw himself to death.'

'You've got a number of...' Dermot paused, not wishing to offend, 'I won't say pimps...'

The black whoremaster waved a generous hand. 'Be my guest, it's all they are.'

'Anyone in particular you rate a little less than price've gold?'

Malleson knew one or even two but made a great show of imitating Rodin's thinker. 'Eerm...' He hesitated.

'Someone not too resolute under pressure, who would shy away from a wave of the whip?'

'I have one guy, sure.'

Dermot smiled and spread his hands. 'Then we are in business, gentlemen.'

All nodded wisely as if they knew what the burly Irishman was on about and what business they were suddenly in. All except Malleson, who requested an explanation, which Dermot was only too pleased to give.

When it was completed Kuldip asked, 'What happens when Kline is overtaken?'

The chairman of the board, austere but elegant in his grey pinstripe, considered then replied gravely, 'Given that outcome I suggest we foreclose on his option to breathe. All in favour say "Aye".'

All shades of opinion around the table agreed 'Aye' and with unity of purpose and policy duly achieved, the meeting adjourned to the nearest drinks cabinet, where all members, with the possible exception of Kuldip, were most happy to toast the newly formed triumvirate and to wish it well in its various undertakings.

*

'You OK, boss?' the dwarf asked.

Kline lifted his head from beside the whisky bottle on the bar.

'Yeh.'

'The other guy, the Asian geezer, he's gone t'use your phone.'

'Right.'

He'd been thinking of the dead girl again, remembering the warm flesh, the brief time they had together before Mallenson took the initiative and killed her without waiting for Rawlinson's orders. Bad enough that, but Kline could still have called it fate if, after waking that first night in Dinah's bed, he had left her sleeping, gathered his clothes, tiptoed across the lino and out and away through her door. That was the course he should have taken but, without a woman for almost three years, he wanted more. So much more. All the fucking he'd had throughout the night and then some more.

Never let your prick rule your head,' Kline muttered to himself. 'Never.'

'What?' enquired Archie. But seeing the set face and abstracted eyes of Kline across the bar top he didn't bother to ask again.

Obvious, so bloody obvious, Kline accused himself for the umpteenth time. The danger to anyone found helping him escape from Rawlinson's clutches was obvious yet he'd chosen to ignore it, at Dinah's peril.

Kline shook his head, tilted it from side to side as if to dislodge a weight of conscience. Failing to do so he concentrated upon the stage, as if a Billy Brody story could ease the burden of his troubles.

The comedian, three parts pissed as usual, was galloping through his Roy Rogers Saga.

'Ey yow, Roy Rogers, I've got a message.'

'Message, sir?' Brody, as Roy Rogers answered himself.

'Ar, seems rustlers've run off with y'herd...'

'Good golly, sir. I must ride home...'

'Wait, Roy, another thing, y'ranch house burned down n'all...'

'Let me go, sir, let me go home to my wife n' family.'

'Just a minute, Roy, y'kids, y'kids were inside... burnt, charred t'death, Roy.'

'My... my wife, sir?'

'She escaped, Roy...'

'Thank the good Lord, sir. I must ride to be at her side in this time've torment...'

'Roy... Roy... she escaped the conflagration but those goldurned rustlers done raped her good then shot her daid.'

The comedian paused for breath, assumed a horror-stricken face, turned an imaginary horse's head and made to exit across the stage and out of town. Then he reined in and turned back to his imaginary tormentor.

'Yuy've no further news t'give, I hope, sir.'

'No, Roy, but me an' the boys were a wonderin' if y' could give us a song before y'go?'

Kline knew the joke. He'd heard Brody tell it better. Idly, he glanced around the grinning punters and noticed the outline of a woman's slim figure in the shadows near the exit adjacent to the stage. In shape and height it could have been Dinah Carmichael. Kline grimaced at the trick of light and shadow but kept his gaze focused upon the unknown woman while Billy Brody introduced the Shadettes' final fling of the evening.

'*Who?*' the Shadettes sang as they thrust three rounded hips at the centre tables.

'*Who?*' they asked the leering punters on their right. Then they swayed across to the left of the stage ready to repeat the themselves in time to the music again.

The boy on the spotlight did his best to follow the bouncing brown bodies across the stage but overcompensated downstage right and for a moment poured white light into a corner of the club and illumined the face and figure of Dinah Carmichael coolly watching the Shadettes start their chassé back towards centre stage.

Kline did not believe in ghosts but he catapulted from his stool and hurriedly made his way down towards the mysterious presence by the door.

A hand caught his arm. He tried to shake it free impatiently.

'Mr Kline,' a voice said.

Kline recognised Khan.

'Later.'

'Now.'

'No.' Kline shook himself free and zigzagged through the tables, just missing a waitress with a tray of newly gathered glasses before he reached the door and found no beautiful brown and breathing body waiting there.

The corridor outside the exit door was empty but Kline went searching along until he reached what had been her dressing-room. For some reason he knocked once before opening the door and half hoped to find that face, gold star on cheek, turned expectantly towards him.

The dressing-room was in darkness. The light when he switched it on revealed only a dirty mirror with a square of intermittently broken bulbs, an empty tissue box, an overturned chair, a rack with a western costume thrown carelessly over and an open wicker laundry skip.

Once Kline had been glad to reach the refuge of this room. Now it seemed like his life, sordid and empty. Kline leaned against the door jamb, closed his eyes, listened to the thump of his heart subside.

Khan found him slumped against the door.

'What is it?'

'Thought I saw Dinah.'

'We put her aboard a plane for Trinidad...' Khan reminded the dejected figure gently. 'She was in her coffin... you saw that for yourself.'

Kline nodded to himself.

'I know... I know.'

'The whisky, perhaps?' Khan suggested.

'Yeh, that's it.'

'Take a room in a hotel,' Khan urged the big man. 'I will pay. Then tomorrow we will meet here and start afresh on establishing your new persona.'

'What?'

'As Rawlinson.'

'Another ghost.'

'Let me give you a lift away from here. Your partner, Dermot, can put the club to bed. Yes? Come on, Mr Kline.'

Khan put an arm about Kline, who shook it off and walked only a little unsteadily alongside the Asian and towards an exit door that opened into the night air.

Khan pushed the bar up and the door rattled open.

'We meet here tomorrow, Mr Kline. Sleep well. We have many mountains to climb if you are to replace Rawlinson.'

Kline said nothing, only walked into the darkness.

Khan, who always took silence for acquiescence, yawned pleasurably and contentedly, more than satisfied with his day's work.

John Kline heard the exit door scrape closed behind him and felt for a moment a sublime pleasure in being where no eyes could see, where no arms could reach. He huddled down among the discarded debris of the Maverick Club and shed his tears of sorrow and self pity. Then he walked away from them and towards the lights that signified the streets of the city.

Chapter Five

Malleson came awake with an ache in his head, a bad taste in his mouth, a throb in his injured hand and a raw, unsatisfied sensation in his groin.

'*Gorjeeze!*' he shouted at the morning light, whose feeble penetration made grey an area of gloom about the barred window of the basement flat.

Beside him a ridge in the bedclothes stirred and Malleson remembered the limp body, cold lips and the hard, unrewarding labour of humping the dry white stick of a woman called Anne Darracott.

'You!' he said accusingly and kicked her pointy bum bone with his big toe.

'Ow!' exclaimed Anne and Malleson in unison. Startled from sleep, the blonde tousled head surfaced angrily.

'What?' Anne said, glaring at the brown face frowning at her.

'Get some bleedin' tea.'

'You said I was t'screw not brew.'

Malleson sighed. 'So I got it wrong. A mistake for which I've paid by producing too much sweat for too little spermatozoa. So Annie, baby, consider your duties reallocated and go get some friggin'…'

Anne felt the foot move back ready to expel her ignominiously from the bed. To avoid this indignity she sat up and swung out of the warmth of the blankets and into the cold morning air.

'Man, you're skinny!' Malleson stated, appraising the bones and angles of her skeleton body and noticing the dark purple blotches that disfigured each inner arm. 'Yes, indeed, Orphan Annie, I doubt if even Belsen would cop f'you.'

Anne said nothing; she had to be careful of this guy who held all the shots available to her. She'd meant to try and please him in the body rubbing stakes the previous night but had lost interest and journeyed instead with the brief phoenix of euphoria that grew from the heroin she had begged from Malleson on his return from Rafiq's house.

'Tea, you said?'

'Right.'

Anne picked up a bedcover that had fallen to the floor and draped it toga-like about her before wandering off into the small kitchen.

The man in the bed watched her trail away, stroked his head, stared up at the ceiling and wondered how best to exploit Orphan Annie.

Maybe she was nothing more than what she seemed, a junkhead. But she had been Rawlinson's secretary-cum-knocking piece. What *had* the dead bossman got out've that tight, dry little crevice. Maybe it was the overall appearance of her. The blonde waif, the underage child thing. Innocence despoiled, all that perv-flage stuff. He'd never catered for that side of the human condition, just the 'Dip-your-wick-it's-paynight brigade' and the 'Hoof and horn can't-get-it-any-other-way trade'. Yeh, he could put this lady to work, for sure. Break her down. Feed her needs; then, if he needed her knowledge or contacts to help his drive to be the best in Brum, he'd know just where to find her and just how to make her talk. He must get up soon – busy-busy day t'come. Malleson smiled to himself as he considered each step of the perfectly feasible if somewhat elaborate plan Dermot Macavoy had devised for the delivery of John Kline.

When Anne brought the mugs of tea in to her lord and master she found him still a-bed and absently clicking the fingers of his good hand to the progression of his thoughts.

'Tea,' she announced and placed the hot base rim of the mug down upon the bare brown chest.

'*Urhh*! You stupid bleedin'... *uh*!'

'Sorry,' Anne said without much sign of contrition. She smiled secretly into the warmth of her heavily sweetened tea, not realising that her slight act of rebellion had hardened Malleson's inclination into a resolve that would find her, that coming night, a resident of what he termed a palace of pleasure but was in fact a crumbling three-storeyed house in Handsworth where girls screwed men for money and paid Malleson for the privilege of doing so.

'Can I have some stuff?' she asked suddenly.

Malleson smiled. 'Course you can, baby.'

It was too easy.

'In return for what? I've money...'

'I told you,' Malleson said patiently. 'We're very primitive. We still use a barter system – y know, one service in exchange for another.'

Anne gave no thought to the implication of this remark; for the moment she only knew she had accomplished an immediate goal.

Putting her mug of tea down she looked around the room eagerly, a child agog to find a hidden present.

Malleson said nothing but pointed a long forefinger towards a cabinet containing record albums and piled cassette tapes.

The waif, unable to contain herself, ran to the stacked tape boxes and hunted down their number until she found one that contained not a coil of brown recording tape but enough grains of white skag for a day's supply. She tested the drug by taste and then felt a surge of elation. That guy Malleson was all right.

'Thanks,' she said gratefully.

'That's OK, orphan Annie,' Malleson said smoothly. 'You go to that bathroom and get your little self all fixed up. Then maybe Daddy'll let you come out with him for walkies.'

Anne nodded, now only too happy to do his bidding.

Watching her hurry away Malleson smiled to himself; already he was in front – a new whore for his stable and he hadn't even got up from bed yet. It was a good omen. Yeh, yeh. That bastard Kline's luck will have to be more than just good to hold out against mine today, thought Malleson as he sat up and swung himself out of the big bed.

On reaching the Maverick that afternoon Kline had been surprised to find Khan not yet arrived. Dermot was, however, in attendance and Kline caught up with his partner in their office.

Something bothered Kline. What?

'C'mere, Dermot.' Kline beckoned his partner.

Worriedly the Irishman came across then frowned in puzzlement as Kline sniffed at him in intimate proximity.

There was the fragrance of exhaled lunchtime Guinness, a surface aroma of Brut aftershave from the broad expanse of chin but not the scent of musk that permeated the office.

Then Kline remembered.

'Dinah's perfume. Why can I smell it in here?'

'I dunno, do I...' Dermot spread his hands. 'Unless, oh yeh, I've just had a bird in askin' about the stripper spot...'

'What did she look like?'

'Oh, more brown than black, big tits, tight little arse on her, like the two halves of the same apple...'

'I meant her face.'

'I dunno.' Dermot gestured vaguely, his interest waning. 'She wore dese big shades an'... an' a turban thing... Ah, who th'hell looks at a stripper's face, f'Chrissake?'

'You give her the job?' Kline asked, wishing he had never started the conversation.

'No. I'd already booked Julie Del Roi. She's put on weight but...'

'OK,' said Kline, deciding on an explanation of mere coincidence. 'F'get it.'

'This black bint left her name an'number... Where? Over there...' Dermot pointed.

Kline picked up the sheet of notepaper from the edge of the desk indicated and read the name and number.

Dermot saw the expression of shock come to his partner's face.

'What... *what*?'

Silently Kline handed the paper across.

Dermot glanced down at the name and telephone number written there.

'Dinah Carmichael!' he yelped in surprise. 'She's dead, int she?'

'That's right,' answered Kline coldly.

Each man looked in puzzlement at the other then turned to gaze at the large publicity photograph that displayed the dead stripper more or less naked, retaining only a wisp of veil and white stockings and suspenders from her bridal strip routine.

The two men stared at her image on the wall. The dark eyes returned their stare, mocking her trade then and haunting Kline now.

Dermot shivered. 'What's it mean, John?'

'Let's find out...' Kline said, picking up the nearest telephone and dialling the number scrawled on the paper.

The *burr-burr* tone sounded again and again, its constant pulse denying the opportunity to speak the name on the paper and hear a husky voice say, 'Speaking'.

Finally Kline lost patience with himself and the situation, banged down the receiver and turned on Macavoy.

'C'mon, babes, we've other things t'do today besides piss about with practical jokes. I want the accounts I didn't see yesterday. Also, I want a rundown from you on each and every bouncer we employ. I'm looking to pick a team of guys who don't mind how they earn some extra change. Tell those interested they'll be expected to guard my person and help me settle my score with Malleson. OK?'

Dermot rubbed his chin. 'Fine, John, fine, will do.' He didn't like the sudden snap of authority in the Kline sod's voice. It meant trouble for everyone.

The Irish eyes tried to express only goodwill to all his best buddy's schemes. It wasn't easy; the resentment glinted through.

'You seen Malleson lately?' Kline asked suddenly.

'No!' Dermot said indignantly.

'Not yesterday or last night?'

'Dear God, no. I was out on club business. Fixing strippers. Do us a favour, John – I mean, that *coon* an' me... me who's tryin' t'reclaim the Maverick for the white races. Why would I mix with the likes a him?'

Kline nodded slowly. 'So if I wanted to move against him, you'd be willing to lend support?'

'Course I would, Johnny, course. Just say where and when...' Dermot answered, confident that if his gambit worked that night the only service required of him would be as a pall bearer at Kline's funeral.

'OK. Good,' said Kline.

Macavoy rubbed his big hands together.

'Now then, you were wantin' t'cast y'eye over the books?'

Not if you want to show me them, Kline thought, but said, 'Yeh, right,' then sat down at a desk purposefully.

There was something he did not fancy about all this. Not just the seeming purposelessness of the Dinah re-incarnation but also the sly jauntiness of manner that Dermot unconsciously displayed.

'Here y'gi,' Macavoy announced and dumped three years' accumulation of accounts almost into the lap of his partner.

'Thanks,' acknowledged Kline wryly then coughed at a catch of dust from the mound of paper before him.

In the small interview room at the back of the Birmingham police building, Mangit, an attractive Indian woman in her early twenties, adjusted the lower folds of her peach-coloured sari and tried to find a comfortable position on a hard wooden chair.

Small-boned and fine-featured, her beauty was of a kind that appealed to western eyes rather than Asian. Sometimes she suspected her husband worried about the whispers from her village about the possibility of mixed blood in her ancestry, and although he denied that this was so, Mangit sometimes thought that he would have preferred his marriage to have been arranged with a girl who, on reaching maturity, would have been unremarkable and hence nearer to the mould of Punjabi womanhood.

Thinking of her husband made Mangit's apprehension at being brought to this place all the greater. She thought of how her children would discover that their mother was a thief. To avert her thoughts from such disgrace she took from inside her bodice the airmail letter from India and began to read it once again.

She had reached no further than the second line, which read 'You must send more money', when there was a sound of voices outside the door.

Hurriedly, Mangit concealed the letter in the moist palm of her hand.

The interview room door opened and the immaculately dressed figure of Zaheer Mohammed Khan entered. The Pakistani man and the Indian woman stared for a moment at each other.

'You were Jashir Singh Mahall's wife?' he started.

'*Am* his wife.'

'Yes.' Khan paused. 'The shop owner will not take this shoplifting matter any further. I have talked to him.'

Mangit said nothing, cast her eyes modestly down away from the handsome policeman before her.

'You receive money from the state?' Khan asked.

The woman shook her head firmly.

'From work?'

A nod.

'Why steal food when you could buy?'

Mangit lifted her head.

'My husband was sent back to India by immigration authorities. He cannot get work. I have to send money earned from my job to him.'

Khan remembered the Sikh's deportation for illegal entry. Recalled Jashir's last frantic wave towards the observation platform, to this wife of his and their two children. Little wonder he should be upset at being wrenched away from such an attractive woman. Khan concentrated his thoughts back into official channels.

'I looked for you after he was sent away but you had moved your address. Where did you go to?'

'Cousins. They put up with poor relations for a while and then they say you and children must go.'

Khan nodded. 'What will you do now?'

Mangit looked to the one forlorn hope in her present life. 'Wait for my husband to return to us here.'

'How can he?' Khan asked, puzzled.

The woman made no reply but transferred her gaze from Khan to her hands clasped together.

Khan moved a step nearer to the seated woman and looked down upon the lustrous head of black hair.

'Mangit... how?'

The head lifted, the dark eyes stared up at him.

'He will, you see,' she said with certainty. 'The same way as he entered last time. It gives him hope and me too. Hope that he will be meeting up with the men who betrayed him to the immigration officials.'

'Why not join your husband in India?'

'To starve?' Mangit tightened her lips and spread them into a hard, bitter little smile. 'It is better this way. Even if Jashir does not succeed it will be something if he manages to kill some of the people who have brought this thing to us.'

Khan glanced at his watch. 'What are their names?' he enquired.

'Rafiq, Kuldip...' Mangit paused and spat the final name contemptuously across the bare room, 'and *you,* Mr Khan.'

The last of the chosen bouncers shouldered into the Maverick office. Kline looked them over as Dermot rapidly introduced each member of the squad. Jackman, Pollard, Frampton, Miller, Gary, Sturt.

All nodded with the exception of the last named, who held his voice box to his throat and vibrated a resounding 'PLEASED-TA-MEETCHA.'

'Shuttit,' said Dermot, from force of habit, before launching himself into a fulsome speech of welcome that introduced Kline to all present.

He did not know what to say about Khan lounging there in the bleedin' corner as if he owned the joint, so he said nothing.

'…John Kline!' Dermot finally concluded, giving what little floor there was left to the tall man in grey who lounged back in the boss's chair behind the big main desk.

Kline stood up and walked around the desk in order to inspect the calibre of each recruit Dermot had brought before him.

Watching his partner make his silent tour of assessment, Khan made a mental tally of all the battle scars visible along the lineup of battered bouncer faces.

Khan counted four split eyebrows, three drooping eyelids, two broken noses, one shattered cheekbone, a newly stitched jowl and a cut-throat whose throat had apparently once been cut.

Looking at the assembled bunch of heavies as a whole, the agent was reminded of the Duke of Wellington's famous remark about not knowing if his men scared the enemy but by God they certainly frightened him.

'OK,' Kline said at the end of the inspection parade.

'Relax… smoke… Here, help y'self t'cigars…'

Watching the thick fingers diminishing the contents of a box of Dermot's cigars, Kline ordered his thoughts. When the cigars were alight, when all eyes were upon him, he began his speech.

'I brought you guys here tonight to hear a few things from the horse's mouth. First, I'm back to stay. No more runnin'. I've decided everyone in this town has me tagged killer so I've decided to act like one.'

'How, like?' asked Dermot with a jangle of alarm sounding in his head.

'Like *Rawlinson*…' Kline smiled at the sudden attention of all staff in the room. 'That punk had this town sewn up tighter than a Jew's purse. He could do it, so can I. Right?'

No one answered, though Dermot shuffled a little then muttered, 'Lot've people want t'run this town, black, white and khaki.'

Kline folded his arms, smiled with confidence, then rapped out, 'To get into prostitution I need only take Malleson over. Drugs I don't know but I will. Gambling, pornography, protection and all the bread and butter stuff, from scrap metal to the passing of stolen goods, is down for takeover by a team of talents led by me.'

'An' him?' said Dermot, jerking a thumb at Khan.

'Him I need for what our brown brothers call the Blackbird run. The illegal immigrant area. Khan works f'me. He takes his orders from me. You all see sense, all of you will take the gospel only from me!'

At this climax of egocentricity someone shouted, 'Yeah,' and the heavy ranks heaved and jostled each other with some enthusiasm.

Realising what the moment required, Dermot thrust himself forward as if propelled by a surge of fervent emotion.

'John... John... put it *there*! I'm proud t'shake the hand of a man with guts in his belly. I'm proud t'follow you, proud t'help, proud t'act in any capacity y'care t'name!'

'OK, Dermot, y'know what they say about pride...' Kline replied dryly as the Irishman tried to wring one last brotherly squeeze from his right hand.

Macavoy relinquished his handclasp with Kline and glanced around the faces in the room.

'I take it youse boys're happy t'find y'selves founder members of my friend Johnny's little firm?'

Some of the mob nodded. Dermot frowned then remembered the procedure for such matters.

'All in favour say "Aye".'

'Aye!' every bouncer bar one shouted.

'Sturt?' Dermot warned.

'OHAYE,' said the voice box as its owner suddenly remembered where he had last heard that word 'aye' shouted in that sort of unison.

'John...' Dermot said humbly, 'let me be the one to organise the ranks for y'...'

Kline hesitated.

'Y'know y'c'n trust me now,' Dermot wheedled with a sly glance at the scatter of account sheets on the desk.

Kline nodded.

'You got the job, Dermot.'

'You won't find y'selves the losers, and dat's a promise,' said Dermot as the members of the new team filed past him and out of the office.

When the last man, Sturt, had shambled out into the corridor, Dermot summoned up one last gush of reassurance for the new gang leader.

'Y've made the right decision, John. Y'c'n trust me t'look after y'interests, hope y'know dat.'

Kline waited until the door closed then said cynically, 'I'd sooner trust my balls to a barracuda.'

'Don't underestimate the Irishman,' Khan said cautiously.

Kline relaxed, lit a cigar. 'How'd it sound?'

Khan rose from his corner, stiffened to attention and straightened his right arm into a fascist salute.

'*Schön, Mein Fuhrer.*'

Then he clicked his heels as Kline bowed in acknowledgement of the apparent success of their charade.

Chapter Six

In the darkness of a small shabby room in Malleson's house of pleasure the woman came awake and waited for the slight sway of her houseboat as it reacted to the waters of the canal. But the bed remained still and the dark room became a thing of menace as she remembered Malleson's words: 'You've a habit to support, I've a living to make.' Then he had thrust her inside while his henchmen sniggered and looked her over with eyes that showed only contempt.

What would she be required to do to qualify for life support? Prostitution. What form, with whom, for what and how often? The woman on the bed began to cry, but no tears came though her eyelids clenched and her thin body shook as with a fever.

When the dry sobs subsided the itching began to intrude upon her flesh. Hoping to frighten the ants away Anne reached for a bedside light, clicked a switch across and lit not the bedside lamp but a red spotlight in the ceiling that bathed the bed on which she lay in a circle of blood.

To Anne it was as if a pail of offal had been emptied upon her. Screaming and rubbing her skin in an effort to remove imagined stains, she ran from the ruby red pool of light that covered the bed.

At the door, the handle rattled but the tenon of the lock held tight and when she hammered at the wooden panels they hurt her fists. When she cried out for help and asked to be allowed to return to the world, no one answered, only the beat-beat of her heart that echoed somewhere down deep in the old house from where a pulse of reggae music could just be heard.

Anne turned back to the room, pressed herself against the door, slid down, hunched up and began to cry salt tears, as might a child who found herself locked inside a cupboard to which no one had a key.

*

The reception room on the ground floor of the brothel contained much of Malleson's pride and investment. He was proud of the deep-purple carpeting, the black leather and chrome-framed furniture, the expanse of mirrored panelling and the recently installed Bang and Olufsen stereo system on which the sounds of Bob Marley's 'War' came throbbing and wailing through.

It was the slack, quiet time of the early evening when the girls would be resting, gossiping, sleeping, fixing and flexing for the rigours and passions of the pay night to come.

Madam Eva eased herself unobtrusively into the chair that was sited inside the reception room but close enough to the door to give a view of stairs, hallway and the entrance from the street. Once possessed of striking looks, Madam now wore a mask of make-up and had seen her once slim body disappear beneath a fall of fat. It toppled from her chins, cascaded into the slopes of breast then spread to the ultimate girth of hip and buttock before sweeping into plump thighs that merged into surprisingly shapely legs, which supported both her bulk and her assertion that once her shape had been something to see and sell dearly.

As she settled herself her 'nephew', Denny, tall, thin, in his early twenties, entered flicking a duster first to one side then the other. Madam, noticing Malleson in conference with his assistants in a corner of the room, motioned Denny not to intrude but to busy himself in tidying the salon.

'Midnight, no sooner an' certainly no later,' instructed Malleson. 'You make the Maverick. Head for the main corridor, go down it 'till you find a door marked "Manager". Open that door. The office'll be empty. So will a side drawer on the desk opposite; put the package into this drawer, clear?'

Pitt, young, black, pulled at the peak of his baseball cap uneasily and stared at the small oblong parcel in apprehension.

'What I do then, boss?'

At Malleson's shoulder, Hunniford sniggered. 'Get your arse out've there, baby.'

'Yeh,' Malleson said casually. 'There's a delivery of goodies at Snow Hill Station t'morrow night at eight. I want you t'be still in one piece t'help collect it, 'kay?'

Pitt, already sweating, nodded.

Bryden pursed his lips seductively as Madam's nephew fluttered by.

Hunniford looked towards the door past Madam in the hope of espying passing pussy.

Malleson concentrated upon the unhappy Pitt then set the trap for Kline in motion by waving a hand of dismissal.

Watching the youth carefully carrying the brown paper package away, Hunniford said – not very originally – 'Wouldn't fancy being inside his shoes t'night, man. '

Malleson grinned. 'Or his underpants, given his usual loss of bottle at the first pinch of pressure.'

'Kline'll take him apart,' Bryden stated.

'Let us hope so, brother,' Malleston said, moving to adjust the balance between speakers on his beloved hi-fi. 'Let us sincerely hope that Mr Bastard Kline does precisely that.'

Kline watched the stripper Julie Del Roi. Dressed in hunting pink coat, black stockings, riding boots, Julie pranced to and fro on the stage riding a cock horse suggestively up and down between her naked plump thighs.

'I'll get that horse its penicillin jab,' an Irish accent sounded down his ear.

Kline nodded. ' 'Kay, Dermot.' He didn't bother to turn his head as his partner moved away towards the swing doors that led to the main corridor.

Now then, Kline thought, looking at the emerging flesh of Miss Del Roi, who had dismounted from the stick horse and was divesting herself of her outward garments at a seductive rate. Thing was, Kline paused, how much do I need that piece of arse up there? Maybe enough to...? He became aware of the metallic Dalek voice grating away beside him.

'OFFICE-MR KLINE-NIG-NOG-IN-SUSSY-CIRCS.'

'What?'

Sturt pointed towards the swing doors and then followed his own instructions. Kline sighed. Pushing himself away from the bar, he acknowledged the free fall of Julie's white, pink-tipped mamelons and followed the solid figure of Sturt through the exit and down the corridor towards his office.

Inside, he found an assorted group of Dermot, Khan, Sturt and another bewhiskered bouncer, Gary, who held a young, terrified black up against the wall by means of a forearm held firm across a windpipe.

'What's happenin'?'

Cary eased the pressure on the black throat and cleared his own.

'Ermm, Dermot... Mr Macavoy, that is, asked us to keep an eye out for loiterers, like, n'I copped this 'un sneakin' in 'ere, like. So I waited f' 'im t'come out so I could jump 'im... which I did...'

'That's how I found them,' Dermot said.

'OK.' Kline went across to the young man pinioned against the wall and indicated that the pressure should be relaxed.

Pitt straightened his baseball cap, rubbed his throat, croaked out, 'Lookin' f'the toilet, any harm in that?'

Before Kline could reply Cary said, 'Not sure if he didn't 'ave some sort've parcel with him when he come in 'ere, Mr Kline.'

Khan frowned. 'Not when he came out?'

'No.'

Suddenly the mood of those in the office became less relaxed.

'You been plantin' anti-personnel devices, matey?' Kline asked the scared youth, who shook his head but without total conviction.

'Keys, Dermot,' Kline snapped authoritatively, then, conversationally, said to Pitt, 'Not that I don't believe you but I'd like to take a look around outside. You won't mind if we leave you locked in here f'a while, will you?'

The eyes in the brown perspiring face moved one way then the other as Kline took the office and safe keys from Dermot and ushered the personnel from the office.

'Shouldn't be more than an hour or two,' Kline said, cool and detached as he closed the door on the hapless Pitt.

Left alone in the empty office, Pitt shook the sweat from his brow and with dithering fingers pulled back his left sleeve to catch sight of his wrist watch. It was twenty-one minutes past midnight, twenty-one minutes past safety. Waves of panic crashed and pounded inside his head, driving him towards the door, there to hammer and hammer for release.

'Room service,' said Kline, poking his head into the office.

'There... there!' Pitt squealed. 'Over there, side drawer, bottom!'

Kline went to the drawer indicated and eased it open. Saw the brown paper parcel and carefully lifted it out.

'Knife, he said to Khan, who had followed Kline back into the office.

Silently Khan handed across his pocket knife and watched as the tall figure of Kline stooped over the desk and adroitly cut the string wrapping to reveal a shoebox that was then shown to contain a battery, with coils of wire, sticks of gelignite, all attached to a ticking clock mechanism whose alarm was set for thirty minutes past the hour of midnight.

'A bomb, Mr Kline?'

'Nothing but, Mr Khan.'

'Live?'

'Ticking over,' Kline replied absently, trying to remember past instruction in disarming such explosive devices.

Anxiously, Khan watched Kline move the knife towards a connecting lead.

'Should not one leave the handling of such devices to more expert hands?' he suggested.

It was a simple mechanism but effective enough to destroy the office and all inside.

'I've handled this type before in Ulster,' Kline explained. 'But move yourself and the rest out've range.'

Khan nodded, took Pitt by the arm and was about to lead him away when Kline said, without looking up, 'Not him. If I'm to blow skywards I'd like him along as company.'

'See you soon, I hope, Mr Kline,' Khan said as he released the trembling arm of Pitt and withdrew, closing the door carefully and quietly behind him.

Pitt was too terrified to breathe, even to move. He thought of that roar, that searing blast, the heat, the sight of limbs separated from a body, his body. Pitt closed his eyes and swore to whichever spirit might hear that he would atone if only given one more chance.

On the desk top, Kline had decided which wires led where and to what connections.

Gently he placed the point of the knife blade into one slotted screw head and began to turn its thread slowly to free it of contact with the wire that linked the clock with the bound gelignite sticks. To calm his fingers, he talked casually to the petrified youth behind him.

'If I succeed in disarming this little fella, you an' I are going to get our heads together, so gather y'thoughts. If I do a butterfingers they'll be gathering up more than our thoughts.

'You've got to be from Malleson...' Kline realised the clock was still ticking away despite the release of what should have been the connecting wire – nasty. There had to be another. Kline's eyes scanned the jumble of wires, trying not to become transfixed by the inexorable movement of the main finger towards the half hour past midnight when the alarm would sound not with a ring but a roar of detonation. Ah, there – the knife blade dipped in again and began to turn as Kline started the opening sentences of what could be his last speech.

'Where were we? Malleson. I'm becoming more and more anxious to meet... to meet that guy... perhaps you will be able to suggest the best place to surprise him?' There was no more time. This *had* to be the right wire. 'OK, babes, here we go. Say your prayers, shake hands with the devil...'

The silence after Kline loosened the wire was blissful for both men. Breathing deeply, John Kline took up the shoe box, crossed past the swaying Pitt to the door and banged once with the flat of his hand.

After a pause, Khan appeared.

'Here,' said Kline, pushing the silent shoe box with its contents at the Asian. It's all yours. I'd like t'know everything you can find out about it. Fingerprints, the full SP.'

'All right, John?' Dermot asked as he came back into the office.

'Yeh.'

'Was there a bomb?'

Kline looked at the black. 'Timed to go off just as we'd be thinkin' about cashin' up.'

'Black bastard!' Dermot spat, and backhanded the bomber across the mouth.

Flattened against the wall, lower lip cut inside and bleeding, Pitt regarded the hard-set faces that stared their loathing of him.

'What's y'name?' Kline asked.

'Uh!'

'Mr Uh has promised to converse with me about matters of mutual interest,' Kline said with a glance at Khan.

'Did Malleson send you, shine?' Dermot said pugnaciously.

Receiving no reply, the Irishman raised his fist again, which brought the feeble denial of 'Who's Malleson?'

Kline sighed. 'Don't be difficult' was what he was about to say when from the tannoy came not the usual farts and crackles but a high pitched, nerve-grinding whine.

'What's that, Dermot?'

'The engineer. Silly sod f'gets... I'll switch...'

'No, leave it.' Kline remembered where last he had heard such a sound. In the interrogation unit at Long Kesh.

Picking up the keys and opening the safe he took out a black sacking bag used for holding banknotes.

'C'mere, babes.' He beckoned Pitt across the office.

With the help of a rough hand the black was brought face to face with Kline.

With a series of swift decisive movements, Kline hooded Pitt with the black sacking bag, turned him about towards the wall, spread the arms, pushed the body forward, and spread the legs apart so that Pitt could only retain a precarious balance by resting against the wall on splayed fingers.

Kline took a tissue from a box on Dermot's desk, ripped it apart and rolled each section into a tight plug. Before placing a plug in either ear he leant into the hooded figure.

'I hate all this and you will too, but when you're ready t'chat, just raise your arm and y'll be restored t'the wonderful world of sight n'sound.'

The figure at the wall said nothing. The whine grew ever more intense to the unprotected ear. Khan drifted into the corridor. Dermot indicated by mime he was going for a drink and left, well pleased at the outcome of events.

With the door closed the noise seemed to reverberate and grow ever more penetrating. It was bad enough through the wads of tissue that half protected Kline's hearing; for the man cut off from sight and dominated by the high level of jarring sound it was infinitely worse. Pitt swayed against his aching fingers and wondered how he could possibly be expected to hold on.

Seated at the point furthest from the source of the sound, Kline watched the quivering muscles in the spread legs. He had hated this technique in the army but had carried it through then. Now, when his own life had been attacked, now he would use the techniques he knew to obtain the information that would enable him to strike back at Pitt's bossman, Malleson.

*

'Bring my clothes,' Malleson ordered.

Obediently the girl got up from the bed and gathered the dandy's attire, carefully laying each item in sequence of dressing.

From the bed Malleson watched the flow of red hair down the naked white back and tight, pale, slightly parted arse; he liked the style of this one. What was the name she'd given? Claire. Young and fresh and all of fourteen years, she had been on the run from an approved school and had been given shelter and passed along to Malleson's house for breaking in. Now, with this task accomplished, it was time to move along. Lazily Malleson stretched out a brown arm to lift his Omega watch. Jesus! It was a quarter to one! Flinging the covers aside hurriedly he took his clothes from the startled girl and began to dress rapidly, thinking all the while of whether he could make it home before Kline came looking for him.

Anne Darracott listened to the noises of the house. The comings and goings. The heavy feet ascending and descending wooden stairs. The grunts, groans, laughter, argument. The rhythm of sexual endeavour transmitted through the ceiling above. And always there was the distant music below sounding like the beat of a distant heart. She had called for a while. Someone had mimicked her cry for help once but that was hours ago. Now she was in the drowsy yen period before the bad times of withdrawal really began. Sleepily, she yawned, rose stiffly from her crouched position at the door, drifted across the thin, worn carpet and lay down across the width of the bed and opened herself to the baleful scrutiny of the red eye that glared down from above.

Two floors below in the hallway, Malleson instructed Hunniford of the care to be afforded Anne Darracott, while Bryden tipsily stood nearby, attempting to don his jacket and drink a tumbler of scotch at one and the same time.

'Let the blonde bitch sweat f'a few hours. Then fix her up. Madam knows where the stash is.'

Hunniford nodded. He fancied being in charge of that snooty lady very much.

'Keep an eye out for Kline. Doubt if he'll attack here. But who knows what classified level of information Pitt'll give him. Anyway, keep the door bolted. Telephone for help if necessary, 'kay?'

Hunniford nodded. Bryden, with a whisky-sodden sleeve, tried to

Vendetta

look as if he understood what was happening.

'C'mon, Bonny.' Malleson tugged his arm, unlinked the chain across the heavy front door and thrust Bryden in the direction of the darkened streets of Handsworth.

Hunniford bid his boss goodnight, hooked the chain across the door and considered what he most wanted to do. He had saved his energies for just the possibilities that had now been tossed his way. OK. Soon enough every dude with a fiver would be riding her ladyship to oblivion. He'd slide into her saddle first. Yeh.

Already feeling a stir of anticipation Hunniford walked purposefully towards the stairs.

The hooded figure at the wall shook its head from side to side. Kline watched. The whine went on.

Inside the black hood Pitt felt lost in a world of screaming noise that would not let him think one thing. He could not remember anything, not even how he was supposed to signal to stop the torturing sound that grated through him. Pitt tried to concentrate. To feel. To think. But all was scattered, jumbled, frightening. Pitt felt a sob lump up in his throat.

He tried to hold it down but it fought its way out. He contained the next but then the sobs came up and out, up and out... until all at once there was a blinding glare of white neon light and deliverance from the tyranny of sound.

In the silence the eyes of the young, disorientated black jerked about trying to focus, his mind trying to decide what it was the tall white guy now staring at him had wanted.

'Where can I find Malleson?'

That was it.

'Now or... or tomorrow night?' Pitt said dully.

'Both.'

'OK.'

The music from the salon stereo was late night mood stuff of the James Last vintage that Madam much preferred. Not that she could hear it for the whining voice of the Brummy who stood before her perch complaining that his needs had been too zealously attended to and that a precipitate end had been attained that was of less duration than he had anticipated.

'Short times short as you make it,' Madame said succinctly. 'S'up t'yow t'control y'bollacks, not come cryin' f'a refund...'

'Bollacks, t'you, Madam!' the Brummy said, turning away sourly to survey the group of girls, black, brown, white, who stared at the spent punter without interest.

In the far corner, a Pakistani whose wife was far away in a village across the sea tried without success to raise the head of his companion, who had succumbed to the joys of Brew Eleven before sampling the pleasures of the flesh.

'Bollacks to you, ladies, bollacks to you, gentlemen, and bollacks to all creatures in between,' the punter said at the sight of Denny flapping towards him.

'See y'next week,' Madam said impassively as the punter was ushered to the front door by a reproving Denny, who disliked common language.

When they reached the front door, the punter was searching for a suitable parting insult concerning the propensities of hermaphrodites to onanism but it wouldn't come out right.

'Come on, dear, you've had your five penneth,' Denny said, impatiently holding the door open.

'Go fuck yourself' was what the punter was about to pronounce when from outside came a rush of rough men in evening dress who thrust punter and ponce aside and charged into the reception room, there to be confronted by an indignant Madam Eva, who trembled from jowl to belly with outrage.

'How dare you enter here!'

'Where's Malleson?' Kline asked, taking in the room and its occupants.

'Not here, this is...'

'A respectable whorehouse, sure.'

Kline turned, Madam tried to protest but was thrust aside.

'You...' Kline indicated Sturt. 'Come with me. You an' him...' This taking in Dermot and Cary. 'You can do a demolition job down here.'

'Right,' said Cary, who enjoyed the destruction of other people's property.

Shit, thought Dermot to himself, Malleson is going to love this turn up. But there was no choice, knowing Kline's mood, so he upended a settee, which deposited a bunch of fillies arse over tip into a screaming, yelling scrum of bare bums and split beavers.

Kline, with Sturt following, raced towards the stairs.

'Stop!' said Denny imperiously, barring their way. 'You can't go up there!'

Surprised, Kline paused, raised a fist. 'Why?'

'People are busy...' Denny said in tremulous explanation, but seeing the determination on the butch face before him, he added weakly, 'Be discreet then,' and stepped aside.

As Kline and Sturt reached the first landing the sounds of destruction grew from the reception room below, culminating in a shattering crescendo when Cary put the stereo deck to his shoulder and hurled it against the centre of the mirrored panelling with all the force he could muster.

In the first room that Kline entered, he interrupted a round of reverse pleasure.

Through the arch of spread legs of what was obviously a female, an irate red male face glared out at Kline.

'Sorry to interrupt y'meal,' Kline said and shut the door.

Across the hall Sturt came out of another room. Kline caught a glimpse of black and white bodies busily enmeshed.

'NEVER-EVEN-NOTICED-ME!' said Sturt into his voice tube, grinning broadly and closing the door on the interlocked couple.

The next room was empty and its opposite number across the landing contained only a sleepy little girl who rubbed her eyes and said, 'Where's Mamma?'

'Go to sleep. It's nothing to worry about,' Kline said gently as the child turned over and settled again into her sleep.'

On the second floor, there was a room where a lady gave a gentleman a geography lesson by means of a trip around the world; another room where exhaustion had set in; and finally Kline recognised a naked black, pumping up and down on an anonymous passive white lady whose features Kline had no opportunity to examine for Hunniford effected a speedy withdrawal and launched an attack by vaulting from the rumpled bed and hurling himself against John Kline.

'Always thought you were a prick,' said Kline and hit Hunniford a blow to the belly that took the remaining starch out of what remained of that gentleman's erection.

Hunniford shook his head, came back jabbing, punching, hooking in at Kline, who grabbed at the sweating, slippery torso and tried to manoeuvre an advantage.

Anne, seeing the open door, decided on a run for freedom which coincided with Hunniford freeing himself. Kline, off balance, was unable to prevent Hunniford halting the woman's escape by means of a backhander that sent her crashing and screaming against a wardrobe.

The shift of Hunniford's attention gave Kline the chance to recover and mount an attack whose impetus and impact sent Hunniford reeling back to make sickening contact with his head against the wall. When his senses started to clear Kline had one strong hand on his scalp, the other under his chin and was seemingly intent on twisting in opposite directions with the object of breaking the attachment of Hunniford's skull from his spine.

'Malleson here?' Kline brought out from between clenched teeth. 'Uh… uh?'

'*No!*' yelped the black, frightened at the sudden jerk of painful pressure. 'Just gone… Just… home… Gone home.'

With the neck so twisted, it would have been simple to make it go *crack*! Kline resisted the temptation but relieved his frustration by ensuring, by means of his knee, that no further sexual pleasure would be enjoyed by Hunniford that night or the next.

It was time to scarper before reinforcements came running. Kline stepped over the groaning, retching man at his feet and made towards the doorway. As he went out of the room he heard a woman's voice call chokingly from the room behind.

'Kline?'

Who would know his name here? And that voice…

Kline returned to the room as the tousled blonde head came around the foot of the bed. The hair was stained with sweat. The eyes sunken in the wan face were full of tears. From the nose a trickle of blood and mucus dribbled down to lips made swollen by the blow recently suffered.

'Please… please!' the hoarse voice jerked out.

With a sense of shock he realised who this was. Difficult to believe that the cool, beautiful, assured blonde who had engineered their first meeting was now this naked, distraught creature crawling towards him across the dirty carpet.

Anne looked up, pleading for his recognition to restore even the memory of who she once was.

'Anne,' she said. 'It's Anne.'

'I remember,' Kline said and offered her his hand.

Chapter Seven

Khan nosed his yellow Datsun into a parking space opposite the big gate of Winson Green Prison. Beside him Kline seemed preoccupied. He was thinking of Anne Darracott.

'I took her back t'that boat've hers...' he said suddenly. 'I thought maybe she'd have some junk stashed there. She didn't. She just got worse n'worse. Mainlinin' right down into hell. Y'd never believe a human body could throw off so much sweat, bring up so much vomit, suffer so much pain. I couldn't stand it so I brought her to the All Saints Drug Rehabilitation Unit.'

'It's just down the road,' Khan said gently, thinking to encourage the man beside him towards a relationship that could bring information. The pale, blonde ex-secretary must have known of the uses to which corrupt money had been put across the Midlands by her old boss Rawlinson.

'And Malleson?' he asked. 'Missed the twat by a minute.'

'I've arranged for last night's would-be bomber to be looked after for a few days. I believe he intends to leave Birmingham in order to escape from Malleson's anger. He's really quite grateful to you, Mr Kline, for giving him the chance at a new start.'

'The bouncers at the club think we took him for a swim in a cement waistcoat.'

'Let them.'

Kline nodded absently. His thoughts and eyes were on the prison in which he had spent almost three years of his life.

Anything was better than a return through that gate. Even if it meant playing puppet to a master from the Security Service. Kline cleared his throat, turned back to Khan.

'Malleson's expecting a consignment of something worth more'n fifteen guineas an ounce. Brown Bomber said he thinks it's to be passed over tonight at a disused railway station called Snow Hill.'

'It must be cocaine.'

'That's not bad.' Kline acknowledged the pun and threw in a few of his own. 'So, if we've made the right connections, Malleson's tracks n'mine are due t'cross t'night, right?'

'Yes. It will go some way to creating the gangster image we need for you to attract the attention of the consortium of oh so dishonourable men.'

'Anything on the bomb?'

'Not yet.'

'One other thing.' Kline felt for the slip of paper in his jacket pocket, smoothed it out. Read the name Dinah Carmichael and the telephone number written alongside. It still didn't make sense. 'Can you use your influence with the hidden powers of government to find an address or who pays the bill on that number now?'

Khan took the scrap of paper, read it with some surprise.

'Some black chick left it at the Maverick. I'd like to meet up with her.'

'Ah...'

'To kick her arse not to screw it.'

'I'll check it out it out.'

'Fine. I'd better get this visit over. See you.'

Kline ducked out of the car. Glanced once more at the prison gate across the way, said 'Bollocks' to the world, the gate and the prison beyond and made his way down towards the gates of All Saints Hospital and its Drug Rehabilitation Unit.

In the car, after watching the tall figure stride away, Khan looked again at the slip of paper Kline had given him and began to wonder, not about dead Dinah Carmichael but about the Indian woman he had recently interviewed, the Sikh's wife, Mangit. I must pursue my enquiries, discover if her husband really did plan a return to exact revenge. Yes. It was his duty. Khan started up his car and waited for a gap to appear in the stream of traffic, a small unconscious smile of anticipated pleasure showing on his handsome brown face.

'Relationship to patient?' the nurse at the desk questioned.

Kline frowned. He couldn't think.

'Friend?' the nurse suggested.

Why not. 'OK.' Kline shrugged.

'I think you can perhaps visit briefly. I'll see.'

The nurse disappeared. As doors opened Kline thought he heard a shrill defiant voice crying out in refusal, but he couldn't be certain that it was the voice of Anne Darracott until the nurse reappeared wearing a faint smile of apology.

'I'm awfully sorry, Mr Kline. Miss Darracott is being a little wayward. The doctor thinks perhaps your visit would be more valuable at a later time.'

Kline wondered why he had bothered to get involved in the first place.

'I'll call again, if I can. Tell her I came today just to, y'know, see how she was and...'

Kline paused not knowing what else there was to say.

'I'll tell her.'

Still Kline hesitated, not knowing why he felt a reluctance to leave.

'She's OK?'

'Yes. It's a resistance to the idea of an ordered course of treatment. Quite usual.'

'But voluntary – she doesn't have to stay?'

'Any patient can leave anytime.'

She probably didn't want to see him anyway. Kline raised a hand to the nurse and went from the reception area, pausing only to step aside at the door as a taut, tense young man, sweating, pushed past and approached the desk.

'Hello, Stephen...' he heard the nurse greet what must have been a former resident. Then he was out into the open air and experiencing the relief and momentary sense of well-being that comes to those of good health as they leave the confines of a hospital. Whether he would still be in good health after this evening, he had no way of knowing. But he had the element of surprise and this time there would be a meeting with Mr Malleson and a chance to express his dissatisfaction at being made the target of a time-bomb. Yeh.

Jauntily, Kline smiled in anticipation, not realising that he had obtained just the information that Malleson had wanted and was intent on following precisely the strategy that Dermot had hoped for when he had conceived the gambit.

*

Pete Malleson kicked the heavy carved wooden cabinet that contained the absent Mr Rafiq's booze. The glass tinkled inside; the assorted members of the alliance stared in varying degrees of apprehension as the black ex-boxer glared his rage at the bodies seated at the table.

'My bleedin' place looked like a bomb'd hit it. Those customers interrupted in the middle of what they'd paid for ain't going' t'come back!'

Malleson paused then, his voice lowering ominously.

'I want to know who's responsible for causing excessive fragmenting of my mirror, the doing-in of my new stereo and the general mangling of Madam's nephew's mush by means of a fast flung fist?'

The voice tube held to Sturt's throat intoned, 'KLINE!'

Malleson tried to maintain a small measure of self-control.

'And nicked off with Lady Anne Hophead?'

'The same,' Dermot answered before Sturt did.

'I really am a little tired of hearing that motherfucker's name – Kline, Kline, bleedin' *Kline*!'

Malleson kicked the foot of the cabinet again, hurt his own foot in the process, and tried to hide his discomfort with a scowl of outrage.

Dermot, misinterpreting the reaction of pain for suspicion of motive, went into his prepared explanation.

'We had to give your place the works, Pete. When that guy you sent ran off at the mouth, Kline took off after you like a bat out've hell. We had to follow or the whole plan would've blown there an' then.'

Limping to the table, sitting drumming with the fingers of his undamaged hand, Malleson realised there was nothing to be gained by further enquiry from this bunch of uncaring sods.

'Aye, aye, all right… all right. Snow Hill, is it on tonight? It better be!'

The Irishman smiled the smile of the hunter who knew his prey was certain to enter the prepared trap.

'Kline said the Maverick will have to get by with half its strength've bouncers t'night.'

'Just make sure he picks the right half dozen.'

'Don't worry,' Macavoy said soothingly.

Malleson's glance shifted to the small, stocky Asian seated

diagonally across from him.

'What about you, Kuldip – you in on this?'

Kuldip spread his hands to emphasise his non-involvement.

'Kline has done little to hurt me.'

With a jerk of his thumb Malleson indicated the Asian to the Irishman and said with irritation.

'Tell him.'

'The Blackbird's next on Kline's list. He's said as much. No more life've Riley collectin' dose peaceful pickings from your illegal immigrants unless Kline gets stopped dead in his tracks tonight.'

Kuldip refused to meet anyone's eye. He was thinking about his master's reaction. He could perhaps justify the secret meetings, but to commit men and resources even to what appeared a certain victory might be called insubordination and qualify for instant dismissal at the very least. He really did have to tread more than warily.

'How many dum-dums you goin' t'donate to the cause, Kuldip' Malleson asked quietly.

'Not so bloody easy, you know. I know lots've bloody Asian boys but I would need Mr Rafiq's name to instigate them.'

'Your boss? He's in Rotterdam.'

'It go wrong on Kline again, Mr Rafiq not enjoy my getting involved.'

'It's not going to go wrong. But put it this way, baby – in you're in. Out you're into the next ice age far as this alliance is concerned. Right, Dermot?'

'It's a true statement of fact,' the Irishman agreed.

Kuldip knew he couldn't win. If Mr Rafiq found out he had missed an opportunity to make an alliance with a future source of profit he would never be forgiven.

'OK.' You can have some boys... but if Mr Rafiq—'

Kuldip stopped, listening to what had sounded like a car swishing in on the gravel of the drive outside. No, no. Nothing. Imagination. Come on, he urged himself, stop all shally-shillying, show all present that nobody was more fearsome and ferocious than he himself. Kuldip's lip curled. His eyes flashed malevolently.

'How many Asian boys you want, uh?' he said with an ugly snarl and sneer of expression. 'Just say, just *say*!'

'How about eight at eight?' Malleson asked the now increasingly agitated Asian.

'Arms?' said Kuldip, jumping to his feet. 'Knives? A gun? Just say, just *say*!'

The black paused. 'Kline armed?' he asked the big Mick across the table.

Dermot shook his bullet head. Kuldip, now fully wound up, bared his teeth and started to jab fingers at those present to emphasise his scorn for what he took to be their lack of resolution. From the side of his jacket he produced his knife. With a theatrical flourish Kuldip began to wave it back and forth, like a conductor before an orchestra.

'You want to play for real or not?' he cried out in scorn.

'You going to act, *act*! That's what I say, you want Kline sod dead you kill him...'

The main doors opening interrupted the flow of Kuldip's exhortation to murderous consummation. His jaw dropped. His knife stopped cutting patterns in the air. His confidence ran away as sand through a sieve. The reason for Kuldip's consternation stood in the doorway.

A dapper Asian of middle years wearing a camel hair coat, carrying a hide suitcase, pulling on a pipe with a curled stem, now surveyed the scene of bodies sprawled about his table.

'Mr Rafiq...' Kuldip said to the apparition.

'Yes, Kuldip, you were saying?'

Kuldip knew that calm tone that Mr Rafiq now affected. It presaged a cloudburst of angry invective: the longer it was contained, the greater would be the force of abuse, the sharper the retribution. Kuldip shivered, his bombast burst and scattered by the impact of Rafiq's return. What could he possibly say to retrieve the situation?

'Welcome home, Mr Rafiq,' was what he said, in a small voice as he sheathed the knife and slumped down into the refuge of the chair at the point of arc of circumference that lay farthest from the door.

'Thank you,' said Rafiq. His contempt for those present gave a layer of frost to the ice of his outrage at this betrayal by a subordinate.

The members of the board around the large circle of the table became uneasy at the little man's approach. Dermot and Malleson made a movement towards standing as Rafiq came towards them.

'No, no...' Rafiq held up a plump, manicured hand.

'Please. I have heard rumours about these secret meetings held in my home. I have brought myself all the way from Rotterdam to attend this one. Please sit down. Please allow me to attend as an interested observer.'

Hearing such calm assurance in Rafiq's voice Kuldip began to rise from his seat with the intention of pleading his case but his employer would have none of it.

'No, no. Kuldip, you are obviously the chairman – remain in my chair.'

'Not a chairman, not me...'

'Of course you are. Please do continue, I insist,' Rafiq ordered as he withdrew from the table to stand, a brooding presence to disconcert the company.

Heavily, Kuldip lowered himself back into Rafiq's chair. He scanned the faces around, then pronounced flatly, 'This meeting, I declare it finished!'

Malleson, surprised, leaned forward.

'The decisions stand or what?'

Uneasily, Kuldip looked askance at Rafiq who, impassive, began to fill his pipe without sign or comment.

Dermot scowled. All this fuckin' deference to a little jumped up, greasy wog. Do something positive, he decided.

'We go ahead,' he said firmly. 'Right down the line.'

'You?' Malleson asked Kuldip, sharply.

After an awkward pause, Kuldip said in humble apology and explanation towards his boss,

'We have a Kline problem, Mr Rafiq.'

The flame of the match sucked down into the pressed bowl of tobacco. There was a moment's flare of flame before Rafiq replied, his voice tinged with sarcasm.

'When you use the term "We", Kuldip, it is not in a royal sense but in the sense of this... this multi-racial conglomerate of petty interests around my best table. Or does "We" mean law abiding members of the Asian community such as myself?'

Kuldip stared around at the board members. 'Kline hasn't attacked us, we, the Blackbird, not yet he hasn't, not yet.'

'But he will,' Malleson said.

Rafiq smiled his bland smile.

'Why? What have I done to provoke him?'

Dermot replied, 'He's out to take over from Rawlinson.'

'Sorry, who?' Rafiq seemed to have forgotten the name of his dead partner.

Malleson was about to say, 'You slimy bastard, you know who,' when Dermot kicked him, as a warning against needless provocation, under the table.

'Ow!' Malleson yelled and, thinking Kuldip was the culprit, reached across for the startled chairman's lapels and got ready to deliver a nut job. But before Malleson's head could make contact with Kuldip's face, two Asian helpers sprang from the shadows.

'OK, OK,' Malleson muttered up at the huge Pathan and his weasel-faced companion.

'All right, Kuldip, we'll forget it. We can manage without your bleedin' legions.'

Before Kuldip could reply Rafiq asked with worried concern, 'You have already made a commitment on my behalf, Kuldip?'

'We can get out've it.'

'No, no. Do you think I have gained a reputation as a respected leader of our community by "getting out of" agreements?'

'They only want to borrow a few of your boys, Mr Rafiq.'

'Against this one Kline fellow, do I understand it aright?'

'They may not even be used,' Malleson said.

Dermot put in his two pence worth. 'Just as back up. Insurance, like, you know.'

Rafiq puffed on his pipe, thoughtfully. 'Very well. I leave the decision to my self-appointed plenipotentiary.'

This last word started a chain reaction of puzzled enquiry.

'Ey?' Malleson questioned.

'Who?' Dermot grunted.

'Me?' Kuldip asked.

'You,' Rafiq confirmed.

Kuldip searched the face of Rafiq for an indication of what he should decide on his own initiative. Finally, with relief, he detected a slight almost imperceptible nod.

'OK,' Kuldip said grandly, relief mixed with an attempt to regain his lost assurance.

'We keep our word like we always do. You got some boys if needed.'

The commitment of forces made and accepted, the members of the board began to stand and drift from the table towards doors politely held open by their host, Rafiq, who nodded pleasantly to each departure in turn until only Sturt remained to make a shambling exit.

The battered, ugly face bent in to the Asian leader, the voice tube cocked.

'BOLLOCKS!' it said succinctly.

'And good luck to *you*,' Rafiq replied as he closed the doors carefully together and turned, trembling with outrage, upon the unhappy Kuldip, who had remained transfixed in the chairman's chair as if its authority might protect him from the wrath to come.

The thunder rumbled in the room. The black clouds gathered. The storm broke.

'What have you done, Kuldip, what have you *done*!'

'Trying to protect your interests is all…'

'Making deals on my behalf, you, Kuldip. Committing our resources to black thugs and Irish gangsters. Inviting them to confer in my home, in my name, *you,* Kuldip!'

The recipient of Rafiq's rage tried to halt the flood without success.

'Mr Raf…'

'If you find yourself cleaning vans out on the Blackbird run you may consider yourself blessed by fortune, Kuldip!'

'Listen, Mr Rafiq, please, I play along with them. I promise nothing, not before tonight. I promise you, I know everything but that everything cost us nothing.'

Rafiq looked down at his assistant, all Indian arrogance.

'Stand up when you speak to me,' he said, quietly but with the authority of his power and position.

Hastily Kuldip scrambled up, watched as his master moved away to an armchair, there to view with distaste an ashtray overflowing with the noisome evidence of the intrusions made into the sanctity of his home.

Pushing the offending ashtray from him the Asian leader settled into his chair and stared at his assistant. Finally, after long minutes, reason damped the fire of his anger. Placing the fingertips of his left hand against those of his right, he said calmly, 'Disclose details of this "everything" you have discovered.'

Kuldip sighed with relief and began to outline the plans and strategy of the plot against Kline that was to reach fruition that evening in the precincts of the disused railway station at Snow Hill.

Three hours later, on what had once been a busy platform twelve, John Kline stared down at the weed-grown tracks from which the rails of the permanent way had long since been removed.

Behind him, parked on the section of the station platform still used as a public car park, Khan sat watching Kline from behind the wheel of the yellow Datsun.

Kline regarded a torn poster of a ten-year-old timetable. Something bothered him; he was early in order to view the terrain and pick a place of ambush. Trouble was there were so many. The waiting rooms on this platform, broken, dirty glass scattered across their wooden floors. Maybe too obvious a place. Try somewhere else. Kline walked down the platform past a barred and shuttered refreshment kiosk, jumped down onto the wide trench between platforms and moved towards the Stygian black rectangle that lay beneath a bridge over an area where buffers must once have been.

Whatever was inside that darkness Kline could neither see nor guess at. It must have been without an outlet, for not a scintilla of light showed. A sudden flap of sound made Kline stand away, alert, tense. But it was only a pigeon disturbed by the man. Turning to survey for vantage points, Kline noted a signal box, but it was too high, too difficult to ascend and descend without losing the advantage of ambush. It had better be the main waiting room on platform twelve.

The decision made, Kline quickened the tempo of his walk and approached the elevated signal box that once had been the nerve centre of a busy station complex. Now it was a dead brain in a rotting body.

Inside the signal box cabin stood Kuldip, trying to see Kline by peering down through windows made opaque by city grime. Then through a gaping hole in the floor near to the rusting levers, Rafiq's lieutenant caught a glimpse of grey suiting as Kline passed by below. Kuldip gave himself a minute to allow Kline to clear before he picked up the heavy sawn-off shotgun and thrust it through a broken window as a signal of standby to those who dwelt in the darkness beneath the bridge. No sign of acknowledgment was made in return but that was as it should be.

Kuldip peered next towards the windows of the main waiting room.

Waiting in his turn for the signal of a pickaxe handle raised up and down by Malleson as a sign to stand by to enter the Battle of Snow Hill.

Along the trackway that led into the station from the other side came the members of the mob recruited by Dermot at the Maverick. Dermot himself, Sturt, Gary, and three others who had been instructed to scarper at the onset of battle.

'Arm up!' Sergeant Dermot ordered, pointing at the British Rail debris of wooden struts and pieces of discarded metal fencing.

Duly equipped with clubs of metal and wood, the ugly brigade marched down to face inspection by the hard blue eyes of Captain Kline.

'OK. Follow me,' Kline said, thinking he would brief the troops on their duties when billeted inside the waiting room.

Watching the back of Kline's head, Dermot found it difficult to restrain a smirk of satisfaction. Any moment now Malleson would raise his arm. There was no way it could possibly fail. Kline was a dead man.

From the driving seat of the Datsun, Khan watched the motley mob assemble and begin their march down the litter strewn platform.

Intent on Kline's progress, Khan noticed the grey Mercedes only when it glided into the next-but one parking space. Instinctively Khan slumped down out of sight and cautiously reached up to alter the angle of his driving mirror in an attempt to identify the occupants of the neighbouring car.

The mirror located the chauffeur. White face, dark glasses, blue uniform. Khan did not recognise the man so he changed the angle of reflection and with a start of surprise saw the smooth brown features of Rafiq. Hunched down in his seat, Khan frowned in bewilderment. Why had Rafiq returned to Birmingham and why was he interested in the outcome of low-level gang warfare? Puzzled, Khan decided that he would allow events to take their course and maintain a watching brief on the reactions of Mr Rafiq.

Three paces from the entrance to the main waiting room, Kline saw the door swing open. Holding up a hand he halted, waiting tensely for whoever it was to appear. Grinning, gripping his pickaxe handle at either end as though it were a staff, Malleson waved first to the far signal box then to the black duo of Hunniford and Bryden to join him in confrontation with John Kline.

'Hello, Cunthooks,' Malleson said softly to the big white man before him.

The confidence of the black's manner warned Kline that something was all wrong. Outnumbered two to one they should have been off and running, not watching him with wide grins and slavering relish.

From the black hole beneath the bridge, the headlights of a Dormobile flashed on like two eyes of a baleful nemesis. Kline saw the lights lurch in the darkness then the van emerged at speed, headed up past the signal box and bounced towards the platform where the opposing gangs now stood. Not good, thought Kline, seeing the van brake to a halt between the platforms and start disgorging a host of knife-waving, wild-eyed Asians. They were led by a giant Pathan whose blood chilling war cry disturbed profoundly all who heard it, from the pigeons roosting in the roof to the gang of men grouped on the platform below.

Kline raised his arm to wave his men into battle but before the gesture could reach fulfilment a sickening blow below his left ear sent him stumbling sideways up against a torn poster that invited him to sample the joys of Scarborough.

Kline wished he could, for through waves of nausea he saw the man who had clubbed him from behind was Dermot Macavoy and that three of the bouncers were beating an ignominious retreat, leaving the blacks moving in on him from the left, Dermot, Sturt and Cary closing from the right, as all the while the hordes of Asia charged ever nearer. Kline rubbed his head, doubled his fists, knew he had been duped, trapped, bamboozled by an expert.

'You Irish Mick bastard!' he spat.

'Should've fucked off from Brum when y'had the bleedin' chance,' Dermot said, raising the wooden strut and aiming to cleave his partner's skull in twain to illustrate his assertion.

Malleson noticed something odd: the Asian onrush wasn't slowing; the war cries weren't dying away – they were bloody well *increasing*!

Led by the giant bearded warrior at their head the Asian army fell upon the unprepared group outside the waiting-room door with maximum impact. Dermot was the first to suffer the shock when carried past an equally startled Kline by an Indian who seemed to have a great desire to insert a sharp-pointed knife into that portion of the Irishman's anatomy where he was wont to put his Guinness.

Why events had taken the surprising turn they had, Kline had no idea, but he grabbed the unexpected opportunity to escape by charging through a gap in the fray and legging off towards a downward slope that led into the bowels of the derelict station. Hard pressed under the stranglehold of an Asian assailant, Malleson finally broke the grip of the hands at his throat, bent the fingers all the way back into dislocation. As the wog screamed Malleson threw his hard woolly nut into the brown face, which gave him a moment's respite in which to retrieve his pickaxe handle and glimpse the figure of John Kline just before it disappeared down into the underpass.

Seeing his enemy about to escape, Malleson yelled out in rage and frustration and, with a surge of adrenaline driving him on, began to wield his club against foe and friend in an effort to clear a way to allow pursuit of Kline.

Finally, only a big Irishman with an Asian coiled around his head and shoulders, barred his way.

'Duck, Dermot!'

Fortunately the bullet-head did so just before Malleson's hickory handle smacked into the Asian head on Irish shoulders.

Feeling the grip of the python loosen, Dermot shook himself free and hurried after Malleson to join in the hunt for Kline through the gloomy regions of the station below.

Kuldip, sauntering between the platforms, shotgun over his arm, saw the black and the Irishman running towards the underpass. The Asian knew there was only one way through the dark labyrinth of corridors and offices below. He must hurry to be at that exit to greet whoever emerged from the maze. Kuldip jumped up on to the platform, paying little attention to the flailing fists and cries of pain that continued along the platform where his men were gaining the upper hand and using it to hammer black and white mercenaries right into the ground.

Arrogantly, Kuldip waved the Mercedes into smooth activity and before ducking inside made a circular movement with his hand to indicate to the chauffeur that he wished to progress towards the outer circumference of Snow Hill Station.

As soon as the Mercedes had left its parking space the driver of the yellow Datsun sat up and made ready to follow the progress of Rafiq.

The corridor was dirty and dark, with unidentified debris

underfoot. Kline wondered what was the best direction to take towards an exit that might allow him out onto the streets of the city and safety. At a junction of corridors he paused, then heard, close behind, the footsteps of pursuit.

There was an office nearby. Kline pulled the door open; it stuck halfway across but with enough space for Kline to slide inside. Pushing the door back Kline noticed that the floor of the office had several boards missing, giving a rutted, uneven surface from the door to the centre of the room. Kline decided not to bother to close the door fully but picked his way carefully to the middle of the office, there to await the arrival of whoever was anxious to catch up with him.

Clattering down the corridor, Dermot saw the door of the office and heard a dry cough from inside. Without pausing for thought Dermot charged towards the partly opened door.

In the gloom of the office, Kline saw Dermot shoulder the door open and attempt to run at him. The rush only lasted one step for Macavoy's foot sank into the space of the first missing floorboard and down went Kline's partner with a bellow of surprise and pain.

Malleson, following, was brought down over the broad back struggling to raise itself.

In the confusion Kline hurdled the fallen pair and ran into the corridor, almost into the arms of Hunniford and Bryden, who had finally managed a retreat from the debacle on platform twelve.

Surprised, they paused, and Kline turned teetering on one leg around a corner that revealed another long dark corridor but with a box of light showing at its end. Kline began to sprint towards this, chased at varying distances by Hunniford, Bryden, Malleson and a limping Macavoy.

Kline could feel the air fresh on his face and see the dust swirl in the fall of evening light getting nearer; he felt he was increasing his lead on those behind and had achieved escape when, with only yards to go to the exit, a stocky man stepped out to block Kline's exit with a jerk of the snub nose of a sawn-off shotgun.

Jesus… what's this? Kline asked himself, pulling up as quickly and as completely as he possibly could.

Kuldip grinned. He really liked this game.

'Please to stand aside, Mr Kline.' Kuldip jerked the shot-gun again.

Pleased to comply with the instruction, Kline did as he was

requested, leaving the Asian to face the oncoming rush of those pursuers now ganging up and advancing from behind.

BOOOM! Kuldip released an explosion of sound, shooting into the confined space of the underground corridor.

Cries of fear and consternation ensued in the darkness. 'Holy Mother of God!' an Irish voice yelped in tune to the diminishing sound of retreating footsteps.

What happens now? Kline wondered, and in answer to the question the grey, gleaming wing of a Mercedes encroached upon the exit from the station corridor.

Kuldip waved the shotgun towards the car.

'Your carriage is awaiting you.'

'Who's driving it, a big brown rat?'

The Asian winced in superstition at the word.

'Don't use that word. It bring bad luck.'

'What word?'

'Ra...' Kuldip almost said, then snarled out, 'Bloody well move, smart bastard, you!'

The rear door to the car opened, a plump brown hand beckoned.

'Mr Kline?'

Kline looked in at him.

'Aslam Rafiq...' the Asian leader said by way of introduction and held out his hand.

Seeing Kline not accept the handshake of his master, Kuldip dug the shotgun into Kline's back to emphasise the protocol required.

'Take Mr Rafiq's hand in common politeness, then get into the car. And remember, any survival ideas and you find your brains sprayed about for interior decoration. Get in!'

'OK,' Kline said, touching the proffered hand, and got into the back of the car.

When they had settled in with Kuldip riding as shotgun, Rafiq indicated to the chauffeur it was time to go home then turned his attention to his guest.

'This is an unexpected pleasure,' he said affably. 'I have so looked forward to meeting such a resourceful chap. If but a fraction of what I hear is true I will be truly pleased to make your acquaintance.'

'Likewise, I'm sure,' Kline said in dry reply, wondering where exactly they were going and what this rescue might imply.

Watching the Mercedes pull away Khan pondered the same question. There was only one way to find out. Follow the grey car to its destination.

Some little time elapsed before Malleson and his mates felt it safe to emerge from underground. Seeing only the soft light of a fading dusk on the street outside the station, all relaxed at release from the anticipated second blast of shot and began moaning in high dudgeon each at the other.

'Soddin' shootin' war, that's what it's got to now. That's where we're bleedin' at, thanks t'you, Dermot!'

Almost incoherent with rage, frustration and the consequences of his partner's escape, Dermot finally spluttered out, 'Not my fault. We had him. Had Kline but for that... that triple crossin', double dealin', piss ballin', arse crabbin', woggin' little twat, Kuldip!'

'Maybe not just him. Maybe someone pullin' on his strings. That occurred t'y'brilliant brain, uh?' Macavoy rubbed the bristles on his big chin. One way. Then the other.

'Who?'

Smiling bitterly, Malleson mocked the white.

'You're the planner, the strategist, the Bobby Fischer of men an' their motives, so you tell me, Thickey Mickey.'

After a few minutes thought: 'Rafiq. But why should he want Kline all in one piece all of a sudden?'

'Why should an' Irish Paddy like you need a black spade like me?'

'Dat Kline wants the money out've me n'the breath out've you. In my book that reads mutual interests callin' f' mutual measures've protection.'

Malleson looked sourly at the sweating face of the Irishman. He really was rather disillusioned at the turns events kept taking under Macavoy's management. Perhaps a few terse orders wouldn't go amiss.

'Find out what the mutual attraction is,' he ordered the hapless Dermot. 'N'while y' doin' so, General, I'll get my spades dug in for a state've siege. You want to see me, no passwords necessary, just information and a plan of campaign that will not only recover lost ground but also make certain that this time Kline gets buried beneath it. OK, let's go.'

Watching the three disillusioned remnants of his army troop away, the disgraced general felt a surge of panic. Jesus but he had really screwed up. He'd lost everything. Malleson's trust, the link with the Asians. Kline could well be free to come at him for revenge and money. Dermot licked lips parched dry with apprehension. He experienced an overwhelming desire to be inside the Irish Club with his own kind. But that was another thing: the bomb he'd borrowed – sooner or later the boys in the black berets would be demanding an explanation not only for the unauthorised requisitioning of the explosive device but also the lost cover of the Maverick Club. Macavoy felt his gut tighten and turn over. What to do about that? What to do about them? Where was Kline? Why the rescue by Rafiq? It was obviously a three-crate problem. Dermot just hoped that at sometime during the lowering of those thirty-six black bottles a solution would occur that would at least stem, or at best turn the tide of forthcoming events that seemed certain to engulf him.

Chapter Eight

'Cigar?' Rafiq offered.

'Ta,' said Kline taking a dip into the silver box.

'Forgive me if I do not join you. I prefer my pipe.'

'Be my guest,' Kline said ironically, glancing across the width of the opulently furnished room to where Kuldip sat nursing the shotgun across his knees. 'What about Kid Curry. He smoke?'

Rafiq snorted in derision.

'It would be a criminal waste; he could not differentiate the cured tobacco leaf of Cuba from a dock leaf dipped in turpentine. Cutter?'

Kline shook his head, bit the end, spat the stub into a nearby ashtray, lit up.

Anxiously his host asked, 'It is acceptable?' as if it really mattered.

'Not a bad bit've burn.'

'Brandy?'

'Thought you'd never ask.'

'Of course I would, of course...'

At the brandy decanter, Rafiq paused at its low level and shot a look of irritation towards his assistant, who, anticipating the accusing glance, had already looked away.

'When the master is away in Rotterdam my minions imbibe more than a little brandy.'

'He organise that all by his little self?' Kline asked sarcastically.

'Shut up your trap, Kline, if not for me you dead down a Snow Hill tunnel!' Kuldip shouted across the room.

'He is right for this once,' Rafiq said as he handed the glass bowl with its two fingers of brandy to Kline, who said nothing in reply but sniffed then tasted the cognac. 'How is it?'

'Never beat best bitter!'

Smiling politely, Rafiq returned to the drinks cabinet, closed its doors. Went to his favourite chair. Sat down. Regarded Kline. Kline stared back. Drank. Smoked. Said nothing.

After a while Rafiq said with a chuckle, 'You contain your curiosity extremely well.'

The long body stretched out in the armchair opposite.

'I'm happy 'n' content t'be able t'follow one breath with another just like it.'

Rafiq inclined his head modestly.

'For that privilege I must allow a little credit for myself. I ordered Kuldip and his boys to rescue you...' Rafiq paused for thanks but Kline said nothing, just gazed steadily across the room awaiting further elucidation. A rough diamond, Rafiq thought, becoming more and more convinced that he had made the right decision for the future.

'I do not expect thanks,' Rafiq went on, 'or trust between us, not yet. But our little rescue, will you please accept it as a small gesture of goodwill between us in case circumstances should ever arise that may work to our mutual advantage?'

'Like what?'

The rotund little Asian held up a hand in amused surprise.

'How direct you are. You and the late Mr Rawlinson, you do share the same direct approach.'

'To what?'

The plump manicured hand waved languidly.

'Should we say, business? My information is that you are intent on a little empire-building. That your sights will soon be focused upon those unfortunate illegal immigrants who are prey to blackmail and extortion?'

'Seems easy pickings f'someone,' Kline offered just to prod Rafiq on a little.

'Yes. But not worth your trouble. Believe me, Mr Kline, I have cases brought to me every week...'

From his seat at the door Kuldip coughed warningly at his chief's choice of words.

'Cases brought to my *attention* every week,' Rafiq rephrased. 'Only someone in my position in the Asian community could possibly know how many or how few immigrants are involved or have the slightest chance of knowing where to find these poor, unfortunate creatures once they are placed in employment and therefore in a position to earn, you understand?'

Kline understood a little.

'A little,' he said.

'Good,' said Rafiq standing, a sense of relief bringing added ease to his manner.

'You seem an intelligent man who would not wish to blunder into areas that could only bring disaster to community relations. I wish you good fortune with all of your other adventures.'

Kline regarded the hand offered to him in slight bewilderment.

'You mean I c'n go?' he said in surprise.

'If you so wish. I must hurry away – a radio interview. Merely local but it is expected.'

Kline touched hands then followed the little Asian towards the door and into the hallway after smiling mockingly at a scowling Kuldip.

At the front door the men shook hands again.

'It is a pleasure to do business with an intelligent man. We keep in touch, Mr Kline,' Rafiq said in farewell as Kline left via the front door into unexpected freedom.

When Rafiq returned to the main room of the big house he found Kuldip sullen and uncomprehending of the finer ramifications of his strategy.

'Funny bloody...' Kuldip started, then paused to bring order to the chaos of his thought. 'You want Kline not to attack the Blackbird, let the spades kill him. He attack no one then... then worms attack *him*!'

'And Malleson and the Irishman?' Rafiq asked gently. 'What about those gentlemen and their limited intelligence? They gain a little power, all they would do is abuse it. The law would stamp down on their activities and if we should be connected, even as associates, we might be crushed too. No, Kuldip, the last thing required in the Midlands is anarchy. My hope is that Kline has the potential to realise what the last big gang leader, Rawlinson, forgot: crime is no longer a matter of bursting heads and blowing up banks. Crime is now too complex and creative an activity to be left in the bungling hands of the common criminal.'

'That Khan has been seen with your newfound Kline friend.'

Rafiq dismissed the agent's role with a contemptuous gesture.

'He is a factor in the equation that has not been forgotten. If Khan is seeking retribution against the smugglers of illegal immigrants, if he has definite evidence against us, why has he not used it? What can he offer Kline that I cannot triple or quadruple – whether it be prestige, position, power or money?'

Kuldip, having lost himself a little during his master's monologue, was suddenly alerted at the mention of money. 'Money, yes, money. The Blackbird, when it start to run, Mr Rafiq?'

A smile played about the lips of Mr Rafiq. Of course his assistant knew nothing of the latest means devised to bring illegal immigrants into the UK.

'Run... *run*? The Blackbird will no longer *run*. The Blackbird must spread its wings, Kuldip, and commence to fly!'

Then he began to laugh, to spread his arms and flap them up and down as would a fat little bird.

Last joke, last joke, one to wrap up the evening. Not that there was anyone left in, thought Billy Brody, 'cept f'th'boss. Kline there at the bar and an Asian guy... Joke? Oh, yeh.

'This Asian...' Brody started. What about him? 'Wanted to spend his holidays in India, so he goes to his nearest railway station in Birmingham and says, "Please to tell me what train I should catch to send me to Delhi, please?"

' "How the bloody 'ell should I know? 'Ere, tek this and bugger off t'Euston."

'So the Asian goes there an' asks again and this time they give him a ticket to the coast and so it goes on until finally he arrives at the station in Delhi. Before joining his relatives he thinks, why not be prudent, why not make sure of your ticket back to the UK while you still have money in your pocket? So he goes to the ticket office and asks for a ticket from New Delhi to Birmingham. The wog clerk looks up at him. "Oh, yes," he asks, "which station in Brum do you want, New street or Birmingham International?" '

There was no one to laugh or snigger – only the bouncers, who'd heard it before, and the big boss, who obviously hadn't been listening.

'Goodnight, everybody.' The comedian bowed to the empty club and to the bouncers, who were already carrying heavy chains to lock around the push-bars of the half-dozen exit doors.

'You've been a fabulous audience,' Brody quipped to a passing cigarette girl.

'Anyway…' Brody said, slotted the mike back into its groove and called it another night.

At a table left of the stage Kline sat smoking a cigar, a pint of bitter before him. Khan, seated beside him, drained the juice of an orange and nagged on at his man.

'Think, Mr Kline – Rafiq does nothing without some purpose.'

Kline sighed, drank. Watched the club being put to bed. 'Indian talk with forked tongue. I dunno, he seemed to be saying, "Now I've scratched your back, baby, keep off mine." '

'Off the Blackbird?'

'Yeh.'

'Ah. He must be reactivating a route.'

'Yeh.' Kline yawned, feeling suddenly tired and far from a warm bed.

'This Anne Darracott,' Khan said abruptly.

'What about her?' Kline asked sharply.

'All the information her head must contain about Rawlinson, Rafiq… the drug and smuggling networks in and out of the UK. If I might suggest something, Mr Kline, I would be pleased if you would become a friend in deed and later a friend in need of her information.'

The corners of Kline's mouth turned down in distaste – at his companion and at the role that required his crawling through the undergrowth of society.

'Sometimes you an' your job give me an overwhelming urge to spew my ring, Mr Khan.'

'Sometimes I share your reaction,' Khan replied grimly. 'When I see the degradation, the misery brought to ordinary lives by the trafficking in drugs, prostitution and illegal immigration.'

Kline yawned again. Khan pressed on.

'Tonight you have only won a skirmish and survived a minor battle. If you are to succeed Rawlinson, you must gird yourself for a continuing war, Mr Kline.'

'I want Dermot,' Kline stated. 'I really want Malleson and I wouldn't say no to those baby bouncers who switched sides at Snow Hill. But I also wouldn't mind a last pint and a kip before we sing "We'll Meet Again" an' assault the beaches of Normandy…'

'And see Miss Darracott?'

No reply.

'Mr Kline?'

'Tomorrow, Mr Khan. If I do see her. It'll have to be tomorrow. OK?'

Someone switched the lights out. In the darkness Khan breathed out. 'OK.'

The following morning, Anne Darracott lay against the white soft pillows of her bed in the All Saints Drug Rehabilitation Unit. Earlier she had been asked by a well-meaning social worker whether a change of clothes could be brought in to her. For some reason she had agreed, handed over the keys to her barge and now there they were on a chair, her smart blouse and fawn skirt from yesteryear. Why?

Why those particular clothes? Why a change of clothes at all, she wondered, but knew herself well enough to know that she often altered the course of her life without conscious decision, her actions preceding a shift of thought.

The last two nights had been the worst of her life. Following the rescue by Kline from Malleson's house of pleasure, she had discovered that the lifeline of her roll of money had been lost in transit, left behind or stolen by person or persons unknown. She had accused the staff here. Ranted at them. Refused their treatment of a substitute for heroin. Scorned that there ever could be one. Finally, last night, she had succumbed to treatment, but only under extreme protest to the taking of the methadone tablets. It had little kick but kept down the symptoms of withdrawal.

Why not? Anne thought. Why not use this place? Show the doctors what they want to see. Why not? First step, get dressed. Make the bed. Be a good girl. Huh. She raised her thin body from the bed. Made herself think practical things about her appearance. Like hair shampoo. Peering at her appearance in a round mirror almost sent her scuttling back to bed but she forced herself to go doggedly about the first steps that a woman would take if she genuinely wanted to travel the route towards rehabilitation.

Down in the pad beneath the pinball parlour Malleson listened to the seductive female tones purring down his ear. American, he thought. She sounds something. Concentrate. Speak.

'You want t'see me, baby? On business? I'm always ready to do that. What's y'name? Sarah what? Gant? G-A-N-T? Gotcha. Yeh, call in anytime, baby. I'm having a little security applied at the pinball but just say you've an appointment an' you'll be ushered down. Right?'

Malleson hung the telephone back on to its cradle. For some reason the hard tones of the unknown woman caller had turned him on a little. Wondering what exactly was the business Sarah Gant had to offer, Malleson swung to and fro on his suspended wicker chair. He felt safe here, his helpers all about him. Few days to recuperate, find what was going on then he'd bounce back. No more alliances – only the brothers and their sisters.

A knock on the door followed by the entrance of Hunniford and Bryden and someone else. Uh! Dermot Macavoy. Malleson stopped swinging. Left his chair and circled the room with a Groucho prowl of wary menace, circling all the while towards the big scowling Paddy Mick at the door. Finally, with a start of affected surprise Malleson deigned to notice his visitor.

'Ah, Generalissimo Shamrockorosa...' he said mockingly. 'Welcome... Search him,' he instructed his bodyguards.

'They did that upstairs,' Dermot protested.

'I don't trust you Micks.' Malleson gestured for the search to take place. Bryden shook Dermot down quickly with expert hands.

'No bulges, boss,' he said, shaking his head.

'Not even in his Y-fronts?' Malleson asked innocently.

Bryden laughed. 'No-ooo way!'

Dermot glared at the black faces with their white teeth bared in laughter. Laughing at him. Why? Find out.

'What gives, Malleson – why'm I suddenly persona non grata at the turn of a card?'

'Cos every one you deals got t'be the ace've spades, babe.'

'Bad luck, that's why you're freezin' me?'

'Thank some've the saints you worship that it's just freeze not ice.'

Dermot Macavoy sensed a definite change in his former ally's manner. As if he was no longer needed. Redundant. Superfluous to requirements. Macavoy wished he had stopped at the second dozen bottles of stout last night instead of plodding on into the hinterland of black despair that was the only respite he could achieve from the free flow of troubles that poured through his life at present.

'I came with a plan to get Kline,' he heard himself suddenly blurt out.

'Who?' Malleson asked politely.

'Kline!'

'He still livin'?' Malleson affected surprise.

'Bleedin' know that, dontcha,' Macavoy muttered savagely.

Malleson nodded decisively, remembering his wrecked house and stereo. 'Y'could say. Y'could say, yeh.'

'You want to hear my ideas or what?'

Malleson turned away from the Irishman.

'Anythin' on the box?' he asked Hunniford, who shook his head.

'OK.' Malleson walked to the big bed, flung himself across it with the abandon of an absolute boredom brought on by the prospect of listening to yet another Macavoy scenario. 'Right, General.' Malleson waved his permission. 'Let's hear your latest pantomime script. Shoot.'

Dermot took a big breath, prayed for inspiration. 'We wait a day or so, lull Kline into a false sense of security, then get as many soldiers as we can muster and mount an assault on the Maverick. Smash it up if we have to. We capture Kline, transport him out t' somewhere like, I dunno, Chasewater, where we court-martial the bastard, carry out the sentence. Tie him to a rock, ferry him out 'n' commit his body to the watery deep.'

In the deafening silence that greeted the proposal Malleson sighed heavily and enquired of Bryden, 'Correct me if I'm wrong, but didn't Rommel use the very same tactics in his initial desert campaign?'

'Probably,' said Bryden diplomatically.

'I'm sure he did,' Malleson went on in tones of heaviest sarcasm. 'It has that subtle stamp of tactical genius. Yeh, the wadin' in, the smashin' up puts me in mind of another master of siege warfare, Marshal Zhukov.'

'Tell me one bleedin' thing wrong with it!' Macavoy blustered.

Malleson frowned. It was truth-telling time. He levered himself up from the bed and approached the Irishman directly.

'You've been too long at the Guinness. You've had so many bad results, y'not even bothering to enter the starting stalls. Kline has a base. He'll strengthen it. Advertise for bouncers, pick them over 'til he's got just the right blend. You don't believe it? He's already advertisin' in this morning's paper. Soon he'll have just the right type of mob t'both defend his territory and sally forth beyond. If he fancies doin' that, Dermot, which he will, he simply calls up Mr Rafiq and Kuldip and says, "Hey, man, send over some legions. We goin' huntin' Thickey Mickey and Pickhandle Pete!" '

'I don't think so.' Dermot shook his head.

'You don't thinkin' so just confirms everythin' I've spelt out. Oh, did I ever thank you fully for gettin' my house smashed up? Madam an' her nephew have departed; half the girls have leglock from havin' their coitus so rudely interrupted and the rest have gone off freelancin' while their lords and masters recover from the battle that will go down in history as the Shambles at Snow Hill.'

'D'y'want me in or not?' Dermot asked, in an almost humble tone.

'Not,' said Malleson in flat reply.

'Why?'

'Y've no bleedin' help to give. Advice? F'get it. Position? Y'no longer inside the Maverick Club, are you? I mean what can you give? A division? Can you throw a division into the field against Cunthooks Kline?'

Sadly, Dermot shook his head.

'A battalion? A cricket team? Anyone?'

Dermot sighed. 'No. No I can't. Sorry.'

Malleson put his lips to the Irishman's jug-handle of a right ear.

'There's lots've Irish in the Midlands,' he said seductively. 'It's not unknown for them to join underground armies. I suggest you hire yourself a recruitin' drum an' hit' the taverns of the town. An' as you wend your merry way, remember – a general without an army is no greater than the extent of his own privates.'

Malleson moved away. He snapped a salute, made a trumpet of his hand and blew the sad slow strains of the 'Last Post'.

Bryden and Hunniford formed a guard of honour to the door, watched as a crestfallen Irishman shuffled from the room. Then all three threw salutes at each other and collapsed with laughter at the last sad retreat of Generalissimo Shamrockoroso.

Anne looked at herself in the mirror again. With her hair washed and the clean clothes she seemed transformed into someone she used to know but couldn't quite place. Inside she felt the same aching, desperate longing for the means to total euphoria and the golden warmth of escape from the world of memory, pain and trouble.

A discreet cough behind her. Whirling around aggressively, she then remembered the demands of her new persona.

'What is it?' she asked the male nurse, black face above white coat.

'Visitor.'

'*Visitor?*'

Around the door of the rectangular room the white face of John Kline appeared with a broad, confident smile.

'No grapes, no flowers, just Dr K and his sunshine manner,' Kline said breezily.

Anne folded her arms. 'How'd you get in here?'

'Well, y'see, I explained our special relationship – how fate keeps throwin' us together an' how we decided not t'fight it any longer. So, for the sake of your emotional welfare, here I am.'

Uncertainly the West Indian nurse ventured to Anne, 'OK?'

Anne shrugged. 'What can happen?'

They waited for the young man to withdraw, but when they were alone neither could seem to relax.

Anne looked at Kline. 'What's with the Blarney?'

'What's with the change to looking like a human being?'

Anne answered with another wary question. 'Why're you here? Tired've counting your take at the Maverick?'

'All of two minutes that'd take.'

'Rawlinson called it a goldmine.'

'I've yet to find the seam then.'

'Why you here?' Anne asked again.

Kline looked away. 'Nothin' better to do.'

The man wanted to say, 'Sorry, I wasn't thinking beyond you and Rawlinson', but instead another question came out.

'You gettin' enough?'

'What?' Anne frowned.

'You know...' Kline made an awkward gesture; he could never remember the slang in vogue. 'Drugs.'

Anne's hazel eyes suddenly hooded.

'I would if you'd kickback my money.'

'Money?'

'I had a roll of it.'

'You must've left it in Malleson's knockin' shop then.'

Anne compressed her lips in tight disapproval. 'What a choice turn of phrase you do have.'

'It's where you'd arrived at – the bottom.'

A blaze of hatred carried her forward.

'This is the bottom, Kline.' Then, to emphasise her desperation, she pointed her index finger like a dagger at the floor. 'Here. Here. When you turned me in *here*.'

Kline could not work any of it out. With an expression of genuine puzzlement he said, 'They said you'd been difficult at first but today...' he spread his hands in a small gesture of bewilderment.

Anne couldn't resist putting the guy right. She placed her hands on her heart, fluttered her eyelashes and said demurely, 'Today I'm their perfect little unit of rehabilitation.' Then she dropped the pose, adopted her usual veneer of frankness tinged with aggression. 'One thing old Annie isn't is slow on the uptake. I know when someone has me with a leg up. Right. Like in here, you conform, they give you good reports 'n' you're out on the streets with scripts arriving at regular intervals to keep the worst from happening. I need to get myself together... I need to get on their mailing list, get my life sorted out. So I conform. I wear this...'

Kline saw, for a moment, a bright eager expression of vivacious life light up the gaunt face of Anne Darracott.

'I do their tests...'

The counterfeit smile of enjoyment faded, the eyes became hard with determination, the attractive face of a moment before ferocious now with her real intent.

'I swallow their methadone and I wait.'

'Wait?'

Anne smiled her contempt – for him, for the unit, for everything.

'To get back on the skag,' she said lightly. 'What else?'

It was hopeless. Kline knew it but he began to speak awkwardly anyway. 'Look, one thing I can't take is people pontificatin' about what other people should do.'

'But...' Anne mocked.

Forget it, Kline decided. 'OK, it's your death.'

'You fixed?'

Kline shook his head.

'Ever fucked then?'

'Once or twice. Never with you.'

Anne ignored the implication.

'Take one orgasm. One.' She held up a finger. 'Multiply it a thousand times and that's what "H" does for me.'

A faint grin, almost boyish, appeared on Kline's face as a reply occurred to him. 'I'd dig a thousand orgasms but one at a time. It's the same thing only it takes longer.'

Anne pursed her lips, looked his tall frame up and down. 'You're pretty boring, you know that?'

'Sorry.'

'Don't be. This straight talk is all good practice. I'm down to see the shrink here sometime.'

Kline doubted there was a way to reach her but he started to try. 'I thought you maybe needed help, encouragement. When I first met you I figured you were sent as a decoy but I didn't care. I would've taken greater risks to touch an' feel an' have all of you.'

Anne remained untouched and unimpressed.

'Lust's a terrible thing. Now you've no doubt screwed your rocks off you can see me for what I am.'

'Sorry, I can join you in memories of things past but that night I was hyped to my eyeballs.'

'OK, OK.' Kline sighed, wondered whether if he was not under orders to persevere with the acquaintanceship, whether or not he would have stayed this long. He wasn't sure. 'I can see you for what you are, Anne. You're always hiding behind clouds've heroin,' he said in exasperation and truth.

'What kind've metaphor's that?'

'I don t love you or anything but I do find myself wondering who you are.'

'Those clouds blow away you wouldn't want to know.'

Kline looked down upon the oval face with its fine features and surrounding fall of fair hair. He sensed the self-contempt was a frail defence that could be breached not by charm or guile but by genuine sentiment. But as he was unsure of the extent of his own feelings, he hesitated to press the relationship further. Almost delicately he drew away to the door, looked back and said, seriously, 'Try me some time.' then departed, leaving Anne Darracott to puzzle on the problem of what was meant and said and of why anyone should take an interest in a casualty case such as herself.

Zaheer Mohammed Khan sat on the little wall outside the terraced house where he knew the Indian woman, Mangit, lived with her two children. He knew the time that her shift ended at the local clothing factory and how long it would be before she appeared. Khan stroked his moustache in a familiar gesture. He wondered whether the woman had had any further communication with her deported husband. It was a difficult matter – without trust in or even involvement with the woman he would very likely gain nothing; therefore this was very likely a waste of time. Probably not worth even waiting to catch a glimpse or receive the rebuttal he was bound to suffer. Then he saw the glossy black head, the small graceful body and the gentle, modest manner as the woman came towards him, eyes downcast.

Mangit was remembering the words of her husband's letter as she passed the handsome Pakistani seated outside her house; repeating them silently, she turned into the doorway of her house. The words of the letter from Jashir had read, 'I read in your letter the mention of the man Khan with heartbreak and dismay. Remember who he is and from what country he comes. All their history tells of capture of other races, other religions, other men's women. Smile sweetly on him if it will keep him there long enough for me to return and exact revenge.'

Khan watched Mangit unlock the door and go into the house. He decided he would approach her not with questions but with a request that he be allowed to help alleviate the social deprivation of a one-parent family in Birmingham. Khan stood up, went through the gate and was about to ring Mangit's bell when he noticed the door had been left ajar. Khan pushed it open and went inside.

The Plumber's Arms sheltered Sturt and Gary from the storm of Dermot's scorn.

Cary, his leg in plaster and resting on a stool, sat beside Sturt, who, left arm in a sling, was raising a pint of bitter to his silent mouth. Both refused to meet Macavoy's desperate eye.

One push an' we're back in the Maverick,' Dermot repeated.

'Sorry,' Cary said. 'I can't walk, let alone make another run at Kline.'

The pint went down, the one good hand fumbled for the voice tube.

Sturt said,

'DOCTOR-SAID-I'M-TO-REST-MY-ARM!'

Dermot found their excuses somewhat lame.

'Seein' as y've only two arms n'two good legs between y', maybe one could hold Kline while the other kicked him?'

Both ex-bouncers smiled uneasily.

'Bout all we could do, Mr Dermot.'

'Ah, y'fuckin' chickens,' Dermot pronounced, draining his stout and slamming the empty glass down on the table.

'ANOTHER-GUINNESS?' Sturt grated.

'Before y'go,' added Gary, then smiled in relief when Dermot Macavoy took the hint and with much muttering and dire departing threats left them to recuperate from the wounds suffered in the slaughter at Snow Hill.

Later that afternoon, while Macavoy was combing the clubs and pubs of Birmingham in a fruitless attempt to raise recruits to his cause, Malleson had rested and was now deep in the complex matter of evaluating the effect of Brighton's downhill gradient upon a round-actioned horse whose form had hitherto been shown as effective only on right-hand tracks of a galloping nature. He'd just decided to oppose the animal when another class of creature entered his life with a bound through the doors. She was accompanied by two panting, discomfited bodyguards. Malleson saw a slim, medium height, heavy breasted, trim, black, sophisticated lady dressed in a space suit of silver lamé.

'Bette Davis had a line for this place!' a voice heavy with the accents of New York twanged across at the startled Malleson.

He stammered back, 'Whu-what?'

'You don't know, I'm not gonna tell you.'

'She won't submit to a search boss,' Bryden complained.

'Where'd you get those two morons?' the American asked. 'Dr Frankenstein's summer sale? You want to know if I'm armed?'

'Yeh,' said Bryden pugnaciously, watching her zip open her shoulder bag.

'I am, so what?' replied the lady in silver lamé. She whipped out a small calibre pistol and pressed it to the black male forehead under the white beret of Bonny Bryden.

'What y'gonna do about it now?' she asked.

On receiving no reply, she looked over her shoulder at Malleson. 'Great security. Congratulations.'

'Who the hell are you?' Malleson asked, wondering whether the gun, now held on him, was loaded and sure somehow that it was.

The pistol disappeared back into the bag. A small white card appeared in the long, scarlet-tipped fingers.

'Seein' this here is a business call...'

Malleson took the offered business card and read the name printed.

'*You're* Sarah Gant,' he said, remembering at last the telephone call of early morning.

'Mrs Sarah Gant,' the black beauty said with an elegant arrogant timing and emphasis that would have done Mae West proud.

Dermot pushed moodily out of the last pub on the hopeless round of recruitment Malleson had set him. There was nothing to report. He was alone. All the favours done, all the drinks bought went for nothing when you needed them refunded in commitment to a cause. Bastards, he thought and began to trudge wearily down the hill that led towards the Golden Grove drinking club. Deciding to cross the Alcester Road, Dermot paused to wait for the traffic to clear, which allowed a black Ford to sweep up alongside. Dermot recognised with a start of fear who it was now reaching across to open the door and to invite Mr Macavoy to please get in and accompany the company for a little ride.

There was nothing for it. The two soldiers in the rear of the car would be armed. There was no choice but to get into the black car. Close the door and try to stop trembling as the driver gunned the car and drove them all away to meet the unit leader of the Irish Republican Army, Birmingham Division.

The lady in the space suit lounged on the big bed. Malleson, looking down on her, experienced for the first time since who-knows-when the overwhelming desire to screw someone enticing, experienced and maybe unobtainable. Concentrate, he ordered himself. Business first.

'You want me to provide your agency with my girls. As what?'

'Escorts.'

'Where's the percentage in that?'

'There's a new exhibition centre opened. That's gonna bring lots've tired business men to town. And what does our weary warrior want after a hard day's hustling, hmm?'

Malleson thought about it. Sarah watched the slow train of thought.

'Ah!' said the newly enlightened. 'He hopes to *screw*!'

Sarah Gant's generous mouth and full lips fell open in mock amazement. 'Oh, you really catch on right away, don't you?'

'Where? Ah, hotels... hotels... *their* hotels. I know a few taxi drivers – could get plenty more to recommend our personalised service.' Malleson became more enthusiastic the more he thought of the proposition – and of working in tandem with the woman before him.

'The only reason I'm here,' Sarah said in matter of fact tones, 'is that I've heard you are the man with the merchandise. Those pretty black, brown and caramel ladies without which no evening on the town will be complete. You do have the goods to deliver?'

Malleson thought of his scattered stable. 'Not under the bed. Not here, not just now.'

Sarah nodded. That was understandable. Malleson watched her disdainful stare move about the underground room.

'Look,' she said suddenly, 'let's get out of this dump. It makes me think small. Let's have dinner tonight. The Albany, seven-thirty. Right?'

Malleson wanted to but was wary about leaving the protection of his pad.

'Well,' he said hesitantly.

Sarah Gant stood up from the bed, put her curved breasts in profile to him, moved a leg forward to throw into relief a bulge of ripe sylvan buttock.

'Don't you fancy me?' she asked provocatively.

Malleson swallowed. 'Seven-thirty,' he agreed. Then gazed greedily as the mysterious Mrs Gant paraded her assets towards the door, there to disturb his black henchmen, who had been keyholing on the other side.

'Hang loose, boys,' Sarah said in parting as she left the discomfited pair.

Malleson joined his men at the door. All three gazed up as their visitor climbed the iron gantry that led up above. With the gleam of silver and the garish lights from the pinball parlour it was like bidding farewell to a visitor from another world who must now be whirled away to the exotic realms of her home planet.

'We seein' that lady again, boss?' Hunniford asked, bemused.

'*I'm* seein' her tonight,' Malleson said, already concentrating on the problem of dressing for an evening of business-like seduction.

Khan had found Kline in the main Maverick office engrossed in a close study of a new set of account sheets that had come to light with the forcing of a drawer in Dermot's desk. After enquiring as to the inconclusive meeting with Anne Darracott, Khan indicated the adding machine and scattered accounts.

'A man of many talents, Mr Kline.'

'Book-keeping isn't one of them. But I can add up and take away and wonder about the result.'

'Discrepancies?'

'Too soon to say.'

'Oh, that telephone number you asked me to obtain information on...'

Kline glanced up. 'Dinah Carmichael?'

'It's the number of the telephone at her flat. I checked, it's empty. The telephone must still be connected.'

The man at the desk thought about it but it led him nowhere. 'What about the bomb?'

'Apparently the real thing, couple of pounds, design of recent IRA models but also fixed not to go bang.'

Kline scratched his head with the end of a pencil. 'Why plant a bomb here that can't explode? Ah, to make me believe the information pulled out of Pitt. I get it.'

'Yes,' said Khan, looking at his watch.

'I really must leave you, Mr Kline. I have an arrangement to escort an Indian lady and her two children to the cinema.'

'Glad to hear it. I was getting worried about you.'

Khan was about to say, 'Purely business, I do assure you,' but Kline had already returned to his audit of the Maverick accounts.

The wooden foreman's hut was too small for the crush of Irishmen grouped about the one man seated, Dermot Macavoy.

Half perched on the desk of the gaffer sat a thin, scrawny little man known as Farrel. He spoke quietly, playing with the frame ends of the dark glasses he usually wore.

'Now, Dermot,' he spoke with the softened tones of Southern

Ireland. 'You've worked for us as cashier using the account at the Maverick night club as a means of transferring contributions over to Ireland as artists' fees, copyright, that sort've thing.

'When I could. When I could,' Dermot said, his fear rattling the words out with staccato precision.

'Now these arrangements seem to have stopped. Why's that?'

Dermot held his sweating hands together before him as if in prayer for deliverance; then it came. A chance at a solution to all his problems. He needed time. Time to work it out. 'It's all one... the cause is all the same,' he jerked out.

Farrel rubbed his eyes. 'If it's all the same let us move to the second puzzling occurrence, the requisitioning of an explosive device with instructions that it was not to function fully. Which brings us to today and your attempting to recruit members of the first link on the chain of command for an enterprise of which I and nobody else in this unit had the slightest knowledge or awareness.'

'I'm goin' t'tell y'everythin', everythin'.'

Farrel smiled thinly and without humour.

'Please do,' he invited, then added, 'I trust also that there will be sufficient excuse contained in your explanation to countenance the saving of your life.'

'Yeh... yeh...' Dermot stared up at Farrel, then at the others. He recognised the two men nearest the door. Executioners. Fane and Conlon.

'OK,' Dermot began. 'I've had a British undercover agent planted on me. I wasn't sure before but now I am. It's a fella from the SAS.'

Dermot paused, looked into the dark shaded eyes of the unit commander, and delivered his ace. 'Fella by the name of Kline.'

Chapter Nine

It's beginning to make a pattern, Kline told himself as the answer printed out beneath a column of figures taken from one of his Irish ex-partner's bank statements. Beside his elbow the internal phone buzzed.

'Yeh?'

'Couple of big guys to see about the advert for bouncers,' a voice said.

'OK, Les, send 'm along,' Kline replied absently, still studying figures of the club's profits and losses. Soon he became immersed in the problem again and only a sharp rap on the door brought him back to awareness.

'Come in!' Kline called.

Two burly men, wearing raincoats, entered. The club owner looked at them approvingly. They were the right build and seemed more than able to handle themselves.

'OK. Park y'selves and let's talk about the attendants' jobs,' he invited.

Conlon smiled at Kline pleasantly enough. 'I don't think we'll bother,' he said in a voice whose rhythm contained the rising inflections of a native of Belfast.

'Thanks all the same,' added his companion, Fane, opening a briefcase and producing an automatic pistol.

Kline regarded the gun. Watched in bewilderment as Conlon took over the briefcase and started scooping the papers from the top of the desk into the interior of the case.

'What's this?' Kline asked. 'The new policy of the Inland Revenue?'

Not a vestige of acknowledgement flickered across the faces of the two Irishmen.

When the briefcase was full of account sheets, cheque books and Kline's jottings, Fane waved the pistol towards the door.

'We'd be pleased if y'd come with us now.'

The smooth, affable manner did little to disguise what the consequences would be if Kline opted not to accept the polite invitation.

'OK. Now that you've cleared my desk there's nothin' left to do anyway.'

Kline walked quickly to the door hoping to slam it back onto his would-be captors and escape, but they knew all about that sort of thing, and Kline found himself being escorted efficiently towards whatever fate was to decree.

In the evening light on the small airfield Rafiq and Kuldip watched the light aircraft swoop in and taxi to within yards of the hangar that sheltered the two Asians.

Within minutes half a dozen illegal Asian immigrants had been transferred from the discomfort of the restricted space of the plane to an equally tight squeeze inside a long, grey steel container with trailer wheels attached. It had been designed for the transport of glider wings and bodies but now was to be used as cover for Rafiq's Blackbird run.

While Kuldip was scurrying and harrying and hitching up the glider trailer, Rafiq hurried across to greet the pilot, an ageing Biggles with the obligatory brush of jaunty moustache.

'My dear Miles, how are you, how is everything?' Rafiq asked anxiously.

The pilot shrugged. 'Hunky Dory. No problem with radar. I came in low from France; the cover doesn't extend over all the English coast, fortunately.'

'But radio?'

'Haven't got a wireless have I, Raffy...?'

'No, no. What a pity.' Rafiq smiled. Took a bulky envelope from his pocket and pressed it into the pilot's hand.

'Defray a few expenses, my dear.'

'Much obliged. Ta. So what happens, I drive my car and glider trailer to a point of rendezvous, where the Kuldip chap takes over, transfers the cargo into his van?'

'Yes. Is that agreeable to you, Miles?'

'Fine. What local law around here are well used to seeing are gliding containers come and go at this airfield. I see no obstacle to a profitable enterprise.'

Rafiq rubbed his hands delightedly. 'I sincerely hope that is so, my dear Miles.'

'Depend on it. I'll just put the old Piper lady to bed, then it's wagons ho. Yes?'

'Yes. Oh, yes,' said Rafiq happily, looking across to the long silver box that contained the latest additions to his tally of immigrants brought into the United Kingdom.

At the same time as Rafiq was testing the first flight of his Blackbird, Kline was being blindfolded in the rear of a black Ford Capri 2000S. Head forced down on the back seat, a gun barrel resting on the nape of his neck, Kline soon lost all sense of time and direction.

Eventually, after a final test of the car's suspension across a section of what must have been rough ground, they stopped. Strong hands gripped his arms and he was thrust into a space that seemed to be tightly enclosed, for he could feel the close proximity of gaberdine raincoats pressed up against him on either side. Then came a sudden lurch of movement and the whirring sound of what sounded like a steel hawser followed by a movement upwards. A lift, obviously. Going where? To meet what? Kline could smell... what? The smell of plaster. Feel the draughts of air as successive levels seemed to be reached then left behind during the slow ascent.

The journey upwards seemed to last a long, long time before the lift stopped and he was thrust forward to stumble blindly across a debris-strewn floor. There was the murmur of voices, the fumble of fingers at the knot of his blindfold. Screwing his eyes in anticipation of strong light, Kline was surprised to find that illumination of the bare room was almost non-existent. In the gloom Kline could just make out a little runt of a man wearing dark glasses that must have rendered the semi-darkness of the newly constructed room impenetrable.

'Let's have a side open,' the little man ordered. From the shadows one of the gunmen pulled a rope to unfurl blue plastic sheeting that curled upwards to bring daylight in to what was the penultimate level of a high-rise office block still short of completion.

Blinking, Kline noted the scattered bricks about the floor, the stark grey of the concrete ceiling and the steel girder structure that supported the square of space in the sky.

There was nothing of help within reach. Kline noted a hang of electric wires to his right; maybe if he edged...

As if reading his intentions the man in the sunshades, Farrel, lifted a warning hand and waved it away from him with a little shooing motion.

'Please move a little further towards the light, Mr Kline,' he said in his soft-toned voice.

Kline went towards the edge, saw the sweep and sprawl of Birmingham spread sixteen floors below.

'Further on,' Farrel instructed. Kline's legs refused to function until another Irishman said in a familiar voice.

'What's up, Kline, y'legs taken root?'

'Hello, Dermot,' Kline said before moving to the edge of space as the Irishman brandished a workman's shovel warningly.

'Thank you,' the IRA unit leader said, now satisfied that his prisoner's position was suitably precarious. 'Now, Mr Kline you've bin brought here because certain allegations have been lodged against you by Dermot Macavoy.'

'Like what?'

'Like spying on him and upon our organisation here in Birmingham.'

'What?' Kline started, then light dawned. 'Shouldn't you be wearing a black beret?'

Dermot Macavoy, smoking, wearing a white protection helmet, stepped forward. 'We'll wear black armbands f'you, y'bastard!'

'Be quiet.' Farrel motioned the executioners, Fane and Conlon nearer. Then he concentrated his attention upon the tall Englishman standing against the backdrop of an evening sky.

'Answer these questions. Are you, as Macavoy maintains, a British agent?'

'No.'

'Have you been in the British Army?'

'Yes.'

Kline saw the guns being eased out of the raincoat pockets. Could see the grin of delight forming across Dermot's mouth.

'In Ulster?' The questions continued inexorably.

'Yes.' The guns lifted.

'And were you also a member of the Special Air Service?'

'Yes,' Kline answered. The safety catches clicked off, the guns of the execution squad levelled upon him. 'But one who refused to serve.'

Farrel frowned. 'What does that mean?' '

'I joined the Army to soldier not to spy.'

There was a movement of violent protest from the Irishman in the white helmet. 'He's bloody lyin', lyin'!' Dermot cried anxiously, his voice cracking with tension.

'Someone is,' said the man in dark glasses glancing appraisingly from accused to accuser.

'Don't listen to Kline,' Dermot pleaded. 'He'd talk the devil into givin' him a glass of water!'

Farrel considered this then replied. 'You should know, Dermot. Aren't you his partner?'

Kline saw his chance. 'Delmot's everyone's partner. You might think he's your agent, a cover for the channelin' of funds across the Irish Sea, but I've checked the books at the Maverick...'

Macavoy found it impossible to stand still. 'Lyin' twat...' he muttered, holding the handle of his shovel with hands that gripped with ever increasing tension.

Kline noted the whitening knuckles of his adversary and realised that the calmer he could keep his tone the more liable his erstwhile partner was to erupt into uncontrolled anger.

'Yes,' Kline said coldly. 'You'll find, when you audit those books...'

'Shut your lyin' gob up!' Dermot ground out.

Kline ignored the interruption but focused upon the little man who was obviously in authority over all present. 'Yes,' Kline continued, 'you'll find Dermot's loyalties lie not with the IRA but with the DMA.'

'What?' Farrel asked sharply.

The Dermot Macavoy Account,' Kline explained.

This last statement of truth was the trigger that sent Macavoy blundering forward to still Kline's mouth with a side swipe of his steel shovel. Kline, who had gambled on the move, waited for the last possible second of commitment from his attacker before launching himself into a sideways dive and grabbing for the hanging rope that had held the plastic sheeting in place. He felt the rough fibre of the rope slipping through his hands, gave one frantic squeeze of his burning hands - and then it held his weight and he could swing out over the edge and circle into space over the long drop that lay below.

Kline's attacker saw the ploy, tried to change aim at the leaping body, missed, and teetered on the brink of oblivion while Kline curved back to regain the edge of the concrete platform.

Nobody moved as Dermot fought for balance and lost. Emitting a last '*Basta-a-ard!*' Dermot's dying scream was heard diminishing rapidly as all the Irishmen clustered to the side in time to see the shattered broken body of Dermot Macavoy being bounced away at speed on the back of an empty contractor's lorry heading home to the Black Country.

'Oh, shit!' Gonlon said as the body was borne away. All at once they remembered John Kline and shifted their gaze up to a pair of legs in grey suiting shinning up the rope, already almost within reach of the topmost level of the office block.

'Fire!' Farrel screamed and Fane had the chance of one shot, which passed through the cloth of Kline's turn-up without touching flesh. The gunman narrowly missed decapitation when an avenging Kline hurled down a house brick that swished past Fane's ear to go clang against a girder before bouncing off to fall and land finally on the building site below.

'Let's get out've here,' Farrel decided. 'The lift! Get into the lift!'

Running and stumbling, the members of the unit ran and jostled and stuffed themselves into the steel box of the lift and then began the slow progress down the length of the sixteen floors below.

On the roof above, an out-of-breath Kline rested against tarpaulin-covered cylinders with an oxyacetylene welding torch attached. He heard the whirr of the steel cables on the pulleys of the lift and realised that the driving motor and simple drive mechanism must be close by.

Thinking that the lift was about to arrive, Kline searched for a suitable weapon with which to welcome his visitors. After selecting a length of steel scaffolding and taking up a position of advantage, Kline realised that the lift was being lowered by the wires and pulleys now before him.

By squinting over and carefully avoiding the moving support cables, he could see the square top of the cage down below. It was too good an opportunity to let go by. Kline inserted his steel scaffolding rod into the driving sheave and felt it bite against the brake to jam the works and halt the progress of the lift car abruptly between the tenth and eleventh floors.

The faint sounds of frantic fear could just be heard but Kline hardly noticed. He was more intent on assembling the welding equipment, lighting the torch, and then adjusting it to the correct cutting intensity.

When he had the blue flame flaring to his satisfaction he began his task of severing the steel threads on which hung the lives of the three men suspended below.

Only when a single strand of steel cable remained did Kline hesitate. Then he remembered the planted bombs, the smell of scorched flesh, the mayhem and murder caused by the members of the unit at his mercy below. He pronounced sentence. Carried it out. The steel hawser parted. The cage of the lift, freed of all restraint, plummeted down with ever-increasing speed until it finally smashed into the concrete base on the ground floor with an impact of such force that the screams, pleas and prayers of the occupants of the crushed cage ceased immediately.

The hotel telephone gave a long warble. '404, Sarah Gant,' the woman said. 'Yeah, fine, show the gentleman up.'

Sarah replaced the receiver, glanced appraisingly about the room. Too much light, she decided and dimmed the main lamp. Switched on her cassette recorder to play a little mood music, checked her gun was accessible inside her open hand-bag, sprayed on a little Mitsouko perfume, smoothed the long flow of woollen djellaba-style dress and waited.

When the knock rapped on the door, she called that the gentleman was to enter.

Around the door the wide brim of a low-crowned hat appeared and beneath it a large pair of dark glasses.

'Why, if it aint Zorro himself!' Sarah said in greeting.

'Ey?' Malleson said, who couldn't see a bleedin' thing in the dimly lit room. Ah, that was better; by sliding the shades down, he could see the sexy lady a lot better. Made up. Dressed up. Standing like a tigress waiting to fall upon a passing buck.

'C'mon in, baby. Glad y'c'd find some time to come up an see me.' Sarah held out her hands to him.

'Bit dark in here, innit?'

'Maybe.' The lady pressed a switch. A sidelight came on near to Malleson.

'There. That should help show your feathers.'

'Woh?'

'The suit… it's more than enough.'

'Oh, yeh.' Malleson preened in his best grey pinstripe and tossed his silver-topped stick nonchalantly towards a wastebin, where it rattled and rolled but stayed inside. Malleson considered the reaction to his choice of threads for the evening. You could take it two ways. 'I don't know what y'mean. Whether the suit's too much or, y'know, too much…?'

'It's beautiful, baby.'

'We havin' dinner?'

'Eating makes you fat. Let's go somewhere else first.'

'Fine. Where d'you want to go?'

'It's your town. I'm just a stranger in it.'

'Lots've places. Where – restaurant, disco? Just say.'

'A club,' Sarah decided.

'Lots've them.'

'The Maverick?' Sarah suggested innocently.

Malleson stared over his glasses in sudden surprise. 'The Maverick, why say that?'

'I saw the sign once. What is it, you have to be a ghost to show there?'

'Sumthin' like that. There's a guy in charge of the place I don't want to see just yet. OK?'

'What's his name?'

Malleson frowned. 'Does it matter?'

'He's into you for money?' Sarah persisted.

Malleson shook his head, not wanting to discuss it.

'How come you're so scared of him?'

The man began to become irritated. He hadn't come to this lady's bedroom to discuss the likes of John Kline. 'Too long a story…' he said flatly then, with a build of aggression, 'I'll fix him when all the race conditions are right f'me an' wrong f'him. Right?'

Sarah clapped her hands together once.

'I just love dominant males. One rat in twenty is a leader. An' you're *it*.'

'Yeh.'

'So let's go to this Maverick Club.'

'I told you!'

Sarah grinned. 'OK. Let's stay here. You want to smoke?'

'What've you got?'

'Bit've Mexican... some Columbian Red.'

'Either, any, both.'

'Lock the door.'

Malleson did as he was asked. Leaned his back against the frame, looked across to where Sarah was shredding tobacco and pouring on the dark liquid that promised to relax the strain that had appeared with the mention of the Maverick Club. Malleson watched the pink tip of her moist tongue pass along the cigarette paper – watched her seal the joint and beckon to him from her bed.

'Momma wants you to be yourself, baby. Momma wants you to relax and not worry about one thing...'

Malleson remained unmoving. Sarah lit the fuse.

'Come on, Mr Malleson.' The invitation floated across the room borne on a cloud of cannabis.

'Let's you an' me make a few smoke signals at each other. Huh?'

The man in grey moved away from the door, sauntered across to the dark temptress now reclining on the bed and offering up the joint.

'Ta,' Malleson said, took the bulky roll of impregnated tobacco and drew on its acrid smoke.

Khan sat with Jashir's children between his seat and Mangit's. On the screen the birds sequence from the film *Roop Tera Mastana* illumined the fine profile of the woman. Sensing Khan's scrutiny, her eyes moved to his then darted back to the screen. Curious to see how intent on the film she really was, Khan continued to look at her. After only a few seconds the woman's attention wandered back towards him. Khan smiled slightly to her confused reaction of discovery, then, well satisfied with the progress being made, began to enjoy the film.

The hotel room suddenly dropped several feet, leaving the man and the woman suspended in space. Malleson experienced the breathing of the woman beside him as a long slow wave of sound that seemed sometimes a warm wind, sometimes a wash of euphoric sensation across his body. He thought he should be naked but when he concentrated he could still see the striped cloth that encased legs thrust out before him on the bed. From a distance the accented husky American voice that had first attracted him floated on a warm cascade of exhalation.

'Here,' Sarah said, passing the butt back without having taken an inhalation.

'Uh. Oh. Yeh. Ta. You OK?'

'Sure.'

Malleson, his collar loosened, his hat tilted, moved his head, sucked the last drag down greedily, coughed.

'Good stuff – fast take.'

'I know,' said Sarah, who had, unbeknownst to her companion, taken very few drags from the shared joint.

'Why'd you come to me in my life?' Malleson grunted.

'I wanted the best of the up and comers. There was a white man name of Kline... and you, a black boy with a world to win.'

'Where you from, exactly?'

'New York. But my work's anywhere there's profit to be had from intimate entertainment.'

'Now's the time. Here?'

'Business guys with expense accounts means the nightlife in this town goin' t'go boom!'

Malleson tried to concentrate. 'The law...'

'Pay them off.' Sarah Gant dismissed the problem briskly.

'I will. Sure. If I'm in...'

Sarah raised herself on to her elbow.

'Why if?' she said pointedly.

'We goin' t'be partners... I'll need to know, y'know, you.'

Sarah Gant, hard, confident, looked down at the brown, bearded face. 'I'll prove myself, baby, where it matters, up front, organisin' the hookers an' their action. Me...' Sarah tapped between her breasts. 'I'm takin' the risks with you at my back. I mean, seein' as it's cards face up on the table time, what exactly have *you* done?'

Malleson's mind suddenly attained a measure of clarity. 'My form'll stand scrutiny,' he announced proudly.

'Yeah?'

'I was the arm of the guy who used to run this town.'

'And where's he?'

'Dead.'

'Some arm. Big hand all round.' Sarah clapped.

The man scowled in pique. 'I did all he asked. *More* than that.'

'Muscle, threats... a kicking or two...' Sarah said scornfully. 'Give me a dime an' I'll buy two dozen.'

It was time to state a few facts of life and death, Malleson decided. She thinks you're small time. You better tell her. 'I been all the way and back. There an' back, y'know.'

'No.'

The man sprawled on the cover of the bed raised himself up. In his head events were winding themselves into a reel for playback.

'The man said, "Find this man. This Kline." Me, I sorted it. Found out the lady who'd hidden him. I tracked Kline down, gathered him in, delivered him up and stopped that stripper's mouth for all time. You ever killed anyone?'

'I've brought a few to the point of exhaustion,' Sarah Gant said laconically, not wishing to break the flow of Malleson's recall...

'You say, that life there...' Malleson pointed to the ghost of Dinah Carmichael at the foot of the bed. 'It's got to stop and me, I'm goin' t'do it. How? Heroin OD. Right? Fill the hype. Find the vein, insert the needle into that thin brown arm. /the blood runs, the pure stuff goes in... The 'dermic fills with blood. Her blood. You don't think about it. Your mouth and throat feel dry. You tidy up the flat, scatter a few needles around, then close the door on Little Miss Dinah-mite lyin' dead on the bed.'

Malleson paused, glanced down at the woman, who was obviously impressed, lying staring at the ceiling visualising the scene so vividly evoked for her benefit.

'Anyone can kill anyone,' Malleson added as a final accolade for himself. 'It's gettin' away with it that calls f'somethin' else.'

After a long pause Sarah breathed an almost inaudible, 'Yes.'

Malleson realised the depth of the impression he must have made. 'You realise you'll be runnin' with the real thing, uh?'

'I know now.'

Malleson thought it was about time talk ceased and action began. 'We goin' t'merge our talents?'

Sarah still stared at the ceiling. 'Why not?'

'This intimate entertainment you mentioned. Y'give free samples, Sarah?'

'Not usually.'

Malleson turned to her, went down towards that broad, full, red mouth, paused, his lips an inch from hers. 'Put this down on my company account,' he breathed, then melted in on the woman, kissing, feeling, biting and finally reaching for the naked body beneath the long woollen dress to claim his glistening prize for attaining such a high level of experience in nerve and performance. Now another form of performance was required and Malleson was ready to go into overdrive. Removing the dress, looking down upon the brown, warm body, he undressed slowly, feeling the urgent pulse of his desire lift insistently before him.

Refusing to hurry, Malleson made himself wait. Display the bearer of the standard that this lady obviously required.

Sarah moved a leg open, threw back an arm, turned her head and bit the flesh of her inner arm. It was a signal to her professional self to close the conscious mind, to do exactly what the situation required.

When Malleson lowered himself to the bed he received a moist welcome that was a tribute not to his manhood but to the will of the woman.

Feeling the push of the first inward thrust Sarah went smoothly into the function she did best – that of giving the john as good a ride as anyone had a right to expect in this hard world. Expertly she caressed the sweating back, fluttered fingernails across the driving buttocks, found the tight little entrance that clenched and constricted around the sudden insertion of her finger. Hearing the first moan, feeling the first convulsion, Sarah swiftly became the aggressor until Malleson cried out in long shuddering orgasm.

To culminate his pleasure it was necessary that she too should yell in ecstatic abandon which, having had many opportunities to practise, she did in perfect unison.

Grunting contentedly, Malleson collapsed into satiation, unaware that all he had penetrated was the belly of the woman beside him. Had he been able to follow the run of her present thought or know the true purpose of Sarah's visit to Birmingham he would not have rested so securely on the heavy, dark-tipped breasts of Mrs Sarah Gant.

Kline stood at the bar, newly changed into his evening dress, considering the problems of falling Irishmen and whether to invite the club stripper, Julie, for a drink, with a view to spilling a little seed later in the evening.

'Drink, boss?' Archie asked.

'Yeh, why not.' Then, for no apparent reason, there came into his mind the image of Anne Darracott, vulnerable, trying to hang on to a way of life that for her had changed for the worse with the death of Rawlinson and the end of easy drug supply.

The tiny barman brought his boss a large Famous Grouse whisky. On stage, a black blues singer, Ena, began to croon the opening of 'As Time Goes By'.

To dislodge Anne Darracott from his memory Kline drank most of the scotch quickly but still the image of her persisted. Try something else, he decided.

'Archie.'

'Boss?'

'When Julie finishes her next spot, I'd like to buy her a drink. OK?'

'Sure.' Archie nodded. Had he Kline's height he would have done the same.

'Ashi, Bela,' Mangit said to her children. 'Say good night to… to…'

'Uncle?' Khan suggested.

The children smiled a shy good night then were ushered from the room by their mother.

Khan glanced about the living room, filled with toys, clothes, ironing waiting on a board, and then he saw, by the clock on the mantle shelf above the gas fire, an airmail envelope. Khan crossed quickly to the fireplace, was about to take up the letter when Mangit re-entered.

'Jashir?' Khan asked, indicating the letter. 'Your husband?'

'Yes.'

Deciding it was too soon to press for advantage Khan changed the subject as if he really had the interest of an uncle for the welfare of children whose father was far across the sea. 'Do the children usually got to bed at this time?' he enquired.

'It is much later for them than is usual. The film…'

'They have school tomorrow?'

'Yes.'

'How is the school?'

'They teach them to be English people.'

Khan shrugged. 'Of course.'

'Jashir says…' The woman gestured hopelessly.

'Yes?'

Mangit shook her head, the heavy plait of black hair swinging heavily. Let us talk of you. Why do you molest me and my children?'

'I want to help you. I want to help Jashir to avoid the consequences of re-entering the country and of trying to take his revenge outside the law.'

Mangit trembled, held out her hands in supplication. 'The law. Your law, their law – what about *our* law!'

'Let me be open and honest.' Khan paused, waiting for the eyes of Mangit to settle on him. When they did, he touched his forehead. 'I seek to assist Jashir from here... but from here...' The hand moved to the area of his heart, 'from here I seek to assist you.'

Mangit looked away. 'Please stop this.'

Khan moved nearer, touched her bared inner arm with the tips of his fingers.

'There is a law of attraction between man and woman. I find myself a servant under that law.'

Mangit, flushed with the implication of his words, took an angry step away. 'And me, what about me! For you a night or nights. For me, even should my husband not return to destroy me, I would be cast from my family. Those same children whom you so admire would spit at my memory. When you tire of me, I would have nothing, no family, no relations, no husband, no house, only empty life to live.'

The small delicate body shook within the silk of the sari. Khan wanted to take her into the shelter of his arms but resisted; it was too soon. Already he had exceeded the limit of his planned involvement.

'Please leave, Mr Khan,' Mangit entreated.

'I still wish to help you, Mangit. Please allow me. I promised Bela and Ashi swimming lessons; don't deprive them.' Khan smiled. 'Please let me see them... and you.'

Mangit turned to the clock, took up the airmail envelope, crushed it in her hand.

'We shall see,' she said, then waited until the door had closed behind Khan before she turned from the fireplace and smoothed out the thin paper of her husband's letter. The words she tried to read said, 'I have sold my remaining piece of family land. With the money I will pay the agent to arrange for me to travel the new route into England.' The words did not register in Mangit's consciousness. Her mind was filled with the recall of Khan's handsome features and full, frank smile.

*

Vendetta

Anne Darracott settled down to sleep at the end of the first day of full rehabilitation. Hazily she thought over the events. Kline's visit, the drag of learning the stupid rules, making conversation with the rest of the inmates and the preliminary interview with the psychiatrist, Dr Rai. That had gone OK, she thought. Story of her life recorded on videotape for future analysis. Anne smiled into her pillow. She'd given nothing away. Just the hard facts of her life. Not the reasons, not the reality of it. She would hold on to that. Hold on to it. Hold on. Hold. The little girl-woman slipped into sleep.

Kline listened to Julie Del Roi snore beside him. Somehow it amused him. He had expected nothing but bodily release, which the stripper had duly given But it was all business; keep in with the boss, take him home, give him what he wants, nothing more. Which was just as well. Kline sighed. Decided to duck out. Stealthily he put out a bare leg then body out of the bed. As he dressed it occurred to him that if he had left the other stripper, Dinah, like this, she would probably still be alive. What was happening to him? Kline wondered. This introspection. First Anne in his thoughts, now Dinah. The snoring stopped. The body of the woman turned onto its side. The breathing resumed its deep, slow rhythm as John Kline called it a night and retreated from the room.

Chapter Ten

'How's the property market?' Rafiq asked the long-nosed, saturnine Englishman.'

'Bloody awful. How's the supermarket business?'

Rafiq indicated the poorly packed shelves.

'Bloody awful. Had to tear a strip off the manager.'

'Bloody staff problems everywhere, Raffy. People don't want to work. Anyway, just passing. Thought I'd pop in, give a bit've forewarning sort of thing...'

'Of what? Warning of what?' Rafiq asked.

'Seems the MD's making rude noises about the drop in profits.'

Rafiq waved his hands in protest. 'I have been absent in France and Rotterdam. MD must know why.'

Winthrop picked up a packet of dried apricots, sniffed their stale aroma. Replaced them hastily.

'Yes, well. MD understands to a degree. But how long will it be before normal service resumes is what he wants to know. Rest of us wouldn't say no to some return on our original investment either.'

The Asian retained his composure with an effect of will.

'The Blackbird has had a trial flight, a successful run. No one is more anxious than I, my dear Gordon, that it resume normal service. I can use cheap staffing here, for instance. Yes?'

Winthrop nodded gloomily. 'Be something to tell him, I suppose. But can I also add that other enterprises are to be activated?'

'Such as?'

'Such as narcotics.'

'I have only so much time. My legitimate business interests here, my restaurants, the warehouse, not to mention the extent to which the media pesters me to defend the cause of the Asian against the rise of the fascist and racialist parties to the far left!'

Rafiq paused for breath, which allowed Winthrop to suggests smoothly, 'Then delegate, Raffy, delegate.'

'Yes, yes, but it is a matter of trust.'

'I'm seeing the chairman soon. Should I tell him it's becoming a bit much for you?'

'No, it will be all right. I am considering a new man to replace Rawlinson. I will decide one way or the other very soon.'

'May one ask his name?'

Rafiq paused. It would show he had not been idle. Would show the hidden investors in criminal enterprise that their money was only temporarily dormant. 'Yes, certainly. His name is John Kline.'

'Sorry can't add any more t'th'score, got t'get movin'.' Malleson apologised to the dark head on the white pillow.

Sarah Gant yawned sleepily. 'There's another night t'night. Will I see some girls before then?'

Malleson grinned. His cock felt like it had been scrubbed with a wire brush but somehow its tender fall reinforced his swagger. Mrs Gant wasn't bright-eyed and bushy-tailed either.

'I'm off t'fix it now. They can parade at my place late afternoon before they start their night shift.' Malleson looked at the profile and beauty of his new partner. 'Don't expect them to look as good as you, though.'

'Won't troops of exotic ladies attract busybodies on the vice squad?'

Malleson hadn't thought of that. 'Might. Yeh. Huh. I know a place, just the place f'interviewin' personnel in peace. I'll check it out, telephone later, tell you where to meet an' when. See y', brown eyes.' Malleson raised the silver knob of his cane to the brim of his hat and departed, leaving Sarah Gant to open her eyes, waiting, waiting to hear the click of the hotel-room door. When it came, she swept the bedclothes aside and headed for her shower quite alert; she showed little sign of the weariness displayed to the man but a moment before.

'What have you been up to, Mr Kline?' Khan stormed later that morning. 'The nationality squad has been picking up pieces of Irishmen from all around a building site. The body of Dermot Macavoy has been on a tour of the Midlands apparently.'

Kline put his hands in his pockets, leaned against the grille of the Maverick bar.

'We had a Hooley up on the sixteenth floor. I'm very much afraid there was a general falling out of friends.' Kline regarded the normally cool Asian quizzically. 'Is that what's eating you? Nobody saw me at the site.'

'No, no. It's not just that.' Khan looked grimly around the club, at the cleaners, the black blues singer sorting music at a piano. 'Before coming here, I telephoned the head of my department. An unfamiliar voice answered. The man who was my chief is no more. He suffered a heart attack yesterday. And a final cardiac arrest at four o'clock this morning.'

'This affects me?'

'Yes, Mr Kline, this does affect you. The only reason you are free is on his authority. His replacement might not be so flexible, given our present standard of performance. Things must happen, Mr Kline. I must have names, some proof that this consortium of investors in crime exists. Something to justify your remaining at liberty. Move against Malleson. Involve Anne Darracott. Make a big enough splash and maybe you will attract the attention of the consortium and be invited to join them!'

'If—' Kline was interrupted by the buzzing tone on the internal telephone link at the bar. Ducking under the counter and picking up the receiver Kline listened, frowning with irritation. 'Yeh. Give it to the engineer, ask him to stick it on the speakers.' Kline slammed the phone back on its hook.

'Well?' Khan asked.

'That chick who says she's Dinah left a message on tape. Silly cow, I'll kick her arse when I catch up with her.'

The tannoy whined then relayed the muffled voice of a woman that could have belonged to anyone. Even Dinah Carmichael. 'Hello, John, John Kline. Are we ever goin' t'meet up? I waited such a long time an' you never called. Let's meet up. We've ever so much t'talk about. Old times. How it was. What you got me into. I'll be at this number at four this afternoon – 2468252. Look forward t'seeing you. All my love, Dinah.'

Kline tried to figure it out. Khan watched the play of nagging thoughts that made Kline hook his fingers into the grille of the bar and stare down at the floor.

'You intend to call that number at four o'clock?'

'Bet your boots,' said Kline, straightening and looking aggressive. Khan nodded. It seemed that at last his partner was ready to move against the source of guilt that had beset him since the death of Dinah Carmichael.

'I met a guy...' the blonde bitch shrugged as if it didn't really matter. 'Went down the chute for him. In the sixties, y'know, having a passport stamped in the East didn't automatically guarantee a shakedown at Customs. Well, this guy've mine. He got hooked on heroin, became impotent.'

The psychiatrist sat back in his chair and watched Anne's reaction to seeing the bored manner and cold dismissive attitude of herself as she had been recorded on videotape.

'Impotent,' the flesh-and-blood Anne said to the image of herself on the screen. 'I thought he couldn't get it up because of you!'

The voice of Dr Rai spoke, as voice over, on the set. 'What happened?'

A shrug from the screen. 'I couldn't cure him, so finally, to keep him company, I began to fix too.'

'How did your relationship with Roy finish?'

Another shrug. 'It terminated.'

Standing before the machine, Anne gestured in hopeless explanation. 'I wasn't there. We'd had a fight. He must've used a dirty needle.'

'Septicaemia,' said Dr Rai from behind his desk.

Anne shrugged casually, as if she was before the camera. 'It's another word for death.' Then she realised with sudden and complete detachment that here she was acting before a screen that showed her acting before a camera and herself. The multiplicity of her self-deceit struck her like the thrust from a bayonet. Crying out, holding her belly, she sank down before the persona that in a matter-of-fact manner was summarising a whole period of her youth.

'I drifted around,' it said, 'trying to fix enough courage to take that trip down to London but I never did.'

The sobs choked up and up. Anne began to bawl out the emotion stifled all the years of her life. When the racking sobs drowned the monologue of cool detachment from the tape, Dr Rai turned it off and comforted her before leading his patient, her eyes awash with tears, into the corridor and back towards her ward.

As they passed reception a tall man stood up quickly at the sight of the weeping woman. Recognising the visitor, the doctor shook his head. 'Not just yet, Mr Kline.'

'I'll wait.'

'As you wish.'

Kline sat back on his chair, wondered what had happened. Checked his watch; it was still three quarters of an hour before four o'clock. He could afford to wait for a little while.

'Haven't cried like that for years,' said Anne.

'It's supposed to make you feel better.'

The blonde head shook itself resignedly.

'There's only one thing makes me feel better. And I'm not going to get a supply here. But at least I know now how this place works. If I can get a release with a series of supply scripts for methadone, that'll buy me time to get organised again.'

She paused. Struggled with her inner self. Looked almost shyly at the man beside her bed.

'What d'y'want?' Kline asked quietly.

'You to pretend you're my straight, caring, loving boyfriend. That you'll look after me. If the doctors believe I'm into a relationship that's halfway healthy they'll let me out and put my name on their mailing list.'

Kline thought about it. Anne hastened to add, 'Once you take me through that door you can go one way and me the other.'

'Yeh. I'd figured that.'

'What d'y'say, will you see the doctors?'

Kline nodded decisively. 'Sure. I've some business to attend to but I'll tell them we're going to get married.'

'No. No, there's no need...'

Kline put his fingers to her lips. 'If you're going to tell lies, Annie, make them as big as a house.' Then he smiled at her, checked his watch. Frowned and made to go.

'Kline... uh...' Anne realised she didn't even know her fiancé's first name.

'John,' Kline said dryly.

'Well, John. Y'know… thanks.'

Kline raised a hand before hurrying away. Anne rubbed her eyes with the back of her wrist, lay back and began to cry quietly but this time gently until she lapsed into quiet sleep.

At the reception desk John Kline stressed his commitment to Anne and was told that his desire to accept responsibility would be communicated to Dr Rai.

'Good.' Kline paused. 'Is there a telephone?'

'Just outside,' the receptionist pointed.

With the second hand racing towards four o'clock Kline hurried outside and dialled the number given him by the voice that professed itself Dinah Carmichael's.

His call was answered immediately.

'I'll be at the old Milner place. You want to see me. Be there,' a woman's voice said tersely. The phone went dead.

Kline went back into the hospital.

'Old Milner place. Know it?'

'No,' the receptionist shook her head. 'But maybe one of the taxi drivers does. Should I call?'

'Yes, if you would,' Kline said.

'Is it an emergency?'

'Might be.'

Kline paid off the driver by a factory that was obviously disused. Around the factory perimeter Kline could see broken fencing and a great growth of fireweeds. A movement caught his eye. It was a woman, a young woman, hurrying down a side road towards a gated entrance. As the taxi pulled away Kline ran to overtake the girl. As he got nearer he could see the provocative sway of arse inside over-tight trousers. He realised also the girl's skin tone was as dark as that of Dinah Carmichael. Excited, despite his reason, Kline caught hold of the girl's arm and swung her about to face him.

'Yow in a hurry t'do business or sumthin', mate?' A Brummy voice whined indignantly. Kline had never seen whoever it was before.

'No,' he said. 'Sorry, thought you might be someone else.'

'Bloody cheek. Thought yow was a rapist.'

'No. Sorry.'

'Good job,' the girl said. 'Now, I'm late.' She turned and hurried away, not past the factory but through the rusting gate. Puzzled, Kline followed, some instinct making him take care to keep out of sight. The girl flounced up to a door and knocked. After a moment the door was pulled back. The girl stepped inside. A black face peered out. With a tingle of shock Kline recognised Malleson's helper, Hunniford. What was going on? Kline decided to mount a small investigation. Carefully, he entered the yard of the factory and prowled around seeking an entrance or a sight of whatever the place contained. What windows were available revealed nothing but empty offices. Kline turned a corner and came upon the iron steps of a fire escape. After glancing about and seeing nothing but clumps of weed, Kline began to climb the steps that led towards the roof of the factory known locally as the old Milner place.

Hidden by the fence, Khan watched Kline ascend the fire escape. Having traced the address of the telephone kiosk number given by the mysterious caller, he had waited to follow the woman who had answered Kline's call at four o'clock that afternoon. Now that Kline had arrived Khan decided it was time to move a little closer to whatever was about to happen. Stiffly, he eased muscles cramped by the waiting and watched Kline clamber on to the rent and disappear from view.

Part of the roof was of reinforced glass and halfway along Kline saw that a panel was missing; carefully he sidled along, unaware that his progress was visible from inside the main workshop of the factory below. The scene that Kline looked down on was part of a parade. A gaudily dressed lady would sally back and forth before a khaki-clad figure wearing a forage cap whose peak obscured from Kline's view the features of the face below. Click! The figure snapped its fingers and another black lady detached herself from the press of prostitutes to present herself for appraisal. Kline recognised her as the girl he had accosted outside the factory gate. The angle of his vision allowed him to see only a little of the scene below. Deciding to return to the fire escape and enter the factory at a lower level, Kline began to move back along the frosted glass of the roof.

Down below the whores chattered and giggled as the parade ended. The lady in khaki gave her judgments to Malleson then noticed the shadow of Kline above. Pointing upwards she indicated the intruder, felt in her shoulder bag, produced her pistol and handed it to Malleson, pointing towards a row of offices. Malleson, realising what was required, nodded and hurried towards a door marked 'Personnel'.

Kline found a door that was splintered and easy to force, a little way from the foot of the fire escape.

Inside, he found himself in a long corridor between offices. Hearing a sound, he flattened himself along the wall and saw at the corridor's end a glimpse of passing khaki.

Kline moved swiftly along to the corner in time to see the back of a woman at the door of an office marked 'Personnel'. Kline waited for the door to open and close behind the lady. Then he padded along, took a breath, and opened the door to find a gun trained on his belly; it was held by a grinning Malleson, who leaned against a glass partition.

Behind the door, the lady guerrilla stepped out of the line of fire. Kline took his eyes from the gun and stared at a black face whose eyes were concealed by the slats of wide sun-shades. The sensual mouth, however, mocked him with a cruel smile of anticipation.

'Fire!' she ordered. Malleson did so. Kline spun around as the woman spoke but felt a searing pain as the bullet tore through the flesh below his lowest rib. Grimacing with pain and shock he stumbled and fell to the floor.

'Again, again... Fire again!'

Malleson moved forward; there was plenty of time to level the score with the fallen Kline. A bullet through the head would be the killer, Malleson decided, and he stepped forward to deliver the *coup de grâce*.

Khan had waited for a minute before following Kline into the offices of the factory. As he had ventured inside Kline had disappeared into the adjoining corridor after his quarry, and the first intimation Khan received of his whereabouts was the sound of a shot. Khan began to run at speed towards what he took to be the office from which the sound of gunfire had come. Unfortunately he had miscalculated and the office he opened contained nothing but an old metal file container turned on its side. Then Khan saw through the frosted glass partition blurred figures in the adjoining office. Saw an arm with a gun in its hand begin to extend itself.

Picking up the filing cabinet, Khan hurled its weight at the glass, shattering and showering the occupants of the next room with a rain of splintered glass.

Disturbed in the process of execution, Malleson fired but missed the head of the man on the floor; before he had a chance to aim again, Khan charged into the office to tackle the black in the style of a rugby forward. Both men fell and struggled together amidst the shattered glass on the floor while Kline gathered his strength and staggered after the woman who had almost engineered his destruction.

Malleson held on to the gun, recognised Khan and detected the strong scent of law enforcement. Determined to cut his losses, he scrambled clear of the Asian's clutches and ran through the gap in the broken glass wall and out of the neighbouring office, seeking a speedy return to his helpers and whores before the pursuing Khan could grapple with him again.

Malleson managed to gain enough of a lead to allow him precious seconds in the main workshop. As he entered it he groaned, for from the far entrance two uniformed policemen had entered and were advancing towards the group of girls and their pimps, Hunniford and Bryden.

'Scram... Scram!' Malleson yelled.

Squawking and fluttering like a flock of frightened exotic birds, the whores scattered in all directions.

Running alongside a buxom, bouncing belle named Maxine, Malleson thrust the pistol into her hand.

'Hide it for me,' he panted, then turned to gather Hunniford and Bryden to his side to prevent the progress of the police.

Black and blue were about to confront each other when from behind the West Indians a voice said, 'Hold it.'

Malleson turned to see Khan with the drop on him.

'OK, sure. No sweat,' Malleson said, looking past the police revolver to see if Maxine had cleared the premises. When he saw she had he relaxed and asked haughtily, 'What's all this about?'

With supreme effort Kline caught the woman at the fence; he could feel the blood flowing from the wound in his side. He wanted to retch, to lay down the burden of forcing his hurt body to tackle the surprisingly strong female that now fought, scratched and struggled to break the grip of his unwelcome embrace.

Rolling over and over, the man eventually used his weight to subdue and pin the woman beneath him. Lifting a shaking hand, fighting sickness and a fading control of consciousness, Kline at last pulled off the slatted sunglasses and stared down into the dark eyes of Sarah Gant.

Kline tried to recognise the face below him but it blurred and faded as he tried to place the vague sense of familiarity this stranger aroused in him.

'Who the hell are you?' he managed to blurt out in the last seconds before unconsciousness overwhelmed him.

Sarah felt Kline's head drop on to her shoulder. Almost within reach of where they lay on the rough ground was a stone of sufficient weight to smash a skull, but as she wriggled and reached out a hand, a polished shoe stepped, with light pressure, upon her wrist.

'To repeat that last question and to ask another,' Khan said politely, 'just who are you and why do you wish to kill Mr Kline?'

Chapter Eleven

Kline sat propped up in his hospital bed. Khan sat on the chair beside him and stroked his moustache.

'Who is she? Her name is Sarah Gant.'

'So?'

'*Née* Carmichael.'

After a pause Kline said, 'Dinah's sister?'

'Yes. When her parents emigrated she went to an aunt in America. Dinah came to England. It's not unusual in West Indian family life. When she attended her sister's funeral she refused to believe a drug overdose was the cause of death and came to Birmingham to investigate.'

'Why didn't she come to me?'

'Not that straightforward, Mr Kline. She thinks that your irresponsibility was a direct cause of her sister's death. Sarah gained Malleson's confidence, enticed you as Dinah's ghost and brought you both together; she informed the local police of the meeting and encouraged what she hoped would be fatal results.'

Kline scratched a pectoral muscle. Nodded.

'Neat.'

'I would grant high marks for such initiative.'

'I'm sure you would. Sorry to spoil her game by surviving. Where's Malleson?'

'Your friend is awaiting charges. Unfortunately he disposed of the gun but we can nail him down for ten years with you as a direct witness and recipient of his bullet.'

Kline grunted. 'We'll talk about that when I'm up and out've here.'

'To use your expression, Mr Kline, Malleson has been taken out of the game. That is all I require.'

'You said me an' him could travel all the way. Ten years in the nick's just a stop down the line.'

'No, Mr Kline.'

'I've had a visitor, a Mr Rafiq. He was quite, quite charming. Wants me to come to lunch. Seems I'm to meet some friends of his with a view to mutual profit if they approve me…'

'The consortium?'

'I think so. Part of it anyhow.'

'When will you attend this luncheon?'

'Tomorrow. I've cleared it with the hospital. So long as I don't go berserk physically, I'll be OK.'

'You're sure?' said Khan, his brain racing to evaluate this latest break in their favour.

'Providing I'm not encumbered with police enquiries over Malleson.'

'Yes. I'll do what I can,' Khan said absently. 'Excuse me.'

Kline watched the Asian press a summons bell.

'This could mean a great deal to us, Mr Kline, this approach to you from Rafiq. My new chief is by reputation a by-the-book man who has little time for the use of clandestine agents. Especially unsuccessful ones. But now, perhaps… Well, I am expecting a summons. Anything you can glean from Rafiq might mean the difference between success and failure. Freedom or captivity for you… Ah.' Khan turned to the door, which had opened to admit an elegant brown lady now wearing a haute couture trouser suit in funereal black.

'Ah, Mrs Gant.' Khan stood and became effusive. 'Please do come in. I know you have met but allow me to introduce you formally. Mrs Gant, John Kline.'

'You remind me of someone I used to know,' Kline said, trying to cover his surprise and alarm at being confronted so unexpectedly with the lethal lady from New York.

'I wonder why that should be?' Sarah said coldly.

'Children, children,' Khan chided.

The man and woman continued to stare antagonistically, like two boxers in the preliminaries to a prize fight. Khan glanced at his watch. 'Dear, dear,' he said casually, 'I really must be going. Be good to each other.' He was through the door, leaving them alone before they realised he was going.

After a long pause the lady said, 'They let you smoke in these places?'

'Nope.'

'I thought not,' said Sarah, shaking out a cigarette from her pack.

'Ta...' Kline said in anticipation.

Sarah Gant hesitated, then passed the pack to him 'Just want t'tell you it's not my idea, this working together.'

Kline blinked. 'Work?'

'Mangin' hookers for you. What was to be mine and Malleson's escort racket. Somethin' I dreamed up as bait. It's feasible. I just never planned on it reachin' the operational stage, that's all.'

The man in the bed rubbed his forehead; then understanding dawned. 'You've been talking to Mr Khan.'

Sarah smiled ruefully. 'For days I've been talking to him.'

'So, for playing madam what do you receive in return?'

'The promise that you won't prefer charges.'

Kline sighed in exasperation. 'That one.'

'What?'

'Nothing. What else?'

This time it was the woman's turn to sigh.

'To be satisfied with just half a pound of your flesh.'

'Can we settle on that?' Kline asked, his expression open and serious.

A bitter little smile formed on the wide mouth. 'Would you?'

Kline shifted uncomfortably. Now that he could take a close look, Sarah's resemblance to her dead sister disturbed him. Finally he decided to say what was in his head and heart. 'I feel Dinah's death. Every day. If I could take her place under the ground, I would. All I can do now is make sure the guy who killed her pays.'

'Yeah.'

'About this escort agency... If it's a way to squeeze Malleson out into the open, fine; if not, forget it. And as for Khan and his little schemes, there'll be no charges from me. So why not do yourself a favour, leave Malleson to me.'

Sarah drew deeply on her cigarette.

'I'll split him with you,' she offered. 'Right up the middle.'

Transferring his walking stick from one hand to the other, Kline used it to support the weight of his body as he clambered aboard the *Anne Carol*.

Inside the cabin Anne Darracott felt the sway of the barge and glanced up from her work of restoring a damaged section of feather banding on a drawer from an antique cabinet.

'Who…?' she started to call, then stopped in surprise as John Kline ducked through the bead curtain that divided the main cabin from the kitchen.

'What do you want?'

'Thought I'd see how my fiancée was copin' with life's little problems.'

Seated like an elf, cross-legged on the carpeted floor, Anne looked at the tip of the glue brush. What was there to say?

'OK,' she said wryly. 'You?'

'Been in dock. That's why I couldn't see you.'

'I didn't expect…'

'Least I could have done was carry your suitcase out've that rehab place.'

'You did enough.'

'Everything OK?'

The elf shrugged, pushing the brush back into a pot of glue. 'Prescriptions arrive every day. It's a start. A breathing space.'

'Yeh. What you goin' to do for loot?'

'Dunno. Work. Something like that, I suppose, 'less something else turns up.'

Kline paused. She seemed calmer, more adjusted than he had ever seen her. Probably the alternative treatment she was receiving. 'How'd you like t'work for me?' he asked casually.

A quick frown. 'As what? Hat-check girl? Stripper?'

'More boring than that. Secretary, PA, companion — whatever y'want to call it.'

Anne said nothing but continued to stare up at him in genuine bewilderment. Why he had bothered to visit at all was beyond her. And now this job offer… Searching for an answer, she found herself looking into the eyes of John Kline and realised with surprise that he was maybe offering a genuine commitment, not only as an employer but as a man. Misinterpreting her reaction Kline went on.

'I'd pay as much as your old bossman Rawlinson did.'

Anne smiled in bitter memory of that bastard.

'He paid in kind mostly. A cut of the merchandise.'

'I've a lunch appointment with Rafiq an' some of his fancy mates in an hour. He's interested in the smugglin' of narcotics. You know the names. The routes. The market price. You know why people want the stuff and to what lengths they'll go. I don't and never will.'

Anne remained silent, fighting off a vague sense of disappointment. Perhaps she'd mistaken the man's motive. He just wanted to use her, same as her former boss and lover. Well, what to do?

Kline could think of only one further enticement. 'You re-organise the drug route and no one's goin' to mind a small cut out of each and every consignment.'

The elf stood up from the floor.

Kline watched the pink tip of tongue make slow progress across her upper lip.

'Come an' have some lunch,' he said engagingly.

In the week that followed Kline's release from hospital, Khan had expected a summons to report to the newly appointed head of the department that contained Khan's section of the Security Service.

Since being accepted on a probationary basis by Winthrop and Rafiq, Kline and Anne had brought in several titbits of new information and each day Khan had prepared an ever more detailed account of the activities of the consortium of interests that were ploughing the profits of corrupt business practice into the spread of organised crime throughout the Midlands.

Finally the demand for a personal report on his activities had arrived and Khan now found himself seated on the upper terrace of the imposing sixteenth-century house owned by Sir George Jeavons.

After the knight of the civil service had listened to Khan's report he made no immediate comment but glanced instead over the tailored sweep of undulating lawn and beyond to the horizon of his estate.

Khan waited, studying the slightly florid face of the still relatively youthful man who had achieved such a meteoric rise.

Sir George turned from contemplation of the landscape back to his guest. 'More tea?'

'No, no thank you.'

'Quite right. Like a rose, the first is the best. Sometimes I have a pot of Darjeeling tea brought out to me with the lid removed. I sit alone with that so beautiful aroma all about me and watch my world at peace.

One could still be in rural England. Society stable, the Industrial Revolution slouching forward but still unborn. Our great years yet to be...'

'India yet to be conquered for her tea plantations,' Khan interposed gently.

Jeavons smiled, inclined his head in acknowledgement.

'That's the flaw, of course. How quick you are, Khan.'

'It is my job.'

'Yes. Come, I'll show you the grounds. You can see the house at its best from the lower terrace. And we can talk about your job.'

'Fine.' Khan stood and fell into step with his new superior. Walking away from the house, Jeavons spoke abruptly.

'So, tell me... this gang you call the consortium. You have all their names and occupations?'

'Not just yet but in a matter of days...'

'Days make a week, weeks make up into months... Stop.'

Khan wondered what was expected of him.

'Now, turn...'

The Asian did as he was instructed and saw the striking aspect of the house that soared above them.

'Magnificent.'

'If you were fortunate enough to possess a house and home as beautiful as this, would you risk its loss by giving your authority to an unlawful investigation?'

'It is only stones held together by mortar.' Khan spoke without thinking. Disturbed by the implications of the last remark, Jeavons turned his mouth down in reproof.

'What at pragmatist you are, Khan.'

'I enjoy its beauty, of course.'

'Mmm...' The voice of Jeavons seemed tinged with disappointment. 'Of course, the styles, the different architectural styles, the periods of English history, what they represent would mean nothing to a follower of Islam.'

Khan looked away from the house and beyond the shoulder of the Englishman beside him.

'I follow only what I call truth. One God. Call it Islam. Call it whatever you wish. It is everywhere, in people and also in the splendour of your estate, Sir George.'

'You would be a difficult man to tempt with power, money or prestige, Khan.'

The Asian smiled but did not feel any need to reply.

'But corruption can take other forms,' Jeavons continued. 'There's corruption by idea. The idea of a more fulfilling life, of the greater good, of promotion, of restoring a nation's glory in the way I have restored that house – by destroying some wings, rebuilding others.' Jeavons continued to gaze towards the edifice of his property but with a change of manner and intonation as his official position began to manifest itself. 'I believe you employ clandestine agents. Who they are you will not say. This is not condoned by society, the law, my minister or myself. Your actions, do they not contravene this truth of yours?'

'When a shoal is landed some little fish may swim away, surely?'

'That might seem to be justice but it's not the law and it makes you, Khan, to be no more than an end-justifying-means man.'

With alarm Khan attempted to divert the process of decision that seemed to be flowing against him. 'This is hardly fair,' he protested. 'Today I have reported my successes. Given you names – the property developer, Winthrop; the secretary to the consortium, Norah... the means by which they are bringing drugs into the United Kingdom—'

'But not the top men. The top two. What do you call them?'

'MD – I mean managing director – and the chairman. I have no names yet but given a little more time.'

Jeavons sighed. 'That we do not have. What secrets and deals my predecessor knew and made must lie buried with him in the boneyard. We must start anew. You will turn over the illegal immigration details to the Home Office. The gentleman you say is bringing in heroin by means of the diplomatic bag can be apprehended by Special Branch with the goods in question. I suggest you spend some time on your reports then perhaps take a spot of leave to allow the realisation that from now on illegal investigative methods will not be required.'

'And the consortium?' Khan could hardly contain his anger and disbelief.

'Fraud Squad. CID. Give them what you have. Let them interview these mysterious sources of information you guard so jealously.'

'Sir George, just two days more.' Khan made a last plea. 'Please.'

'Request denied, Khan,' Jeavons snapped in irritation at the persistence of the agent. 'I am now the authority responsible for your activities. I call them unlawful and if persisted in they may render you liable to prosecution and imprisonment. Can I make it clearer than that?'

A wave of frustration engulfed Khan.

'No, Sir George,' he said heavily.

Jeavons slapped him on the shoulder.

'Now... let me show you the other side of the house before you leave.'

At the lock gate, the barge *Anne Carol* bumped and nosed against the wooden barrier as if sharing the impatience of her owner, Anne Darracott.

Screwing her eyes up against the bright sunshine, she peered at the trees of the adjoining copse of trees alongside.

'Relax,' Kline said sleepily.

Anne snorted in derision and stared nervously at her watch.

'You don't realise what we're into. People double cross, steal, lie, cheat, kill for just a speck of the stash we're carrying.'

'You arranged this pick-up point.'

'Yeh. With a Chinese guy name of Yan. Uh...!' Anne made a conscious effort to relax by leaning back on rigid arms. Beside her on the roof of the barge Kline advised, 'Give it five minutes.'

'No more... what are you doing?'

Kline said nothing but raised the wide sleeve of her tunic to reveal the inner arm still blotched purple from her time on the needle. Silently he kissed the bruised flesh. Anne jerked away. 'What is this?'

'Just passin' time. We keep gettin' thrown together.' He waved a hand at the empty landscape. 'This lot is like you an' me. No connection.'

Anne stood over him, legs splayed apart, hands on hips.

'When I agreed to work for you there was no mention of being required to screw. So if you just want a pair've legs t' lie between, there's plenty walking about the Maverick Club who'll he happy to stay open 'til all hours.'

Kline knew it. 'OK, OK.'

But the blonde hadn't finished. Rubbing her inner arm, she went on. 'Two things I'd like to stop. One is maybe dependence on what we've got hidden down below. The other thing is, I'm twenty-five running up to fifty. I've had a lot've guys, all sorts, passive t'massive... I've been passed from hand to hand like a dirty book. An', you know what, baby, I'm sick of it. So lets back off.'

'If y'want.'

Anne took three angry steps away along the roof of the barge. Waved her arms in a gesture that expressed all her confusion of emotion. 'It's not what I *want*!' Then, after a long pause during which the turmoil within her quietened, 'I'm simply saying that if a nice ride on the waterways of the Grand Union Canal is all you're after, pick up some other vessel.'

Kline watched her jump down on to the stern, saw her fumble for the pill bottle and swallow tablets of methadone. Fair enough, he thought. We know where we're at. Me n'her.

Anne started the motor and began to reverse away from the abortive rendezvous.

In the cover of the bushes, two Chinese youths watched the barge begin to pull away Only when it had gone quite out of sight and they were certain that nobody else was in the vicinity did they feel justified in leaving the lock to return to Birmingham and report what they had seen.

That evening Kline stood with his new friend Mr Rafiq at the bar of the Maverick.

'But why would they not turn up?' Rafiq asked anxiously.

'Dunno. Anne's out tryin' t'establish contact. Why the hurry?'

Rafiq lowered his voice carefully. 'The big boys like big profits. The hero... the goods in question are our best chance to produce a quick success before the next full board meeting.'

Do I get to meet the great MD or his mate, the chairman, ever?'

Rafiq spread his hands. 'They reveal neither their names nor faces to mortals such as we, John. Ah, Anne...'

' 'lo,' said Kline, noticing that the blonde lady had changed into a black evening gown with a glittering criss-cross of sequins that caught his eye.

'I've left a message for the guy who was supposed to purchase our supply.' She shrugged. 'Told him we were pretty pissed off at being left hanging like a spare prick at a wedding. All right, Rafiq? Nice t'see you here. Quite like old times.'

'Yes. Yes... I merely popped in to check on progress.'

'Don't worry about it '

'Yes.'

Kline eased his weight from one leg to the other.

'You got a pain?' Anne said, noticing the slight frown of unease come to Kline's face.

'Bit.'

'Why not sit down. Do your wound a favour.'

Why not lie down, Kline thought. In bed with you. 'Tell me,' he started as Rafiq drifted away towards a group that contained Sarah Gant and various attractive ladies recently filched from the stable of Mr Malleson.

'Tell you what?'

'Do you want a drink?'

'No.'

They stood alongside each other looking across the club to where the Shadettes' lead singer sang a straight simple version of 'My Man'.

'That speech you made out on the lock,' Kline said. 'You meant all of that, didn't you?'

'Yes.'

'Thought so.'

'And you? That time. When you first saw me here. About wanting to touch and feel and have all of me. You meant all of that?'

'Yep.'

'I see.'

'So we both know what we're getting into,' Kline said, looking sideways at her. Anne nodded, put a finger to her mouth, grinned impishly, said nothing.

Kline said. 'Let's go to the boat.'

An hour later Khan was about to enter the main area of the Maverick when he caught sight of Rafiq and Sarah Gant in conversation at a table near the bar. Not wishing to alert Rafiq to his connection with Kline, Khan decided it was best to withdraw. The news he had to impart to Kline was only of defeat and that would keep until tomorrow. Walking out of the club left Khan with the rest of the night looming empty ahead. Having spent the day clearing his desk and writing reports, he felt drained, resentful, angry at having to leave a job half done. What to do? Whom to see? He remembered Mangit. Moodily he thought that there was more unfinished business. Her husband perhaps somewhere along the route of illegal immigration, perhaps at this very moment in possession of facts and names that would ensure closedown, convictions that would pay the long-standing debt for the death of a police colleague who had been murdered while working undercover for Mr Rafiq. Khan suspected Kuldip, of course, but proving it? It was too much. But Khan couldn't walk away; he had lived with it for too long. He decided to pay a visit to Mangit and to let the course of events run wild for a little longer.

Frantic for each other, Kline and Anne started pulling off clothes and loosening buttons before even reaching the bead curtain. At the bed Kline bent to kiss the lips held up to him. Suddenly he thought he heard a sound from outside. He hesitated. Anne's lips parted to reveal that attractive gap-toothed smile.

'You've too good a memory, matey,' she said. 'No one's going to—' she stopped as two Chinese youths thrust aside the curtain of the cabin to allow the entrance of a middle-aged Chinese who bowed politely. 'Miss Darracott.'

'Mr Yan,' Anne said acidly, advancing from the bed. 'How nice to see you at long last.'

'Forgive my caution. You understand, after losing so many tried and trusted Triad colleagues to the drug squad, I must be extra careful. My nephews observed your frustration at our not-meeting out on the canal. Now I come to you with the hope that we may do business.'

'Good,' said Anne decisively.

'You have a sample?'

'You have the money?'

'Yes.' Yan indicated the nearest youth, who tossed a hold-all bag to Kline.

'Check it,' Anne ordered.

Watching Kline open the bag and fan out the bundles of bank notes, Yan said smoothly,

'May I also be as cautious when I receive *my* purchase?'

'Of course.' The woman moved to the trunk, opened the lid, touched a spring and took from the compartment that jumped open a small package of Number 4 heroin. She handed it to the Chinese, who already had a slip of polythene and a bottle of chemicals to test the purity and validity of the sample.

From watching the Chinese huddle over the serious business of the sample, Anne glanced across at Kline enquiringly: holding all ten fingers up, Kline indicated the ten one-thousand-pound bundles scattered on the bed. It wasn't street prices but at this link in the chain it was a fair profit, she decided.

Satisfied with the test, which changed white grains to purple, Yan bowed. 'We will do business again. Next time you will not be kept waiting.'

'Good. See you,' Anne called after the departing Chinese.

Delighted with the success of the transaction and tingling for the things to come, Anne and Kline decided that clothes were surplus to requirements.

Seeing the dark run of irregular stitching around the side of the white torso, Anne asked anxiously, 'You be OK?'

'Don't worry.' Kline pulled off a last item of clothing, which revealed hard evidence to disprove any doubts the woman might have had about the validity of her sexual attractiveness.

Regarding what was now Kline's most outstanding feature Anne experienced for the first time in years the full flow of excitements that came not through the point of a needle but from inside her brain and belly. Seeing John Kline about to clear the spread of banknotes from the bed, Anne said with relish. 'Let it lie. It should be so lucky.'

Kline grinned. C'mere,' he ordered, opening his arms to an embrace that soon led them to fuck with fine abandon on the mattress of money.

In a garage halfway between the airfield and the house of Rafiq, Kuldip pulled the first of the latest batch of smuggled Asians out of the glider container. There was something familiar about this one, Kuldip thought as he scanned the face of the illegal immigrant now before him.

Thankful that he had taken the reluctant decision to discard his beard and turban, Jashir Singh Marshall stared back into the eyes of one of the men who had betrayed his name to the immigration authorities. Jashir's hand tightened on the hilt of the short kirpan sword his religion required him to carry.

Kuldip decided there was nothing to bring a name to mind. 'Move!' he shouted and pointed to a Dormobile with open doors.

Thankfully Jashir hurried to the van. He would deal with Kuldip and Rafiq in the course of time. Now, after his long journey, he wanted only to be carried on this final lap that would end with him back in the city of Birmingham, there to reunite with his children, Bela and Ashi, and his wife, Mangit

In the large bed in the small room the Indian woman clung tearfully to the Pakistani man.

'It is all right,' Khan said soothingly.

'I am unfaithful now as a wife, Mangit said. 'What will happen to me?'

'Nothing, darling,' Khan said and held her to him.

Chapter Twelve

With her children out of the house it seemed ominously quiet as Mangit cleared the breakfast table. The knock at the door startled her. Since she had moved to this flat few friends or relatives came to visit. Behind the panelling, she called, 'Yes. Who...?'

'Jashir.'

Mangit's heart began to beat like a bird at the bars of a cage.

'Open the door,' Jashir urged. 'Open the door!'

Trembling, she had to obey. When the Sikh entered, there was no rush of welcome, only a guilty averted glance. Without need of explanation Jashir intuitively understood the loss of his wife's honour and loyalty. His thoughts ran with panic to the silence in the rooms of the little flat.

'The children?' he said with a tremor of rage in his voice, despite his every effort at control. 'Where are my children? Where?'

Anne was awake before Kline. Refreshed, released, she felt permeated with the juice and essence of the man asleep beside her.

As if feeling her warmth of gratitude Kline turned in sleep, winced at the pull on the stitches of his wound and half awakened to the woman's caress stealing down from chest to belly.

'Huhm. You'll be lucky, Annie,' he said but then realised, feeling the sudden lurch towards tumescence, that luck had nothing to do with it; that he was in bed with someone who had made it a pleasure to stay through the night into this most pleasant morning.

Feeling the slow roll and rub of her hand on his penis made the ache in his side recede. Having to protect the wound had made for restricted and controlled movement that had meant for the most part lying back and bringing Anne onto him.

This was the position they now adopted – Anne mounting the pole, riding the cock horse back and forth, up and down all around the town until she found herself at a junction of multiple orgasms.

Anne shuddered, straightened, felt the brace of legs and caressed the balls that lay behind her. She did not want the act to end any more than did Kline, who knew that the cries and sobs of his lady rider and the pleasure welling up and out of him might be the last act before a bitter parting. For Kline had decided that Anne must be told the full story of what he had enticed her into.

Lost in the flood and flow of orgasms, Kline gently brought the small shoulders, the little-girl breasts, the blonde head, down to rest. Made the white body lie along on his, coupled and, for the moment, content.

In the benign exhaustion of this post-coital embrace Kline kissed the side of the face resting against his. There was the salt taste that could have been from tears. Experiencing a wave of compassion Kline sought her mouth.

Anne opened her eyes briefly at the strength of his pressure. When she could speak she propped up on an elbow and looked wonderingly at the man's face below.

'That's one to start the screwing not to end it.'

'It's all right,' Kline said and looked away.

'What is?'

'Everything.'

'Good,' said Anne, feeling the last of her hold on him relax and the now softened penis fall away to, she hoped, fight another day.

'Coffee,' she announced. 'Eggs?' she asked.

'Yeah. Love it,' Kline said reaching for his cigarettes and deciding that he would not condemn himself by explanation until after breakfast.

On the balcony of the swimming baths Jashir sat and brooded, looking through the ornate Victorian ironwork down towards the blue water in which Khan played and cavorted with Anhi and Bela. The question was not whether to kill but where. Where? As if in answer to the Sikh's inward question, Khan pulled himself out of the water and entered a cubicle to re-emerge almost immediately bearing a brightly panelled plastic beach ball with which to entertain Jashir's children.

The Sikh could not bear to watch the happiness of the scene below;

there was only one thing that the situation demanded he should do.

Jashir stood and moved purposefully to the steps that led to the changing cubicles below.

In the swimming bath Khan held the little brown body of Bela and let her legs kick and thresh the water in one last burst of energy before leaving the pool at the end of the lesson.

With the water splashing and the children laughing, Khan did not see Jashir slip into the cubicle that contained his clothing.

'That's enough,' Khan said eventually and lifted first one child then the other onto the damp-pitted edge of the swimming bath.

Holding a small hand in each of his, Khan walked towards the cubicle.

Inside the milky light of the small wooden space, Jashir took out his kirpan sword and waited for the swing doors to part so that he could thrust the point of the blade into the belly of Mr Khan.

It was Bela who saved the agent's life, for, within yards of the changing room, she broke free, danced away, then tossed the beach ball she was holding to her 'uncle'. Khan caught it and stopped momentarily as the child ran ahead into the cubicle.

Khan saw the man with the sword but did not recognise his identity until Ashi shouted shrilly, 'Da-Da!'

That was all the warning Khan had before the first thrust of the broad blade came lunging at him. Parrying the wrist beyond the hilt was all Khan could do, and with the force of the charge both men went stumbling towards the slippery side of the bath and plunged headlong into the water.

Having only recently left the swimming bath Khan was more adaptable to the change of element, and having seen the sword fall to the floor of the pool, he immediately lured the Sikh away from an attempt at retrieval by swimming as if to reach the steps that led up out of the pool.

When Jashir struck out in pursuit Khan swam for the steps using just enough power to keep out of reach of the flailing arms behind. Within reach of the side, Khan suddenly spurted, dived for the tiled wall, turned over underwater, felt his feet touch the side, then kicked and launched himself torpedo-like back at the oncoming Sikh.

Khan's head came up and under Jashir's solar plexus to connect with sickening impact. Unbalanced and with the breath forced out of him, Jashir panicked, gulped water and went under. By the time he surfaced Khan was almost out of the water. Jashir surged towards the side and caught hold of the agent's ankle. Khan, within reach of a stiff bristled yardbrush used for cleaning the pool, managed to grasp and bring the handle to him. When the Sikh tried again to hoist Khan back into the pool, he received the sharp stab of a hundred bristle ends from the brush head. Crying with pain and with the shock of having eyes stung into temporary blindness, Jashir felt hands haul him from the water.

Unable to see out of blurred and streaming eyes the Sikh shook his head from side to side in angry acknowledgment that his attempt at vengeance had ended in failure.

Leading Jashir along the side of the baths, Khan saw the frightened children, Ashi and Bela. 'It is all right,' he called, but the children would not come to the man who had blinded their father When Khan extended a comforting hand, both children, as one, backed away.

They had breakfasted quietly. For Anne it had always been that euphoria was disturbed by comment, but slowly it came to her the growing period of silence might be because of something ominous. Worriedly, she began to gather the crumpled banknotes scattered in the melee of the night before.

Kline watched her. When she had two hands full of money, he said almost shyly, 'You were worth it.'

'Maybe we should just take this lot and skip merrily out of town, mmm?'

Kline thought about it. 'I dunno what muscle this consortium's got behind it.'

'Let's find out,' Anne suggested, lightly.

'I need more than money to get off the hook.'

'What's that mean?'

In the pause, Kline shrugged, looked away, tried to change tack. 'Who gets the loot?'

'The secretary to the board, Norah.' Anne imitated a precise business-ladylike tone. 'Ladies lavatorium in the city centre. We go in adjoining stations and pass the loot under and along. What's the betting she pushes a receipt back underneath?'

Kline smiled slightly. 'Written on bog paper, right?' The smile faded. 'You're going along with all this?'

'Beats the hell out've office work.'

'There you punch a typewriter, no one punches you.'

Anne Darracott placed a doubled fist against the hard belly of John Kline.

'I got protection, see,' she lisped in imitation of Humphrey Bogart.

Kline looked steadily at her. 'You got me,' he said simply.

'S'what I mean, kid.'

'You got nothin'.'

'Nothing?' Anne asked, indicating the rumpled sheets of the bed as witness to the irony.

'I'm on the end of a line, a decoy to hide a hook.' Kline's mouth set into a hard line. 'I've pulled you into more than you think... here's your chance to duck out.'

'Of what?'

'Khan's some kinda cop. He saw me send your old boss-man down the Swannee. For takin' Rawlinson's place n'findin' out names of his backers maybe I'll miss out on a return trip to HM's nick. Maybe. It's all I've got. A promise from the Security Service. Nothin'.'

At first the implications of her own involvement did not occur.

'How many names you need?'

'The whole consortium. The two guys who run it.'

'This MD?'

'An' his mate, the chairman. Everything that I can discover will or could help.'

Then she realised. Like a backhander across the face, she realised. Why she had been invited to become involved, why she had been taken in and fucked over in every sense.

'Means of Class A drugs entering the country?' she said coldly.

'That's why I recruited you.'

'Only reason?'

'Then.'

'Now?'

Kline would not decide for her. 'You've got a choice,' he repeated.

Anne rubbed her inner arm with nervous fingers that followed the fear of her thought.

'Your nothing or mine?' she asked.

Across an abyss of loneliness Kline looked at her set face, the amber eyes hard yet brimful of tears. It had to be her choice. He could do nothing until Anne moved to him or away. Then she put a foot on the fragile bridge that might span the abyss and ran to join Kline in the middle.

They stood for a long time swaying slightly in an embrace that was a commitment to support each other in their bid to traverse the dangers ahead.

When her frightened children had been brought home in a police car, Mangit had learned of the happenings at the Moseley Road swimming baths. She had found it difficult to hide her elation at what she had heard. Now Jashir would be deported. Now Khan would have success and she would have him. Him. Khan. Through the hours that followed, through the afternoon and into the evening, Mangit had waited for the man who now held dominion over all her thoughts.

When at last Khan arrived Mangit had hugged him, led him to the small settee, then looked at the handsome face of her lover. A distant string of discord jarred her happiness. Khan sighed, looked dully at her.

'I was with Jashir.'

'Are you hurt?'

'No.' Khan sighed again.

'Is he?'

'Not badly.'

'But he is locked away.'

Khan nodded.

Another silence before Khan said, 'Your husband refused to co-operate with me.'

Mangit smiled tightly to herself. 'He will be deported then?'

'If his position remains unchanging.'

'Good!' Mangit pronounced fiercely.

Khan did not seem to approve of her tone for he glanced reprovingly at her.

'That is what we want?' Mangit asked bewilderedly.

Her lover looked away. The woman thrust a hand to her breast. 'It is what *I* want.'

The man, staring ahead, refused to meet her pleading eyes until she said. 'What *you* want?'

'My personal wants are secondary. My job demands that I do everything to persuade Jashir to disclose names and details of the immigration route.'

'Then he will stay here. You... you wish for *that?*'

The voice of the police agent remained steady, an official tone of formality bringing a chill foreboding to Mangit's heart. 'Part of his price would be that of amnesty, the other is the return of you.'

'He would destroy me!'

'No. Jashir knows where violence has taken him.'

Mangit began to wail, to emit the sound of her inner pain. Khan felt its edge of anguish but made no move towards comforting her. When the cry subsided, Mangit said in a low stubborn voice, 'I will not go to him. He is my arranged husband, you are my chosen lover. I will not persuade Jashir, not with one word.'

'It is not necessary. No one can speak for another's heart.'

'How much do you love me?' Mangit asked quietly.

'Jashir asks that I promise not to see or entice you ever again.'

'How much do you love me?' she repeated.

Khan stood. Looked down into her eyes.

'I have a choice to make.' Then he looked away and Mangit knew what her fate was to be.

'Forgive me, Mangit,' Khan entreated, knowing that she never would.

Shocked, Mangit would not reply. Would not move.

'I must go, Mangit,' Khan said eventually.

'To Jashir?'

'Yes.'

'Do not go!' Mangit called across the chasm now between them.

Khan said nothing in reply but obeyed the dictates of duty and closed the door on the woman.

For a while he stayed with his forehead pressed against the wall outside and listened with regret to the sounds of weeping from within. But there were things he had to do. Statements he had to take. Duty to fulfil. Zaheer Mohammed Khan stood away from the wall of the room that held the woman who had loved him. Then he turned and walked quietly away.

For the first few days after his release from custody Malleson had stayed within the confines of his flat and licked his wounds and nursed the damage done to his self-esteem by the contempt and constant abuse of his police interrogators. He had found the confines of a prison cell less than delightful and was determined that in no circumstances was a return to be contemplated. This last resolution did not mean renunciation of his criminal ambition, far from it, for Malleson had realised that the only reason for Kline not making charges must be that he wished to exact a personal revenge. Well, that that was OK. He was safe here. All he was awaiting now was the return of the gun he'd given to Maxine and he would then move against Mr John Kline for a final act of assassination.

A quick rap of knuckles on the door interrupted the run of Malleson's thoughts. Going from bed to door he called, 'Who?'

'Atty.'

'Bonny.'

Malleson let his helpers in and held out a hand to receive the gun.

'Ain't got it, boss,' Hunniford said. 'That Maxine moved without tellin' her address. She in with that Sarah Gant-Kline team, long with th'rest've our hustlers.'

'Man,' Bryden took over the narrative, 'down the street the whores they all wearin' new clothes, talkin' about their medical checks.'

Atty nodded. 'I wouldn't be surprised if Sarah Gant an' Kline don't run a pension fund f' when they all shagged out.'

Bryden giggled. 'Pay as y'lay.'

'I'll do the jokes,' Malleson muttered sourly while moving to occupy his wicker chair. He had to do something. Say something. He could feel the doubt even in these, his most loyal of monkeys. What to do? Whip himself into action. Yeh. Go!

'This is some losin' run I'm into,' Malleson began. 'Jesus, the fix is in on every race. Now, you seen me lose n'lose before...'

'Right,' they said. They had indeed seen that.

'But I've blasted clear.'

'Every time. Every time.'

'Got those losses back.' Malleson began to swing the chair to the rhythm of his rebuilding confidence.

'An' more,' Bryden encouraged. 'Got those losses back an' *more*.'

'It's the same with this. Defecate or abdicate, shit or bust. No way am I goin' back inside.' Malleson slowed the arc of his chair. 'I'd sooner they scrape me off a wall than surrender to that.'

'Yeh... Yeh!' his buddies shouted in unison.

'Right,' Malleson stood up and out from his basket chair.

'That guy with the short-barrelled shot guns – pass the word along I wish to buy. Also, I want what the scum call "surveillance" on Kline. I want to know when and where I can get in another shot that won't just wound but will cut him clean in half.'

Kline sat on the long settee in Rafiq's main living-room and popped a peanut, threw it up in the air and caught it on its downward fall. He was bored by the programme on the massive TV set, before which Rafiq stood totally engrossed in the debate between himself and a prominent member of a new party of the far right. Across the room, also immersed in the programme, sat Gordon Winthrop.

Idly Kline wondered about the meeting called for that night. No PAs or secretaries, Rafiq had said conspiratorially, adding that he had a feeling they were to meet with the mysterious MD. Kline hoped so. He had seen nothing of Khan for several days and the name of the managing director of the consortium would be a notable offering.

On the screen a craggy white face was in close up. 'British jobs for British people…' it was saying with bull-dog pugnacity. 'Let the people of the new Commonwealth create their own wealth instead of stealing ours.'

The camera switched to Mr Rafiq. 'Stealing, is it?' he replied, pointing his pipe. 'Stealing. Manning your hospitals, your transport, your night shifts…'

'The British Alliance Party intend to have over four hundred candidates at the next election. The white population will vote for a party that will abolish immigration and arrange for repatriation of those strangers who require it.' In the studios the camera pulled back away from the participants and the sound faded from Mr Rafiq's reply to his opponent, Nairn Wendell.

'Same old arguments ' Rafiq said, turning the sound down as the screen showed the background to the issues raised. Kline watched the film clips of fascist rallies; the faces of Mosley, Hitler, Mussolini passed across the screen, ogres of yesterday strutting in uniforms, saluting flags and banners.

Rafiq was a little disgruntled; he felt he should have been given the last word in the debate.

'What are they showing this stuff for?' he asked Winthrop,

scornfully. 'Neo-Nazi gangsters have discarded uniforms and now desire to look like you and… well, like you anyway, Gordon.'

Winthrop drained his whisky. 'What did you think of that British Alliance chap?'

'Not a fool, fast in debate. I'd never met Mr Wendell before but next time I will be ready for him.'

'Really?' said Winthrop and held out his empty glass to his Asian host.

At the drinks' cabinet, Rafiq asked. 'Norah, she is accompanying the MD?'

'Oh, yes. Should be here any time now. There was a news item or something they wanted to watch.'

The TV set now showed footage of the Nuremburg rallies. On his return with fresh drinks, Rafiq switched the programme off. As the dot disappeared the door opened and in stepped the immaculately groomed secretary to the board, Miss Norah Garwood. 'The MD won t be more than a moment,' she announced.

'Excuse me,' Winthrop said and hurried out to greet the great man in person. Kline looked over towards the door, Rafiq waited by the television expectantly.

Winthrop returned. 'Gentlemen, I have the honour to present our managing director.'

In walked Nairn Wendell.

Rafiq's lower lip dropped in surprise as he recognised the man who had opposed him only hours before in a television confrontation on race. Inadvertently Rafiq's eyes moved to the blank screen beside him then back to the craggy-looking face of the man in the doorway.

Kline watched the Asian's double-take of shocked surprise and, as the realisation of just who MD was struck home, Kline began to laugh aloud.

The *Anne Carol* shifted under the swell of a passing craft. Inside the cabin Anne lay curled on a couch reading a book on nineteenth-century furniture. She felt uneasy, her mind skittering away from the text and photographs. For no apparent reason she felt a great thump of anxiety for herself and for Kline. But then she remembered this was the end of the four hours since her last treatment of methadone. That was it – take the stuff, get changed and make for the Maverick, where John had arranged to meet her. As Anne put the book aside she heard a light tap on the port side window. Pulling back the curtain she looked into the brown face of Rafiq's helper Kuldip.

Gesticulating, the Asian silently asked if he could come in. Shrugging a why not, Anne closed the curtains with a swish then went to unlock the hatchway.

In the darkness of the towpath Kuldip waited to gain entry to the barge. In his mind he recalled Mr Winthrop's secret and explicit instructions. Kuldip knew this was an opportunity for personal advancement and no bloody white chit of a lady was going to stand between him and success.

The hatch opened. Anne peered out. 'Kuldip?'

'Yes, Miss Darracott. May I come in?'

'My, aren't we formal?'

Kuldip clambered down into the brightly lit kitchen area and faced Anne, who raised an eyebrow of enquiry

'Mr Winthrop... got new drug buyer to meet for you.'

'Sorry, got a date With your best buddy, John Kline. He should be here soon.'

At the mention of that name, Kuldip became somewhat agitated and under the excitement and apprehension of Kline's imminent arrival his tenuous hold on the Queen's English became spasmodic.

'Mr Winthrop, he said what? *What?*'

'I don't know.' Anne watched the brown eyes roll around their sockets in agony at the effort of recall.

'Yes... Imperial... *No!*' Kuldip wiped the tape, started again. '*Imperative*, yes – you co-operate tonight or all hope of future profit gone.'

The stocky little Asian indicated his person with pride. 'He said that to me, not Mr Rafiq.'

'They'll put you in pinstripes next,' Anne said dryly.

Kuldip frowned. 'Not unless you help me cause a meeting with this buyer man nearby.'

'How nearby?'

'I take you. I have my van, very comfortable. I put a cushion for you up in its front seat ready.'

Anne clasped her hands together in simulated minor ecstasy. 'Oh, well then, how can I refuse?

'OK. We go. We go!'

'Just hold your water.' Anne went into the cabin and towards the bedside cabinet for the lifeline of her pill bottle. She had almost unscrewed the metal top when Kuldip started yelling from behind her, 'No! No good. Refuse. It is forbidden!'

Starled at his vehemence, Anne asked in annoyance, 'Who by?'

'By me. Kuldip!' he insisted, grabbing the woman's thin arm to emphasise his authority.

'Ow!' Anne cried, twisting about, the bottle falling, the precious methadone tablets scattering like a shower of hail. 'What is this, Kuldip?'

'You come with me.'

'You stick your head up your arse!'

Kuldip disliked such talk from ladies so he smacked her filthy mouth. Anne cried out at the blow then glared at him in outrage.

Kuldip smiled. 'Now we take our tracks away from here, Miss Darracott.'

'My tablets…'

'You will not need them. They are not good for you.'

'But—'

Kuldip raised his hand again. Anne decided not to complete her question.

'Move,' Kuldip ordered, pointing towards the kitchen.

Praying for Kline to appear, Anne moved slowly to the kitchen. Waited at the foot of the iron stairway that led to the hatch above. Looked hopefully upwards, but nothing happened – only a shove in the small of the back and an angry exhortation to 'Bloody move!'. There was nothing for it but to comply. With a shiver of apprehension Anne began to climb the stairway.

'Nice pay packet.' Kline weighed the envelope in his hand; it felt heavy with a goodly weight of banknotes. But of what denomination? Kline saw a picture of the Bard of Avon duplicated some fifty times on the twenty-pound notes.

'Of course, that includes Miss Darracott's share of the drug proceeds,' Norah said fussily. 'And would you please sign to say you have received payment for the initial consignment.'

Kline regarded the slip of paper with amusement. 'You haven't deducted income tax,' he said teasingly.

'No, no, I just like to keep things clear and straightforward. A reference to settle any disputes should they arise at a future date.'

She really was a pain in the buttocks, Kline decided as he signed and watched her slip the pay receipt away into a cardboard file. 'Thank you,' she said primly and turned to a group that included her boss, the MD; Winthrop; and an unhappy Rafiq, who was questioning Wendell in puzzled tones.

'But as managing director you are accepting profits from the Blackbird run of illegal immigrants.'

'Aren't you?'

'Yes, of course, but I try to bring in those families stupid immigration laws have put asunder.'

It was not the only reason for the Blackbird run but it was true in part.

Wendell drew the bush of his eyebrows together. 'We've no time to waste on playing the Brown Pimpernel, Rafiq. Take 'em out, take 'em in, I don't care anymore than you do. They've a purpose to serve for both of us. Get me another drink, Gordon,' he said abruptly thrusting his empty glass at Winthrop.

Momentarily alone with Rafiq as Norah accompanied Winthrop, and seeing Kline stretched out on the long settee, Wendell said in a low, serious voice. 'This Kline trustworthy?'

'Yes. Why?'

'The chairman wants a little favour of him.'

'Should I...?' Rafiq indicated the reclining figure.

'All in good time,' Wendell said and looked over towards John Kline with a glance of hard appraisal.

Throughout the journey Anne had remained mute, trying to restrain her fear and to contain the convulsive shivering that threatened to assail her. Whether the chill she felt was from fear or the onset of withdrawal from the methadone, she wasn't certain. Not that it mattered, for when Kuldip pulled into the garage and locked the doors he explained at last the reason for her abduction.

'Mr Winthrop wants to know who you working with and why also.'

Anne smiled derisively. 'Why also?' she mocked.

Almost nonchalantly Kuldip slapped her insolent face, first on one side then the other.

'Now. He most anxious to discover if you feeding information about drugs running to police. Seems a courier was arrested yesterday at airport with heroin in his diplomat bag. Now he trust me with secret task of deducting information out of you.'

'I work for Kline,' Anne began, but then she remembered what she had been told that morning about the role of Khan. 'Nobody else,' she finished the sentence quickly and defiantly.

Kuldip wondered about the pause. The flicker of thought it conveyed. It was a sign of having information to hide.

'I heard Mr Rafiq say once you liked to shoot up your arm.'

Even her burning cheeks and broken lip could not prevent Anne laughing at him.

Surprisingly Kuldip did not seem to mind.

'You think I'm thug only? Me, I got a nice surprise cooked up for you.'

'What?'

'Ah....' said the Asian and pulled her about to face the interior of the driving cabin.

Reaching into the glove compartment he brought out a familiar object that caused Anne suddenly to feel as if all the ladders climbed so far were for nothing. Now she was to be swallowed up by a serpent from her past and deposited back onto square number one.

Kuldip held up the primed hypodermic needle tantalisingly. 'Best of French heroin... That should be suitable bait to make you shoot out all of the truth of what you know. Yes? *Yes*?'

Anne did not hear him. All her attention was on the needle.

With little else to do John Kline listened to the continuing debate between Rafiq and the managing director of the consortium.

'May I ask you, Mr Wendell, how it is that you can reconcile the policy of your party with your role as MD to our company here?'

'You have already stated the word. Policy. My Alliance Party needs the Asians the way Hitler needed the issue of the Jews, to construct a platform to power. As our society crumbles, the white Briton looks about for a scapegoat. He sees brown faces, he sees black. He sees only one party that proposes a radical solution. He is ready to act, to vote.'

'The more immigrants, the more fascist votes,' Kline said succinctly.

Nobody answered him. Wendell, after a sharp look in Kline's

direction returned his attention to Rafiq. 'The money your fellow Asians pay for the privilege of entertaining Great Britain illegally pays my party workers, my campaign funds. And for that and your help in organising it, I am most grateful, Mr Rafiq.'

'Thank you,' Rafiq said unhappily. Watching Wendell turn aside to Winthrop he could just hear what was being said by the Alliance leader. 'Let us get a base of a parliamentary party and we can see about shipping back the brown brothers to where they came from.' Then, seeing one of the leaders of the brown brothers listening intently, he gave an easy chuckle. 'That doesn't mean *you*, Mr Rafiq.'

'I will be in favour with your new regime?'

'We always repay loyalty.'

Rafiq did not believe it. Filled with doubt and foreboding he looked from Wendell to Winthrop and then back again. He could not define why exactly but he sensed that in some obscure way he was being tested. Why? For what purpose? And why tell him about the uses to which profits were put? They must know he would find that revelation unpalatable.

'Everything all right, Aslam?' Winthrop asked smoothly.

Rafiq smiled blandly. 'Oh, yes, everything's all right. Extremely so, my dear Winthrop.'

But when the chaps turned away, Kline watched the smile of the Asian faded to pursed lips of annoyance.

Kuldip placed the hypodermic needle carefully on the engine cover of the van, just a little out of reach of the addict. After a pause he picked the needle up and offered it enticingly. The blonde head shook vigorously. Kuldip laughed. He knew enough of what he had to offer and was certain that victory and promotion would be his. Returning the hype to its former position he settled back to wait for time to turn its trick.

At last, thought Kline, the bums are about to get around to me. Looking up at the men clustered about him he waited for whatever was coming. Wendell opened the proceedings.

'The chairman has long talked to me of the need for expanding the main board. There could be an opportunity soon for you, Mr Kline.'

Seeing Rafiq's expression of discontent at this overture, Winthrop added quickly, 'And for Mr Rafiq.'

'Thing is,' Wendell continued, his eyes never having left Kline, 'there's a chap whose services we'd rather do without…'

'Yes indeed,' Winthrop said. 'I believe the underworld phrase is to contract him out.'

Kline said impassively, 'You want me to do it?'

'We would be delighted if you could.'

'Who is it?' Kline asked Wendell casually.

'Norah has the particulars.'

From her file the secretary produced a sealed brown envelope for the MD to present to Kline.

'You'll find his details and photograph in there.'

Kline could sense an air of expectancy about the room. Like a poker player betting blind and about to view his hole card, Kline opened the envelope and looked down on the features of the man they wanted him to kill. Not a movement or change of expression betrayed the sudden surprise Kline felt as he stared down at the face of Zaheer Mohammed Khan.

After a moment, Wendell asked, 'You are prepared to enforce the contract upon that particular party?'

'Sure,' Kline agreed without a trace of emotion in his voice.

It seemed to be cold as a morgue inside the garage. Anne leaned against the side of the Dormobile and rubbed her arms. There was no chance of holding out; already she could feel the insidious build to panic and betrayal of all she knew. Of Kline, of Khan. It was only a question of time before she reached for the golden panacea that Kuldip would then snatch away and withhold until her knowledge became his. All she could do, Anne thought hopelessly, was to hang on for as long as she could.

As if reading the intention Kuldip said suddenly. 'It is early nights yet. We stay 'til morning lightens if you like… It not going to upset my mind; I'm used to working away all my night.'

'Yeh,' Anne said and closed her eyes sleepily. Something sharp digging into the back of her hand roused her. It was the point of the hypodermic lightly jabbing her into wakefulness.

Anne began to yawn while Kuldip giggled and replaced the shot of heroin within her sight but out of reach.

*

The brown envelope lay on the desk before Kline. Deciding that Anne would already be at the Maverick he had gone directly from the house of Rafiq to his office at the club. There he had found the man he was contracted to kill waiting for him and Anne not yet arrived.

Kline watched his fingers toying with the envelope as Khan concluded his explanation of why he was finished with the case of the consortium.

'On the dole, Mr Khan, that it?'

'I have spent the last two days clearing my desk, assembling statements from an illegal immigrant, passing on what I have to different agencies of the law. They'll act straight away, of course, scoop up a few little fish, and without properly documented evidence yet to hand, our friends in the consortium may happily swim away to re-form again.'

'What about me n'Anne. Do we sink or swim?'

'I have not passed on your names.'

'Why?'

'Because nobody has yet asked me.'

'But they will?'

'Yes. Then I will do what I can. Explain your help, put what success we have upon the scales.'

'See what it weighs?'

'Without the full consortium…' Khan spread his hands in apology. 'Sorry, not enough.'

The tall man stood from his desk picked up the envelope and advanced angrily towards the agent.

'That's comfortin'. That really makes me feel hunky bleedin' dory!'

Khan watched Kline's agitation as he walked in a small circle about him.

'I repeat. I will do what I can.'

'Which is sweet fuck all now. Less than nothin' now. Well, I'm not goin' t' wait for your mates t'lift me off the street. Your power might be kaput, babes, but I've cards to play. Chances to take. Prestige to win.'

Now in close proximity the two men stared at each other.

'The only witness to my misdeeds, such as they are, Mr Khan, is you. Eliminate you and maybe I'll be baskin' out in the bay with the sharks of the consortium.'

'No, Mr Kline.'

'So sure, Mr Khan, so bleedin' certain?'

'You can only play the killer against your enemies, Mr Kline; your friends you can only threaten.'

It was true and the knowledge did not help the growing frustration Kline felt well up within him. Finally realising that he could never kill without reason or passion, Kline slammed the brown envelope given to him by Wendell against the chest of Khan and turned away.

'My identity photograph,' he heard Khan say in surprise.

'I'm supposed to execute a contract on you to ensure my advancement to full board status. They gave me that mug shot.'

Khan looked at the photograph again. Now that the initial surprise had passed, his mind turned over the questions it raised.

'When did you pass on the case?' Kline asked.

'Yesterday.'

'Who to exactly?'

'Various people in the Home Office, Special Branch, immigration squad...'

'Someone in that lot wants you over the side.'

Khan agreed. The question was who? Then a solution occurred. After sighing for effect he said dolefully. 'Well, what can I say, you're right – someone wants me dead. What can I do? I have nothing now, no power or position, no real success to offer. No hard evidence against the consortium. As you say, nothing. So...' Khan sighed, shrugged resignedly. 'You may as well kill me, Mr Kline.'

It was two in the morning when Kline burst into Rafiq's home.

Panic-stricken Rafiq was lifted up forcibly by the lapels of his silk dressing-gown.

'Mr... John... please. I do not know where Anne is... *please!*'

'I've been all over town, asked everybody 'cept for you.'

'Why are you certain she is missing?'

Kline produced the methadone bottle he had found on his return to the houseboat.

'She wouldn't go anywhere without this. It's a lifeline she still needs.'

Rafiq wanted to help and said so. Kline assessed him with eyes that expressed his worry and aggression.

'You cross me, Rafiq, and you're down for the same treatment as

Mr Bleedin' Khan.'

I understand. Unfortunately, or fortunately for me, I do not know anything of Anne's disappearance. Perhaps Kuldip could assist, but he is not here.'

'Where is he?'

'Where? Gone to a private cinema. It is extremely late but I could disturb the manager, see if he talked with Kuldip.'

'Do that,' Kline said. It was some action at least.

Waiting for the number to reply, Rafiq explained. 'It is small, a sordid place with late showings of very lewd films... ah...'

Kline heard the Asian switch to Urdu or Hindi or some such. Anyway it was unintelligible to him but sprinkled with the name of Kuldip. Eventually Rafiq replaced the ornate telephone.

'Odd. He has not been there at all. Why should Kuldip make a point of telling me he is going to the pictures then not go?'

'Where else would he be?'

Rafiq thought for a moment. Then said, 'He has had some problems with his van.'

Anne felt her hand being guided to clasp an object. Despite an effort of reason her fingers grasped and brought the hypodermic towards her. Kuldip would have something to bind her arm. Yeh. Then the needle would not come any closer, for a strong brown hand with hair on its fingers was preventing further movement by gripping her arm.

'You work for Kline?'

'Right. Right.'

'And who does that man work for?'

Anne looked at him, shivering. Without hope of rescue, why prolong the torture?

'Well?'

Anne summoned the last dregs of will and shuddered with the effort needed to place the antidote to her anxiety and fear back onto the van.

Kuldip found it all highly amusing. Giggling at her plight and pathetic attempts to resist the panic of withdrawal, he said softly. 'It is a long night, Miss Darracott. Let us talk, then you have beautiful fix and, me, I can prove that I am up to task given by Mr Winthrop. Let me prove my fitness for promotion from bloody van driving. I tell you, in this world, you get opportunity, you better bloody well not take no for answer.'

'I work for Kline,' Anne said, rubbing her itching nose and watery eyes. 'No one else. I work for him and... and heroin.' The last word of betrayal slipped out. Kuldip picked up the hypodermic, offered it one more time.

Anne was just reaching out for its comfort when they both heard the rattle of the locked garage door and Rafiq's voice calling the name of his assistant.

Swiftly Kuldip put the needle down, clamped a hand to Anne's mouth and eased his knife out to place its point against the throat of his prisoner.

In the silence the door rattled again.

'Kuldip?' the muffled voice of Rafiq called.

Head pulled back by Kuldip, Anne started a slow search with her free hand across the engine cover of the Dormobile. Kuldip, with all his attention directed to the door, failed to notice the slow movement of the groping fingers.

Outside the garage, Rafiq and Kline stood in front of the locked door.

'Don't you have a key?'

'It is Kuldip's province, but it is obviously empty.'

'Yeh,' Kline said, looking at the door for a moment longer before starting to follow Rafiq back towards the Mercedes.

Anne's searching fingers finally located the hypodermic needle and fastened around its thin barrel, waiting for the Asian to relax his grip around her neck.

Hearing the footsteps recede Kuldip took the knife away from the white throat and began to breathe again.

Feeling the grip about her slacken, Anne used all her strength to twist away from the man who held her captive.

Grunting in surprise Kuldip staggered back on to his heels, which gave Anne the chance to drive the hypodermic needle point into the Asian's groin with all the force she could muster.

With a scream of pain Kuldip folded up over his pierced testicles, allowing Anne to yell with all the urgency and desperation of her being. 'John! Help me! In here... help me *now!*' she screamed then watched transfixed as Kuldip straightened up from his anguished crouch and began to stagger towards her, knife poised for revenge.

On hearing Anne's shout Kline charged towards the Mercedes, thrust himself into the driving seat, paused to clip on the seat belt, gunned the engine and aimed the car at speed towards the garage door.

Before Kuldip could reach Anne the doors buckled then burst inward under the impact of the Mercedes' power. Driving on through the wreckage into the garage Kline released the belt from his smarting shoulders and climbed out to be greeted by a panic-stricken Anne.

'I didn't say anything. I didn't fix... I didn't...'

'No, baby.' Kline kissed the top of her head and tried to locate whoever else was inside. There he was. Kline saw the stooped figure of Kuldip moving back to the far wall.

'Stay here,' Kline said and passed Anne gently to Rafiq then went into the garage and towards Kuldip.

'Knife! Knife!' Anne called in warning.

Kline saw the blur of Kuldip's arm and ducked instinctively sideways, which was a fortunate move, for not half a second later a knife sliced through the space he had formerly occupied.

Now there was nothing to prevent Kline advancing upon the unhappy and apprehensive Asian pressing himself against the wall.

Kline lifted his right hand, balled it into a fist with every intention of extracting retribution. But when the moment came to smash his fist into the sweating brown face, Kline had a better idea.

'Let's have a chat, kid,' he suggested, lowering his fist. 'Then perhaps I'll take you along to meet a mate of mine.'

Surprised at receiving an invitation to open his mouth rather than a punch to stop it, Kuldip began to talk.

On the journey towards Rafiq's home Kline insisted that Kuldip make a telephone call. When a sleepy English voice finally answered, Kline gave the receiver to Anne's interrogator.

'Mr Winthrop?' Kuldip gulped for air in the tight confines of the kiosk. 'So sorry to disturb your slumbers but Anne Darracott knew nothing. I put her through the wringer, pity bloody good but she A-One and OK all the way.'

'Yes. Fine. Well done,' the voice of Winthrop acknowledged.

Kline depressed the cradle points then dialled again.

'Khan,' another sleepy voice said.

'Good morning, Mr Khan. I think I might have a little present for you.' Kline glanced at the unhappy Kuldip and grinned. 'At Rafiq's, yes. Soon as you like. See you.'

Within the hour Khan had arrived and had been acquainted with the happenings of the night and morning.

Khan considered the facts of the situation; addressing an uneasy Rafiq he asked, 'Winthrop instructed Kuldip to abduct Anne. This "MD" sent Mr Kline to kill me. Why?'

'A test, I think, to ascertain who was loyal. If Kline killed you, if Anne was cleared of suspicion, things could proceed.'

'And why didn't they tell you about this test?'

Rafiq shook his head and smiled shyly.

'Perhaps they consider my loyalty to their company and its aims a trifle suspect.'

'Because of the uses to which the profits of illegal immigration were being put?'

'I assure you I had no involvement, no...'

'No idea. All right.' Khan paused, weighing what advantage to take of the situation. 'I lost a colleague who travelled undercover as an illegal immigrant. I wish to solve his murder above all else.'

'How did he die, Mr Khan?' Rafiq asked innocently.

'By knife thrust.'

The eyes of Rafiq shifted towards his unfaithful servant, who was drowsing in a luxurious armchair. 'Kuldip carries a knife I believe, Mr Khan.' Rafiq muttered.

'Here.' Kline tossed the knife onto a low table before the settee on which Khan sat.

'You could elaborate upon that statement if so required?' Khan asked.

Rafiq inclined his head.

'I believe so, given the right circumstances.'

Interesting, Khan thought. Since being taken off this case circumstances seemed to be unfolding that made an ultimate solution, if not certain, at least possible. Maybe he should let events continue their course for a little longer. Taking Khan's momentary silence as a setback Rafiq decided to play his trump card. 'Might I suggest a little ploy? If you can hold Kuldip out of circulation and hide yourself as if eliminated by Mr Kline...'

'Great minds,' Kline said in acknowledgement that Rafiq's ideas duplicated those of Khan.

'There is a general board meeting to be held,' Rafiq went on, feeling the perspiration dampening the palms of his chubby hands. 'Profits review... figures... facts... documents... and new members to be introduced to the chairman of the board.'

'All we need,' Kline said to Khan, who nodded briefly before asking the most important question. 'Where will this board meeting be held, Mr Rafiq?'

Chapter Thirteen

K line sat in the Organisers' Suite of the exhibition complex with Anne beside him. Across the room four unknown executive members of the consortium discussed area profits with Winthrop. Around the rectangular table, where the board meeting would be held, fussed Norah Garwood, straightening papers, placing pencils. She paid meticulous attention to the space reserved for the chairman, placing and replacing the glass tumbler and carafe of water so that his nibs would need not stretch an iota more of muscle than was necessary to reach for the glass. Kline looked at his watch and glanced at Anne, who, with her hair drawn back, looked severe and intent on the serious business before them. Catching her eye, Kline could not resist winking like a naughty boy.

Anne smiled in reply. During the past four days she had thought often of the hours of nightmare experienced while being held prisoner by Kuldip. That she had held out for so long against the pull of an easy fix was a cause of hope to her. Silently she vowed to herself that if they made it through the dangerous present she would be happy to create a life mundane in its domesticity.

In the hotel lobby Sarah Gant cocked one long leg across the other and returned the stare of a gentleman from Texas. Maybe it was the accent bringing nostalgia but she really felt like turning a trick just for the hell and profit of it. Sarah had accompanied Anne and Kline to the exhibition area ostensibly to check out the location for the whores on the team. But one professional appraisal was enough to jettison the idea.

Any lady out for profit from her sexual attributes would find herself lost in the horde of secretaries, PAs and girlies whose job it was to decorate the exhibition stands. With all that spare cunt about why would a sales guy need to buy it here, she thought, watching the hard-nosed

Texan keep on reading the legend emblazoned across her tee-shirt. From one nipple to the next stretched the word 'Stardust' in letters that glittered as would particles from an astral body.

'Pratt. Bob Pratt,' the traveller in heavy machinery from the Lone Star State introduced himself abruptly.

Suck, fuck, or whitey reviling the nigger's woman. Sarah bet the first with probably the contemptuous 'Black Shit' as he ejaculated. Well, it didn't bother her and it would cost him. She smiled in reply to his introduction.

'Gant. Sarah Gant.'

'How are you, Sarah?'

'Available.'

'I've not that much time.'

'I'll take no time at all.'

'You're a business lady?'

'The best.'

'Let's...'

'Go?'

Sarah stood and walked ahead. Knowing she had a good ass, she used it for effect.

Feeling the thud of her shoulder bag she was pleased that Maxine had returned the pistol to her and not to Malleson. Yeah, Sarah thought, as they approached the elevator, it was good to have a friend at your side and a client admiring your behind.

In the car park, opposite the Organisers' Suite, with a good sight of the exit, Malleson sat with a loaded shotgun across his knees. Concealed by newspapers it lay ready and waiting to wipe out the man he had tailed from the Maverick to this isolated exhibition site. Malleson wondered how long it would be before Kline reappeared. However long it was he was determined to wait. To act. To recover his losses with a devastating blast of shot from first one barrel then the other.

The lift in the corridor halted, the doors opened and Aslam Rafiq hurried along the corridor.

From a side cloakroom further down the corridor Khan watched the plump figure open the door to the bathroom and go inside.

Khan stepped into the corridor and signalled to his hidden

uniformed helpers by holding up a finger to warn that there was one more personage to come. Withdrawing to his vantage point Khan settled himself to await the arrival of the chairman of the consortium.

Inside the boardroom the executives seated themselves at the table. Finding himself alongside Winthrope, Kline asked, 'Why exhibit yourselves in this place?'

'What better camouflage than to be out here, just one of any number of similar groups who hire suites to meet and confer?'

'That makes sense,' Kline acknowledged. He looked at the time. 'This chairman guy own a watch?'

Norah overheard the remark. 'He is invariably punctual,' she said frostily.

'Couple of minutes yet before you meet the great man,' Wendell said affably, accepting Kline's directness as an attribute in a man who fulfilled contracts with such speed and efficiency.

'Be about time,' Kline said, curious as to the identity of the chairman and tense with the hope that whoever it was would walk into the trap set. The final two minutes dragged around the clock on the wall, a slow double circling of a red second hand that would either bring their schemes to fruition or send Kline back through the gate of Winson Green Prison.

Waiting inside the cloakroom, Khan contemplated the possible end of his career. He had gained the use of police help on an authority he did not hold, and this compounded the disobeying of an explicit order of his head of department. The sound of the lift along the corridor put an end to the Asian's brooding thoughts. Tensely he edged an eye around the alcove and saw with a sinking feeling that all his calculations, all the chances taken, everything staked on this final throw were lost, for striding purposefully down the corridor, dressed in familiar pinstripe, a red rose in his buttonhole, was Sir George Jeavons.

Inadvertently, Khan flattened himself against the inner wall and prepared for the wrath to come. Deflated, he supposed uniformed branch had decided to verify his request for help and it had reached the desk of the chief himself. Ah well, Khan thought. Face what's coming. Get it over. And with that he stepped into what was now an empty corridor.

*

The chairman's first duty was to be introduced to the new members of the board. First an Asian gentleman was presented and then Winthrop ushered forward a rough-looking individual.

'Sir George Jeavons... er, John Kline.'

Both men looked each other over. Neither seemed overly impressed at what he saw.

'Kline.' Jeavons held out a well-manicured hand.

'George,' Kline said, touching the offered hand briefly.

Jeavons' expression sharpened as he glanced up at Kline, but then he turned to the business of chairing the meeting.

'Shall we begin? First let me welcome our members from the North East and North West and also our charming new associate member, Miss... Miss Darracott, and not forgetting the latest and, I am sure, most valuable full members of our board, Mr Rafiq and Mr Kline. To business.'

Jeavons took up his order of business paper and had time to say, 'Now if I may draw your attention to item...' before the door opened and Khan, followed by a number of uniformed officers entered the board room.

Khan cleared his throat diffidently.

'If I may interrupt your proceedings, Sir George,' he said, then paused to watch the flutter of paper fall from the startled hands of the head of the clandestine consortium.

Even after the boardroom had been cleared of everyone but Sir George Jeavons and himself, Khan could not believe that his duty now was to escort his chief into custody.

Khan turned from the window. 'We must go,' he said quietly.

Jeavons stared ahead. With his confidence drained he seemed nearer fifty years of age than forty. 'The thing is,' he started, 'the thing I dislike most, Khan, is that it should end out here in this concrete monument to twentieth-century anonymity. If you would have been kind enough to arrest me at home I could have left with perhaps a little style.'

Khan, feeling little pleasure in his capture, stared unhappily at the crestfallen man hunched forward in his seat at the head of the long table.

As if Khan had asked the question, Jeavons began to answer for his motives. 'Not politics, not belief in anything. Romance, if you like. But above all I wanted money. And that's what I created here. You have the documents, the details: drugs, illegal immigration, prostitution; corrupt payments invested in crime brought me a yield of money for the building and maintenance of my estate. Money to pay the drones for the upkeep of a last piece of Old England.'

Khan remembered the pride of Jeavons' ownership on that day when they had stood on the lower terrace and gazed at the splendour of the stately old house. Then he also recalled that on that same day he had been warned off the case. The instructions passed to Kline for his murder must have emanated from the man now slumped at the boardroom table.

'We must leave now,' Khan said firmly.

'Yes, of course.' Sir George pulled himself up from the table and began to walk towards the door. After several paces he suddenly stopped, a bitter smile hovering at the corners of his mouth.

'What?' Khan asked.

A cloud of weariness seemed to envelop the knight of the civil service. 'Just a look into the future. A bleary photograph of my beautiful home and a caption. No doubt some fool will be unable to resist labelling it "A monument to corruption". Shall we go, Khan?'

As he and Anne sauntered out of the suite entrance and into the triangular area between car park, exhibition hall and railway station, Kline began to chuckle again. 'Khan's boss,' he said in derision.

'Yeh, what a crew,' Anne said, looking towards the spiral of yellow metal that curled upwards around steps that led to a bridge across the railway line.

'Where's Sarah?' Kline asked.

'I said we'd see her by the station steps.'

'OK,' Kline said, stopping to light a cigarette between cupped hands.

Malleson eased himself out of his car, rested the short-barrelled shotgun on the edge of the door and aimed carefully at the man and woman waiting near to what looked from a distance like a helter-skelter painted in a shade of bright yellow.

Swinging along the bridge that spanned the railway tracks, Sarah considered on what item of clothing she might blow the hundred bucks just extracted for her suction service on the hard-talking but fast-shooting Mr Pratt. Something outrageous, Sarah decided as she began to descend the stairway towards the agreed meeting place with Kline and Anne.

Looking down on the expanse of concrete below, Sarah saw the man crouching behind a car door and about to blast Anne and Kline from a range that made a hit more or less a certainty.

'John, Anne, behind!' she yelled and began to hurry around the descending spiral of the steps fumbling in her bag as she ran.

'Down!' Kline shouted, pushing Anne to the ground and flattening himself beside her as the shotgun exploded its charge towards them.

'Goddamn fuckin' bastard,' Malleson screamed as the bodies of Anne and Kline did not stay sprawled on the ground but scrambled to their feet and began to run for the cover of the structure containing the spiral staircase.

Malleson was about to advance for another try from closer range when he caught a glimpse of Sarah Gant holding a pistol and pointing it at his head at an angle that left him unprotected by the cover of the car door. Malleson stood, raised the shotgun to his shoulder and released the second barrel. The sound of the shot hitting on yellow metal sounded, *spaaang*! People screamed. There was no sign of Sarah Gant.

Kline realised that both barrels had been fired and ran towards Malleson with great speed. He was going to wreak havoc; he was going to end this once and for all. Malleson hurled the empty shotgun at Kline, halting his advance momentarily, giving Malleson a chance to sprint away toward the main exhibition hall with Kline in pursuit a little way behind.

Anne, sheltering behind the bridge, saw Sarah emerge from behind the boot of the car. Both looked at each other. Silently Anne pointed after Malleson and Kline. Pistol at the ready, Sarah Gant hurried away in the direction indicated.

Hurtling around a corner, Malleson came across an electrician about to close a door to an access tunnel that led beneath the great hall.

'Hey!' the man started to protest as Malleson advanced menacingly towards him. 'Wha—' His question was terminated by a blow that sent him staggering and allowed Malleson to enter the corridors that contained the circuits and lines that brought light, heat and power to the huge complex.

The groggy electrician had enough time to give his jaw one rub before another hard-looking character shot round the corner and without a by-your-leave shunted the sparks aside and also entered the interior of the tunnel.

Gooin' tow report this, the Brummy decided, and he turned a corner to be almost bowled over by a black bit of stuff with 'Stardust' on her tits who asked him about having seen two guys.

'In there... in there... everyone's gone in bloody *there!*' he complained, pointing at the dark square entrance that led below. 'And they've no more bleedin' right than you,' he called after Sarah as she ran to follow the others.

Inside the maze, Malleson glanced back along a corridor banked with jumbled wires, electric fittings, buzzing machinery and saw Kline appear and hurtle after him.

Galvanised at the sight, Malleson ran in a straight line away from his enemy. Fear giving him speed, he gained enough of a lead to take an advantage if it occurred. Halfway along the underground passage he spotted a spanner and a workman's bag and in the ceiling above a hatchway half open. Seizing on the spanner, Malleson turned and hurled its weight of metal at his pursuer.

Ducking, Kline heard the crackle and saw the flash of blue as the steel smashed into a meter on the wall alongside his head. Malleson glanced up into the face of a startled maintenance man in the act of connecting a power point in the floor of the hall above.

With Kline coming at him bent on murder, with the bolt hole above blocked by a Brummy, there was only the option of straight ahead. Malleson began to run again. He had travelled only a few strides when he saw from a junction of corridors ahead the cool black lady Sarah Gant step into his path and level her pistol at the heart of his precious person. Uncertainly Malleson pulled up, turned to the oncoming Kline, looked back at Sarah Gant; then he saw above him what could be another access hatch cover. Clawing his way upwards, he felt his foot slip, frantically he grabbed for a wire, felt it pull away, reached for another and became entangled in a mesh of cable. As Malleson struggled to free himself he made connection with the main supply of power. Death passed instantly through him. No scream came, only his dead weight slowly untangling itself from the coils of electrocution. The body of Malleson fell silently to the concrete floor of the passageway below.

Kline reached Malleson first. He felt little sense of triumph, only a feeling of tired gratitude that it was now all over. For him, for Malleson.

Sarah Gant looked down upon the body of the man who had destroyed her sister, Dinah. 'Now I can go home,' she said in a hushed voice, while the power buzzed its satisfaction all about them.

Chapter Fourteen

On the observation platform of Elmdon Airport Anne waved and Kline raised a hand as Sarah climbed the steps of the aircraft that would start the first leg of her journey home. Sarah waved once then was gone.

Leaning against the rear railing, Rafiq finished reading an article on a consortium of criminals that featured a picture of an imposing house in illustration of the corruption exposed.

'Let's...' Kline took Anne's arm then noticed the man who had joined them on the platform. 'What you doing here?' he asked Khan.

'My job,' the agent replied. 'I am to meet with a colleague from a crown colony. Does that interest you, Mr Kline?'

'Oh, yeh, fascinates me. But unfortunately we got a meetin' with the gamin' board, right, Aslam?'

'Yes, oh, yes.' Rafiq put away his newspaper hurriedly.

Khan looked at all three in turn.

'Everything is all above board now, is it?' he asked sardonically.

'What else?' Kline said.

'Boring, isn't it?' Anne said and nudged Kline, with an expression that believed her words.

'Mr Rafiq?'

'My dear Khan, one does not wish to share a cell with that scoundrel Kuldip.' Rafiq shuddered.

'Yes.' Khan regarded the Asian leader thoughtfully. Kline and Anne deserved their freedom, but this one?

Hurriedly Rafiq pushed out his hand.

'Do feel free to visit our club,' he invited.

Khan stroked his moustache and raised an eyebrow at the tall man.

'Mr Kline?' he asked.

'Mr Khan,' Kline raised a hand in a gesture that could have meant anything and turned and began to descend the steps followed by Anne and the portly Mr Rafiq.

Khan observed their descent towards a waiting Mercedes.

Watching the trio enter the car below, Khan felt a pang of emotion. Whether it was envy, or regret at losing such useful pieces from the board, he was not at all sure. At least,he insisted to himself, it was not because of Mangit. And then the feeling of loss welled up again and he knew the truth for what it was.

Khan stood and watched the Mercedes drive away. He remained on the platform for a long time until at last the light aircraft carrying the man from Hong Kong taxied in on the runway below.

With an effort Khan wrote *finis* to one story and walked down towards the start of another.

John Kline
will return in
Death Touch

Following is an excerpt

Chapter One

From outside it seems nothing more than a Birmingham engineering workshop that has seen far better days.

Approaching the large, closed, heavy wooden door are a crowd of Chinese workers, all carrying lunch boxes. Harry Sen jostles amongst them, just another stocky Chinese guy eager to joust with the gods of chance.

The crowd passes a solitary glass kiosk that sells burgers and hot dogs. Inside sits a watchful Chinese who surveys the side streets that lead to the grime-tainted workshop. Beside his left hand sits a red alarm button.

Harry Sen is familiar to the gatekeeper, a burly ex-boxer, Roy 'Stinger' Sturt, also known as 'Shtum' on account of having had his vocal chords slashed by an assailant's blade. Leaning back against the door, Sturt holds a voice amplifier tube to his scarred neck, intones, in a metallic boom,

'HELLO-HARRY- GOT-SOMETHING-FOR-ME?'

Harry greases the palm of the doorman with a fiver and is allowed inside through a creaking wicket gate.

The workshop smells of machine oil, stale cigarette smoke, human sweat. The ceiling is high; morning sunshine leaks in through grimy windows, casting a dim light on the crowds of Chinese gamblers hunched over their games of chance. There is a low hum of activity, the click-click-click of mah-jong tiles, the shuffling of banknotes, the passing of wads of money back and forth, occasional stifled squeals of delight over a winning play.

Harry places himself next to a giant Butler Combined Planing and Milling Machine, upon whose broad table the main gambling action is taking place.

Watching the lines of play is the plump figure of Mr Yan. Harry, too, studies the game. Then his gaze shifts towards a bench that holds a drill and a small hand press. On this a more sedate game of dominoes is being played. Leaning against the bench, not taking part in the game, is a Chinese man with a hollow look that suggests a love affair with an opium pipe. Harry nods across to the thin man, indicates a move towards the back of the workshop. Mr Yan, alert, watches Harry's progress intently. A jerk of his head sends two henchmen after the stocky figure.

Between two benches there is a swift exchange of a sealed package before both Harry and Chen are seized from behind. There is a fracas, a struggle. Harry knees the guy who seeks to grapple with him, darts away as his attacker squeals in anguish. Chen is punched in the gut. He sinks to the greasy factory floor.

Outside, in the hot dog kiosk, the lookout sees an official-looking gent striding purposefully towards the building that houses the illegal gambling operation. He jams down on the red alarm button, hard.

Inside, a hooter blares out a warning. Instantly, games are halted, boards hidden, money stashed away. Gamblers become workers, machines are activated. An extractor fan starts up with a whirr of grating sound. The table of the Butler planing machine begins its stately progress, forward and back, forward and back…

Roy Sturt presses his voice activator to his throat, booms out instructions.

'MASKS!'

Four young Chinese 'workers' step forward. They raise metal welding masks to their faces.

'WEAPONS!'

Four flaming welding torches point towards the door, which shakes under a pounding from outside. Sturt turns towards the entrance, Harry, panting, joins him, points, asking to be let out. Sturt eases the wicket gate part way open, lets Harry through before glaring at the uniformed official who attempts to enter.

'WHAT-DO-YOU-WANT? the voice box intones.

'I've come to read the gas meter.'

'WE-DON'T-HAVE-GAS-PISS-OFF!'

Anne Darracott follows John Kline out of the council offices, watches him crumple the application document then hurl the ball of paper back at the Victorian building.

Hurrying along Colmore Row, dodging through the morning traffic, she tries to keep up with the tall, muscular guy in the grey suit.

'It's not over,' she says. 'We can appeal. John, it's early days. The business doesn't even a name yet.'

Kline's voice is bitter, his hands bunched, knuckles white.

'The authorities have it in for me, first at the Maverick, now at the restaurant. Without a booze licence, we're just a hash joint.'

'What was the reason for the turn down?'

'Police objections. No detail.'

She trots along beside him.

'What about, Khan? You've done that bloke favours, ask for one in return.'

'Khan? Mr Khan has taken a powder, disappeared, out of the country.'

Birmingham seems a world away as Zahir Khan waits for the train to stop outside his home village of Jallundar, Pakistan. The land lies flat, open, a vast sky above; a few white cumulous clouds, precursors of the monsoon season, litter the sky. On the heavy air the faint aroma of spiced cooking mixes with the acrid smoke of the engine driving the train.

Stepping down at the small country station, Khan sees his father waiting to greet him. Smart in white linen suit, club tie, hat, the old man seems a little more stooped than Khan remembers, but still proud of bearing.

Father and son embrace, awkwardly but warmly. The elder Khan gazes up enquiringly.

'How is Queen Elizabeth?'

'Well.'

'And England?'

'As ever.'

'What brings you here?'

'I'm investigating Asian highway drug traffickers. The trail starts here in Pakistan, goes through Hong Kong, Amsterdam into England and perhaps on to America.'

'Opium?'

'Heroin. There is an influx into the UK. A flood from a new source of supply.'

'Crime never sleeps.'

It is a phrase the ex- inspector of police often used as his son was growing up. It gives Zahir Khan a comforting sense that he really had arrived home.

They begin to stroll towards the village. Behind them the four-carriage train chugs away, sending a smudge of grey smoke up into the azure sky. Struck by a sudden worrying thought, the old man halts, grasps his son's arm.

'It's topping to see you, of course, but you mustn't waste time visiting me if duty calls elsewhere.'

'There's little I can do at present. We suspect the new influx of class A drugs is from Chinese gangsters. Their Triad societies are difficult to penetrate but we have seconded a pair of undercover agents from Hong Kong. I hope to receive their findings when I return to the UK.'

'Good, good...'

Khan senior pauses as he sees, running towards him, an eight-year-old boy.

'Here's your nephew, come to greet you.'

Zahir smiles, opens his arms to greet the excited youngster. A little way behind, racing along the dusty track, he can see other village children shouting cries of welcome. Soon they are surrounded by a throng of youngsters bubbling with questions.

'Are you really a policeman?'

'Have you caught many crooks?'

'What's Britain really like?'

'Tell us...'

'Tell us...'

Khan's father holds up his arms.

'England is exactly as I say it is.'

The children cheer.

Holding a half smoked cigarette, Anne Darracott leaves a public toilet cubicle. The cistern flushes behind her. About to douse the ciggy in a bucket of sand she sees used hypo needles lying amongst the fag ends. Her expression darkens. She hears, from behind a closed door, a cry of pleasure as a hit strikes home. The door of the cubicle is covered in obscene graffiti saying who did what to whom and in what way. Anne hears giggles on the other side of the barrier, wonders who is shooting up inside. Veteran junkies? School kids? Anne feels an invisible hand move her towards the cubicle. She puts her arms out, presses her hands against the door, makes herself breathe, turns herself about, heads out to re-join John Kline.

The church of Saint Stephen is empty of worshippers except for a visiting organist who plays a few bars of 'All Things Bright and Beautiful' before sashaying into a thunderous version of Bach's Toccata and Fugue in D minor. The sonorous notes fill the church with glorious sound.

The music seeps down into the crypt below. A musty space rented by a group calling themselves 'The Hong Kong Charity Foundation', in reality it is a setting for rituals that have no foundation in charity.

Chen lies spread-eagled on the dank flagstones of the basement. He groans under the weight of two gravestones pressing down on his chest.

Shen T'ang, middle aged, conservatively dressed, in appearance more a member of the Chamber of Commerce than the leader of the murderous mob variously known as 'Hong Ming' or 'The Red Disciples'. With him is his second in command, Mr Yan.

A little to the side, gazing down at the suffering Chen, is Shen T'ang's daughter, Lily Li T'ang. Tall, not yet twenty years of age, she is beautiful in a cold, contained way. Impatient for action, she gestures to Jian and Chang, two would-be members of the Triad society. They lope over to a pile of abandoned gravestones that lie stacked around a pillar. With an effort they lift a stone that faintly reads 'Robert Sinclair, Man of God, 1847-1899'. The Chinese youths stagger out of the shadows, wait for further instructions. Mr Yan bends down, stares into the bloodshot eyes of the infiltrator.

'Chen, what did you give to the man who ran away?'

Struggling to fill his lungs against the weight of the stones bearing down on his chest, Chen spits his defiance.

'Something that will destroy you all. You will never find Harry Sen. He hides in a place without a name.'

Yan steps aside, Shen T'ang takes his place. With a polite smile he addresses his victim in slow, measured tones.

'We know your Hong Kong police colleague works undercover as a cook. We will search him out. His betrayal, like yours, must be avenged.'

The Triad leader gestures to the initiates. Carefully and slowly they place the gravestone of the long dead parson onto the others. The added weight soon takes effect. Chen's eyes bulge, blood surges up into his throat, fills his mouth, chokes him. Unable to breathe, his legs kick out in a final spasm of agony. Lily smiles, turns to speak to her minions, issues her orders in a cut glass English accent.

'Thus perish all traitors. There are stone coffins back there – hide the remains of this creature inside one of them.'

Khan's father leads his son into a graveyard with rows of sun-bleached headstones. Around the perimeter lie unruly grasses that may contain cobras. In the oppressive heat, shrubs and trees wilt, bowing down towards the parched earth. The elder Khan removes his hat, holds it to his chest, bows his head in a gesture of respect. His wistful gaze travels along the lines of gravestones.

'I often come here. It is rather how I imagine an English graveyard to be. Here they sleep, the British dead. Some of them are the fathers of the chaps I instructed in the ways of India. They would have become able administrators had not the blunder of '47 put an end to the order of things.'

The old man begins to wander among the graves, pausing from time to time at a name he recognises.

'Ah, yes, Captain George Fowler, died of a fever, poor fellow. Well, let's not become morbid. We are alive, you have a fine job working to uphold the law in that most green and pleasant land across the sea.'

'Father, why not visit England, compare it to the land of your imagination?'

'No, no, that is not necessary. With the help of Rudyard Kipling, I have created England here...'

He smiles, taps his temple.

'Yes, yes, the downs, the valleys, the hills, the towns whose children have slept secure for a thousand years.'

Zahir looks down at his father, but this is not the time to disillusion him. The old man notes his hesitation.

'Am I to assume you will shortly be recalled to your duties?'

'Yes, I must soon return to England's green and pleasant land.'

The confines of the church crypt have become a place of initiation. Between stone pillars stands an altar on which is arrayed a pantheon of Chinese gods and demons. Their contorted features are illuminated by candles and flaming torches that flank the display. Joss sticks fill the damp air with the scent of sandalwood.

Before the altar stands Shen T'ang, wearing red satin robes and the snake's-head crown of high office. Lily Li Tang, on his right hand side, wears a white and crimson robe; around her plaited hair is coiled a brown, tasselled headpiece. She holds a ritual brass bowl filled with blood.

Below them, the master of incense, Mr Yan, dressed in a white ritual robe, sports a ruby red headband. He holds a thin, curved, sheathed knife. He makes a beckoning sign towards the far pool of darkness.

From the shadows, two Chinese youths crawl across the stone floor towards the waiting Triad leaders. Both initiates are naked except for scarlet loin cloths.

On reaching the feet of Shen T'ang they are summoned to rise by Mr Yan. The youths stand, each extends an arm, joining their separate thumbs together. Lily steps forward to hold the sacrificial bowl beneath their hands. Mr Yan unsheathes his knife, slices across the undersides of the offered thumbs. As the blood of each novice drips down into the receptacle, Shen T'ang intones the ritual response.

'Know that I am Shen T'ang, president of our most honoured society, Hong Ming.'

Lily offers the bowl to the man called Chang. He drinks. His companion, Jian, waits his turn. When both men have drunk deep, the Triad head continues his blessing.

'Know that your blood is now one with the true disciples. Pray that one day their blood will honour yours, pray that their courage will become yours. You may now call yourselves initiate but be aware that the next step required to seal your entry will be one of great hazard.'

Lily takes the bowl of blood away. The arms of the youths are lowered. With bowed heads they prepare to receive the benediction of Shen T'ang.

'May you survive to wear the red robes of honourable membership.

May old age and wealth be yours in the service of this, our most ancient and revered society, Hong Ming.'

Mr Yan and the initiates slowly retreat from the altar. The shadows flicker and dance in celebration.

Lily takes up a soft-headed drumstick and gong. As Yan and the recruits bow with respect and obedience, she strikes the gong. The resulting boom fills the underground space with an ominous resonance.

A thunder storm has swept the streets of Rawalpindi clean. Khan and his son, on their way to Islamabad airport, have decided on a brief sightseeing visit to the busy town.

After the downpour, Saidor Road soon returns to its customary bustle. In a recess, under a sign that reads 'English Typing Done', the Writer sits next to the typist, a middle-aged Asian with a neatly trimmed white beard. The typewriting machine is a vintage model that P.G. Wodehouse would have recognised. The Writer watches the crowds passing by, listens to the buzz of the auto taxis plying their trade. He plays with his sun glasses, thoughtfully. The typist waits, the Writer begins to dictate. The keys fly and print his words on paper.

'Exterior. Rawalpindi. Day. Khan and his dad, killing time before his flight back to the UK, stroll past the camera on Saidor Road. Camera follows them as they skirt a large puddle then...'

He pauses. Where should the next scene should take place?

'CUT TO: Interior. Chinese Ritual Basement, Birmingham. Day.'

Inside the basement of Saint Stephen's church, the two new recruits, Chang and Jian, now fully dressed, stand before Shen T'ang and his daughter Lily. Mr Yan waits behind. It is the final stage of the initiation. The torches splutter and spark, the candles burn and shine their light on the demonic gods of chaos and destruction. Shen T'ang displays a photograph of Harry Sen.

'This is the man whose life you must claim to prove your worth to our society.'

'Who...?' Chang starts to ask.

Yan thumps the taller recruit between his shoulders.

'Do not question, obey!'

Jian and Chang bow to the Triad leader.

'Please, master, where is this man to be found?'

'Our information is he works at a restaurant.'

'Of what name?'

'It has no name.'

Chapter Two

It is lunch time before Anne and Kline return to the restaurant. Anne can sense Kline's frustration. The sale of the Maverick club has raised enough funds to make a fresh start but without a liquor licence it will be so much harder to make a profit.

Not talking, they walk past the lines of empty tables. In the kitchen, they are greeted by Harry, their Chinese cook.

'Bit've lunch, boss?'

'Great.'

'Drink?'

'Best thing I've heard today.'

'Miss Anne?'

'Soda water, on the rocks.'

Kline seats himself at a table, long legs sprawled. He undoes his neck tie as if he were casting aside a hangman's noose. Anne watches him, senses it is the time to keep her mouth shut. Their drinks arrive, she fumbles for her methadone tablets, takes one down with a swallow of soda water. Her companion notices but makes no comment. Behind them Harry is busy creating their lunch. Anne decides to break the silence.

'Is it the licence thing that's pissing you off or is it something else?'

'Something else like what?'

'Me?'

'Just not used to having to do things by the book.'

'It's what we decided.'

'I know, I...'

He stops. Staring at him through the oval window of the kitchen door is the face of a Chinese youth. Kline waves a dismissive hand, calls,

'We're not open yet!'

He frowns as not one but two Chinese guys shoulder their way into his kitchen just as his cook brings bowls of noodles, prawns and vegetables to the table. Jian, the smaller of the two visitors, addresses Kline as Harry ducks out of sight.

'We desire to see the owner of the restaurant.'

'You're looking at him.'

'Yes, what is name?'

'Kline.'

Anne grins. 'He means the name of the place.' She spells it out. 'It hasn't got one.'

'Yet,' Kline adds, helping himself to a mouthful of food. 'You waiters?'

'We look like waiters? We wish to talk.'

'No charge for that.'

Jian looks around the kitchen.

'I worked here once. Before it was closed for illegal gambling. You know Chinese bet hard?'

'I've heard.'

'Heard, have you? Now, since bigwig judge close down dens, we need places. You have store rooms behind kitchen. Let us use them, we give you cut from every game.'

Kline glances across at Anne; she gives him a stony look in return. 'No.'

The taller Chinese rubs his fingers together under Kline's nose.

'You not like money?'

'Not if it's as fishy as your fingers.'

Chang helps himself to a prawn from Kline's plate, sucks on it.

'Not bad. You have good cook.'

He reaches for another helping. Kline grabs his hand.

'You've no manners, want me to teach you some?'

'Want your hair parted with a meat axe?'

From the corner of his eye Kline sees Anne wince at the growing aggro. The smaller thug pushes himself forward.

'Lots of restaurants in this town need protection.'

'Is this what this is about?'

'Rent out your space, we pay you; refuse and you must pay us.'

'For protection?'

'Hey, you catch on pretty good.'

Kline sighs, looks towards Annie.

'This is where I came in.'

He stands, fills his lungs, exhales. Grabs the intruders by the scruffs of their necks, marches them towards the swing doors that lead out of the kitchen.

'A word in your ears.'

He pushes them through the doors, propels them towards the street.

'Beat it!'

Jian stumbles and falls; Chang pulls out a knife, steps towards Kline threateningly. Anne emerges from the kitchen as Kline grabs a decanter, lifts it ready to crack open the first skull that comes within range.

Jian scrambles to his feet, pulls Chang away from the growing confrontation. They retreat into the street. The door bangs behind them. Kline relaxes, chuckles to himself. Anne is less than impressed.

'Enjoy yourself?'

Kline shrugs.

'That pair of yellow perils used the word 'protection'. I did three years because of that word, you know.'

'Yes, I know, you keep telling me.' Anne says, her voice hard as ice.

In the crypt of Saint Stephen's church Lily Li T'ang is alone with her father. Both still wear their ceremonial robes. Lily lifts the brass bowl, sniffs at its contents, wrinkles her nose.

'Ugh, daddy, what a ghastly smell.'

Shen T'ang looks up from his *Financial Times.*

'The real thing would be worse. Blood of a rooster, cinnabar, wine. Knowing Mister Yan's obsession with economy that is probably the blood from a frozen chicken.'

'How disgusting.'

Harry Sen can smell danger. He suspects the visit of the Chinese duo was only a scouting mission. Are they in wait for him outside? What has become of his partner, Chen? Murder? What of their mission? How could he protect their findings? The cook looks around the kitchen then down at the chicken he is preparing. He takes out a wad of papers from his pocket, rolls them tightly, inserts the document deep into the innards of the bird.

Holding the carcass by the neck, Harry places the chicken next to the other frozen poultry within the freezer. He moves to the back door, eases it open, checks the alley for danger. Seeing none, he steps outside.

Kline and Anne are perched on stools at the restaurant bar. Both are leafing through lists of names, consulting dictionaries. Kline looks up, a gleam of triumph in his eyes.

'Got it.'

'Go on.'

'Kline's Cuisine.'

His fellow researcher thinks about it. Shakes her head, her blonde hair swirling. Kline gives up, slides down from his stool, heads behind the bar, pushes an optic, brings down a shot of scotch.

Anne ploughs on. She reaches the letter 'N' in her dictionary; 'N' for what? Narcotics? Oh, sure, thanks a lot. Nefertiti, the Egyptian queen? Décor would be, what? Funeral masks? Hieroglyphics decorating the menu, waiters in loincloths? Nah, bad idea. Then she sees it. Reads the definition and knows the search is over. Kline sips his scotch, looks quizzically at Anne as she gives him a seductive smile.

'Ready?'

'Hit me.'

A pregnant pause.

'Nirvana.'

'Nir... What?'

'Nirvana. Where all desire is extinguished. The consummation of bliss.'

Kline pictures her naked on his bed.

'I'm all for that.'

As they raise their glasses, the door that leads to the kitchen crashes open. Harry, their chef, stumbles in. He attempts to speak, blood froths on his lips. He turns, they see the profile of the knife buried between his shoulder blades. Anne cries out with fear, Kline rushes to support Harry, catches him as he falls.

'Harry, who did this?'

The cook stares up at Kline, tries to mouth a message.

'Roo... Heart of the rooster...'

'What?'

Kline feels the life ebbing from the body he holds in his arms.

'Harry...'

There are no more words, only a dark gush of blood from Harry's mouth. Gently, Kline lowers Harry Sen to the floor.

'He's a goner.'

Anne begins to shake, trying to make sense of the horror.

'Why this, for Christ's sake?'

Kline frowns.

'It can't be to get back at me, not for a few quid's protection.'

'What was he trying to say?'

'Something about a rooster, heart of the rooster.'

'What?'

'Why make those his... his last words, it doesn't make sense.'

John Kline watches the blood of Harry Sen slowly form a pool on the floor. He feels an anger, a need for revenge, a desire to discover the truth behind the last words of a man who had become his friend.

Anne senses his growing excitement. How can she stop him from being drawn back into a dangerous world of mystery, mayhem and murder?